Praise for *The Fair Botanists*

'Sheridan creates an evocative, enjoyable portrait of
1820s Edinburgh and of two women determined
to lead independent lives.' *Sunday Times*

'Completely enchanting and fascinating . . . a rollicking and
immensely readable tale . . . Sheridan succeeds in what very few have
attempted before; in imagining early 19th century Edinburgh as a
genuine if imperfect city of enlightenment, a thrilling, optimistic
and romantic landscape where science flourishes, beauty is created,
wrongs are righted, possibilities are infinite, and women can begin
to dream, at last, of how it might feel to be free.' *Scotsman*

'A vibrant mix of history, romance and mystery' *I Paper*

'Lush, seductive and scandalous, this is a gorgeous read.' *Daily Mail*

'A beautiful, immersive gem of historical fiction' *Good Housekeeping*

'An absolute treat for fans of historical fiction and rich storytelling' *Red*

'Compelling, fascinating and incisive about
its social context. A cracking good
read' Val McDermid

'Dazzling, original, full of wonderful characters
and so interesting' Katie Fforde

'Joyously seductive prose with evocatively-drawn characters . . .
a beautiful tale of scandal and intrigue firmly rooted in the
capital of 1820s Scotland' Susan Stokes-Chapman

'A charm of a book. A spirited tale of female empowerment set amongst the blossoms of enlightenment Edinburgh, it is suffused with the rich perfume of its historical era. Lively and generous-hearted, with an array of utterly engaging characters, this enchanting novel reads like a warm tonic for the soul' Mary Paulson-Ellis

'Delightfully original, sensuous historical fiction, led by a charge of female characters as captivating and complex as the brightest of botanical flowers' Cari Thomas

'Enchanting and absorbing . . . [I enjoyed it] because it's about women and women's lives, people I know and talk to, and am' Anstey Harris

'As rare and lush as the Agave flower itself, *The Fair Botanists* is a richly realised, transportive delight' Rachel Rhys

'Beautiful . . . Every sentence is a gift' Miranda Dickinson

'A seductive, sensory romp through Georgian Edinburgh. Hugely enjoyable' Ambrose Parry

'There's no enlightenment without enlightening women, and Sara Sheridan gives us two great ones to reckon with in Belle and Elizabeth. *The Fair Botanists* gives us a glimpse into the complex life of Edinburgh in the 1820's with joyous female characters at the heart of the story' Annie Garthwaite

'A beautifully written, enchanting, escapist delight, peopled with wonderful characters. I really enjoyed the exploration of growing female independence in a male world – Belle and Elizabeth will stay with me for a long time.' Caroline Lea

'I loved this vivid evocation of Enlightenment Edinburgh – a city in the throes of tumultuous change – filled with a cast of fascinating characters, both real and imagined.' Fiona Valpy

Sara Sheridan

THE FAIR BOTANISTS

HODDER

First published in Great Britain in 2021 by Hodder & Stoughton
An Hachette UK company

This paperback edition published in 2022

4

A CIP catalogue record for this title is available from the British Library

Paperback ISBN 978 1 529 33622 1
eBook ISBN 978 1 529 33623 8

Typeset in Adobe Garamond by Hewer Text UK Ltd, Edinburgh
Printed and bound in Great Britain by Clays Ltd, Elcograf S.p.A.

Hodder & Stoughton policy is to use papers that are natural, renewable
and recyclable products and made from wood grown in sustainable
forests. The logging and manufacturing processes are expected to
conform to the environmental regulations of the country of origin.

Hodder & Stoughton Ltd
Carmelite House
50 Victoria Embankment
London EC4Y 0DZ

www.hodder.co.uk

This book is dedicated to the lovers who vowed to wed in secret during lockdown and ran away to do so as soon as they possibly could. To you. To love. To family.

Where the bolt of Cupid fell . . . upon a little western flower –
Before, milk white; now purple with love's wound – and maidens
call it love-in-idleness.

Oberon, *A Midsummer Night's Dream*
by William Shakespeare

But pleasures are like poppies spread, You seize the flower, it's
bloom is shed; Or, like the snow-fall in the river, A moment white,
then melts forever.

'Tam o' Shanter' by Robert Burns

His cheeks are like beds of spices, mounds of sweet-smelling
herbs. His lips are lilies, dripping liquid myrrh.

Song of Solomon

Prologue

1 June 1822: The Old Royal Botanic Garden, Leith Walk, Edinburgh

A small crowd gathers on the street outside the McNabs' cottage on days when the trees set off for the new Garden at Broomlaw, a mile and a half distant. The dew is fresh on the leaves, shimmering in the sunshine as the first of eight carts bearing precious cargo rolls through the gates onto the road. A barefoot girl of no more than six years of age jumps up and down in excitement, her face traced with grime though she must be on her way to the dame school. 'Look, Jamie! Look!' she squeals.

It is an extraordinary sight. Alder and ash, cedar and fir, oak and willow, trees of twenty, thirty and forty feet transplanted into huge wooden barrels proceeding one behind the other, the carthorses bent to their task, hauling them up the gentle slope, the huge wheels turning slowly as they make their way towards town. Twigs quiver and branches sway though there is no breeze on this summer morning. The gardeners smirk. This work, they know, is historic. People will remember seeing it their whole lives, the transplantation of acres of ground, shrub by shrub and tree by tree, backbreaking work though it is. They have been pioneering the process for several weeks. Nobody has ever attempted it before – not on this scale.

The head gardener, William McNab, watches each cart as it leaves, checking that every tree is secure before taking his place on the last wagon. He looks up and waves goodbye to his wife, Betty, standing at the window of the upper floor, holding their youngest so the infant can see the spectacle as it recedes up the hill towards town. The child will remember this as a fairy tale, unsure if the mass of moving leaf and branch that dwarfs his father's frame is any more real than the kelpies, goblins and fairies whom his sister Catherine spins into diverting stories for her younger siblings every night before bed.

'Hold her steady, man,' McNab directs the coachman. It is all about momentum. More than four miles an hour, and the trees could overturn the carts, for the weight of even the largest convey-ance is far less than the tree it bears. He tries not to fuss. There are only a couple of hundred trees in the old arboretum and over the last year the men have hauled thousands of bushes and flowering shrubs, aloes and cacti – but the larger ones still cause McNab concern. In spite of this, he endeavours to leave his men to their business. If he's honest, he likes accompanying the processions because of the stir they cause. The trees are some sight. A veritable wonder.

The ragged children fall in behind the carts, running in the strange, long shadows the trunks cast onto the beaten earth. They stare up at the foliage as it passes overhead. 'Hey, mister!' one boy shouts, indicating the spectacle. 'How do you put them up there? Do you have a giant to do it?'

McNab has no time to tell the lad that the trees are not like dande-lions, pulled from the ground in an easy movement. The roots must rest for weeks after being carefully dug out, and they will need to rest again before being watered and replanted at the new site. He invented an entirely new machine to lever the barrelled trees onto each cart, but it seems too flashy to admit that the success of this operation is down to him – both his knowledge and his inventiveness. He is only doing his job, after all. It's nice to be stretched. William McNab would not be satisfied with a job comprised of fripperies – the task of growing pansies for the side tables of aristocratic drawing rooms or running the kitchen garden of a grand house to make sure the master has pineapple for the dining table when he requires it and grapes from his own vines. The Botanic Garden is dedicated to science. To medicine. Each plant bears properties vital to the apothecary's art.

'If you don't get to your lesson the master will skelp you,' McNab scolds the lad who asked the question. 'Go on now!'

The forest rumbles towards Edinburgh as the children lose heart and turn in the direction of Pilrig, where the school bell is pealing.

Chapter One

Warriston Crescent, Canonmills, Edinburgh

Belle Brodie is often amused by society's reaction to her. The illegitimate daughter of the granddaughter of a duke, she was brought up in the country, for it is to the country that the women of wealthy families are sent when they disgrace their good name, and it is there that their mistakes are educated by extremely strict governesses in the hope that those mistakes will not make further mistakes and family honour can be recouped.

This morning, having in her twenty-five years confounded all the meagre hopes that the elders of the Brodie clan had of her, Belle rolls over and yawns as her maid, Nellie Patterson, opens the embroidered Chinese silk curtains and folds back the shutters. Belle squints into the grey morning.

'Eugh,' she says and falls back on the pillows. Nellie fetches the breakfast tray. Her mistress is unusual, spurning the hot chocolate and buttered rolls that most wealthy women favour when they rise. Instead, Belle breaks her fast with smoky Chinese tea, a shot of whisky and a plate of oysters scooped out of the Firth of Forth and delivered to the kitchen by a Newhaven fishwife who carries her wares in a basket on her back three miles to and from the harbour. This time of year, the job is even more tedious – the oysters are breeding and the fishermen charge extra, to sort the mature shellfish from the new season's crop. Some refuse to do so, maintaining the oysters should not be harvested over the summer. Belle considers this an affront – she wants nothing else for breakfast and if this causes extra work, does it not also create gainful employment?

'I'll wear the blue spencer with the brocade over my muslin,' she says and yawns once again. Through the uneven glass, a mottled duck with five ducklings floats past on the foamy swell of the Water of Leith which runs along the bottom of the garden. Since the tannery closed on the other side of the bridge, the water has become more congruent with nature. When Belle first moved into the house at Warriston Crescent, it was not unusual to wake to what looked like a river of blood. Now the water seems practically rural.

She turns her attention to the tray, knocking back the whisky with a smack of her rosebud lips. Nellie moves silent as a shadow into the dressing room to lay the outfit her mistress has chosen onto the chaise longue.

'Put out the ox-blood boots,' Belle calls after her, for today she is going out. Nellie appears in the doorway.

'Shall I tell Jamie to fetch the carriage?'

Belle spoons vinegar onto her first oyster.

'Later,' she says. 'I've a message to run.'

Nellie doesn't ask. Messages are usually her province but if the mistress wishes to undertake a maid's work, who is she to question her? She is paid, after all, 6 shillings a year more than any other girl of her acquaintance, and in addition has her share of a guinea from each of Miss Brodie's gentlemen at Christmas, which is given for the discretion of the staff. Nellie, Jamie, Mrs Grant the cook and Claire the understairs maid all take this seriously and never utter either of the men's names, in the house or out of it.

As the oysters slip down, Belle takes in the room with satisfaction. This little house (for the crescent is certainly not as grand as the Perthshire estate where she was sequestered for the first sixteen years of her life) is pretty, and Belle has, she feels, appointed it well. She takes in the image of herself in the gilt mirror on her dressing table, propped on plump pillows in an almost sheer gold nightdress edged with dark lace. Her auburn hair is still in ringlets from the night before and her sky-blue eyes are brightening. She smiles.

It gives her pleasure that here she is, nine years after she left home, at twenty-five years of age, where she never ought to have been – only a few yards north of the municipal boundary of Edinburgh – in a property bought with the money she extracted from her half-brother, Joseph, in exchange for the destruction of inappropriate letters their father sent to her mother two decades before and building her own fortune by means of generous allowances paid by two married men who are happy to have even half her attention.

This is not to say that Belle Brodie makes her living only by selling her body. She is fully aware, flirting aside, that her brain is her greatest asset and, as she grows older, she knows this organ will determine her prospects far more than her pretty eyes or slim ankles. Even the most talented courtesan has not much more than a decade to make enough money to last her whole life – from whoring, that is. But in addition to the activities she undertakes with her gentlemen, Belle has other plans.

To this end, an hour later, wearing her new velvet hat with the ostrich feather trim and a military jacket, Belle crosses the main thoroughfare at the end of the street. Slim and only five feet and two inches tall, the overall impression is of an attractive but determined fairy general. Masonry dust hangs in the air and coats the leaves of the bay trees planted at the end of the terrace. The dust has been an habitual problem in Edinburgh since the end of the last century, when the town council started building the Athens of the North on farmland beyond the old Nor Loch. It has, however, only seriously troubled the residents of Canonmills more recently as investors have begun to build on sites further down the hill, now the first phases of the New Town are complete.

As Belle approaches Tanfield the smell of urine rises from the mud, though the tanners are long gone. Some enterprising businessman will build on this site, no doubt (there are rumours that a gas company has entered negotiations to secure it and that they plan to light up Princes Street and after that the rest of the town). But for now, Edinburgh's byways abide in darkness at night and Belle has rented one of the sheds. She knocks and is admitted by a studious-looking lad called Edzel McBain who grins as he pushes his tiny reading spectacles down his nose and peers at her over the top of them.

'Good morning, Miss Brodie,' he says reverently and locks the door behind his mistress. Belle has rescued this boy, and he is indebted to her. The son of a drunken Thistle Street porter, Edzel was eleven when he began delivering parcels on his father's behalf. Every time Belle saw the lad he reminded her of an owl desperate to escape the nest. A misfit. As he tarried awkwardly on the doorstep one day, she questioned him.

'Have you no other messages to get on with?'

'Naw, miss,' he said, shifting from foot to foot, not wanting to go though she had given him his penny.

Belle can read people and she read Edzel admirably. She made enquiries. The boy excelled at school but had no prospects and fewer friends. Belle offered to pay for tuition to see if he might gain a place at the medical school. She likes the idea of a doctor who owes her his living – not that she would ever be graceless enough to put it that way. For the last three years she has covered Edzel's expenses and twice a week the boy undergoes lessons given by a minister housed in a single, attic room in Cumberland Street. At night the boy crams by the light of two tallow lamps until well after midnight here in the shed, where he now lives.

Beyond Edzel's tidily made box-bed, the other fittings in the shed betray activities halfway between a laboratory and illicit still – Belle's manufactory. While Belle knows that a woman who makes her own money can never be a lady, she also knows many ladies residing in the New Town have slaves to make their money for them. Belle, on the other hand, has different ideas, and if they come off, she will secure her position just as well as any girl of her class might hope to do by marrying the heir to a large fortune.

Today the air in the shed smells of a herbal concoction with the faintest whiff of tar. Jars of oil line a set of shelves, reminiscent of a rogue surgeon's museum, though the shady yellow liquid contains not the severed heads of babies or the detritus of major surgery with its tumours and cankers, but a selection of barks and roots. Small barrels are piled to one side marked with chalk. Two stills are set on the bench. In the corner is a table stacked with books and a single chair tucked beneath it.

'Did the orris come?' Belle asks.

The boy shakes his head.

'I went to the port twice, but it wisnae there, miss.'

Belle sighs. She rarely wants anything for long before being satisfied. At first she found it intriguing to be denied, but the shipment they are waiting for has taken too long. Edzel, nervous that Miss Brodie might be disappointed, cuts in.

'Miss?'

Belle smiles reassuringly. 'There is nothing you can do,' she assures him.

'Will Dr Brodie be angry?' Edzel asks.

Belle takes a moment. It has not occurred to her that Edzel, who is a bright lad, might not have reasoned that she is the intended recipient of the packets and letters arriving for Dr Brodie. The boy has had a great deal to overcome in life, but not that, she thinks. No serious botanist would correspond with a woman, at least not one without prodigious family connections and a decent garden from which they might receive seeds and specimens in return for their assistance. Women who sell themselves are seldom taken seriously by anyone other than their lovers. Edzel is a little in love with Belle himself – the crush of a schoolboy – and cannot, it comes to her now, imagine that she has obstacles of her own and that the gentlemen across the country, or indeed, the world, with whom she corresponds believe her to be a gentleman too.

'I will try something else in the meantime,' she says. 'We will have it in the end, Edzel, by hook or by crook.'

With that she motions towards the door and the boy jumps to open it.

'Good day,' she says smartly, enjoying the sudden waft of scent from a pine box crammed with lilacs, which Edzel has somehow disturbed in opening the door. 'And don't let anyone in, mind,' she adds.

'Oh no, miss. Never.' The boy almost salutes.

Chapter Two

The self-same morning, four miles to the north, Elizabeth Rocheid stands on deck waiting for the Port of Leith to come into sight. This far north, the haar clings to the coastline like a wet shroud, so there is no view to be had of the shore along the firth. The short voyage to Scotland has been turbulent and the other passengers (all three of them) have been sick. Elizabeth feels proud of her sea legs – a tribute to a childhood pottering on rafts on the River Wye. Now she tries to ignore her nervousness about what Scotland will be like, and instead focuses on the sails being trimmed.

As the ship nears the dock and a waft of foul water rises to the deck, Elizabeth returns to the cabin to check her things – two trunks and a portmanteau, which are not much to show for ten years in the house at Richmond her husband rented before he died. She sold almost everything in the run up to her departure – most of the furniture and even William's clothes – but careful management allowed her to keep a maid until the end. Now she needn't worry any longer. She runs her palms up her arms to smooth her long, unlined tan leather gloves that have seen better days and pats her portmanteau. A long, shrill whistle sounds on deck. She has the letters from William's cousin, James, in her reticule and now that she is close to meeting him, she feels both nervousness and relief. She will be safe. Provided for at last.

When the ship docks, the port is misty. Elizabeth squints, making out a carriage with mulberry livery waiting by a shabby warehouse. It looks fine, if a little old-fashioned. A heraldic emblem is emblazoned on the side. She remembers seeing a similar design once on a gold signet ring that William wore when they were courting – he took her hand, kissed it and then apologized for forgetting himself. She brushes the thought aside. She has left London now, and never intends to go back. The gangplank in place, she steps down to inspect the carriage. The driver is a lad of no more than sixteen – blond, pink-cheeked and angelic.

'Rocheid?' she asks.

'Yes, ma'am.' He jumps down. 'Are you for Broompark?'

Elizabeth eyes the boy. She glances through the small window into the empty carriage. She thought James would come to meet her. *We are looking forward to your arrival.* Is that not what he wrote? Still, she does not like to ask.

'I have trunks,' she gestures towards the ship.

'I'll see to it.'

'Are you . . . the footman?' He is not wearing anything that resembles a uniform. The boy stares sheepishly at his feet.

'I'm the undergardener, ma'am,' he admits. 'The stableman's mother isnae well and he went to Liberton. I've a way with horses, so they sent me.'

'Mr Rocheid keeps only one stableman?' Her stomach sinks. Has she jumped, she wonders, from the frying pan into the fire? The letters spoke of an estate. She resists the urge to remove the pages from her reticule and double check. The boy shakes his head.

'Mr Rocheid keeps a separate coach house, ma'am. You'll be staying at Inverleith House with Lady Clementina and this is the carriage stabled there.'

She feels relieved and decides, for now, to leave the question of who on earth Lady Clementina might be. She does not wish to advertise that she is anything other than a fully informed member of the Rocheid family. Come to think of it, when James Rocheid wrote to her, he used the word 'we' instead of 'I'. Lady Clementina, she thinks. It is an old-fashioned name. She gestures towards the carriage door and the boy opens it.

'Two trunks and a portmanteau,' she says.

As they set off, he informs her that he is not taking the turnpike road, for he has a message to deliver. Elizabeth does not object. She watches the streets of Leith as the carriage passes. They are remarkably clean, she thinks. The road looks new. There is some industry on it and one or two fine houses set back from the traffic. Elizabeth strains in her seat, keeping her eye on the sea, now in the distance across the fields. Squealing beggar children run alongside the carriage – a dangerous game. She is aware she is trundling uphill and that it is getting sunnier as the journey progresses. She wonders when she will first glimpse the famous silhouette of Edinburgh Castle. At a terrace of recently completed houses marked Picardy Place, the carriage halts and she peers outside as her driver disappears into a wide basement to deliver his message. On the other side of the carriage there is a hill with an unimpressive building on its summit, but that, she tells herself, surely cannot be the castle. When the boy returns, she hails him out of the window.

'That's the observatory, ma'am,' he says. Then he smiles. 'The Broomlaw is not much further. If it's the castle you wish to see, there is a bonnie view from the house.'

Elizabeth's hands feel weak. This is a big change, and it suddenly feels very real. She is so nervous she cannot clasp her reticule and it slips down her skirts to the carriage floor. Making two soft fists that would hardly crush a butterfly, she retrieves the bag as the carriage turns right down a steep hill and stops so suddenly that she is jolted almost out of her seat. She stares out of the window with increasing impatience. Why can't this lad just get to her destination? Surely they would have been there by now had he taken the turnpike road.

The street, however, seems engaged in some kind of spectacle. Further down the hill several well-dressed people have come outside and are pointing at whatever lies ahead. Cooks and maids have climbed the stairs from their basements. Hall boys are tarrying in doorways. From the carriage Elizabeth can make out three jam-smeared children, diverted from their breakfast, who are hanging out of a window. Deciding to investigate for herself, she knocks on the box above her head where the boy is sitting and calls, 'I'm coming down!'

She doesn't wait for him to open the door. Beneath her feet there is only a beaten track, so she is careful not to mark the hem of her dress. Elizabeth has worn her best outfit to meet James Rocheid. What she sees, however, puts all thought of her absent benefactor and her place at Inverleith House out of her head, for in front of her there is a procession of trees moving slowly down the street.

'Oh,' she says, as if her voice were not her own and another, delighted woman has uttered the exclamation. All she can think of is Birnam Wood moving to Dunsinane in *Macbeth*. Perhaps in Scotland such things are possible.

The trees halt abruptly. As she stares she realizes that this has been caused by one particular tree, which must be, at her reckoning, over thirty feet in height. It is some kind of evergreen, a fir perhaps, though she does not recognize the exact species. Two men jump down to secure the ropes with which it has been tied to a cart while another settles the four horses pulling this massive load. 'We must go slower, Tommy,' he instructs. 'Like Mr McNab said.'

Elizabeth gawps. There are seven trees ahead of this one. She recognizes a sycamore, an alder and a willow among them, the roots contained in huge oak barrels like bulky travelling skirts, all on carts.

'Excuse me,' she calls to a fellow who is watching the men secure the cargo. 'What is this?' Her voice trails. The man smiles and doffs his hat.

'We are moving the Botanic Garden, ma'am. Have you not heard?'

'A botanic garden? Indeed. I am lately arrived from Richmond and have often visited the garden at Kew,' she manages to get out.

The man introduces himself.

'I am William McNab,' he says, 'the head gardener. I was trained at Kew.'

'How do you do. I am Mrs Elizabeth Rocheid,' she tells him. Her surname has an immediate effect. A look of respect passes across McNab's face. Then he catches a glimpse of one of the men who is tying a knot incorrectly. His blue eyes flash, as if the fellow were hurting a small child.

'Not like that,' he snaps, then to Elizabeth, 'excuse me.' He steps in to tie the knot himself and as he does so, Elizabeth notices that two young ladies have rushed out of one of the houses carrying an easel. Setting it on the ground, one begins to sketch the strange procession while the other looks over her shoulder. She will have to work like lightning, Elizabeth thinks. The plants will be off in a minute. How often can anyone say that?

As Mr McNab returns to her side, she notices the comforting scent of soil, which emanates from him as if it is in his blood.

'I imagine that we are neighbours. If your destination is Inverleith House,' he says.

'It is.' A flutter in her stomach as she remembers.

'Will you be staying long?'

'It is my new home, Mr McNab.' She wants to ask him about it but the most she can get out is, 'I was not aware that the property bordered a botanic garden.'

'We are not yet, ma'am, what I would call a garden.' He smiles. 'More a large open-air potting area.'

She gestures towards the parade of trees. 'This is impressive. I would not have imagined it possible to move such mature specimens.'

McNab grins. He decides to own the achievement. Why not? 'It is a process of my own design.'

'Well, it is impressive. You must write about it, Mr McNab. In a monthly magazine? Or even a book. It is quite the amazement.'

He nods. 'In time,' he says doubtfully. 'In truth I must understand the process fully first. We have lost a dozen trees or more. They did not survive.'

'How many have you moved?'

McNab pauses as he makes a reckoning.

'We have near three thousand plants at the new site. Not all trees, of course. I'd say we have over a hundred mature specimens in the arboretum. And several smaller.'

Elizabeth laughs. 'I would like to see this "potting area" of yours.'

'You would be very welcome.'

'At Kew I helped upon occasion. I drew for Sir Joseph Banks for four years – until his death. Recording the plants and helping in his herbarium. Perhaps I might be of assistance?'

McNab's demeanour becomes serious. 'We are always in need of botanical illustrations, ma'am. The Garden belongs to the university and is principally used for the purpose of instructing medical students. To be able to demonstrate in winter how the plants look when they flower, for example, is a boon. We have several unusual items that remain unillustrated.'

'I will call once I am settled,' she promises. She feels less nervous now she has a task ahead of her. 'When I knew I was coming to Scotland I had not thought . . .' She starts. 'I mean, I knew there would be heather. And thistles, of course. But I did not expect such . . . variety.' She chooses the word carefully though what she means is that she did not expect such civilization.

It is McNab's turn to laugh now.

'We are still building greenhouses, but,' he lowers his voice, 'I think you will find our range of exotics rival what you have seen in London, though perhaps we are less in funds.' That flash of humour again. Solid but good-natured. She likes Mr McNab.

'Hey!' he shouts to one of the drivers. 'Be careful now. Go slowly.'

'Yes sir,' the man says. He gees up the horses and the cart moves off at a gentle pace. McNab doffs his hat once more.

'We must get on,' he says. 'We don't want to hold you up any more than necessary.'

Back in the carriage, all Elizabeth can think is that if the grounds of her new home border a botanic garden and there is a lawn with a view of the castle, surely it will not be so bad. It is no great matter that James did not come to meet her. And she is sure Lady Clementina will be delightful. *We are looking forward to your arrival. It is not appropriate that as William's widow you are at present unprovided for by the family.* Yes, that is what it said. That they wish to provide for her.

The carriage jerks as it moves off slowly. Above, the jam-smeared children disappear into the nursery and the artist strains to catch the last glimpse of the trees as they move down the hill. At the foot of the slope, the driver halts and pays a toll of a penny ha'penny for the horse and carriage. As they make their way down the loan, Elizabeth realizes that she is no longer afraid. This is an extraordinary place. She is excited to have arrived.

Chapter Three

Three maids and a cook cannot contain the old lady, who howls, barefoot, as they chase her across the grass.

'You will not get me,' she shouts. 'I will not be silenced.'

But they do catch her. 'Lady Clementina,' the cook scolds. 'You will catch your death out here.'

'There will be famine. They cannot continue like this.' The old lady starts to weep. Tears trickle down her soft, pink cheeks. 'The poor, hungry bairns,' she says. She is almost eighty years old and the maid clamping her in place cannot help think that the old lady's skin is marvellous. 'What will they eat?'

The cook is having none of this nonsense. 'Nobody is short of food who has the coin to buy it and you, my lady, will have rolls and butter and hot chocolate if only you will let us serve your breakfast.'

As Elizabeth's carriage rolls up on the other side of Inverleith House, the place looks deserted. It is not that she expects a welcoming party, but it seems odd there is nobody here. The boy hands her down. 'Thank you,' she says and stands at the door, frozen like a princess in a fairy tale. The house is large, double-fronted and built in pale stone darkened in patches by smoke from the chimneys. It reminds her of one of the fancier residences she saw in the village of Hampstead when William and she made an expedition to the heath.

Certainly, the little cottage in Richmond she has recently abandoned could fit inside this place several times. Yes, she thinks, this will do very well.

The boy unloads her luggage and she decides to simply enter as there is no bell nor any knocker on the door.

In the hallway the light is astounding. The place is huge but not overly ornate, as if a gentleman had moved his worldly possessions into a monastic building. The staircase is of stone with a rush runner and a simple mahogany balustrade elegantly curving as it rises. The walls are painted ochre. To her left there is a dining room with traditional red walls topped with a white plaster cornice garnished with bunches of grapes. To the right lies a large, bright drawing room, and ahead, a music room. Curious, she steps inside. It is furnished with a harpsichord painted with pastoral scenes, and a carved wooden fireplace with flutes and lutes in relief. The walls are hung with hand-painted paper – narcissi and peonies. Elizabeth's cheeks burn momentarily at the memory of her husband mocking her interest in plants, but the thought is quickly interrupted by the view out of the French windows of the city laid before her. As promised, she can see the castle and, stretching beyond, the whole of Edinburgh, the rooftops cutting prettily into a wide sky, far bluer than at the docks. And, on the lawn, a huddle of women in white aprons. What on earth are they doing?

Briskly, she steps outside, making out that the staff are crowded around a woman in an old-fashioned, orange day dress. The outfit makes Elizabeth's slightly worn sprigged muslin feel as if it's at the cutting edge of fashion. The maids look up as she approaches. One of them steps forward. She is older, with dun-coloured hair showing beneath her cap. Understairs staff, Elizabeth surmises – probably the cook. The woman curtsies.

'What's going on?' Elizabeth asks brusquely. She will not stand by while someone is bullied, not by the staff.

'Mrs Rocheid?'

Elizabeth nods and the old lady in the orange dress peers at her, past the cluster of women.

'Are you sweet William's wife?' The old lady sniffs.

Elizabeth nods again. 'Madam, might I assist you?' she offers.

The old lady regards her bare feet as if she has only just realized that she is standing directly on the grass. It must be cold.

'Perhaps you should fetch this lady's shoes?' Elizabeth suggests to one of the maids, who nods and sets off for the house.

'I am Clementina,' the old lady says. 'These girls were bringing me to my breakfast.'

Ah, Elizabeth thinks. This is she.

The old lady smiles kindly. 'William is one of my favourites,' she says. 'So handsome.'

Elizabeth concedes this. Her husband cut a fine figure, especially in his uniform. Truth be told, he was a man more suited to the military than to marriage.

'He died bravely,' she says. It is what she has taken to saying. The war with the French is over but William was dispatched to Paris anyway, and ended his life there in somewhat mysterious circumstances. She decided from the moment the news came not to look into it too deeply. Clementina's eyes widen as if she is startled.

'Little William is dead?'

'He is, ma'am.'

One of the maids lets slip a smile. Not, Elizabeth realizes, at the death of Captain William Rocheid, but at her own sudden understanding of the situation – a lady meeting an elderly and mercurial older relation for the first time. Then the penny drops further. She had thought perhaps Mr Rocheid had offered her sanctuary out of pity or even pride. It may be the case that he did not want a woman with the Rocheid name falling publicly into poverty, living on an inadequate army pension. But now she can see there is a more practical purpose to her coming to live here. She sighs. The view is beautiful, and the house is airy and grand. She has nowhere else to go. She might as well find out what the food is like.

The maid brings Clementina's footwear – low-heeled velvet pumps embroidered with oranges. She helps the old lady slip on pale stockings and stows her feet as the others shield her from view for modesty's sake – though it appears there is nobody but Elizabeth to see. The sun is out now. It is almost warm. Elizabeth glances back at the house and the long windows of the dining room. From here the walls are darker than wine, the colour of the most fragrant summer roses.

'Would you serve our breakfast outside?' she says. It is a whim, but she feels like celebrating, and a cohort of maids to do her bidding is certainly something of which to take advantage.

'You may set up a table by the French windows.'

The girls stir. Clementina's face splits into a delighted grin.

'What an excellent idea! Rolls and butter and hot chocolate on the lawn,' she says and claps enthusiastically. 'A picnic!'

'Yes,' Elizabeth confirms. 'And some fruit, perhaps?'

The cook shifts. It is June and the apple barrel has been empty for weeks, though this year's harvest will come soon enough.

'I have last year's cherries in brandy,' she suggests.

'That will be lovely,' Elizabeth confirms. 'Thank you. Lady Clementina and I will promenade for a few minutes while you make things ready.' She motions to the city beyond them. 'This is a lovely view.'

'They have built over the farms,' Clementina tells her. 'I have watched them disappear these last years, one by one. The Earl of Moray had a wonderful home farm that supplied his household. It is all gone now. Even the dairy. Built upon for coin.'

Elizabeth motions to the staff and the maids disappear back into the house in the cook's wake, down a run of hidden stairs that drop out of sight at the edge of the path.

'Lady Clementina,' Elizabeth asks gravely once they have gone, 'were those women roughhousing you?'

Clementina laughs. 'I am in charge here, my dear. I became upset, is all.'

'About the farms being gone?'

'Indeed. The men are fools. My own nephew among them. They could not run a country fair, let alone supply a whole new city. I fear famine is coming.' She leans in and whispers, 'Thousands of new residents settle every year. Thousands of mouths to feed. Thousands of stomachs. They say there are over a hundred thousand people now in Edinburgh and the imbeciles have built over acres of farmland.' She lets out a low sigh and then adds, 'I never use my title in company. It was given in grace and favour. My brother was Sir James and they thought if I also had a title it would help me find a husband, so they petitioned the king.'

'And did it help you find a husband?' Elizabeth asks, taking the old woman's arm. She likes Clementina already.

'Not at all,' Clementina chortles. 'I have an array of opinions and from a young age I was too set in my ways to wed. I had a fondness for Mr Hume, but he was thirty years my senior and I was not the only girl of my generation to find him diverting. Far from it. He was, after all, a genius.' The old woman steps back and peers at her newly discovered cousin. 'You will catch your death,' Clementina pronounces, gesturing towards Elizabeth's muslin dress, her own feet, so recently bare, clearly forgotten. 'You are a bonny-looking woman.' She gives this not as a judgement but as a fact. 'You could be a figurehead with your deportment. Such fine, blue eyes – like porcelain.'

Elizabeth smiles. 'Thank you.'

'They have sent for you to keep me company. To quiet me,' the old lady continues as if amused. Elizabeth silently agrees with her but does not reply. 'Do you like to read?' Clementina asks, genuinely curious.

Elizabeth nods. Of late there has been no money to buy books or for a subscription to the library.

'Novels? Yes, novels, I imagine,' the old woman titters. Elizabeth blushes. Clementina seems to consider her, almost as if she is inhaling everything, body and soul, and coming to a prognosis. She decides, it seems, that the younger woman will do. 'We have some novels on the shelves. I can show you later. My own taste runs to philosophy and politics. Mrs Wollstonecraft – such a tragedy. Such a pioneer.'

At the French windows the maids have assembled a card table on the grass and covered it in thick, white linen onto which they place various silver and porcelain tableware. Clementina turns to make for her breakfast. The old woman is eccentric, but she has probably been bored, Elizabeth thinks, and as there is nobody else here, perhaps also lonely.

'When do you expect Mr Rocheid home?' Elizabeth asks. Clementina turns.

'My nephew scarcely ever visits. He has rooms in town,' she gestures towards the view. Elizabeth slips into her seat as a pot of chocolate arrives. She can smell it. Curls of creamy butter and a small tureen of brandied cherries appear in front of her beside a carved horn bowl of sweetened cream garnished with an elegant silver spoon. Then the rolls. Clementina pours. 'It has changed the sky,' she says. 'That's the thing I object to. Foolish, grasping spires to the glory of a deity nobody can prove. Chimneys belching smoke. Such arrogant buildings shield the real beauty. That of nature. The sky. The source of all our light.'

Elizabeth raises an eyebrow, though perhaps criticizing the church is not so unthinkable for a woman who harboured a crush on David Hume in her youth. While Elizabeth certainly believes in God, she has no intention of doing battle on his behalf. A person's faith is a private matter. She picks up her cup and lets the chocolate slip luxuriantly over her lips. It is the most delicious thing she has tasted in a long while.

Nibbling enthusiastically, Clementina chatters on about the neighbours – especially the Fettes family, who, she says, have large glasshouses and have grown a crop of pineapples. 'Nasty, spiky fruit. They had six of the damn things last year,' she wrinkles her nose, 'but they always were showy.' Elizabeth wonders fleetingly what the Fettes women say about Lady Clementina Rocheid and feels a state of relaxation come over her person as she realizes it does not matter. Unlike at Richmond, here there will be no appearances to keep up. The house is not directly overlooked. The family's place in society is secure. It seems there is enough money to pay for everything. She feels almost lightheaded as she realizes that in this place, and in this company, she can do whatever she likes.

After breakfast the women ascend to the first floor, where there is a library with a curved wall and hundreds of leather-bound books stamped with gilded titles. A thin light washes the room. Elizabeth laughs with joy as Clementina guides her through the contents of the shelves. 'Many women favour the work of poor, dead Miss Austen but we have quite the selection of novels by other ladies, if you enjoy that kind of thing. One of my sisters was fond of women's writing,' the old lady sniffs. Elizabeth strokes the tan book covers as she peruses the titles to which Clementina has led her. She has come to Scotland expecting to build a new life, but first, it seems, she will have a retreat. Food and reading. A recovery.

Chapter Four

Two days later

It is night, the moon is full and there are no clouds to speak of. Up the hill, the windows are alight in distant Edinburgh, the dark outline of the castle regal, a tiny Union flag flying over the city, visible by the icy light of the moon. Through the warmly lit windows of the New Town the cream of Scottish society eats, drinks, dances and debates, but in the Botanic Garden all is still. A fox and her three cubs cut across the arboretum and disappear into the bushes. Tonight, these have the air of monumental gravestones. The greenery is ready for planting like a ghostly regiment camped in waiting, casting strange, inky shadows onto the soil.

A pale-faced, thin boy, perhaps eight or nine years old, picks his way past the gate and through the greenery, moving so smoothly it is as if he were floating, following a circuitous route round the bushes and past the herbaceous beds. He lights a candle using a tinder box, illuminating in the process his tidily patched breeches and boots. that are remarkably clean for a lad who is dotting about a garden in the dark. Leaning forward, he peers inside one of the glasshouses. The panes glow yellow, as if the glass and iron structure were a giant lamp fallen to the ground.

Following the boy through the gate, William McNab accompanies a white-haired woman in a mop cap. The lady is old, but she is strong, striding ahead of him in a pair of well-worn, sturdy boots. She seems curious, if perfectly at home here, like a bulldog sniffing out new territory.

'Take care, Mrs Dickson,' McNab warns. 'The ground is uneven. We are not yet finished our work.'

'I'll be grand, Mr McNab,' she says. 'It is braw tonight with the moon so full. How is the nursery coming along?'

McNab considers this question before answering. It is a serious matter. Mrs Dickson has more expertise in growing seedlings than any of his gardeners, or indeed himself. 'I'm having difficulty getting the alliums to germinate,' he admits. 'It has been warm weather and with the move I am perpetually short of hands. For now the nursery seems less important than the removal, but I'm sure after it's done, I will curse myself for not taking on another man or two. The budget is very tight as you know . . .' his voice trails.

Mrs Dickson nods. This is why she is here – or, to be more accurate, why she has been allowed to come. 'They never want to pay for what they get,' she pronounces. 'Not unless they can show it off.' She lets out a dry, low laugh, for she knows this works in her favour.

As they approach the glasshouse, the boy appears with the candle and the greenhouse dims behind him. McNab puts an arm round the child's shoulder. 'Well, James,' he says, 'will you show Mrs Dickson our prize?'

'Yes, Father,' James replies.

'He's a strong wee lad,' Mrs Dickson comments, as if the child is not right in front of her. 'Will he go into the business of gardening?'

'We hope so, don't we, James?' says McNab. 'He is studying Linnaeus already. He has an interest in plants and is not shy of work.'

'It's work all right.' Mrs Dickson's hair is so white it seems almost luminous beneath her cap. 'Show me the plant then,' she says, following him into the glasshouse. When she sees it, a smile breaks out on her face. 'It's huge!' she exclaims.

'It's thirty years of age – it was here before my time at the Garden.'

'And it has not flowered in all that time?'

'It only flowers once. So it only seeds once. It will die immediately afterwards.'

'The Black Widow of the garden, eh?' Mrs Dickson chortles. 'All the grand houses will want one. Oh yes. I can certainly use this – the catalogue it will appear in will be collected, you can be sure of that.' Even in the low light it is easy to see the old woman's eyes are sparkling. McNab gestures to James, who leads them back outside.

The scent of the burning wick casts itself around the dark doorway like a spell. An owl hoots. 'Well, Mr McNab, you have a deal.' She offers her hand. 'When it flowers, you will keep one seed for yourself, but I shall have all the others. All of them mind. There should be ten, you say? I will pay you five pounds a seed, so twenty-five pounds in advance, which I will give you now. If for any reason the seeds are not forthcoming, you will owe me the money.'

McNab hesitates. He is desperate for funds. He feels soiled and looks around guiltily as if he might be watched. Mrs Dickson is always generous, but this is the greatest liberty he has ever taken with the Garden's stock. She approached him on a day when he discovered his wife rooting in the almost empty potato patch at the cottage because there was nothing else to eat. The move to the Garden's new site has put pressure on his empty purse, for the gentlemen who used to tip for guided tours of the old place no longer have a garden to come to – the old premises being depleted and the new not yet fully stocked. What with prices rising and his wage too low to start with, he has been falling further behind his family's needs for a long time. The truth is that he scarcely earns more than some of his experienced men. As a result, it is not that the McNabs are short of fancy ices or the luxury of white bread, but a simple piece of meat to stew and clothes for the children. When the old woman said she wished to treat with him for something extraordinary that would appeal to her more aristocratic customers, he grasped the lifeline. Now, if he cannot deliver the seeds, he will be more than three months' wages in debt to her. But he has little choice. He shakes the old woman's hand.

'Where will you say you got them?' he asks.

Mrs Dickson understands his dilemma. The arrangement they are making must not be uncovered. 'I'll say a seaman brought back seeds from the Americas,' she says. 'And be sure, Mr McNab, I'll send you a wee gift to sweeten the arrangement. I'm glad you gave me this.' Mrs Dickson lets a thin smile escape her as she hands over a leather pouch containing twenty-five pounds in coin.

'I can take you up to the Walk in my cart. I have business in Leith tonight,' she offers now the deal is done. 'You're on my way home.'

'Thank you,' McNab replies. He and James walked from the cottage at the old Garden all the way in the dark. A lift on the cart will mean they will be home in good time for James to get to bed. The younger ones will be asleep now, or at least under the covers. He's glad he brought the boy with him, for such meetings are, he supposes, a kind of training. He knows he must above all else educate his sons.

'Come on, then,' Mrs Dickson insists. 'We best get the wee lad home. If you want him to visit the nursery one day, I can show him round. It is all good experience. Perhaps not too far in the future, I will be doing business with you, my boy.'

'Yes ma'am,' James says obediently. To him Mrs Dickson seems absolutely ancient but perhaps like some kind of eternal monument she will always be in charge of the seed merchants on London Road.

McNab lingers only momentarily before following them to the cart, untethering Mrs Dickson's horse and handing her the reins. At this time, the road will be all but deserted and he is glad of that.

High above, Elizabeth Rocheid lingers on the other side of a long, low line of newly planted holly bushes, young and sparse enough that she can see through the jagged branches. She is not sure what she has just witnessed while out on her evening stroll, discovering as she has the limits of Mr McNab's open-air 'potting area'. Since arriving at Inverleith House she has hardly slept. It is not that she does not feel safe, but this is a new place and both its noises and silences are unfamiliar. It will take her a while to get used to the rhythm of the household, much of which revolves round Clementina. The old woman retires early – the first evening she lasted until eight of the clock, though tonight she only stayed up until just after seven. She looks suddenly older when she tires and disappears upstairs at once. The staff, accustomed to this, melt into rooms in the attic, the basement, a crib in the wash-house and the hayloft, where the gardener's boys have their dormitory amid the bales. Elizabeth finds the night-time stillness of the upper house soothing and walks from room to room by candlelight, possessing it.

Tonight, curious about her new home, she ties on her cloak and bonnet and crosses the threshold. Walking into the night air feels like diving into a pool of cool, clear water. Outside, her footsteps on the gravel are the only sound. It feels as if she is disturbing the world at slumber, yet it is only nine of the clock. In Richmond, the ton would not yet be rising from dinner to make calls to whoever is receiving or to settle to the evening's entertainment – cards and music before supper and bed.

The house stands on a hill and the moonlight illuminates the papery remains of daffodils in the undergrowth between the trees as she walks down the slope. In Richmond she would not dare walk alone at night, but in Richmond her estate comprised a flat patch of earth ahead of the cottage and the same behind. The last two days have been a dream. Elizabeth has drunk her fill of pink claret at dinner and port afterwards – a pleasure that, Clementina observed drily, is usually reserved for men. They had fish tonight – salmon and cod and caviar on toast and cheese from the goats. Abundance.

Having found the eastern reach of the Rocheids' land, Elizabeth stops to take in the city of plants casting moonlit shadows on the lower ground. The garden is smaller than the site at Kew, where Elizabeth drew botanical illustrations for Sir Joseph Banks – tiny alpines and huge oaks. Walking slowly along the holly boundary, she spies the partially built greenhouses, home to eerie succulents and strange cacti nestling in the dark. Beyond the glasshouses lies a small lake, on the bank of which she recognizes the willow tree carted here on the day of her arrival, and beyond that a stone wall. Then she spots Mr McNab, a stocky old woman, and a young boy in conversation. Something going on.

She considers moving away but, afraid to draw attention, crouches behind the bushes instead, peering at the trio's progress to the greenhouse and back. What are they doing here at this time of night? A gardener does not keep a carriage. Did they walk in the dark all the way from town with a child in tow? She watches as the old woman hands something to McNab. Or perhaps they are only shaking hands. She cannot make it out. Maybe the lady is Mr McNab's mother. Of course, that might be it. She smiles at her foolishness. It has been a trial, she tells herself, but she will recover from always thinking the worst. She must control her feelings. If it is possible to move three thousand plants on carts from one garden to another then surely she will succeed in moving her life five hundred miles north and settling in a well-provisioned and respectable household.

It has been strange for her, being treated like a lady again. Clementina insisted Elizabeth must have her own maid and promoted a girl from the existing staff to the position – a thick-set redhead called Margaret with a snub nose and freckles. Plump at nineteen, anyone could see that she is set to become pursy, Elizabeth thought as she looked her over and silently nicknamed her Currant Bun. The girl will require training but has aptitude and a cheery disposition.

As Margaret unpacked the portmanteau in Elizabeth's airy bedroom on that first day, which now, strangely, seems weeks ago, Clementina insisted on showing Elizabeth the farm. The carriage was called, and an outing made to the other side of the estate where almost sixty acres belonging to the Rocheids runs down to the Water of Leith.

'The farm is worked by three men,' Clementina announced proudly. 'Though we cannot defend it,' she added. 'That is the thing.'

'Defend it?' Elizabeth asked, admiring the goats in the pen, the tattie fields and the orchard where fluffy chickens grubbed between the gnarled fruit trees, prettily in blossom.

'When the famine comes. There is fencing but that will hardly keep out a person who is starving. I have Cook provision the household stores at full capacity and that will feed our own people for a month at least, even if we must make a fortress of the house.'

Elizabeth mulled on this for a moment. As far as she could make out, beyond the Rocheid estate were only open fields – other farming concerns. From where she stood, she could see a flock of sheep in the distance.

'But there is all this land . . .'

Clementina waved the suggestion away. 'Fettes land. Yes. And the land around Wardie House, where they have some interesting berry frames, I grant you.'

Elizabeth wondered how interesting berry frames might conceivably be.

'We shall be as ready as we can,' the old lady said with finality.

Later, Elizabeth asked Currant Bun if there had ever been a famine. The girl nodded as she brushed Elizabeth's hair.

'My mother talks of it,' she said. 'The crops failed so they stormed the distillery to steal the barley and the militia were called. Two men lost their lives.'

'Here?'

'Yes ma'am.' The girl pointed out of the window to the south. 'The distillery is on the river. Down there. There is a blind girl in charge now. A Highland witch, they say. She casts spells across the mash to improve the whisky.'

Elizabeth ignored this – historical fact is one thing, local gossip quite another. 'The militia? And the distillery's defences were broken? When was this?'

'Before I was born. And I am near twenty,' the girl volunteered. 'But Lady Clementina maun remember it.'

The next morning Clementina ordered breakfast to be served outside once more. The staff set up a canvas shelter for it was raining. Plump drops of water dripped off the scalloped edges of the tent onto the thick, lush grass. The maids muddied their boots as they drooped Indian stoles around the women's shoulders to the soft tattoo of raindrops. The food, Elizabeth has come to understand, is passable, but Cook has no way with baked goods. On the first night, the crust of the game pie was inedible and at breakfast the rolls were tough as rusks for the second morning in a row. She and Clementina dipped them into hot chocolate to soften them. Afterwards they sat in the drawing room by the window and watched the weather.

'We will have ham tomorrow,' Clementina said. 'The chocolate is all very well, but the rolls are gey chewy.'

'Ma'am?' a voice cuts into the darkness.

Startled out of her reverie, Elizabeth jumps and lets out an undignified squeak. She swings round. The undergardener who fetched her from the port is behind her. He smells faintly of beer but he is not swaying like a drunk man.

'I thought it was you,' he says.

Elizabeth draws herself up.

'Mr McNab was working late,' she explains. 'His candle caught my attention. What are you doing here?'

The lad grins. 'It's my monthly half day, ma'am,' he says. 'I went to visit my brother on the Cowgate.'

She cannot chide him for that.

'Well, don't go sneaking around,' she chastises him. 'You gave me the fright of my life.'

'Sorry,' he apologizes. 'I didn't know it was you. I just saw someone crouching by the new hedge.'

Elizabeth blushes. He has caught her snooping.

'The land the Garden is laid out upon was part of the house's grounds, was it not?' she asks, pointing through a gap in the holly. The boy nods.

'Mr Rocheid sold it to the university and feu'd out the acres beyond to a builder. Cook says she cannot imagine respectable folk wanting to come and live out here. The nearest church is as far as Trinity. But they will start construction soon – at least that's what they're saying at Canonmills.'

'It will be a terrace of houses?'

The undergardener nods.

'They will have a lovely view,' Elizabeth says. 'Once the new Garden is planted.'

The boy shrugs. This kind of detail is beyond his care.

'Does Mr McNab have a son?' she asks.

'Yes. The eldest is often around the Garden. He'd be a lad of nine, I should say. They will build a house by the gate for the McNabs but the plants must come first. It is some job his father has taken on, moving all that.'

'And does Mr McNab have a mother?'

'He must have.' The boy smiles at his own joke.

Elizabeth ignores this and continues. 'I saw Mr McNab with an older lady tonight. His wife, perhaps?'

'Mr McNab's wife is Mistress Whiteman. She is not old by any measure and I've never known her to come here.'

'White-haired?'

'Brown. She is with child.'

So Mr McNab is a married man and clearly fond of his son – she could see that even from this distance. She likes him even more.

'Shall I accompany you back to the house, ma'am?' the boy asks.

Elizabeth nods. She finds herself wishing for a cup of tea and something to go with it. In Richmond there were occasionally vanilla friands. Not that Cook's repertoire here will run to that – if you cannot manage bread rolls, then cake is out of the question. The memory of her little house filled with the smell of baking is almost the only pleasant memento she has of the life she left behind. At Inverleith House she comforts herself, the fire is still lit in the drawing room and earlier today she found an interesting novel, the pages uncut, which was written by a woman of Clementina's acquaintance who she refers to as 'poor, dear Mrs Brunton' but has not explained why, adding only 'They say that book took Europe by storm, the poor soul.' Clementina pities everyone, Elizabeth thinks. Probably she pities me. I am a widow, after all. *Poor, dear Elizabeth Rocheid.* She gestures up the hillside. 'Yes,' she says to the boy. 'Let's go home.'

On the path she notices bats swooping between the trees to the east of the house and grunting badgers in the bushes near the icehouse and the smell of woodsmoke from the fire that makes the air feel warmer. She smiles at the spiders' webs caught in the moonlight, threaded like festive garlands round the yew bushes beside the laundry.

'Goodnight, ma'am,' the boy says as she peels off towards the front door.

'Goodnight,' she calls after him. 'What is your name?'

'Calum. I'm Calum, ma'am.'

'Goodnight, then. Thank you for seeing me back safely, Calum.' Scottish names sound strange to her but she is getting used to them. It is a sign she is settling in, she thinks, as she disappears into the warmth, where she breaks the moratorium she has laid down against troubling the staff at night and rings the bell for someone to bring her a pot of Darjeeling.

Chapter Five

As the lacquer clock in her hallway chimes midnight, Belle Brodie clatters across the flagstones and up the stairs, throwing off her fur-edged cape and kicking her green satin dancing slippers under the sopha. She waltzes round the sitting room in stockinged feet, humming Beethoven's Six Ecossaises as she glides through the double doors to her bedchamber and flops onto a chair upholstered in powder pink paisley velvet. 'Nellie!' she calls and the maid rushes in.

'Can I get you something to eat?' the girl offers.

Belle shakes her head. She had a cup of white soup not half an hour since to warm her before the carriage ride home from her half-brother's house on Charlotte Square. It is to both their credits that Belle and Joseph Brodie get along famously, having spent very different childhoods that shared a common theme – that of the Brodie family's attempt to drill the niceties of polite social conduct into them. However, conformity, it turns out, is not in their blood, no matter how hard their family tried to make it so. Belle has, after all, long since sold her virtue and Joseph, while living more conventionally than his sister, espouses radical politics from the safety of his well-clad drawing room. He even spoke for the men in Glasgow two years ago who rose against their conditions. 'Why shouldn't they form a union?' he objected. 'I'm sure I would do the same, for they have no power individually to better themselves.' This outburst of opinion shocked the Lord Advocate who was visiting that evening. But that is why people accept invitations to Joseph Brodie's house. To be stimulated. To be challenged. They say two hours at a Brodie salon will keep you thinking for the rest of the year.

This iconoclastic strain, Belle and Joseph joke, must come from their father, a man hardly known to either of them for he made his fortune in sugar in the colonies, where, having married Joseph's mother and accompanied her to Scotland to set up a home, seduced Belle's Mama the very week he arrived.

In the havoc that ensued, Mr Brodie Senior promptly left both women behind and set sail once more for Jamaica, where Joseph vows that he kept a 'dark mistress' until his death. Belle understands that what her brother means by this is 'a slave of whom our father took advantage'. That this is considered less shocking in society than the arrangements Belle has arrived at to keep herself means that Miss Brodie is discreet in her brother's company. To maintain the peace they never discuss their late father or the matter of Belle's occupation, pretending that the money Joseph paid her to hand over her father's letters has sustained her living for the decade since they met.

Joseph tailors his invitations on the occasions his half-sister attends his social events – ensuring foreign visitors aplenty, a few distant, poorer relations and a smattering of his more liberal-minded friends. In company they intimate that she is a widow. Joseph's wife, meanwhile, objects to Belle's invitations. 'Belle is my sister,' Joseph counters and there is nothing the poor woman can do about her husband welcoming a courtesan into their home, for all the reasons that Belle herself chooses not to marry. That Belle sold her virginity in her brother's drawing room several years ago is a matter Mrs Brodie only suspects and will never be able to prove, for a quiet conversation and a discreet visit to a lawyer to draw up the terms on which Belle coolly insisted happened so smoothly that it was only afterwards that Mrs Brodie began to wonder. Her husband's ideas may challenge the orthodoxy but for her, as for many people in society, a young lady being in charge of her own person is the most challenging idea of all.

In the bedchamber Nellie helps Belle out of her clothes as her mistress chatters excitedly about dancing with her cousin and sitting next to a French fellow of Joseph's acquaintance who has written a book about the nature of reality. She might as well be talking about fording rivers in the Amazon or touring the streets of Madrid in an open carriage. Nellie has no experience of supper dances or writers, but she nods enthusiastically as she fetches the mistress's peach satin nightgown and ties her auburn hair with a ribbon the colour of jade.

'And the music,' Belle enthuses. 'Joseph had a string quartet in the drawing room.' Here Nellie's eyes light for she loves a tune. It is the reason she walks two miles there and two miles back to attend church on a Sunday. Belle starts singing. Her voice is as sweet as a thrush. They taught her well in the schoolroom. Sometimes when the mistress sings, Nellie tarries on the stairs to listen. She sighs as Belle pipes the final chorus with a flourish and waves her away to stow the evening dress and its attendant finery in the dressing room.

Alone, Belle checks her appearance in the glass and sits at her writing desk. The patter of late-night rain on the window provides a pleasant percussion. She fumbles in the drawer for a fresh sheet of paper and considers what to write. This, she smiles, is not the usual position of a whore earning her living, but then Belle is not in the business of providing expected services. A young lady of considerable education, she approaches her professional duties with the imagination of somebody with more than a passing interest in the arts and sciences – a true child of the Enlightenment. Daily, she bends nature to her will, drinking a cup of pennyroyal tisane at bedtime, which so far has been successful in preventing the kind of error that her mother made – not the mistake of making love with a married gentleman but of falling victim to the affair. The poor woman believed Belle's father would stand by her. Such naivety sets Belle's teeth on edge.

Growing up, Belle's governesses called her wilful and tried to beat it out of her.

'I worry that you are possessed by an evil spirit,' Miss McCarthy said so often that Belle began to wonder if it was true. But she is now unconvinced that good or evil exist, as she confided this very evening to the writer who sat next to her at dinner.

'Kindness,' she added, 'is another matter. Whether something is good or evil is a judgement in the mind of men, but kindness must involve two people, which makes it tangible.' The French gentleman's eyes shone – he had heard that Edinburgh was full of ideas. It is one of the reasons he came here.

'Madam,' he said, 'this is charming. Tell me more.'

Later he asked her if she had ever been in love and Belle admitted to him quite candidly that she had never embarked on such a venture. 'I don't believe in love – only desire and, of course, pleasure,' she said, leaving him slack-jawed, even though he is from Paris.

Now Belle draws a crow's quill from the box and flips open the lid of her De Lamerie inkwell. When she set upon her course, she instinctively understood her chosen role – her plan since that day in a distant family attic when she came across a trunk containing a dead uncle's papers. A night guide to London that included shocking, if stirring, details of hundreds of whores of different classes – most enlightening for a thirteen-year-old girl who had been brought up to believe that enjoying a hot bath was a sin. The trunk also contained the memoir of a person who Belle's nanny would call a fallen woman, printed on paper so cheap Belle feared it might tear as she consumed it by candlelight, propped up in bed. And letters from Uncle Samuel's mistress, Lucy, to whom he paid sizeable sums of money and who – to his frustration, it seemed – would never tell him that she loved him.

Belle had always known that she would not become a wife, though that is what her mother had hoped for her. 'You will make up for me, won't you, darling?' she would ask. Such conformity, however, was not in Belle's nature. She was a pretty girl and enjoyed conversation and by the time she found the trunk in the attic her mother was long dead, and Belle was already aware that men were interested in her. One man quite forwardly introduced himself in Perth when she was out shopping. Another had tried to take her aside at a Christmas party. Now, she learned, she could earn her living, not as a fallen woman in a desperate, dingy garret but, as Uncle Samuel's mistress did, as an independent woman in charge of her own money and living in style. Examining a map of London that Belle found in the house's library, she discovered that Lucy resided in Westminster next door to an earl.

The real profit, she understood immediately, was not to be made in the momentary spreading of legs and opening of mouths. Over the years following her discovery of Uncle Samuel's legacy, Belle educated herself about the golden age of London's courtesans – the beautiful Sarah Pridden and the incomparable Lady Hamilton – icons in style, with taste as excellent as the best of wives and sisters, yet answerable only to themselves. Accomplished ladies earning their fortunes with their intellects as much as their bodies. Sophia Wilson succeeded, after all, in marrying Lord Berwick and her sister, Harriette, in bedding the Duke of Wellington. Coming to an arrangement with a bookseller in Perth, Belle had pamphlets smuggled in with the newspapers – scandal sheets, every one. One day the bookseller offered her a banned night guide to Edinburgh and Belle lit up, realizing she need not go to London at all. Instead, she resolved, she would reside fifty miles south of her childhood home. In Scotland's capital city. Near her half-brother, who she once overheard her governess telling Nanny was quite as bad as Miss Isabel, though born on the right side of the bedsheet.

As she continued to study for her future occupation, Belle became resolved that in addition to being a willing partner in the bedroom, or indeed in any room of the house, it was her job to touch the depth of a fellow – to understand him through and through. From the start she decided to be available to only a select number of men. Two, in her case. For, like most Scottish women of her class, she had read Adam Smith's treatise *The Wealth of Nations* and understood the laws of supply and demand on the price of any commodity.

When she finally escaped the Brodies' Perthshire estate at sixteen, she took herself to market with two aims: to sell her virginity and to choose her own clients, money not being the main item in either decision. Firstly, she did not want an aristocrat. Perthshire was full of aristocratic gentlemen, flighty creatures who regarded her as if she were a juicy steak, lucky to be eaten. No, Belle desired fellows who had earned their fortunes and had been married for some time – no flibbertigibbet youngsters who were likely to fall in love with their own wives or behave rashly in the matter of their mistresses. She also chose men whose tastes would provide her with the greatest opportunity for her own entertainment. For all work and no play makes Jill a dull girl and nobody wants one of those.

Belle, it turns out, has chosen her profession well. It brings her more satisfaction than she imagines she would derive from a marriage, where she would be as good as owned by her husband and entirely dependent on his generosity. She likes carnal intimacy too much for that.

Belle met both her present lovers at her brother's salon. Both made their fortunes in the building trade – one as an architect and the other as an investor. Older, in their forties, both were troubled by their marriages and happy to pay for her discretion. She does not lie to them about her arrangements, so they know about each other. And, to be clear, the men never visit Belle together, or, as one of them put it when he believed himself to be laying down the law, 'This is not to be an Italian affair, Miss Brodie.'

Now she dips the crow's quill in the iron gall ink and begins to write to this very gentleman. She expresses herself in the most forward terms, for there is nothing he enjoys more than receiving unexpected erotic demands. He peruses Belle's letters at his New

Town breakfast table and pretends to be annoyed over the legal detail of a transaction.

'My lawyer is a fool,' he says, 'I shall have to call on him this afternoon and may be late for dinner.' His wife takes his blushes for anger and instructs the cook to make something that can be kept warm. The mistress of his house never demands anything of her husband, which is perhaps why he is so partial to Belle's missives, and why they compel him to rise, as it were, to her requirements. He is a man who wants to be wanted. For his visits Belle waits by the door like an eager puppy.

'What shall we do, Ruari?' she asks, ever at his convenience. When he makes love to her, she squeals with delight.

Belle tuts at a smudge of ink on her finger but continues writing, finishing the letter with a saucy flourish. *I long for you, deep inside me, to make my rivers flow and flood so you, my love, might quench your thirst in my passion.* Yes, that will do it. He has visited as usual of late, but it has been a couple of months since she wrote to him. The letters must be infrequent to have their full effect – two arriving in two days and then nothing for weeks to add spice. Satisfied, she drops the crow's quill into its box and, using a candle, seals the paper with melted red wax. Then she sits back before picking up the book she is reading on the botany of the Americas. Belle's studies are of vital import to her longer-term plans – her real security. Miss Brodie subscribes to the maxim of John Hope, Regius Keeper of the Garden in the last century, President of the Royal College of Physicians and associate of the Marquess of Bute, who founded the Botanic Garden that is moving a few hundred yards up the main road from the house in which she now sits. 'I believe we derive more knowledge from the senses than all books together', he wrote. Exactly, she thinks, although, as a businesswoman, she believes she will get not only knowledge from the fruits of her senses but also money.

As a scientist she always pays attention to the best conditions for her encounters. Cotton sheets or silk? In the morning or afternoon?

With enthusiasm or with hauteur? It is this passion for enquiry that has led her to have her most interesting and potentially lucrative idea – the notion that has fired her interest in botany and that will, in due course, make her fortune beyond the endeavours of her whoring and see her well-provided for when old age robs her of the bloom sought by gentlemen in their mistresses.

It started with a plate of strawberries three summers ago.

The berries were a gift – the latest thing after years of the world exciting itself about pineapple, a fruit that makes the inside of Belle's mouth tingle unpleasantly. The berries were not the wild, native species, tiny woodland fragoli, but a new, larger and more fragrant kind, grown exclusively by a farmer in Pencaitland under the auspices of the Royal Caledonian Horticultural Society. It so happened that she had kept a plate of them by the bed on a day when both her gentlemen came to call, one after the other. She could not be sure it was the strawberries, but both men were unusually energetic that afternoon. 'I feel very good,' the second gentleman announced, somewhat mystified, but leaving nonetheless an unsought-for stack of half a dozen guineas on the mahogany table beside the armoire. This from a man who speaks so rarely that Belle's staff have never heard his voice. Not the man who wants to be wanted, but the other one, who longs to possess her without explanation. Whose heart sings when he crosses unspoken boundaries, a traveller in the bedroom, if nowhere else. Sometimes he cries when he holds her afterwards and she knows not to ask him why.

Belle put the guineas in her reticule and took a note in her journal. In the following days she ate strawberries and did not eat strawberries. She removed the strawberries from the side table and replaced them. She tried raspberries, her favourites, to no avail and a fold of red cloth in case it was the colour that was stimulating. It was not. She put back the strawberries but this time under a glass cloche.

After a month of experimentation, and at the end of the berry season, Belle concluded it was the scent of the fruit that had this promising effect on her lovers. So, in the spirit of enquiry, she tried other smells. Both peppermint and rose gave her a surprising edge, but not the men. They liked it, however, when she smelled of citrus. She bought a parcel of pummelos and lemons from the Danish Consul at Leith and another of blood oranges, pipping to the prize the chef of the Melville family, who had hoped to make his famous bloody marmalade pudding. With these treasures Belle had her young protégé, Edzel, concoct a perfumed oil that she drizzled liberally into her bath. Her gentlemen, always well disposed towards her, became suddenly avuncular. They sent presents – the silent man a set of silver combs fashioned by Charles Dalgleish, the city's greatest silversmith, the other an ornate gold brooch set with garnets and pearls in a dark leather case trimmed with purple velvet.

That first winter, ever resourceful, Belle began to correspond with spice dealers in Spitalfields and botanists in Bombay, whose names she discovered in the esoteric books she borrowed from the subscription library on George Street. She invested in cinnamon bark and star anise in quantity and conducted experiments in shops and at masked balls at the Assembly Rooms. She had Nellie dress like a lady and promenade along George Street wearing different scents, and Jamie, the coachman, in a borrowed suit of clothes, buy costly accessories for the carriage at the forge on Rose Street Lane wearing by turns the scent of pine mixed with ambergris and a dark perfumed oil concocted from leaf tobacco and cedar.

After almost a year she concluded that while she could not make anybody do anything they did not want to do, she could certainly enhance their natural feelings. The smell of leather made people respect a man more readily. Lavender calmed them. Rose made women more loquacious, but not men. All this was interesting, but Belle understood quickly that the true prize was a scent that could encourage a man who liked you to fall in love. And by God, she was determined she would find that scent. Not for her own use, for Miss Isabel Brodie means what she says and has no time for love. She will never be a wife – she could not bear it – and it is only wives for whom love has a purpose. No. Instead, she determines to find this scent, to make it and to sell it in Edinburgh for three thousand guineas at least, before taking a vial to London and, if she is lucky, doubling her money. The potion will make her fortune as surely as sugar made her father's. It will secure her old age. And with such funds comes safety. Respect. Absolute freedom. Even for a lady.

Nellie brings Belle's night-time tisane as the clock in the hallway strikes one. She puts away her writing things. There is a rare swan's quill in Belle's chest – another present – but it does not demarcate the letters as well as the short, black crow's feather and while Belle does not object to beautiful things, she is nothing if not pragmatic. Yawning, she lays aside the book. The tea smells faintly of peppermint, which focuses her mind as Nellie fusses round her.

'Anything else, miss?' the maid asks.

'Have that sent by courier, would you? In the morning?' Belle indicates the missive propped on the bureau. It must go by the common message boy, who, although none too bright, will raise no suspicion. She climbs into bed, catching a satisfying glimpse of herself in her vivid satin nightgown as she considers the merits of the aloes about which she has been reading. They are soothing plants despite their spiky appearance. Perhaps she will be able to use them. She stretches out like a cat.

'Snuff the candle,' she orders. Nellie does as she is told and engulfs the room in darkness, the glow of embers from the fire lighting her skirts as she bustles out of the door.

In darkness, Belle sips her tea from a Rathbone china cup with dusky roses around the rim. She sinks deeply into the pillows before falling asleep. She will dream, as she does every night, of flying through the sky in a basket under a balloon made of paper and silk – a story she first heard in her nursery, regaled by a nursemaid who was later dismissed for being, frankly, too pleasant. The maid showed Belle an engraving of the famous Vincenzo Lunardi taking off at Heriot's Hospital more than three decades before, in his pink, green and yellow balloon, before he flew across the Firth to Fife, where he landed on farmland at Ceres, to be welcomed by an overexcited local priest and a crowd of farmhands who had abandoned what they were supposed to be doing to marvel at his descent.

'That is a wonderful story,' seven-year-old Belle whispered, her blue eyes bright.

'It is a story, but it is also true. Imagine that, Miss Isabel,' the maid replied. 'Someone has flown like a bird, up there, among the clouds.'

Belle took the image as a maxim for life, soaring above earthly cares, striving for sunlight and freedom, riding the currents that she revisits in her dreams. She is a woman who always sleeps well.

Chapter Six

Elizabeth Rocheid has not ridden in a long while. Clementina offers her the use of an old side-saddle. 'It has sat in the stable these several years,' she says. 'At my age I always have the coach brought round, but you are just a lass. You can ride, can't you?'

Elizabeth nods. As a girl she rode to hounds. The undergardener saddles one of the elderly black mares that drew the coach the other day. Its coat is well-tended but fading. Clementina claps her hands. 'This fine old creature is called Glenzen,' she says. 'Which means "to glisten" in German. The Rocheids own a great deal of land in Germany. My grandfather kept a house there. It was beautiful,' she sighs. 'I don't expect I shall ever see it again. When I was young, I had a bay but now James keeps all the sprightly horses for himself. He's bought an Arabian stallion, I heard. Quite the thing. Glenzen will do for you, will she not?'

Elizabeth watches as the boy checks the buckles are secure. She circles the mare. Calum hands her a riding crop.

'Whenever you're ready, ma'am.'

'Where shall I go?' she asks. She knows nobody and is not the type to ride over and introduce herself to the Fettes or the Wardies, the nearest neighbours, though she will undoubtedly meet them once she has settled in. Everyone around here seems to know everybody else – from the grandees to the parlour maids.

'Och, take a turn about the grounds, lass,' Clementina urges. 'Try her out.'

The lad helps Elizabeth mount and she and Glenzen set off gamely at a trot. She finds that she is laughing at being so high and moving so directly under her own command. It has been a long time since she felt so free. She looks back and waves at Clementina, standing with the house behind her. Then the old woman falls out of sight as the horse follows the natural curve of the land towards the farm and Elizabeth uses the reins to steer the mare in the direction of the water. She has heard the torrent in the night through her open bedroom window but has not yet seen it.

'Come on,' she gees the horse. 'This way.'

The Rocheid land runs down to the river and Elizabeth feels entirely in charge as Glenzen fords the stream, dousing the hems of her dress. On the other bank the public road is well worn with the distillery ahead and a good-sized cottage opposite with a bed of onions in the garden. Elizabeth's ankles are wet and her skin stings with the cold. She did not dress for riding this morning.

Glenzen continues towards the junction, past the ragged huts that make up Tanfield. Ahead, a pretty blonde girl is picking her way along the road. When Elizabeth nears her, she realizes the girl is blind. Could this be the witch from the distillery? She could not look less like one.

'Good morning!' she calls as she crosses the footbridge past Warriston Crescent. She tries not to remember that William berated her once for speaking to a serving girl who appeared to have lost her way on the street. 'It is beneath my station to have my wife pay notice to a maid. Don't you understand how it looks?' he snapped.

Elizabeth tears her mind from the memory and turns it to the enjoyment of the gentle sweep of the crescent. Clementina has mentioned this development – the first land to be sold to builders across the city boundary. 'Only very few rooms, my dear,' she said. 'Homes for the families of well-to-do tradesmen.' She dismissed this notion with a sprightly flick of her wrist. 'We have used one or two of them for jobs on the estate.' The old woman likes her status. Lady of the manor. Saviour of the starving. Perhaps all the Rocheids are snobs of one kind or another.

The road ahead is deserted, with fields on both sides. To get back to Rocheid land, Elizabeth must take the entrance that she took the first day, in the carriage. To the right, two surveyors are laying rope boundaries on one of the plots set aside for more houses (Clementina swears they will be grander than the little crescent and attract doctors and the like. She says this with a shudder, not because doctors are beneath her, but because they evoke illness and while she thinks of little else than the prospect of being hungry, Clementina does not care to imagine being ill.) The men doff their caps as Elizabeth passes, but this time she says nothing. The works will commence soon, she thinks, and slows Glenzen as they come to the entrance of the Garden – a laneway to the left with a wooden gate that is currently gaping. Elizabeth takes this as an invitation, turning the horse off the main thoroughfare. 'That's right,' she says brightly. Glenzen dips her head and does as she is bid. This must be more fun than drawing the carriage, Elizabeth thinks. More fun for me too.

The yard beyond the gate is all mud with a shed of the type used by gardeners countrywide to shelter from the weather. An iron chimney belches a thin stream of smoke, carried off by the lightest breeze. Ahead, up the slope, she sees the holly hedge, dark against the sky, more imposing than last night, for from here it seems to be bearing down. Glenzen halts. In the distance Elizabeth makes out two men wearing tweed trousers, waistcoats and caps digging by the lake, their shirtsleeves rolled to their elbows, and beside them two young, well-dressed gentlemen, one with a book in his hand – students, she imagines. They are standing by a bed of rushes arguing about something until one reaches down and splashes the other and they start squabbling like children. She slides to the ground and tethers the horse. 'Stay here,' she directs the animal, muddying her shoes and hems further.

From the pathway she can hear the voices of two more sensible-sounding gentlemen than those down by the lake and she heads towards them, coming into a glade where William McNab is in conversation with another man. The gardener sounds impassioned.

'But sir,' his voice rising, 'This is not the arrangement agreed with Mr Rutherford. There was to be a review.'

The gentleman wears a greatcoat the colour of chocolate and a sleek, black top hat.

'Rutherford is dead, McNab.'

'Respectfully, do you expect my children to go without education?' McNab presses him. 'It is not tenable.'

The gentleman is about to reply when he catches sight of her.

'Madam?' he asks, and she hears the relief in his voice at being interrupted.

'My apologies,' she says as she steps closer.

'The new Botanic Garden is not open to visitors,' the gentleman announces. His cheeks are like pink apples and his hairline, as he tips his hat, is receding. 'Are you lost?'

McNab cuts in. 'This is Mrs Elizabeth Rocheid of Inverleith House,' he introduces her. Elizabeth feels a sting of pride that she has been remembered.

'Rocheid? But James is a bachelor, is he not?' the other man retorts.

'Mr Rocheid is my late husband's second cousin,' she explains.

'Mrs Rocheid illustrated for Sir Joseph Banks at Kew,' McNab continues. Of course, she thinks, he has remembered me because of that.

'Indeed?' The gentleman now appears interested.

'That is the purpose of my visit,' Elizabeth says. 'I met Mr McNab on the day of my arrival and being more settled, I came to offer my services.' She assures herself that while this does not accurately represent the haphazard nature of her decision to visit, broadly it is true.

The gentleman makes a deep bow. 'I am Robert Graham,' he says. 'The Regius Keeper.'

'Mrs Rocheid is interested in the removal of the trees,' McNab says. 'I thought to suggest, madam, that you might illustrate the process.'

'Ah yes,' Elizabeth says. 'I would be delighted.' It was, she thinks, such a wonder to see.

'As you rightly pointed out, we may find a journal that would print such material to educate others about the method which we have developed,' McNab adds enthusiastically.

Mr Graham's eyes betray his opinion of this idea, and it is not high.

'Not trees again,' he says, dismissively. 'The flora is where the public's interest lies, McNab. It is why I have been endeavouring to comprehensively classify Scotland's flowers, Mrs Rocheid. Last summer I led an expedition to the Highlands where we discovered several unknown species. My students and I will return this autumn. To have an illustrator such as yourself, that Sir Joseph Banks has sanctioned, would be an honour indeed. We may place a piece in the *Edinburgh Review*.'

McNab scowls but before he can say anything, from beyond the greenhouses, two children run, laughing, into the opening. They are younger than the students – and their clothes are dry, their wearers not being foolish enough to splash in the pond even on a sunny day.

'James! Catherine!' McNab chides them.

The children come to an abrupt and guilty halt. The boy is the pale, dark-haired child from the other night, the girl is a redhead attired in a pretty, if worn, pinafore. Her arms are like sticks.

'Are these your offspring, Mr McNab?' Elizabeth asks cheerily.

'James, my eldest son, and Catherine, a year older,' McNab introduces them.

Catherine drops a curtsy but James freezes. Elizabeth crouches.

'Hello,' she says. 'I think I spotted you, James. From up there on the hill. The other night. Your father was working late. You must have been helping him.'

James relaxes. He grins. 'Yes,' he confirms. 'The plants look strange at night.'

'I imagine you are a tremendous help,' Elizabeth encourages the boy.

Mr McNab, however, tenses. 'You were watching us, Mrs Rocheid?'

'Yes,' Elizabeth points towards the holly, 'from up there. I was taking a promenade after dinner. You were in the greenhouse.'

The gardener's pallor grows.

'I'm sorry,' she says, 'I did not mean to offend you. Who was the woman you were with? Was it your grandmother?' she asks James with a smile.

McNab cuts in. 'The children have no grandparents living.'

'I'm sorry,' Elizabeth apologizes. James's shoulders are almost at his ears once more – his father's good graces are, it appears, everything to him.

'A woman with you, eh? In the Garden?' Mr Graham leers at McNab. 'And with the boy too.' He chortles. 'That's rum, McNab. Very rum.'

'I don't know to whom Mrs Rocheid is referring,' McNab objects. 'James and I were here but there was no woman, I can assure you.'

'It was very dark,' Elizabeth says apologetically, though she knows what she saw. Still, she has no wish to cause difficulties. She smiles once more at the children. 'You must be proud of your father's garden. You certainly seem to be enjoying it.'

'I can show you around, if you would like,' McNab offers stiffly.

'I would not take up your time, Mr McNab, but perhaps James and Catherine could give me a guided tour?' she suggests.

This being agreed, McNab and Mr Graham disappear towards the Garden's northern boundary to inspect beds of legumes in which Mr Graham has an interest.

'The pea flower has a regal colour,' he says, as they walk away. 'We should consider the dye and the paints that might be made. Professor Munro doubts the flowers have medical properties, but the apothecary tells me they relieve swollen limbs. That is the thing with flowers . . .' and the men disappear, obscured almost immediately by a copse.

The children show an interest in Glenzen, tethered in the yard. Elizabeth wanders back with them and lifts Catherine onto the side-saddle while James leads the horse by the reins, clippety-clop in the direction of the pond. The young men have now deserted it and moved towards the arboretum.

'She's a good old girl, this horse,' Elizabeth says.

'I can see everything from up here,' Catherine exclaims as they come to the row of greenhouses. 'All of God's great works!'

Elizabeth lets out a laugh and the little girl glares at her. Her cheeks redden.

'Sorry,' Elizabeth says. 'That was an unexpected thing to say when your Papa has worked so hard to form this Garden by his industry.'

'It is God that guides him, ma'am,' the little girl says. 'Who else?'

Elizabeth wonders whether Mr McNab prefers God's guidance to that of Mr Graham, for it is clear the men do not get along. She hopes she has not caused a ruction. Meantime, she puts the matter out of her mind as James takes on the role of tour guide.

'Father has seen to it that the Garden is laid out in the manner favoured by the great botanist, John Hope,' the boy announces, somewhat formally. 'Dr Hope eschewed traditional geometric design and the plants are displayed in mixed beds so we might experience them in concert.'

These are strange children, Elizabeth thinks. They are clearly used to being around adults, as if they are on display.

'And what is in the glasshouses?' she asks.

'Succulents,' James trots out.

'In this one?' Elizabeth indicates the glasshouse that was lit like a lamp the night before. James nods.

'Do you know at Kew some of the glazing is green? Sir Joseph Banks was of the opinion it is better for the plants, imitating the sunlight through the canopy of a tropical forest,' she says.

'Indeed.' James's gaze is serious. It would not surprise Elizabeth if the little boy removed a notebook from his pocket to write the information down.

Elizabeth peers inside. The greenhouse is warm, fired by a coke stove at the far end that heightens the smell of freshly hewn stone and whitewash of which the beds are constructed. The plants are alien with their fleshy, engorged leaves. Some are covered in what appears to be blond hair and spikes, protecting their sap. In the various deserts that are their natural home, all moisture is treasure. She would like to draw these, she thinks, and chides herself for being contrary, for this is the very thing that neither gentleman has asked.

'Do you know the names?' she enquires.

James pipes out genus and species according to the Linnaean system.

'That big one is *Agave americana,* but it is known as the century plant for it only flowers once in a hundred years,' he says, pointing it out.

Elizabeth regards the plant. It is by far the largest in the greenhouse, taller than she is and as wide as a small carriage.

'Really? How interesting.'

'The flower is due,' James adds. 'It is the plant that may save our bacon, if Father can time it right.'

'Save you? What do you mean?'

James bites his lip. He has said too much, but he is rescued by Catherine who, from the saddle, gives a little squeal.

'Let me down!' she insists, as if in a panic. 'Help me.'

Elizabeth can tell that she is feigning distress, but she unmounts the child. Again, she decides not to press the point though there is clearly something afoot. 'Let's walk round the pond,' she says. 'There are several trees waiting to be planted there, are there not?'

'The roots must rest,' Catherine says. 'That's what Father says.'

'And they must not be over-watered,' James adds. 'Madame de Sévigné has written on the subject, but Father has learned more.'

Elizabeth realizes that McNab is a kind of god to his family. 'Your father has asked me to make drawings of his process,' she says.

'Perhaps you can show me the trees that arrived earlier this week. That would be a start.'

'Oh yes,' Catherine endorses this heartily. 'Come on, James.'

Later, when she comes to take her leave, she finds McNab alone. He stands straight as a chestnut tree and quite as unyielding.

'Mrs Rocheid,' he says coldly.

'I did not mean to . . .' she blushes and finds she cannot continue. The gardener's face does not betray any reason for this bad feeling, and she does not wish to discuss it. 'Can we put it behind us? I most ardently wish to be friends and friends do not pry into each other's business,' Elizabeth says warmly. She begins to wonder if the woman she saw in the night was some kind of wraith. There is clearly more to Mr McNab than she thought and yet her instinct is that he is a good man. One way or another, the Garden is a boon and she wants to be part of it.

McNab nods curtly. 'I would like that,' he says.

'And my drawings would be useful?' she checks.

'Yes,' McNab concedes.

'We will say no more of it then,' she replies and, mounting, turns Glenzen towards the road.

As she rides through the estate gates, Elizabeth hopes Clementina will have no objection to her bringing down her painting things, which remain as yet unpacked. She suspects that if the ensuing illustrations are for publication, the old lady will surely approve. She can set up a workplace in the music room, where the light from the French windows is exactly what she needs.

The driveway curves along the perimeter of the estate before sweeping towards the house in a generous arc and Glenzen takes the approach at a canter until Elizabeth pulls her up, catching sight of a smart closed carriage at the front door. It's a fancy conveyance, festooned in brass fittings with two exactly matched chestnut stallions attached to its limbers and two footmen in dark blue livery standing alongside. The coachman, also in uniform, is talking to one of the maids. Elizabeth halts by the stable and dismounts. The maid disappears inside guiltily as Calum comes to fetch the horse.

'Who has come to call?' she asks. She looks forlornly at her stained hems and filthy boots, hoping it isn't the Fettes or the Wardies, all enquiry about Mr McNab's mysterious night-time visitor now put entirely from her mind.

'It is Mr Rocheid, ma'am,' the boy says. 'And he is in a terrible temper.'

Chapter Seven

The hallway smells of pipe tobacco as she sneaks inside and gazes longingly up the stairway, wishing that she could tidy herself before going to the drawing room.

'Is that you, Elizabeth?' Clementina calls, scotching any such idea. Her heart thumping, Elizabeth enters. The man ahead of her is younger than she expects – perhaps only in his late twenties, wearing a sober tailcoat with brass buttons and smart silk pantaloons that match his dark waistcoat. He bows curtly. Elizabeth blushes, his dapper outfit putting her to shame. He looks like Beau Brummell in his heyday, she thinks, at once exquisitely turned out and almost invisible. Smooth-skinned, his hair is mid-brown, his eyes slightly darker, his features so regular that they feel somehow restrained. There is nothing remarkable about him, and yet he looks the very gentleman. 'Starch makes the gentleman, etiquette the lady,' she remembers someone saying as she drops a curtsy.

'Mr Rocheid,' she greets him, trying to conjure something more to say – perhaps to thank him for his kindness in bringing her here or to apologize for being out when he arrived. But before she can formulate a graceful sentence, she is distracted. Behind her, Clementina is stood next to the fire, an embroidered screen between her skirts and the flames. The old lady is hooting with laughter, her eyes mere slits. Joining her in merriment is a portly fellow with bushy, greying hair, wearing a red jacket and buff breeches. Splayed on a comfortable chair, he puffs on a pipe as he chortles.

'Elizabeth!' he hails her as the two elders finally stop giggling. 'I am James Rocheid. This is Johann von Streitz, our guest. All the way from Germany by way of London.'

'Mrs Rocheid,' Herr von Streitz gives a formal bow. 'I am pleased to make your acquaintance.' He kisses her hand. His palm feels dry, as if it is made from paper. His accent, she notes, is almost perfectly English – a little flat on the vowels, but that aside he might have been raised in Mayfair. Her cheeks flush.

'I'm so sorry,' she says. 'I can't apologize enough.'

Clementina waves the mistake away. 'Herr von Streitz insisted on coming to see me,' she cuts in. 'His grandmother was a great friend in my Leipzig days. The flower of my youth. Though I have never before met Herr von Streitz, I feel as if I know him already.'

'Indeed, my grandmother remembers you fondly, Lady Clementina,' he replies smoothly.

'Well, you must return to Inverleith House before you leave Edinburgh,' the old woman says, her tone flirtatious for a thirty-year-old, never mind someone grazing eighty. 'I will read your grandmother's letter and write a reply. You will carry it for me, will you not?'

'I return to Leipzig later in the year – perhaps for a month after Christmas. If it can wait, I will gladly take it myself. If not, I can dispatch it for you, madam, in the diplomatic bag.'

'How kind,' Clementina preens. 'But you will stay a while then? Pray tell, what brings you to Edinburgh?'

'The king's visit,' Johann replies, unable to hide his incredulity that Clementina does not already know this.

Elizabeth nods. Currant Bun mentions the visit almost every day, so excited is she at the prospect of George IV coming to Scotland. 'It's not been officially announced ma'am,' the girl gushed only the day before. 'But Sir Walter Scott, the writer, is organizing the programme. We will be allowed a half day to see the king, won't we? For he will be about the town.'

'I'm sure that will be fine,' Elizabeth had replied.

Addressing the gathering she now asks, 'Does the king come to Edinburgh often?'

James Rocheid snorts. 'He will be the first reigning monarch here since the Hanoverians took power. In over a century, girl. Herr von Streitz has come to make sure the arrangements will suit the king.'

'Indeed,' Johann confirms. It is supposed to be a secret, but he realized almost as soon as he arrived in Edinburgh that this city is not adept at keeping confidences and most people seem to know who he is. 'I am usually at court in London,' he adds. 'His Majesty has not yet decided if he will grace the Scottish capital with a visit, but if he does, it's my job to see that it is a great party. My father was second cousin to His Majesty George III, the present king's father. In our family it is common to serve in this way.'

'What way is that?' Clementina enquires.

Johann's demeanour remains as smooth as his perfectly combed hair.

'The English do not like Germans at court. But from the ascension of the first George, the royal family kindly provided a place for one of us to assist the king in his private arrangements. I am the current incumbent. Travel is an experience, that is how you say it, is it not? An education.'

'Johann is staying with Sir Walter Scott,' James adds, proudly. 'Sir Walter is of course close to His Majesty, but you are the king's official voice in the matter of his Scottish arrangements, are you not, m'boy?'

Johann's manners make it impossible for him to admit to such a thing. 'We are working on it together, Sir Walter and I,' he replies. 'And now, if I might be excused to the closet?'

Clementina rings the bell, and someone comes to show him the way.

Once Johann is out of earshot, James Rocheid sighs.

'You are so out of the way down here,' he says, and then turns his attention to Elizabeth as he puffs with ferocity on his pipe. 'Where on earth were you? I brought you here to look after my aunt and the first time I call I find you are out gallivanting!'

'Now, James,' Clementina starts, but Mr Rocheid will have none of it.

'Well, let me look at you,' he motions at Elizabeth.

She steps forward, painfully aware of the mud on her boots. As James inspects her, she imagines him as a giant hedgehog, sniffing her out. He certainly does not look the least like William. He must, she concludes, take after a different side of the family.

'I cannot have you about the town looking like this,' he says. 'Can you not sew?'

Elizabeth nods.

'I can, sir.'

'Well, do so. You need new frocks, madam, if this is the best of your wardrobe.'

'I have been out riding,' she says quietly.

'Well, for that you should have a proper jacket of wool or velvet. And a fashionable chapeau. Have them send me the account, for heaven's sake. Why, you look like a milkmaid.' He snorts at his own joke. 'Where did you get to anyway?'

Elizabeth explains her route, noticing that Clementina is more focused on her nephew's reactions than anything she is saying. Happily, James Rocheid seems interested in the Garden next door when she mentions it.

'I have sold another plot,' he announces, puffing away. 'Smaller. Only eight acres this time.'

Clementina gasps. 'Not land from the farm!' she says. 'James, not the farm.'

'No. Not the farm. The plot is to the south of the new Botanic Garden,' he blusters. 'The government have taken it and for a good price. Calm down, Aunt, it is to go to another horticultural concern, one directed to graft new species to improve agricultural yields. They like the sheltered nature of the low ground. You are in the safest place in the country now, old girl. A medical garden to the east and a scientifically set up kitchen garden to your south. I thought you'd be thrilled.' He laughs, delighted with himself, as if he has caught the old woman out.

The sound of footsteps emanates from the music room as Johann returns.

'A harpsichord,' he says. 'How wonderful. I understand that the lyrics of some of Joseph Haydn's English songs were written by a Scottish woman.'

'Yes,' Clementina enthuses. 'Poor, dear Anne Hunter. Her husband was quite the collector of zoological artefacts.'

'Well, there you have it,' James says getting to his feet. 'We must be off. I only came to have a look at you, Elizabeth. And to accompany Johann in delivering his letter. We had best get back to town. I have business to attend and I can't imagine Herr von Streitz is at leisure. Sir Walter is putting on quite the show, as I understand it.'

'Will His Majesty take an interest in the Botanic Garden?' Elizabeth asks. Her relations seem surprised that she has spoken but Johann replies easily. 'I believe there are beautiful grounds at Dalkeith Palace where His Majesty will stay if he chooses to make the trip.'

This does not satisfy her. 'I mean the new Botanic Garden which borders us here. It contains a great many plants used in medicine – for teaching,' she says. 'It is an extraordinary endeavour: they are moving thousands of plants, including mature trees, to a plot of fifteen acres that Mr Rocheid has sold to them. They have a new process that uproots the trees into barrels and allows relocation by cart. It is most innovative.'

'His Majesty is little interested in botany,' Johann replies. That is not entirely true. His Majesty is interested in promenading in attractive gardens. But there his interest ends. This woman, however, seems keen and there is something earnest about her. She is, unlike most women he comes across, clearly not particularly interested in the king. 'He likes flowers, I suppose . . . as an ornament,' Johann adds.

'I'm sure it would make a difference to the venture to have a royal patron,' Elizabeth continues, feeling a strange loyalty to McNab.

Johann turns.

'I will look into it, Mrs Rocheid,' he finds himself promising.

'They have a century plant, you see. Which is about to flower. It is extremely rare.'

'Hush,' Clementina snaps, suddenly short-tempered. 'The gentlemen must go.' The group falls to silence as the party removes to the hallway where the gentlemen's greatcoats are fetched.

Clementina and Elizabeth wave from the door as the carriage draws away.

'We must buy cloth today.' Clementina keeps her eyes trained on the retreating footmen. 'For your new dresses. And this riding jacket. It has become fashionable to patronize some of the newer shops peppered around the New Town, but I find those establishments overpriced and much prefer the traditional booths, at the Royal Exchange. I shall accompany you.'

'I thought to bring down my watercolours and portfolio,' Elizabeth says. 'I promised I would illustrate some of the plants next door. For the head gardener, Mr McNab.'

'We will charge everything to James's account,' Clementina continues without acknowledging that Elizabeth has spoken. 'I may buy a hat. There is a tolerable milliner at the Exchange.'

Inside, she rings the bell by the fireplace. 'Have Duncan ready the carriage,' she orders the maid. 'And fetch our cloaks and bonnets.'

'Duncan?' Elizabeth asks, her curiosity roused. The boy's name is not Duncan.

Clementina sits in the chair recently vacated by James Rocheid. She pushes away the Venetian glass ashtray on the side table into which he unloaded the contents of his pipe. 'Pah,' she says, wrinkling her nose. 'In all the excitement with James and Herr von Streitz, you did not hear the news. Our coachman is returned.'

Elizabeth nods. 'I see.' She gazes towards the music room door, thinking that the light today is of a pleasant quality. She would rather stay and paint, but she cannot bring up the matter again. Clementina is set on a shopping trip. The old woman rubs her hands together. 'And that is not all. He comes with news. Or news of him comes, more accurately.'

'About our coachman?'

Clementina leans conspiratorially towards Elizabeth. 'His mother passed away. And on her deathbed decided to unburden herself to him. Poor man. Some fond farewell, that was.'

Elizabeth decides she must be patient. Clementina is evidently enjoying herself. Her eyes flash with delight.

'And what did the coachman's mother say?' Elizabeth asks.

'On her deathbed, mind. In front of the minister and two good women – neighbours – she admitted that she had disgraced herself. That Duncan cannot truly be owned by his father. Long dead now, thank God. She told him that his real father is, in fact, another fellow.'

Elizabeth arranges her features carefully. Clementina is now on the edge of her seat.

'None other than Mr Burns, my dear,' the old woman says breathily. 'It was in some drinking den in the Old Town when he visited. The time he hurt his leg. She was a serving maid in those days at his lodgings and succumbed to Mr Burns's advances.'

Elizabeth's vacant expression betrays her ignorance.

'Oh no! Surely not!' Clementina mourns. 'You must have heard of Robert Burns. The poet of the age. He cut quite the dash and is renowned the world wide still. "My Luve is like a red, red rose, that's newly sprung in June . . . Till a' the seas gang dry." '

'Ah.' Elizabeth recalls this poem. It is, indeed, quite famous.

'I mean he was known for, well, you know how these poets are . . . with women,' Clementina continues. 'Think of Lord Byron. I myself met Mr Burns several times. He wrote my friend's daughter a verse. She and her sisters. The nine muses, he said, could not do better than the Ferrier girls. And I see it now. In the coachman, I mean. Burns was a fine-looking man. I had not thought of it before. Why would I? But there can be no denying it.'

In the doorway, Elizabeth catches sight of him out of the corner of her eye. A tall man, dark-haired with wide, black eyes. His jaw is set to fury. She blushes.

'Ah, Duncan,' Clementina says. 'I have been telling Mrs Rocheid your news.'

'I have not told you my news, ma'am,' he growls. 'I'd rather nobody spoke of it.'

So excited is she that Clementina does not falter at this. 'One of the maids let me know. It will not affect your employment. I was, in fact, very fond of your father.'

Elizabeth steps forward. The poor man, she thinks, everyone between his mother's deathbed and this house has been talking about him.

'Is the carriage ready?' she asks.

'It will take a quarter hour, ma'am. The boy is fetching water. We must brush down Glenzen. She is covered in mud.'

'That is my fault, Burns,' Elizabeth says, trying to be kind.

The man's eyes harden. It seems she can do no right today.

'Burns isnae my name, ma'am,' he says gruffly. 'With all due respect. Lady Clementina has always just called me Duncan.'

Chapter Eight

At last there is time to change. Elizabeth rushes upstairs and swaps her mud-spattered attire for clean, thinking that for Glenzen it is much easier. Currant Bun is in a lather as she fixes her mistress's hair.

'I can see it in his face, ma'am. Not that I ever met Mr Burns, but Cook has a copy of his anthology and there is an engraving of his likeness on the leaf. Who'd have thought it? Duncan looks very like him. Cook says it'll be all over town – in the *Review* and that.'

'Margaret,' Elizabeth lays down the law, 'Duncan himself does not wish to speak of it. This tittletattle is most unbecoming.'

In the reflection of the mirror, Elizabeth can see the shock on Currant Bun's face at the idea of not discussing this, the most fascinating and glamorous piece of news ever to arrive at Inverleith House. In fairness Clementina is clearly going to be just as bad.

'Yes ma'am,' the maid says unconvincingly.

Elizabeth runs a palm over her hair and directs the girl to take down her watercolour palette, three brushes, charcoal sticks and lead from her drawing box and the thin sheaf of paper from her leather portfolio.

'Put it in the music room,' she says. 'And my painting smock.' When leaving the old house, she had debated whether or not to bring her stained linen apron but now she's glad she did. 'And see if there might be a board somewhere. I will need one to lean upon.'

She wonders if she might be able to buy more paper at the Exchange and if there are botanical volumes in the library that will be of use. But there is no time to check.

Outside, Clementina is already in the carriage. Calum stands to the rear like a footman, but not up to the snuff of the suave servants that perched on the back of Mr Rocheid's carriage. Above, Duncan sits on the box with the reins in his hands, his expression no softer than it was in the drawing room. The boy opens the door and helps Elizabeth up.

The ride into town is bumpier than she remembers on her arrival. Up Pitt Street she peers out of the window at the sandstone terraces on either side of the road and the stick-thin trees newly planted behind the railings in the gardens that are being laid out at Heriot Row. It looks, she thinks, warmer than the stuccoed streets of Belgravia on account of the honey coloured stone. Shop boys bustle to and from George Street where the carriage has to wait at the junction, so busy is the city's main thoroughfare. Elizabeth notices two women pointing at the carriage, or, more specifically, she realizes, at Duncan. They move off, giggling, one bursting into a song that Elizabeth assumes was penned by Mr Burns. At the foot of Hanover Street, as the carriage crosses towards the slope of the Mound, Clementina sighs.

'They drained the loch,' she says sadly as they climb and Elizabeth takes in the view of the New Town from the south. Ahead, the buildings are taller and blacker with tiny windows like dark pockmarks. The laneways feel like rookeries. Ragged children beg on the streets. In a doorway, a woman is sat with a tattered grey shawl around her shoulders, drunk. Her face is filthy and her eyes are closed as she mutters under her breath. This surely is an entirely different city from the one they have just come from. Clementina, it seems, is nostalgic for it and entirely at home in this part of town.

'I was brought up in Germany, but I visited Edinburgh three times as a child. The Rocheids have always owned land at Broomlaw but my father also kept a house near the palace,' she says fondly. 'Further down. I returned as a young woman. To come out.'

Duncan pulls up at the Royal Exchange, opposite the ornate façade of Saint Giles High Kirk where beggar children dodge between the blackened buttresses. Elizabeth descends delicately, bringing her handkerchief to her nose. The whiff on the air is anything but pleasant – the stench of shit thick on the filthy streets. Clementina, meanwhile, jumps down like an excited teenager going to her first ball, and heads under the arches into a paved square round which the Exchange's booths are grouped.

Inside the milliner's there is scarcely room to swing a cat and Clementina's wide old-fashioned skirts crowd the space.

'Lady Rocheid,' the serving woman curtsies.

Clementina jostles Elizabeth forward.

'Myself and my young cousin would like to look at hats,' she directs.

A month ago, in Richmond, such luxury would have been a dream but now, even though Elizabeth knows her clothes are dowdy, she is surprised to find shopping tiresome. The assistant bustles and Clementina chooses a hat for herself and two for Elizabeth – adding bows and feathers at the milliner's suggestion. They move to the next booth to buy cloth and Clementina commissions a lilac dress in the style of all her others and turns to Elizabeth. 'You will want muslin, no doubt,' she sniffs. Elizabeth picks a pretty, sheer yellow fabric and is directed by Clementina towards a strong pink gauze in addition, before turning her attention to the matter of the riding jacket, for which she chooses dark red velvet. The assistant measures the women, remarking that Elizabeth's proportions are so perfect she could be a statue.

'You and William must have made a fine couple,' Clementina says. 'He was such a wonderful little boy – so full of energy and excitement. Bright too, as I recall.'

Elizabeth smooths her skirt and says nothing.

'You are not the kind of widow who talks about their husband, are you?' Clementina adds.

'You're quite right. That sort of woman is tiresome indeed.'

They move on again, this time to browse reticules and fans in a glass-topped rosewood cabinet in the shop next door. Elizabeth chooses a pair of bottle green gloves, embroidered with daisies at the cuff.

Outside it has started to rain – only a spit. Duncan carries the parcels to the carriage. 'Thank you,' Elizabeth says as she hands over the boxes. Beside her, it is clear that Clementina does not want to leave the High Street and its memories.

'What else is here?' Elizabeth asks kindly as a costermonger walks by offering early apples.

'Saint Cecilia's Music Hall,' the old woman says dreamily and points down the slope. Elizabeth stares down the muddy incline as a woman leans out of an upper floor and empties a bedpan onto the pavement. Clementina does not seem to notice. 'This place was so alive and look at it now,' she continues. 'It seems so poor. No society, to speak of. It's gone so downhill. And the public concerts have been moved to the new Assembly Rooms where the acoustics are nowhere near as good. It's such a shame.'

It does not seem so far to Elizabeth, that people moved not half a mile to the north into better, more modern accommodation, but perhaps the Old Town was some kind of wonderland in its day. It is difficult to imagine.

'Is the library still here?' the old woman asks, turning up the hill.

Elizabeth takes her arm and they pick over the muddy setts. A fleabitten terrier barks from a doorway and falls to heel behind a small boy, who talks to the dog in Gaelic. Opposite the Tolbooth in front of the cathedral Clementina ducks inside a doorway and climbs the stairs. Sure enough, on the first floor the winding staircase opens into a library – an unexpected haven in the muddy, smelly morass.

'I remember this as a child,' she says. 'I got my first copy of Mr Smith's book here when I was only a girl. I had to wait a fortnight.'

The library is crowded with mahogany shelves, each one crammed full. At the front, periodicals are arrayed on a table. Space here, as in the shops below, is at a premium but it is warm and dry and smells comfortingly of leather bindings and good-quality paper. Elizabeth wonders if there was ever any room on this side of town. No wonder the planners made the sandstone streets to the north so wide and the buildings so grand.

From behind the stacks a librarian emerges. He is so thin that his black breeches would fit a child and his coat looks as if it has been drawn onto his body. He reminds Elizabeth of a thin, black quill. The man peers at them through his glasses.

'Good day, ladies,' he says.

'We are not subscribers,' Clementina avows. 'I was saying to my cousin here that I recall this library from my youth. I am Lady Clementina Rocheid.'

It is impossible to tell if the man has heard of the Rocheids. He gives a little bow. 'How might I help?' he asks.

Clementina moves towards the windows through which she spies a long strip of land that leads down to the drained loch and the newly built houses beyond, on Princes Street. The carriages look like children's toys as they trundle in both directions, carrying people about their business along what was once the riverbank. Elizabeth decides to take her chance.

'I wonder,' she asks, 'do you have any books about botany?'

'Botany?' the librarian appears to be searching a catalogue in his brain.

'Something illustrated, perhaps?' she prompts.

'We have a copy of Mrs Ramsay's botanical lectures and all the editions of Mrs Blackwell's *A Curious Herbal*,' he says. 'You will have heard that story.'

Clementina turns. 'She married her cousin, though he was a ne'er do well,' she tuts. 'He was executed for treason abroad.' Elizabeth wonders if in this city there is anything that everyone doesn't know about everybody else. She is not interested in flowers, she realizes – it is the strange cacti from the Garden that are calling her.

'Do you have anything about American plants?' she pushes the librarian.

'Ah – the new world is a veritable Eden. I have heard that Mr Douglas is writing about the trees of North America, in the footsteps of Mr Menzies as he is,' the man says. 'Though at this time we only have one book, which is principally about a journey across the plains, and I'm afraid that Miss Isabel Brodie has it on loan.'

Elizabeth is disappointed. 'Do you know when the lady might return it?'

'Miss Brodie is a voracious reader. I understand she has a subscription at both libraries,' the man says, his tone of disapproval clear as glass. There is, of course, another subscription library in the New Town. Elizabeth notes that Clementina does not chime in with a story about Miss Isabel Brodie, whoever she might be.

'No matter,' she says.

Outside, Duncan is waiting with a hanway raised to keep off the rain. Already muddy, the High Street quickly becomes a quagmire, the smell of sewage heightened by the movement of the water. They are almost back at the carriage when Clementina spots a gentleman on the other side of the street, shrouded in a navy cape and hat with a silver-topped ebony walking stick for he sports a limp.

'Sir Walter,' she waves.

He crosses the road and bows.

'Lady Clementina.'

'I had the pleasure today of meeting the king's man, Herr von Streitz,' she says. 'He is the grandson of an old friend. I understand he is staying with you.'

Scotland's greatest living writer nods. Von Streitz is residing with him, some of the time at least. Elizabeth thinks she sees a flicker of discomfort in Sir Walter's eyes.

'We are planning diversions for the king,' he says, 'should he choose to make a royal visit to Scotland.'

His eyes turn towards Elizabeth, prompting Clementina to make the introduction.

'My second cousin's widow has come to stay with me at Inverleith House. Mrs Elizabeth Rocheid, this is Sir Walter Scott. Sir Walter, we have just come from the library.' Elizabeth smiles.

Scott grins. 'You are a reader then, madam?'

'There is an excellent library at Inverleith, sir,' Elizabeth replies, 'but I was particularly looking for books on the subject of botany. I have undertaken to paint illustrations for use at the new Botanic Garden. Have you visited it?'

'Not the new one. My uncle, you know, was the keeper until he died – at the old place.'

'Indeed?' Elizabeth realizes this can only strengthen her case. 'Sir, I petitioned Herr von Streitz to bring the work of the Garden to the king's attention. I was held up when I first arrived by the most extraordinary procession of trees. Do you not think His Majesty would wish to know about the innovations taking place?'

Sir Walter has come to understand over the last several months that the king is mostly interested in grand houses, fine dinners and the presentation of ladies. Like von Streitz, since news of the royal visit has become known, he receives requests daily about worthy causes that would benefit from royal patronage, but His Majesty is not greatly interested in dispensing charity. Gifts for the monarch, on the other hand, have already started arriving at Holyrood Palace. Across the country illicit whisky makers are pondering schemes to snare a royal endorsement should His Majesty grace the country, naming their latest blends Highland King and Royal Scot. More bottles of whisky than there are legal distilleries have been received. Musicians have been engaged in Italy and chefs from France are en route. Everyone Sir Walter meets hints that they would like an invitation to something – anything at all. These ladies on the other hand, he realizes, do not seem concerned in the slightest. He finds that an endearing quality.

'Perhaps you might care to attend one of the balls we are planning? With Lady Clementina, of course,' he offers. 'One of the evenings we hope His Majesty will lead the dancing at the Assembly Rooms? Have you a tartan frock? The dress code is Highland.' The king is reputed to be delighted by tartan, which is one reason why Sir Walter has fixed upon it as a theme. Something uniquely Scottish around which sentiment can coalesce even here, in the Lowlands, where it is not traditional.

'Oh yes!' Clementina exclaims. 'It is most kind of you.'

Scott tips his hat, glad she did not press him for a more intimate invitation. Four hundred and fifty-seven ladies are already being presented at the king's drawing room – His Majesty's first public engagement, preparations for which are causing havoc at Holyrood Palace where workmen are converting the guard chamber into a throne room fit for the king's use, just in case. It is said His Majesty will kiss every one of the ladies in greeting and that doing so will take him less than two hours. 'Proficient at kissing, is he?' wags joke about town.

They bid their goodbyes and Sir Walter continues down the hill as Clementina grasps Elizabeth's arm and pulls her back towards the Exchange. The coachman follows, uncomplaining, holding shelter over their heads as they tip over the draper's threshold.

'We require tartan,' Clementina announces with a gleam in her eye. It feels daring to say so. Since the Bonnie Prince's defeat at Culloden the year she was born, the wearing of tartan coats has been banned.

The assistant bustles forward.

'For the ball, madam? Or the drawing room?' Since the prospect of the king's coming, tartan has been workaday for him.

'The ball. Enough for two gowns,' Clementina says.

'I have red shot silk or green. The other colours are gone.'

'Red, of course,' she barks, without consulting Elizabeth. 'There should be no other colour. All the worthwhile tartan was red when I was a girl. Besides, I suit it very well. Let's have a look then. What have you got?'

Chapter Nine

Robert Graham has tried his best to secure even a tentative invitation to any element of Sir Walter's party but to no avail. Few professors at the university are well enough connected to do so, but the Botanic Garden, he keeps telling himself, is a royal garden, originating in Stuart times at Holyrood Palace. As the Regius Keeper – the king's keeper, if it comes to that – he feels his post at the Garden ought to afford him the right to meet His Majesty in person, if only in the company of other worthies. Since he was appointed, Mrs Graham has organized several lavish dinners at his Great King Street townhouse to entertain the great and the good of the city but so far, no royal invitation has been forthcoming.

Graham never wanted the job at the Garden. The shoes of previous keepers are hard to fill. John Hope and Daniel Rutherford were pioneers who changed the way students are taught, advancing the boundaries of medicine. Mr Graham knows he has no new ideas. He is a competent and well-read physician but if he progresses science in any way, it will be through the classification of Scotland's flowering plants, his compilation of which might form a useful tool for others. To the rear of the house he has a small laboratory, fitted with a microscope and chemistry equipment, but he does not go there often, having long ago admitted to himself that the rooms most likely to further his prospects are the dining room and the cellar.

As in most other premises in Edinburgh today, the talk below stairs is of the coachman who has discovered he is Robert Burns's bastard. The news has percolated upwards into the family rooms but Graham is disinterested in poets and does not like Burns's work, be it sugar-coated ditties to please the ladies or (for the gentlemen) drinking songs, frankly too crude for Graham's blood. A footman brings a silver tray with two letters. Robert slits the seals with a letter-knife. The first missive is from William McNab, whose neat writing covers two pages, precisely the length that Graham asked for when they last parted. The letter makes McNab's case for a pay rise from eighty to a hundred pounds a year. It is not an unreasonable request but an irksome one. The university has been difficult about releasing funds for the Garden's move, never mind an extra amount to supplement McNab's wages. Graham peruses the argument and feels a sting of annoyance that the man has made his case well – he took a pay cut when he first arrived in Edinburgh on the understanding his wages would be augmented in time. That was ten years since and the one hundred pounds he is asking for is less than the one hundred guineas he was paid as a far younger man in London as foreman of Kew.

Laying down McNab's letter with a sigh and thinking he will have to do something with it, Graham turns his attention to the other missive. Opening it, he reads the first two lines and guiltily peers over his shoulder. He is alone. Outside the window, the rain patters onto Great King Street, rendering the wide paving stones glossy. Graham reads the first two lines again and blushes. *My dearest one, I have need of you. Such need. I want you to take me on the Indian rug by the fire, and on the sopha where we played cards and then on the chaise longue . . .* Graham turns over the page, and sees, with some confusion, and a little relief, that he is not the intended recipient of this letter. It is addressed to his neighbour, Mr Ruari Innes, an architect and a family friend and, Graham skips to the end, it is from a person signing themselves simply as B. Mrs Innes's name is Flora. Graham sits back in his seat. With a twist of shame, he moves the letter to conceal it as the footman returns.

'This just came from the Inneses, sir,' he says and hands over a third letter. 'It was delivered in error.'

Graham splits the seal on the missive he should have received – a letter from a friend in London, relating botanical news from Kew. However, he cannot concentrate upon it. The Latin names swim before his eyes. The talk is of seeds, herbarium specimens and cuttings. It is no use, he realizes, as he picks up B's troublesome scribbles once more. The seal being split, if he dispatches the missive to the Inneses' house, Ruari will know he has read it. He blushes at the thought. Looking at the fireplace he contemplates burning the thing, but the destruction of somebody else's private correspondence feels wrong. *I long for your kisses in all my secret places.* The letter is dated this morning and addressed simply Warriston Crescent. Mr Graham cannot dispatch a boy to return the letter to the sender, for that surely will result in some kind of gossip. Besides, it is opened now. It comes to him that the fewer people involved the better. In fact, there should be no further people involved. He must deal with this himself.

Rising from the table, he resolves to walk the half mile down the hill and across the Water of Leith, for taking the coachman with him would be a double indiscretion – first in the matter of the man himself and second in the sighting of the Grahams' coach, which is recognizable. Likewise, calling for his horse to be saddled may result in questions. Instead, he has the butler bring his chocolate greatcoat and black top hat and bangs the front door behind him. The rain is not as unpleasant as it looks and the air, if not warm, at least is not cold. He makes it to the bottom of the hill speedily and pauses at the head of the crescent. The letter contains nothing to identify from which house it emanated and there are, as he sees it now, at least thirty in the terrace. The river has flooded and an old man wearing patched tweed trousers and a knitted top is attempting to shore up the defences on Number 1 of the crescent, by piling sandbags at the bottom of the garden. Graham pushes past the bay trees and leans over the wall.

'I say,' he clears his throat. 'I am in search of a lady who lives along here. Initial of B.'

The man's hands are pink and raw as he stops and peruses Mr Graham in an impertinent fashion.

'You don't know the lady's name that you're looking for?'

Graham blusters.

'Well, do you? It is a civil question.'

The fellow looks amused and Graham squirms. The old buffer can't know what I'm here for, he assures himself.

'It may be Miss Isabel Brodie,' the man says eventually. 'Calls herself Belle.'

Graham nods. 'Yes. That may be it.'

'Number seventeen with the shutters of the dining room closed to the street.'

Along the crescent, Graham raps on the front door and waits. He fingers the shameful letter in his pocket and is surprised when the door is opened by a presentable maid with a long, strawberry blonde plait and a well-scrubbed air.

'Sir,' she says, stepping back to let him in.

'I came to return something to your mistress.'

'She will be delighted to see you,' the girl says.

It strikes Mr Graham as he steps inside that he has not been asked for his name before being invited over the threshold. Removing his hat, he notices that the hallway smells strongly of cinnamon and lavender, and he suddenly feels strangely relaxed. Inside, the house is fitted beyond its humble exterior. The hall table is a fine example of a Thomas Chippendale and he could swear the portrait of a lady hanging over it is by Allan Ramsay – a painter as highly thought of as Raphael.

The maid leads Mr Graham up the curved staircase, the rain pattering on the cupola. She opens the drawing room door but does not announce him. The room he enters into is lavish – quite beautiful, in fact – and most beautiful of all is the woman sat by the fire wearing a fine, green dress the colour of spruce leaves. She has been reading – from the cover, a book about American plants. The woman's eyebrows arch as she rises.

'Sir?' she says, dropping a curtsy as the maidservant closes the door.

Graham's cheeks burn as he recalls why he finds himself here.

'Madam,' he bows. 'I'm afraid there has been a mistake.'

'Might I help to rectify it?' Belle replies smoothly.

'I received . . .' but he cannot say more. He pulls the letter from his pocket and offers it to her, worrying momentarily that this beautiful creature did not, in fact, pen the missive and that he is about to offend her. Belle laughs and he relaxes. She takes the letter.

'Oh dear,' she says. 'Might I offer you a cup of tea? Or something stronger? Please, sit down.' She rings a bell and the maidservant appears once more.

'Take this gentleman's things,' Belle says, 'and bring us a tray, would you, Nellie?'

Part of him wants to refuse but this part does not win the internal dialogue upon which he finds himself engaged. He hands over his coat, hat and gloves and, tame as a lamb, sits on the sopha. She is certainly not the strumpet living in chaos that he expected.

'You are reading about botany, madam?'

'I am most interested in the world of plants,' the lady admits. 'Do you think we should introduce ourselves? We can use aliases if you prefer.'

Graham stares blankly. He can think of no other name than his own to offer.

'I am Robert Graham,' he says. 'At your service, Mistress Brodie.'

He notes that she does not acknowledge the fact that he knows her name, though presumably she remembers she did not use it to sign the letter. Belle folds her hands in her lap.

'I am most interested in flowering plants,' Graham posits, his eyes moving towards the book she has now discarded on the side table.

'This time of year they are coming to their most potent, are they not?' Belle says. 'The scent of roses and of lilies is best captured early if it is a good summer. No later than July certainly.'

'Why yes,' he says, not sure where this might lead.

'I'm sure you know far more than I do,' she adds, putting him at his ease. 'I am always keen to learn about flowers.'

'Well, we are about to witness the flowering of one of the rarest plants in the world,' Graham says enthusiastically. '*Agave americana* – it may be in your book.' He gestures towards the discarded tome.

'In Scotland?'

'In Edinburgh.'

'My goodness,' she leans forward, clearly fascinated. 'Mr Graham, have you ever smelled it?'

It is the strangest question he has ever been asked and he converses regularly with medical students, some of whom appear quite witless. 'I have not smelled it,' he admits.

Belle seems disappointed.

'I imagine it must have an extraordinary scent.' She picks up her book and flicks through it. 'Here,' she says. 'It flowers only once before it dies. It sounds operatic, does it not? I mean, the scent of a flower like that must be potent. Surely.'

Graham laughs. 'Perhaps we will stage a perfume party,' he says, letting his imagination stray. 'Open the Garden to the public when the flower blooms. It is common practice in India, I understand, where there are flowers which only release their scent onto the cool night air. *Cestrum nocturnum*. Night jessamine.'

Belle cocks her head. 'You are an expert then,' she says.

Graham hesitates only momentarily to tell her his occupation, but then again, he reasons, he has already given her his name. 'I am the Regius Keeper of the Botanic Garden, madam,' he admits. 'The agave is housed there. Very close, in fact, on land newly procured to the north of here.'

'I thought that place was an arboretum? I saw the procession of trees when they were moving them.'

'Good heavens, no,' Graham replies, shocked. 'I can show you myself, if it would please you. The Garden houses many species aside from the trees. The flowers there are extraordinary.'

'Perhaps after we have had tea, we could fix a time,' Belle says as the maid returns with the tray. 'I have not got the leisure today.'

Robert Graham takes the delicate cup Belle offers him and notes that the shortbread on the matching plate is studded with cumin seeds and dusted with powdered sugar. He tries to ignore the sense of unease that is creeping over him. This woman, he must assume, is Ruari Innes's mistress and yet she appears so pleasant and interested in what he has to say. The house, although small, is furnished as well as, if not better than his own. He sips the tea – a smoked jasmine blend, if he is not mistaken – and takes in everything. As he bites the biscuit, he decides he will tarry a while longer. After all, it would be rude not to.

Chapter Ten

The women did not expect to see Johann von Streitz again so soon. James Rocheid's visits to his family home being few and far between and Clementina's acquaintances being, for the most part, deceased, visitors to Inverleith House are rare. Save, of course, for little James McNab, who, having found a gap in the holly hedge, has taken to calling in the afternoons. Today Elizabeth is teaching the boy to paint.

As Herr von Streitz arrives, all three are ensconced in the music room, Elizabeth painting the picture of the willow tree upon its cart which she intends to present to William McNab as a start to the recording of his project, James drawing a branch of early roses snipped from a bush in the grounds and Clementina, with spectacles propped on her nose, reading Robert Burns's poetry aloud. Elizabeth has not, in the last week, succeeded in dampening Clementina's interest in the bard. At least the poetry is not as bad as the endless reminiscences.

'Ladies,' Herr von Streitz bows.

Clementina rises, visibly delighted. 'Johann. How nice.'

Elizabeth thanks her stars that today she is clean when he comes to call.

'Is this a family group? How charming!' Johann exclaims.

'Not at all,' Clementina sets him right. 'The boy is the gardener's child. Mrs Rocheid has taken a fancy to him. She is very indulgent.'

'Show the gentleman your picture,' Elizabeth prompts James, who jumps up, eager to please.

'Ah. *Rosa arvensis*,' Johann declares at the sketch of the white blooms with their intricate sunny yellow stamens.

Elizabeth laughs. 'There, James, your drawing is perfectly passable. Well done.'

Johann pauses before walking closer to the window to overlook Elizabeth's board. 'Is this tree from the Garden you mentioned?'

'Have you considered my suggestion, Herr von Streitz?'

'That is why I am here. I came to visit the project and thought you might like to accompany me as its champion.' He gives a little smile and then turns to Clementina. 'And of course you must join us, madam.'

Clementina sniffs. 'I am just an old woman. I hardly leave the Rocheid estate,' she says. 'Not these days.'

Elizabeth wonders what she means. Clementina left the grounds not three days since, but then the old woman is always giving dramatic pronouncements.

'A shame,' Johann replies, but he does not argue.

'We shall bring James,' Elizabeth continues. 'He can show you round the Garden as he showed me when I first saw it. He knows the place as well as anybody, excepting his father.'

The child beams.

Coats are fetched and the carriage is called. As Johann goes outside to mount his horse Clementina pulls Elizabeth aside.

'I think he likes you,' she whispers with relish.

'Tosh,' Elizabeth gets out. It is the best retort she can come up with. Von Streitz is ten years younger than she is, never mind anything else. She ushers James outside ahead of her, his eyes shining at the idea of a carriage ride, if only for a few hundred yards. Inside the carriage, he carefully inspects the upholstery, running his pale, thin fingers over the burgundy fabric and breathing in with a faraway look on his face that, she realizes, indicates he is memorizing the experience.

'You have not ridden in a carriage before?'

'No, Mistress Rocheid,' he says. 'Only Mistress Dickson's cart,' he adds, but he does not elaborate further, staring out of the window and straining to hold the leather strap above his head as the carriage sets off, though the ride is not bumpy. Elizabeth notes the woman's name.

Not five minutes later, the clouds have parted and the sun feels warm on her face as Elizabeth climbs down to the muddy yard, this time lifting her hems sufficiently to keep them clean. James runs to find his father. Johann tethers his horse. In his position, many would expect their coachman to do this for them, but he appears unspoilt by his time at court. Once her husband dined with the Duke of Wellington and afterwards he became quite unbearable. Not unbearable, she chides herself – that is the wrong word – but more arrogant than usual, certainly, boasting of every tiny detail of the dinner for weeks. Yes, that's what happened. When he was not posted in the pursuance of his military duty, William frequently insisted she escort him to society dinner parties and even to balls – wherever he could procure an invitation, for he believed connections were everything. 'We must make progress,' he always said and blustered about the position of the people with whom he was acquainted. What would he say now if he knew she was here on an errand with the king's representative?

She shakes off the thought as she and Johann wander silently down to the greenhouses. The trees cast shadows, dappling the uneven clay where paths have not yet been established. William McNab appears behind his son, who is practically dancing with excitement.

'Mrs Rocheid,' he says. 'What a day.'

'This is Herr von Streitz. He is here to see the century plant,' Elizabeth introduces the visitor.

McNab bows. 'Of course.'

'I have started to draw your process, Mr McNab. The carts and so forth. I have chosen to start with the willow that I saw in motion the day I arrived.'

'Good. Good.' She is glad he seems to have got over her intrusion about his night-time visitor. They are square, it seems.

As they reach the greenhouses it is clear they are not the only visitors. Mr Graham's dark greatcoat is visible through the glass and beside him is a smart lady in a muslin frock embroidered with peacock feathers at the bodice to match the one trailing from her hat.

Beside Elizabeth, von Streitz gazes around him, at everything from the trees still cased in barrels beyond the glasshouse to the group of men levering a bush into place a hundred yards ahead. Seeing him against nature is interesting. In the drawing room he appeared so at ease among the fine wallpapers and ornaments but here, too, he has a natural air. She thinks that clearly he is someone who fits in everywhere.

'This is lovely, isn't it?' von Streitz says.

Elizabeth smiles, feeling oddly proud of the Garden. 'I like it too. This place has a long history. These plants have been collected over many years.'

'Almost two centuries,' McNab confirms. 'The Garden started at Holyrood Palace but it has been sited on the road to Leith for many decades. Though the collection has always been impressive, when I arrived ten years ago I was given the job of extending it. Lately there have been many interesting discoveries made by adventurers abroad and the stock had fallen behind what might be expected in a collection of this importance. Since I started in my position however, we have grown near a thousand new species. Many from seed. Hence the present move.'

'How many species do you have in total?' Johann asks.

'Between four and five thousand, sir.'

'My goodness,' he says.

The sun has warmed the greenhouse. As they enter, Robert Graham looks sheepish as if he would bang repeatedly against the glass in an effort to escape if he could, like a trapped fly or bumble bee. Elizabeth realizes this is strange for, if she reads him right, he is a man who values connections and here is the king's own man come to meet him. He should be pleased.

McNab makes the introductions, the two parties not being acquainted. The lady is called Miss Brodie, a name which Elizabeth finds familiar.

'Might you be Miss Isabel Brodie?' she asks.

'Yes,' Belle replies.

'How have you heard of Miss Brodie?' Mr Graham cuts in.

Belle smiles and cocks her head, waiting for Elizabeth's reply. She finds Mr Graham's reaction amusing. He is a man who will be caught out in any wrongdoing, if he panics at a mere introduction.

'It is a guess,' Elizabeth admits. 'The century plant is American, is it not?'

McNab confirms this.

'I was hoping to borrow a book about the botany of America from the library on the High Street. The fellow said Miss Isabel Brodie had taken out a book on the subject. And here you are.'

'What a good memory you have, Mrs Rocheid,' Belle says.

Graham looks relieved as Belle smoothly moves on the topic of conversation.

'We were just discussing the aloe being due to flower. Mr McNab says it is on its way. How long will the flower last, Mr McNab?'

'As far as we know it is only a matter of a month at most. It will be an extraordinary sight,' McNab says. 'Before flowering the plant sends up a stem so long that we will have to remove the glass above it.'

Everyone looks up. The greenhouse is not particularly majestic, but it must be more than fifteen feet high.

'How big will it get?' Belle asks enthusiastically and Robert Graham looks curiously uncomfortable once more.

'I've heard the shoot may grow to twenty feet, miss, on a plant of this size. Perhaps higher,' McNab says.

'And then?'

'It flowers, and when the flower fades, the plant will die. She may only have a few months more in this world, but I hope we will succeed in propagating another from her seed. I have taken cuttings but none of them have taken.'

'May I?' Belle gestures towards the leaves.

McNab nods. 'Of course.'

She leans over and, removing her glove, rubs the surface. Then she sniffs her palm. Dissatisfied with this, she asks, 'Does the flower have a scent, Mr McNab?'

'I do not know.'

'It must be a huge bloom.'

'It will be tall, anyway.'

'I have now read the library book to which Mrs Rocheid refers and it mentions the *Agave americana,* but not the scent of its flower . . .' she persists.

'I suppose,' McNab says, 'we will have to wait to smell it.'

Belle licks her lips and says no more.

'I'm sure Herr von Streitz would be most interested in your process, Mr McNab. The carts,' Elizabeth chimes.

'No carts today,' McNab says regretfully, 'but I can show you some barrelled trees.'

Von Streitz smiles. 'Thank you, Mr McNab. I wonder, if your flower blooms at the apposite time, might you be able to remove it to Holyrood Palace so His Majesty can see it if he wishes? On one of these carts of yours?'

Graham's back straightens. 'The palace? The king?' he says.

'Herr von Streitz is making arrangements with Sir Walter Scott for His Majesty's upcoming visit,' Elizabeth explains, thinking that Mr Graham did not understand the company he was in and perhaps that is why he seemed so much more pleasant. 'I apologize. I should have introduced you properly. This is Robert Graham, the Regius Keeper of the Garden, Herr von Streitz.'

Graham bows with a flourish and the German returns the gesture.

'To be of service to His Majesty, of course we will do everything we can,' Graham says.

McNab shifts from foot to foot.

'Is it possible, Mr McNab?' Johann presses.

'I'd worry for the plant, sir. When would she need moving?'

'The king's visit is expected in August,' Graham snaps irritably. 'That is what people are saying.'

Von Streitz looks nonchalant for he could not possibly say. The king writes to him every second day, but makes no decisions.

The gardener considers a moment. 'August? We'd need to uproot her now. The roots must settle before the plant can be moved. And by my guess, if we were to dig her from the soil, she might not flower. It is a delicate time in the cycle.'

'That is a shame.' Von Streitz does not look disappointed, but then, Elizabeth thinks, he is an ideal courtier. The soul of discretion.

'Perhaps His Majesty might come to the Garden to visit the plant, as it cannot be transported,' she suggests.

Von Streitz is not enthusiastic about the success of such a scheme. It is all chance in any case. His Majesty does not arrange dates – such matters are below him. He will simply write one day that he is coming and set sail the next. As a result, the programme von Streitz is organizing with Sir Walter has no date either – they simply demarcate events as taking place on Day One of His Majesty's Visit or Day Nine, or Upon the First Sunday of His Majesty's Sojourn and so forth. The king will certainly not wish to come to this ramshackle garden to visit a flower that may or may not be in bloom. There was only the merest hope if the flower came to him that he might deign to view it. Von Streitz realizes he would like to please Mrs Rocheid and is disappointed that he cannot do so.

The group moves outside and McNab invites them towards the pond, explaining the labour required to haul the barrelled trees. Mr Graham bustles ahead, flourishing his walking stick showily and commenting from time to time on what McNab is saying. The women bring up the rear in a pool of calm. Belle smiles. Elizabeth smiles back.

'It is like watching children, is it not, Mrs Rocheid?' Belle says quietly. Elizabeth nods. Belle takes her arm and Elizabeth lets her. Miss Brodie smells fresh as a summer morning. She likes her. 'It will be a lovely place when it is done,' she continues. 'Robert showed me the flowerbeds.'

'All these plants are necessary. They are used to make medicine,' Elizabeth replies.

'Yes, it is good that they are also useful,' Belle agrees. She does not elaborate.

Ahead, Elizabeth hears Mr Graham inviting von Streitz to dine at Great King Street, but Belle turns away, so she misses the German's response.

'Poor man,' Belle says. 'He is as delicate as the flowers he so admires. He needs a great deal of watering.'

'Do you cultivate plants, Miss Brodie?'

'I am not a gardener. I do not have the acreage. But I am greatly interested in botany. Hence my borrowing the book, which I returned to the library yesterday, should you still wish to read it.'

'America,' Elizabeth muses. She is miles away, finding it difficult to imagine a country where strange plants like the great aloe grow wild. The English countryside, or what she has seen of it, boasts impressive forests but is for the most part on a more domestic scale.

'I hear it is a place of great opportunity,' Belle breaks her musings.

The men stop ahead and inspect the willow as James darts under the tree's skirts. Graham motions the child out of the way with a sharp flick of his hand, and the boy falls back, shamefaced. Elizabeth beckons him over.

'Go to Duncan, would you? Tell him we will not be long.'

It is an errand that does not need to be run but it gives the child a purpose. Belle regards Elizabeth. 'That was kind,' she says.

Elizabeth shrugs. 'He is a good boy. I have been teaching him to draw.'

The party strolls around the pond. Graham is talking at length now – waving his arms to illustrate his plans for botanical development and crowing about the Garden's history. Von Streitz stops to talk to one of the men who is digging an herbaceous border. He enquires about the Scottish weather.

'I have never known a fellow able to predict the weather with more accuracy than Mr McNab,' Robert Graham cuts in. 'Isn't that right? Tell us what it will be today, McNab.' The Regius Keeper is a showoff, Elizabeth thinks – he will show off whatever he has to hand.

'It will rain later. Within two hours, I imagine,' McNab says patiently.

'And for the king's visit?' Von Streitz is curious.

'August is too far, sir. I am not a seer. But we are accustomed to a traditional Lowland August in Edinburgh, which is to say it will be sunny though it will rain and there will be a storm or two.'

Back at the yard a cart has arrived. A side of bacon wrapped in muslin is unloaded into the gardener's shelter. As the group returns to the carriage and horses, McNab dodges ahead.

'That ought to have gone to the old Garden,' he says. 'The Botanic Cottage. My wife is expecting it.'

The drayman objects. 'Mrs Dickson said to send it here,' he says. At this, McNab pulls the man aside and talks to him low before calling James over. 'My son will show you where to go.'

The boy looks disappointed. He cannot be blamed for wanting to tarry but there is work to be done.

'Mistress Dickson? The seedswoman?' Robert Graham asks and Elizabeth takes note of the name once more.

'Mrs Dickson the butcher's wife,' McNab replies, lifting James up and giving the driver a penny for the toll. 'There has been some confusion among tradesmen about deliveries, what with the two Gardens.'

'We must be on our way,' Belle says, taking Mr Graham's arm. 'I am sure Mr McNab's prediction of rain is accurate and I would like to get home before it comes on.'

'Are you walking? Shall I offer you my carriage? Is it a long way?' Elizabeth asks.

'Thank you. But it is only to Warriston Crescent at the end of the road. We shall walk, shall we not, Mr Graham? It is pleasant to be out in the world and after such a fascinating visit we have a great deal to discuss.'

Graham looks like a child being taken away from a party. There is a hungry look on his face as he watches von Streitz untethering his horse. No, not hungry Elizabeth corrects herself, greedy. Belle drops a parting curtsy. She hesitates a moment, considering. Her profession precludes her having friends both by keeping her busy and excluding her, on the grounds of social respectability, from the general round of drawing room calls that pepper the diaries of respectable women. However, Belle has a good feeling about Mrs Rocheid and cannot yet tell whether it is because she might be useful or because she really likes the woman. Belle does not consider that though her days are full of industry, she might be lonely. However, she is nothing if not adventurous and the chance encounter feels like an invitation to try something new.

'I wonder, Mrs Rocheid, if you might like to join me? I have arranged to call on Lady Liston at Ratho on Friday. She was a friend of my father's and has travelled in America. As you are interested in American plants, it will make a fine outing. She has a garden planted almost exclusively with species from her travels.'

'Lady Liston is not merely interested in American plants, Belle,' Graham cuts in. 'She is Scotland's greatest living expert in them.'

'Where is Ratho?' Elizabeth asks.

'It is a charming village. Ten miles to the south-west. Two hours there and two back. Lady Liston has said she will look forward to me coming. I can easily write and ask her to include you. She will give us luncheon and we can see her garden.'

'I would like that, thank you,' Elizabeth says. 'You are exceedingly kind.'

Belle's eyes shine.

'I shall come for you at Inverleith House on Friday,' she says.

Duncan opens the carriage door and Elizabeth mounts. As they pass the pedestrians on the lane and roll onto the road, Elizabeth notices that Miss Brodie has picked a flower. A tiny part of the stem protrudes slightly from her reticule – one of Mr Graham's cape heaths. At Kew the taking of cuttings is strictly forbidden. She is sure this is also the case at Edinburgh. Miss Brodie, she thinks, must not be aware of the custom. Of course, Mr Graham may have given her permission to snip the plant, though he appears to be a man more likely to keep the rules than break them – unless, that is, there is an advantage to him in the breaking. As Johann pulls alongside on his horse, she is distracted from the matter. He is going to see me to my door, she thinks, and smiles at the courtier's immaculate manners. She feels as if she has been invited to a dinner but it has turned out to be a dance and blushes at what Clementina will make of all this and that it seems not very many days into her life here she has made her first friend.

Chapter Eleven

That Friday morning Duncan meets Mhairi, the blind Highlander. The light is still low and it is too early to be out but he finds it difficult to sleep some nights and wanders about, drawn towards the water. Above, there is a bright star near the last of the pink-edged seed moon. And there she is, lying on the lavender where the housemaids spread the laundry. He wonders if she has slept outdoors, and what it means if she has. Today is the progress of the Cailleach, and the lassies are already fashing, never mind that he has found a tiny, blonde, rosy-cheeked goddess on Rocheid land. Mhairi sits up and grasps a vicious-looking walking stick.

'I won't hurt you,' he says.

'What are you doing here?' Her accent is almost foreign. From a place, he will later learn, so far north that things are done differently.

Duncan is not used to women interrogating him – even before the disconcerting news that has spread about his parentage, his bearing has always engendered respect.

'I work here,' he says. 'You're on my master's land. So the question is, what are *you* doing?'

Mhairi sighs. 'The smell of it,' she says, running her fingers through the lavender. 'I couldnae resist.' She gets to her feet and turns towards the riverbank. Duncan, six feet tall and dark, his father's son, the disdainful conqueror of hearts, follows her. He tells himself it is to make sure she leaves the estate, or at least that she gets off safely, but the truth is, he has fallen in love. Just like that. On sight. Romantic as a poem, not that he would ever admit it.

Women have hounded him since his mother's death. The mistress's maid – a plump redhead, ripe as a peach – cornered him near the icehouse last week. He can't even remember her name, and more, he can't bear the shallowness of all these foolish lassies, chasing the fame of a dead man. Duncan's father (not Burns, the other one) was a good person. Why weren't they as interested when he was the son of a respectable farmer? Mhairi, however, raises her stick.

'Leave me alone,' she snaps and with that, takes his breath away.

As she uses the stick to ascertain a shallow enough crossing place to ford the water, he realizes she is blind.

'What's your name?' he shouts after her.

'Mhairi,' she says. It sounds exotic, the 'Mh' pronounced as a 'V'.

'Where can I find you?'

She turns. 'Why would you want to find me?'

Duncan steps into the water. 'Please,' he says.

'What's your name, then?'

'Duncan,' he shouts back and realizes he is blushing.

'You cannae come and find me at the distillery, Duncan. Mr Stein wouldnae like it.'

'Mr Stein?' Momentarily, he worries that she is Mrs Stein.

'My master,' she says, 'I blend his whisky.'

And with that she is gone.

Duncan has no carriage to ready, but Lady Clementina has ordered that he accompany Elizabeth. Clementina ought to chaperone her young cousin but she has not the energy to be away an entire day and the old woman knows that sending a maid to accompany Elizabeth would inhibit the women's conversation. 'Are you sure you won't join us?' Elizabeth presses her but, though she is acquainted with Lady Liston, Clementina seems disinterested in seeing her. Still, letters have been both sent and received.

'Poor, dear Henrietta,' Clementina says. 'Her feet must have hardly touched the ground these last years. She will be glad to be back at Ratho.'

Elizabeth raises an eyebrow. Clementina needs little encouragement. 'Such a tragedy. She was no sooner home from the Americas than her husband was posted to Constantinople. She must be exhausted.'

Elizabeth finds herself excited, not by this information in particular but by the trip in general. She rises early with the daffodil sun and tarries in her room. Currant Bun helps her dress and she waits downstairs at the breakfast table for Clementina, who today, ever contrary, arrives late. Elizabeth longs for tiny pancakes frosted with rosemary sugar but they eat buttered eggs, ham and tattie scones like leather.

As the clock on the mantle chimes ten, Elizabeth wishes she could look out of the window and see the coach's approach, but she cannot for the drawing room faces the garden. In the end, it is almost eleven when Belle finally arrives. Elizabeth introduces her to Clementina and Belle tarries prettily but does not remove her spencer. Clementina waves them off at the door and Elizabeth admits to herself she is excited to be in such a fancy conveyance. Belle's carriage has every accoutrement that can be imagined and, like little James, she wants to touch it all. The interior smells of black tea and cedar – 'to settle the stomach', Belle explains, as the women cover their knees with thick, tartan cashmere throws.

'I like the smell,' Elizabeth admits.

'I made it. I shall send you some for your coach if you like.'

'Made it?'

'It is an interest of mine,' Belle admits, but does not say more, instead casting her eyes upwards to the box where Duncan has joined her man, Jamie. 'Is that coachman the fellow who . . .?' she asks.

Elizabeth nods. 'He does not like to speak of it.'

'Well, that's good. Men who like to tell you who their father was are generally tiresome,' Belle observes. 'Let us talk instead about the century plant. Is she not handsome?'

Elizabeth nods. 'I too was drawn to her most of all the plants in the Garden, but Mr McNab wishes me to draw his trees and their carts and Mr Graham is quite set on me drawing his flowers – the Scottish ones.'

'I am sure, Mrs Rocheid, like all of us, you have your secrets and might find a little time to draw at your leisure as well as for your hard taskmasters,' Belle replies with a smile.

This is exactly what Elizabeth has been doing. James discovered her in the glasshouse and sat at her feet sketching in the notepad he keeps in his pocket. She smiles. 'I wonder what the flower will look like,' she says.

'It's exciting, isn't it? I had hoped for a red trumpet affair, but Mr Graham says this will not be the case. It is the height that is impressive, not the flower itself. Lady Liston perhaps will be able to tell us more.'

Elizabeth is enjoying this. It is like having a school friend. It has been a long time. She realizes now that she was lonely in Richmond. The women fall into silence as the coach makes time along the banks of the Water of Leith as far as Gorgie village. Turning along the Ratho road, Elizabeth finds herself chatting about Clementina's worries as they pass farm after farm.

'And the old woman believes there will be no food at all?' Belle asks, agog. Elizabeth tells her about the famine that occurred before Currant Bun was born.

'That distillery,' Belle confides, 'is a menace. It was run by Mr Haig for years but now Mr Stein has it. Those gentlemen live for the competition between them, the one desperate to outdo the other. I prefer a Highland malt myself,' she adds.

Elizabeth admits she has never tasted spirits of any kind.

'Not even brandy? Goodness,' Belle says. 'I'm not sure how you will fare your first Scottish winter, Mrs Rocheid, without a warming dram.'

Off guard, Elizabeth replies, 'William was the drinker, not me.'

'William?'

She blushes. 'My late husband. He was brought up in Scotland. He left me little provided for. I am lucky the Rocheids took me in. I should not have said that of him. It was unkind.'

Belle is used to second guessing people. 'But he was the unkind one, I think.'

Elizabeth starts to bluster but cannot continue. Belle's eyes are too steady.

'We should not speak ill of the dead,' she manages at last though for a moment her heart eases. Being with someone so perceptive, after several weeks of little but Lady Clementina's company, feels like a kind of flowering.

Belle nods promptly. 'Very well.' She notices that her new friend's fingers flutter and then come under control, and concludes that Elizabeth's dead husband is a sore point. Still, widows run the gamut from merry to inconsolable and though they say time heals it is not always the case.

The approach to Millburn Tower is quite different from the agricultural land they have been driving through. The house itself is a stone, castellated affair at odds with its name as there is no tower. When they draw up an old woman appears in the doorway wearing a pretty day dress peppered with frills and a long, rose-pink stole. She claps her hands as Belle steps down.

'Isabel, my dear,' Lady Liston says warmly, and kisses the girl on the cheek. 'How lovely.'

Belle hugs the old woman and exclaims, 'You're wearing the jasmine oil I sent you.'

'Jasmine is the greatest beauty, is it not?' Lady Liston confirms. 'I feel, how do the French put it? *Chic.* Yes, that is it.'

Belle introduces Elizabeth.

'Clementina Rocheid's cousin? I am very pleased to make your acquaintance. How is dear Clementina?'

'She is well, ma'am.'

'I am glad to hear it.'

'Elizabeth was telling me that her cousin believes there will be a famine in Scotland,' Belle cuts in. 'For they have paved over too many farms to build Edinburgh.'

Lady Liston laughs. 'Clementina was ever one for a drama. We nicknamed her after that actress – the lady helping Sir Walter stage his play for the king. Mrs Siddons. The toast of Drury Lane. Yes, "Mrs Siddons in heavy rigging", that's what we called her. Famine indeed! Well, my dears, we should walk. I understand you are here for the garden. You must have been cooped up in the carriage since breakfast and it is only a short while before luncheon so let's make the most of it. There is nothing like a garden for cheering the spirits.'

She leads them to a formally laid out lawn area around the south side of the house, with a stone fountain and a sundial.

'This is charming,' Belle enthuses.

The old woman beams. 'It is lovely to have you here. We live very quietly at Millburn.'

'Is this the part of the garden that Mr Parkyns designed?' Belle enquires.

'Indeed.'

'And it is Mr McNab who looked after it when you were away?'

'You are well informed.'

Belle smiles. 'Mr McNab has a century plant, you know. It is about to flower.'

'Really?' Lady Liston leans in. 'He is quite the genius, that man. The university use him very ill.'

'Do they?' Elizabeth cannot help asking.

'I suppose it comes from having spent time in the Americas, but one comes to appreciate one's staff if they are intelligent and hard-working. Mr McNab was so grateful when Sir Robert and I asked him to supervise the garden here while we were on our last posting. He needed the money, the poor soul. I'm sure he could make more tending the great houses of England, but he is a man of honour. He cannot quit the Botanic Garden for he is quite dedicated to it. It is a credit to the nation, after all, and vital to science.'

Elizabeth remembers the side of bacon. 'Do you know Mrs Dickson?' she finds herself asking.

'The seedswoman?' says Lady Liston. 'She inherited her husband's business when he died, and the men said she would not survive a single winter. But her catalogue is quite marvellous. I was reading it in bed the other evening. She has a talent for business, that woman, and she is a maestro with her seeds. How she comes upon some of the rarer species I will never know. They say she has grafted new roses.'

Belle speeds up as they reach a cherry tree which is in blossom. She crumples a few petals between her fingers and sniffs. 'Nothing,' she says.

Lady Liston laughs. 'The fruit has no scent either. Some plants simply do not run to it. The cherries are sweet, however.'

'Have you seen a century plant flower, Henrietta?' Belle asks.

'Once. We were in Bermuda. I can't recall exactly. Small and yellow in clusters about a tall stem. It looked like a weed – quite the giant.'

'Did the flower have a scent?'

The old lady thinks. 'It did. Musty, now I come to think of it. I had a fan, I remember, so I fanned it off. It was not pleasant, I'm afraid.'

Belle is disappointed though she comforts herself that scents work in harmony with each other. An efficacious perfume does not have to be entirely composed of pretty smells. A musty oil can deepen a lighter one and create something magical. She has achieved this before to great profit, though nobody knows it.

'And you, my dear,' the old woman turns to Elizabeth. 'What is your interest in botany? Do you like the properties of plants, like Belle? Or are you a gardener – a seedswoman, like Mrs Dickson?'

'I am an illustrator, Lady Liston. I worked with Sir Joseph Banks for some years until his death.'

'Ah, dear Sir Joseph used to endlessly pester me for seeds and cuttings and goodness knows what. That man was a hound for his herbarium. I sent him some specimens but reserved my rarest for Mr McNab, who, after all, is most concerned with the public good and the important business of education and is here, upon our doorstep.'

The old woman sighs and changes the subject. 'Isabel, I thought you must have come to see me about your father.'

'My father?' Belle says.

'Yes. For my memories and so forth.'

'Oh. That.'

'Aren't you curious about the old fellow?'

Belle shrugs. Lady Liston has offered her this before but there seems little point in pursuing it. 'No more than he was curious about me,' she says.

'You're so like him. He was a passable botanist, you know.'

'He owned a plantation, so I should hope so.'

Lady Liston sighs and thinks that young girls do not understand the treasure of their age. She has weary limbs and her skin is dry and she knows she will not again leave Scotland for the searing heat of the tropics or anywhere else. She did not know her father. He died when she was only nine years of age, though her older brothers and sisters told her a few stories about him. She is the youngest of her siblings and the only one still living, and she regrets not finding out more when she could.

'Really, my dear, are you sure you do not wish me to tell you?'

'My brother may like to know, I suppose. Has he ever asked you about it?'

Henrietta Liston shakes her head. She enjoys Joseph Brodie's salons, which she attends with Sir Robert from time to time, but the only personal conversations she has ever had there have been with Belle. 'The thing is, I truly believe your father came to regret leaving you here. Both of you. He was a man who did not adhere to social conventions but that does not mean that he did not miss knowing you.'

Belle nods. 'Joseph and I expected as much – about his nature, I mean. Neither of us likes to be boxed in. Did you know your father, Mistress Rocheid?'

Elizabeth finds she is not disconcerted by the highly personal turn the discussion has taken – and so quickly. She feels quite at home with both Belle and Lady Liston. This fact surprises her. 'Like you, my lady, I lost my father young,' she admits, although she does not add that this is why she married William Rocheid, who offered her security after her mother had quickly run through the small inheritance her father bequeathed. She was only a teenager and barely knew William when they took their vows though he seemed quite charming. It has, she realizes, always felt that she has had little choice in her decisions – which is to say, penury or marriage. And then penury or coming to live at Inverleith House, which is turning out to be a better bargain. Still, unlike these Scottish women who know what they want and seem to act upon it, she feels suddenly she has had little agency in her decisions. Even here, today, she could not put a name to the life she would choose for herself. This, she realizes, is why she accommodates others so readily.

'You live in Edinburgh now,' Belle says with a smile.

Elizabeth understands what she means. The citizens of this city, men and women alike, consider it the capital of Europe. It is in Edinburgh, after all, as Clementina has asserted more than once, that Alison Cockburn, *salonnière* extraordinaire, hosted on the same night David Hume, the modern world's first atheist, and Adam Smith, the man who pioneered the science of political economy. 'In Scotland we educate our girls along with our boys to everybody's benefit,' the old woman said proudly.

From Millburn Tower the sound of a gong being beaten shimmers across the lawn.

'Ah,' Lady Liston gestures. 'They are calling us.'

Inside, the table is set. It is grander than Inverleith House with an arrangement of wild flowers that includes lush green herbs at the centre. Spikes of rosemary studded with chive flowers snake across the white linen cloth towards rat-tailed silver cutlery and wine-glasses, each engraved with a blooming rose and two buds.

'Will His Lordship be joining us?' Belle asks.

'I think not,' Henrietta answers. 'I arranged a light luncheon for us three alone. Mushroom soup, chicken, cheese and a custard for pudding,' she says. 'In the American style.'

Elizabeth butters a roll. She has missed bread.

Belle laughs. 'You are hungry.'

Elizabeth puts down the bread, guiltily.

'Please,' Henrietta insists. 'It is a pleasure to see a woman with an appetite.'

'Indeed, it is the fashion for ladies to hardly take a bite these days,' Belle adds.

'Not at Inverleith House,' Elizabeth rejoins.

Henrietta laughs. 'Clementina always liked her food.'

'Our cook does not bake often,' Elizabeth adds. It seems kinder than to say she does not bake well.

The butler pours a Rhenish that has been cooled so that the glasses frost, the rose engravings still visible.

'You came to ask me about the century plant then?' Henrietta says. 'Is that it?'

Belle smiles. 'I came to see you,' she insists.

'But you want to know what I know. It is a pleasure, my dear. None of the younger generation in my own family are the least bit interested in botany. My nieces want to source the finest cashmere – which, indeed, we found during my husband's posting to Constantinople. My nephews care for rum and tips on investments. We shall look in the library after we have eaten. I have my notes and copies of the letters I sent home and some rare publications. The dining room and the library are the only reasons I come indoors at all these days,' the old lady declares. 'Sometimes I have them simply serve me in the greenhouses. Perhaps once we have read what there is, I may show you my orchids.'

Belle looks keen. 'I'm sure I shall have a million questions,' she says.

Lady Liston lifts her wineglass in a toast. 'Well, I shall endeavour to answer. To the lady botanists,' she adds. 'And you young ones, so fair.'

'To all the fair botanists,' Belle chimes and, catching Elizabeth's eye, realizes that this is perhaps the first time in a while that either of them has been truly accepted. Henrietta Liston, after all, knows of Belle's employment and has been most understanding about it, curious even. 'I suppose husbands have a variety of needs,' the old lady whispered to her on the night when they first met two years ago and her tongue had been loosened by the copious libation that accompanies all gatherings at Charlotte Square.

Belle had rejoined. 'It is difficult for a wife to understand. Married ladies, after all, only experience one husband. That is, one husband at a time.'

When the women first corresponded it was Belle who was the teacher and Henrietta will always be grateful for her advice. As she takes her first spoonful of mushroom soup she smiles at the ease with which the girl has enabled her to rejuvenate her marriage bed – stuffy old matrons and their moral judgements can hang. Lady Liston likes Sir Robert lying on top of her whispering sweet nothings. And this other woman – she regards Elizabeth – is pleasant, naïve almost. She reminds Henrietta of a cocker spaniel one of her friends once had. She needs looking after.

'We will find you whatever you need, my dears,' she promises. 'You can rest assured of that.'

Chapter Twelve

1 July 1822

In the withdrawing room at Holyrood Palace, where the royal courtier David Rizzio was murdered in front of Mary Queen of Scots, Johann awaits Sir Walter Scott. He wonders if, in different times, Sir Walter might initiate a similar plan to divest himself of another troublesome foreigner with connections to the monarch. Himself. For although the Scotsman is never anything but entirely cordial, in their interactions, he has occasionally noticed a shadow cross the famous writer's face.

Both men are well aware of His Majesty's interests. Scott is one of George's intimates. The king does not read often but he devours Sir Walter's novels. It was His Majesty who unmasked the great man as an author. Scott's first book, *Waverley*, was published anonymously, but upon reading it, George declared that no truly royal personage could bear not to know who had written such a brilliant evocation of his great-uncle's great victory over the Jacobites. In Scotland the Duke of Cumberland is known by both Jacobites and Hanoverians alike as the Butcher.

Unmasked by royal command, Scott enthusiastically befriended the regent – unlike Miss Austen, who, unable to deny George's request for her to do so, dedicated one of her books to him so drily that Scott has heard that her publisher had to rewrite the flyleaf. But Scott is not only a talented writer – he has other advantages to the crown over the merits of a dowdy spinster. Before he left London His Majesty pulled von Streitz aside and told him nobody had Hanoverian interests more at heart north of the border than Sir Walter. Von Streitz was surprised to hear this, the Melville men being, as far as he was aware, the establishment's loyal experts in Scotland's governance. George shrugged. 'Legally that is the case,' he conceded. 'Politically too. But Sir Walter understands the nation's soul'. Johann had never before nor indeed will he ever again hear His Majesty talk of the soul of Scotland (or anywhere else). It is for this reason that he has given way to more of Scott's suggestions, as the king's local representative, than he did the year before when he arranged George's visit to Dublin.

Still, Sir Walter wants more public events. 'The people need to see the king. They want to welcome him,' he insists. This is not demonstrably the case when the sovereign appears in London, and Johann wonders if the writer is using the promise of cheering crowds to insert more public events into the ten-day programme than His Majesty will enjoy (which is to say, more than two, or perhaps three at a push). That said, there is no question that King George's Scottish subjects are excited at the prospect of the royal visit. That is already palpable.

From the window Johann observes Scott's landau arrive through the open gates and waits patiently for Scott to make his way through the hallway. He hears the Scotsman bidding several bright good mornings as he passes the grace and favour tenants who occupy the palace's various apartments, and climbs the stairs to Johann's rooms.

'I hope you're not sleeping in here, old man,' the writer says with a grin as he enters, pulling off his lush, velvet cape and propping his cane against the table leg. 'They say there are ghosts.'

It is a matter of contention that Johann has moved to the palace rather than staying in the well-appointed second-floor bedroom of Scott's bow-fronted Edinburgh home at 39 North Castle Street. 'We are only a short walk from the Assembly Rooms,' Scott enthused when Johann arrived, not understanding that the king's man does not revel in the hoi polloi and only wishes to do his job.

When Johann expressed his discomfort at the intrusion the situation of Sir Walter's house afforded the public, the crown offered to rent a townhouse on Northumberland Street for his use. The handsome young German considered this but decided to go further. For peace of mind, he realized, he must reside out of the sightline of gossipy matrons and gentlemen so desperate for a royal introduction that they will knock on the door of his carriage. Mothers with daughters of an age to come out are particularly determined to gain access to His Majesty's entourage and in Edinburgh two of the great families have such a situation this year – the Melvilles and the Butes. The Butes have already brought their girl to London in search of a husband, the king's visit notwithstanding, but the Melville girl, Jane, is said to be dowdy and the family have decided to launch her at home. Keen to be first with any news of the king's arrival (and his retinue of eligible gentlemen), Anne Melville has pestered von Streitz to call upon her. She is the only mother still writing to him daily despite his move to the unfashionable side of town.

Sir Walter lays half a dozen letters on the oak table. 'These came for you,' he says.

Johann pours two brandies and the men sit. These letters are not important – the real mail arrives from His Majesty by private messenger and in it the king does not censor himself, asking Johann's opinion about fashion or furnishings and advising his cousin of his Scottish requirements or asking questions about the weather in Edinburgh. Most of these queries Johann passes to Sir Walter, but not all. While Johann's brief is to see to the king's personal business, he also answers occasional enquiries from the king's ministers about the political mood of the country, something of which Scott is unaware.

The writer sips his brandy. 'Feel free to open them,' he indicates the missives.

Von Streitz cracks the seals one by one. Three of the letters are from women he encountered while staying at Sir Walter's, asking him to take tea, which he will not. He lays those aside. Two are from gentlemen inviting him to dine – one of them Robert Graham, repeating in writing the offer he made verbally in the Garden a few days before. Johann sighs. He thought he had made it clear that he was not available, but then he finds that people often only hear what they wish to. The sniff of royalty brings out the lickspittle in Edinburgh quite as much as it does in London. The last letter comes from down south. He cracks its seal briskly and ascertains it is from the fellow Lady Banks has employed to work on the late Sir Joseph's herbarium. At Kew Garden things have remained in disarray since the great man passed. Banks was a bully, but the Garden was his passion and Johann is involved because the king has an interest. The site at Kew lies in the grounds of a royal palace, albeit only Richmond Palace, the smallest in the realm. The letter instructs him to obtain seeds from Edinburgh's century plant should it flower and forward them to Kew's head man. Johann thinks it strange that Kew has not petitioned Mr McNab directly.

As he waits for the German to finish reading, Scott gazes out of the window. 'It's an extinct volcano, you know,' he indicates the crags that tower over the south side of the palace. 'At first I thought we might do something with it for the visit. The crags are quite the feature but tartan will be more efficacious on the nation's spirit.'

'The vista is marvellous from the summit,' Johann says.

'You have climbed it?'

He has. Some nights he finds it difficult to sleep. 'I went up Arthur's Seat,' Johann admits. 'A proper pathway would have been helpful.'

This strikes Scott as the very idea he has been casting around for. Of course there should be a pathway – more than that, a road – from which it will be possible to take in the glorious design of Scotland's capital city. He can see it now: the ton in open carriages – perhaps even a racy curricle or two – making a grand circuit round the hill from the pond at the Earl of Haddington's grazing grounds to take in the glorious sight of the rooftops of the Royal Mile and the New Town. 'Yes,' he says enthusiastically. 'There is no time before His Majesty's visit to engineer such a project but it's a capital idea, von Streitz! People will love it.'

'Not the men who have to build it, I imagine,' Johann says drily, still reading.

'Is it the king's business?' Scott nods towards the letter.

'From Kew Garden. They want me to procure the seeds of a plant in the university's new Botanic Garden.'

'They have asked you to obtain these seeds?'

Johann nods.

'Odd,' Scott says. 'I wonder why.'

Johann suggests they leave. 'The men will start hammering downstairs soon. The new throne room is going to look marvellous, but the work is tremendously noisy.' It's smelly too. The stink of lead paint in the hallway is overwhelming some days.

Scott purses his lips – presumably deciding not to point out the relative peace and fragrant nature of 39 North Castle Street, which is, unlike the palace, in excellent repair. 'I'm glad you like what the tradesmen are doing,' he says instead. Scott commissioned Young, Trotter and Hamilton of Princes Street to refit the room. 'An outing? Why not?' he adds. 'I'm interested to see the new Garden and we can make our arrangements en route.'

The truth is that Scott likes von Streitz despite their differences. The writer is a bluff kind of fellow. Besides, the presence of the king's man is a promising sign that His Majesty intends to make the trip to the Scottish capital. At this point, Scott is painfully aware, if the king does not come, the city will resent its monarch and probably him as well. He is honoured to be associated with the visit but this association means, in the minds of many, that it is his responsibility to see it comes off.

Scott rises, leaning on his cane. 'We have much to talk about.' Conversation with the German is like parrying at singlestick. Not that Scott fences. His limp precludes him from most sporting activities. He is not the jealous sort or Johann's physical beauty might irk him. Von Streitz looks like a statue – some kind of god about town. When the writer visited Anne Melville the other day, he noted that she was disappointed to see him and not the king's man. Another fellow might succumb to jealousy over this alone, but Sir Walter is famously fair-minded. He would, however, like there to be more public events in the programme.

In the carriage, as they trundle past the Old Town's slums, they alternate between conversation and silence, Scott raising the stakes and Johann taking his pick of the bids, like an auction.

'We shall have two balls, then,' Scott says confidently. 'And my play performed by royal command.'

'Then three days at Dalkeith Palace with the Buccleuchs,' Johann parries.

'Indeed. And His Majesty's troops inspected on Portobello Sands. The ladies will turn out for that,' Scott adds, sugar-coating the pill.

'So the hunt ball is set,' Scott continues in the landau as they tip the hill and the weight of the carriage shifts forwards. 'It will give us a chance to invite those we cannot fit at the Assembly, which still requires some thought. We must organize contrasting entertainments to distinguish the two events. Tumblers, at the Assembly perhaps? Medieval jugglers. A kind of Highland circus.'

'Yes. Good,' Johann nods. He stares out of the window at the gardens that have replaced the old loch and pictures fire eaters against a colourful, tartan backdrop. His king enjoys spectacle.

'I have moved the presentation of the clans to the day you suggested,' Scott continues. 'The king can remove to Dalkeith Palace directly after that.'

'You will go with him, Sir Walter?'

'I plan to present His Majesty with a watercolour that Mr Turner painted two years since. It is of a picnic. I thought he might be amused by it and as we will, no doubt, picnic with the Buccleuchs, it seems apt to give it to him while we are staying there. It is his birthday during August, if that is indeed when he comes.'

'How charming.'

Scott pauses for there is, as the modern Russian poet Ivan Krylov would say, an elephant in the room. While Turner was painting senti-mental portraits of the view, an uprising took place in Glasgow by the fellows supported by Joseph Brodie. The insurrection lasted a week and was put down as fiercely as Peterloo.

'The thing about public events,' Scott continues tentatively, 'is the engagement of the people. Scotland requires to see its monarch. The king's presence should quell any undesirable factions and to do so the programme must demonstrate the advantages of our kingdom being united.'

Von Streitz manages not to sigh. It is not that he is unaware, but he cannot discuss this with Sir Walter, although the writer keeps trying. Scott is the man to paint a picture – a web of imagining that will overlay Scotland's memory of Cumberland's butchery, but he cannot be made privy to the realities of what it takes to rule. The visit is to be window-dressing and von Streitz has clear instructions not to discuss matters of national security with Sir Walter, for though the king's friend is loyal, he is too open with people.

'I heard from court yesterday,' the German says. It is a lie, but it will divert Scott's interest.

'Is there any news? Has His Majesty decided on a date?'

'No.' Von Streitz will not lie about that. 'But I replied expressing how much he will like to see the New Town. The light and the masonry and so forth. The excellent statues and the views.'

Sir Walter smiles. George loves architecture. He has remodelled every royal palace he has ever occupied.

'I'm doing my best,' von Streitz says honestly. The only thing he hasn't tried is to tell George that Napoleon loved Edinburgh, for informing His Majesty that the toppled French Emperor has a passion for something invariably increases royal interest. Still, that would not be honest either.

At the Garden the men are greeted by McNab.

'It has been a long while, Sir Walter.'

In his younger days Scott used to visit his Uncle Daniel and sit among the medical students arrayed in the room on the upper floor of the McNabs' cottage, where Rutherford imparted his knowledge about medicinal herbs from a dais while the smell of Mrs McNab's bubbling stew pot pervaded the house.

'Sir Walter and I come on a mission,' Johann admits. 'We have been commissioned by Kew to obtain the seeds of your plant. The one you showed me the other day.'

'Which plant?' McNab grows suddenly still.

'The aloe from America in the greenhouse.'

'But it has not yet flowered.'

'When it flowers.' Johann wonders if his English has let him down and he has not expressed himself correctly. He does not think so.

'Will you show me?' Scott cuts in. 'I'd love to see it.'

McNab leads them to the greenhouse in silence.

'It has grown since I was last here,' Johann says, for there is a shoot rising from the centre of the century plant. 'It looks like an enormous asparagus.'

'This?' Scott gestures at the outlandish aloe. 'Is this shoot the flower?'

'It will grow taller and then flower at its height,' McNab explains. 'Kew seem very keen.'

'The aloe flowers only once in its life,' the gardener continues.

'That is why it is called the century plant, Sir Walter,' Johann cuts in.

'Once in a hundred years?' Scott guffaws. 'How extraordinary.'

McNab shakes his head. 'Once in thirty years. The moniker is . . . ambitious.'

'So that is what all the fuss is about. Do we have many of these plants in the realm?'

'Not in Britain, sir. Nor on the continent if it comes to that. There are, I believe, two younger specimens at Chatsworth House but they are a long way from bearing seed.'

'How much will the thing produce?'

McNab pauses at this question. 'We do not know,' he says. 'But certainly very few and my intention is to propagate them here.'

Scott raises an eyebrow. It is a large plant to generate only a few seeds. 'I can sense there is a problem with Kew's request then, Mr McNab. You want to propagate the seeds, is that it?'

McNab nods. It is a lie but is his best chance of retaining control of the matter. 'I know the plant, sir. I've been tending her since I got here. I believe I have the best chance of success.'

'But you did not succeed with the cuttings,' Johann chimes in.

The men pause at this impasse. McNab's hands begin to sweat.

'Kew has written to you already then?' the writer confirms. 'Is that it?'

'Yes, sir.'

'And you refused?'

McNab shakes his head.

'Ah. You did not reply.'

'I did not.'

McNab is making hard labour of these enquiries but Scott persists.

'So this plant has medical properties?' he says.

'You would need to ask Mr Graham about that,' McNab replies.

'I see,' Scott says and gives up. McNab is being unassailable in what ought to be an easy matter. Sir Walter decides that if there is another way to settle the matter, then, they will take it.

And it is for this reason, and this reason alone, that Robert Graham finds quite unexpectedly later that afternoon, that Johann von Streitz accepts his invitation to dine at Great King Street the night after next and says he hopes it will be acceptable for Sir Walter Scott to accompany him. Graham pauses. A grin breaks out across his face, slow and bright as a sunrise. He calls his wife into his study and then his butler and the cook, for it is important that everything should be absolutely perfect.

'We need ladies,' his wife says. 'What is this German fellow like, my dear?'

Ladies are ever the problem, for widows are generally dull and the younger generation, even when they are out in society, cannot be invited without a chaperone.

'First we must ask Lady Scott for she may wish to accompany her husband. In any case you may leave it to me,' Mr Graham replies, thinking that what he has in mind will be an unusual table but one that will feel intimate. Still, he believes it will work. Indeed, much is riding upon it.

Chapter Thirteen

Gardener's Cottage, Leith Walk

It is always mayhem at the McNabs' cottage at mealtimes and today there is a particularly strong sense of excitement among the children. Betty McNab has diced a hunk of the bacon Mrs Dickson sent and stewed it with dried peas and beans. The kitchen smells delicious when William gets home but he has little appetite.

'Don't stand there like a big long streak, Willy,' Betty berates him, curling her long hair into a bun and fixing it in place with a comb as she kisses him on the cheek. 'Have some bread and lard to keep you going.'

The lard will be gone by morning – the children eat it by the spoonful if they are allowed and today Betty cannot bring herself to be strict with them. She is almost six months gone and she is exhausted.

He helps himself to a small slice to please his wife, for if he does not do so, he will have to explain what is on his mind and he cannot bring himself to admit his difficulties when he knows how much Betty has on her plate. Catherine is old enough to help but James is mostly with him at Inverleith these days.

After the family has eaten, he helps wash the younger ones in the chipped enamel sink while Betty stokes the fire so the embers will last till morning. The cottage could use a lick of whitewash but there is no time or money, and besides, ahead of them is a new place at Inverleith, if only Dr Graham will start to build it. The endless waiting is draining. Once the children are down, McNab watches Betty darn socks with holes and threadbare vests beside the fire until she puts away her needle and announces she is going upstairs.

He follows her, donning his nightgown and stroking her hair as she falls as good as unconscious the minute she closes her eyes. William lies awake a while before rising, pulling on his tackety boots and tipping himself into the old Garden, circumnavigating the craters that have been left by the removed trees and dodging the beds of aromatic herbs that he has decided to transplant to Inverleith last for they remain of use to his household. He wishes they were allowed to keep hens, but such activities are forbidden to the head gardener. It would mean fresh eggs though and now nobody visits the old Garden they would probably get away with it. Still, they couldn't take poultry with them to Inverleith. There is at least another year's work in the move and another eighteen months beyond that before the new cottage will be built and that only if Mr Graham gives the go-ahead soon. But he has other matters to worry about, namely this business with the seeds, for he can think of no way to settle the matter.

Disconsolate, he sits on the stump of a diseased chestnut tree that he felled last winter. Under the bright sprawl of Gemini and Orion he runs through his conversation with Scott and von Streitz several times. If he gives the seeds to Kew, he will have to reimburse the money he has taken from Mrs Dickson, which he has spent already paying off his debts. This sounds rather grand, but the money was owed to buy cloth to make the children clothes and keep the family supplied with barley for broth and wheatflour for Betty's soda bread, and to pay grocery bills for butter and cheese. Tuition in Latin for James so the boy can understand the work of Linnaeus. Shoes for Catherine – second hand, of course. And necessaries for the baby coming. He sighs. It is like being a rabbit in a trap. He and Betty promised they would abstain after the last baby was born but they joke that the making of children is their only pleasure. That is not true for either of them. They love their family and their shabby home and for McNab that makes the situation worse, or the guilt, anyway. He is working every hour and still cannot earn enough to feed and clothe everybody. And educate the boys. He must, he knows, adequately educate his sons if they are to have any chance of advancement. It is impossible.

There is, he thinks (and here, were he a more religious man, he would be praying), a possibility that the information he has is incorrect and that the plant will produce more than the ten seeds expected. If he can conceal that from everyone, it would solve his problem, but he has read nothing to give him hope of it. So he must lie to somebody and for preference it will be the fellow at Kew. Though he was given his start at the king's garden when he left his father's Ayrshire farm, he holds little fondness for the old place. Sir Joseph Banks was not popular among the common gardening men and since McNab left to take up his post in Edinburgh, Kew has taken much more than it has given. He is weary of their high-handed demands. Still, Sir Walter's good graces are important to him, though Mrs Dickson brings more regular income and pays a premium. And, he reminds himself, he has agreed that apart from his own propagation (his duty to the Garden to maintain its stock) he will hand her all the seeds the aloe produces. That is most important to the old woman for it secures the value of the plants she will grow. Besides, he must stick to his word for if Mrs Dickson decides to tell Mr Graham about their dealings, McNab will be arrested for theft. And the old witch is more than capable of that if she thinks she has been crossed. She is a tough old bird. Shame twists in McNab's stomach as he considers the public humiliation of such a pass.

Above, the bedroom's casement window opens, and Betty leans out, her dark hair down her back. Her nightgown is almost luminous in the moonlight. The bulge of her pregnant stomach prevents her from leaning on the stone sill.

'I wish you would tell me what is troubling you, Willy,' she says.

It's not like him to forgo his dinner but he could not face Mrs Dickson's bacon in good conscience. He worries that Mr Graham will find out that there is no butcher called Dickson the city wide. Although, he steadies himself, as if Robert Graham would trouble himself with the likes of that. McNab gets to his feet.

'You must not catch cold, love,' he chides her.

Betty has never been ill in all the years he has known her. She is the very definition of the word 'hardy'.

'Come back to bed,' she says, her eyes lingering on his strong shoulders.

He has never been able to deny her. Good times or bad, the best time of his day is always the moment he lies down with his wife and curls his arms around her warm body.

The next morning McNab walks to the new Garden as usual. It is a beautiful day and along Picardy Place the last of the blossom is falling from the late-fruiting apple trees. Workmen saw and hammer inside a house being renovated. Several people wish him good morning and he doffs his hat and returns the favour as he passes. At the foot of the hill a wood pigeon coos loudly over the gurgling of the Water of Leith as it rushes towards the sea, and as McNab crosses the bridge at the top of Warriston Crescent he passes the pretty blind girl walking towards the distillery.

'Mr McNab. Good morning,' she says.

Her voice is like glass. Not the cut glass of the New Town lassies who visit the Garden from time to time, but like freshly blown glass at a workman's forge. Warm and clear and useful.

'Miss MacDonald.' He lingers a moment, remembering how she ran her hands across the bark of a sycamore they were moving some weeks before, and the gardeners stopped the cart to let her do so. She certainly has a way with her. 'Tell me, how did you know it was me?' he asks.

Mhairi smiles. 'Well, sir, you always smell of the earth,' she says, 'and a little carbolic.'

'Don't all my men smell like that?'

She lingers a moment. 'Aye. Though most of your gardeners also smell of whisky from the night before. Cheap whisky at that. And there's something else.' She stands before him, a veritable Cassandra. 'Rosemary. Very faint.'

Betty scents the family's nightgowns and undershirts with rosemary sprigs. McNab blushes. If the girl can tell all that from merely passing him in the street, he wonders what she can tell from the malted barley she oversees for Mr Stein. They say it is down to her skill that the distillery has produced several single malts of surpassing quality of late, as well as the cheap stuff, which they sell to the poor locally, and over the border in England. It is whispered that Mhairi's skill has doubled Stein's turnover and that he paid her twenty guineas as a bonus when she threatened to leave and rented a room for her near the Stock Bridge where she has her meals provided.

Pushing past them Nellie Patterson crosses the bridge swinging a basket containing bread, pies and cheese and wishing them a cheery good morning as she turns into Tanfield.

'And your step, Mr McNab. I recognize the metre of it,' Mhairi adds.

'Have a pleasant day, Miss MacDonald,' he replies, but Mhairi has turned her blank green eyes towards the maid's retreating figure as if she has just realized something, and he could swear she murmurs Robert Graham's name under her breath.

'Goodbye,' he says.

At the Garden the post has arrived, sitting on the ledge inside the gardeners' shed. Two of the men are already at work digging over the compost heap McNab started out of the way of the main planting. He has been forbidden to dig a vegetable patch, but he plans to lay out a small one behind the compost, where no gentleman will ever venture. They cannot pay him so little, he reasons, and forbid him every perk. A gentleman student, one of the more serious fellows, is questioning the foreman about the cultivation of the cinchona tree from which the latest medical advancement in the treatment of malaria is derived. It is said that quinine will save thousands of lives in the colonies. McNab does not join the conversation but closes the door and turns to his correspondence. The letters are mostly predictable. Mr Graham says he is too busy to discuss the trouble with the chamomile bed and that he trusts McNab to take the most efficacious course of action. A gentleman from Stirling writes for advice about a sick conifer. McNab smiles as he recognizes the handwriting of Lady Henrietta Liston and cracks the seal on that letter, which bears a heraldic crest with an outstretched hand.

> *My dear Mr McNab* [Lady Liston starts with a flourish] *I am sure you will not mind me imposing upon our friendship, but I have heard the most exciting news about the blooming of the* Agave americana *at the Garden. I hope it is not too forward to enquire if I might have some of the seeds . . . three will suffice. I know the plant does not produce many . . . I will of course reimburse you.*

McNab's stomach lurches. He thinks he is going to be sick. All he ate this morning was a slice of bread with a smear of jam and a beaker of the small beer Betty brews in the outhouse. He rushes outside to the privy and heaves his breakfast into it. As he wipes his mouth a wave of anger rises in his belly. He has given nothing but service. He should not be in this position but what else can he do? He has no idea how to proceed, he only knows that he cannot satisfy everybody and if they find out what he has been up to, he will lose everything – his family, his position and his hope for the future.

Chapter Fourteen

The night of the Grahams' dinner, Elizabeth sits with Clementina as she dines early on roasted squab.

'Nobody invites company to luncheon anymore,' Clementina says sadly. 'And luncheon is far better than dinner. I could manage a luncheon.'

'You refused Mr Graham's invitation,' Elizabeth points out, but the old lady does not reply, instead neatly slicing her meat, which she sluices in gravy before pushing it to the side of her plate.

She watches as Elizabeth leaves, waving from the front door half-heartedly, having fussed like a mother hen for a good five minutes over Elizabeth's hair and insisted on checking every detail of her appearance. 'Your husband would have been proud of you,' she says. Elizabeth does not know how to reply. She vows to return with details of what everybody wore and what was served. These will interest Clementina more than reports of conversation. Sometimes she feels that she bores Clementina and then something small enlivens the old woman – the sewing of a button or a bird at the window. For all her talk of Mr Hume and Mr Burns, Clementina Rocheid does not like new ideas. Not any longer.

As the carriage leaves the estate it passes three students arguing over some trifle as they pile into a waiting cab. The Garden remains open late for it is light until almost ten in Edinburgh – later than in

London. Poor Mr McNab is at everybody's beck and call, she thinks, as Duncan smoothly overtakes the cab and the Rocheids' carriage rattles south across the bridge and up the hill towards 62 Great King Street.

Elizabeth has never been inside a New Town residence, though she and William once attended a grand at home on Eaton Square. Frustrated that they did not meet personages of the quality he desired, in the carriage on the way back to Richmond he spent more than an hour criticizing her dress. Now Elizabeth tries not to feel self-conscious as Duncan pulls up at the Grahams' door. Through the window she can see the table laid and the candles glowing against the painted red wallpaper. She takes a moment to gather her thoughts as the cold evening air seeps into the box and Duncan opens the door to hand her down. 'Thank you,' she says, and as she climbs the steps to the entrance, two housemaids peer from the barred basement window, not at her, but at him. They giggle. Behind Elizabeth, Duncan grimaces.

Upstairs, the Grahams rise to greet Elizabeth in the drawing room on the first floor. The house is well-appointed, though the rooms are not as large as Inverleith House. She curses herself for being the first to arrive, not that she has ever been the fashionable sort. Mr Graham presents his wife, who offers a glass of ratafia, which Elizabeth would ordinarily consider too sweet but accepts politely. Mrs Graham asks about her botanical illustrations and she is on the point of talking about drawing the Highland flowers that Mr Graham collected the previous summer when the door opens and Johann von Streitz and Sir Walter Scott enter. Scott remembers her and kisses her gloved hand. 'What a charming dress, Mrs Rocheid,' he says of the pink gauze delivered only the day before from the Royal Exchange. 'Are those the Rocheid amethysts?'

Elizabeth nods, touching the rope and fringe necklace studded with seed pearls between the purple stones. Despite Clementina's earlier ministrations, Elizabeth has already forgotten it is there. 'My cousin lent it to me,' she explains. 'She says it has not been worn in a decade.'

'And how fares Lady Clementina?'

'Well, sir.'

Johann bows. 'Mrs Rocheid,' he says and accepts a drink.

'Herr von Streitz,' she replies, noticing that he does not sip from his glass. Perhaps he also finds ratafia too sweet.

Another couple arrive – Ruari and Flora Innes, introduced as neighbours and friends. Mrs Innes sits next to Elizabeth while the gentlemen gather around the fire.

'Mr Innes is one of Edinburgh's most successful architects. I have invested in several of his projects to quite the profit,' Robert says.

'I like a table for eight. It means we all get to speak to each other,' Graham's wife cuts in, swiftly changing the subject. Elizabeth senses that she is used to steering conversation away from her husband's boasting.

Elizabeth wonders who the eighth guest might be. 'Is Miss Brodie joining us?' she asks.

Mr Graham blushes. 'Not tonight.'

'Miss Brodie?' Mrs Graham enquires. It is a name with which she is not familiar.

'Yes. Miss Isabel Brodie,' Elizabeth chimes innocently. 'She is also interested in the Botanic Garden and more of an expert in plants than she would admit. Her current concern is American species.'

Mr Innes starts in shock and tips his glass over his wife's gown. 'Oh, my dear Flora,' he says. 'I'm sorry.'

Mrs Graham fusses, ordering the footman to fetch water. The ratafia leaves a sticky, copper-coloured stain that there will be no getting out of Mrs Innes's pale chiffon gown, water or not. The green ostrich feather affixed to her headdress with a diamond pin shivers, the sole sign of how upset she is by her husband's clumsiness.

'The famous aloe?' Sir Walter chimes, covering Mrs Innes's distress. 'We are all fascinated by that. When will it flower, do you think?'

'I understand it will take a few weeks,' Elizabeth says.

'You are well informed. The head gardener was not able to tell me when I asked the same question.'

Elizabeth blushes. 'Belle – that is to say, Miss Brodie – and I lately visited Lady Liston at Ratho. She has some experience of American plants, having travelled there. She allowed us free rein in her library.'

'Fascinating,' says Scott. 'We must relay this information to Mr McNab, must we not, Herr von Streitz?'

'Indeed.'

Johann puts down his glass on the mantle as Mrs Innes and Mrs Graham leave the room.

'Excuse me,' Mr Innes says, his colour on the pale side even for a fellow with red hair, as he follows his wife. The company settles, Mr Graham's eyes darting repeatedly to the door.

'William McNab is an odd fellow,' he says absentmindedly.

'He is most reliable,' Scott chimes in. 'And extremely talented. We're lucky to have him.'

Mr Graham's lips tighten only a fraction. He did not assemble this company in order to discuss the head gardener, let alone praise him. 'I understand you feel His Majesty will not be interested in the Garden, Herr von Streitz. We are not yet ready for such illustrious attention, nor will we be for some time,' he says, bringing the conversation back to the royal visit.

'His Majesty is little interested in botany in general – it is no reflection on your work, sir.'

'Have you decided so?' Elizabeth says. 'I am sorry. A royal endorsement would mean the world to Mr McNab.'

'It is a shame that His Majesty is not more botanically inclined,' Scott agrees. 'His father was quite the enthusiast as was the late Queen Charlotte. A lady botanist in her own right.'

'I was not acquainted with the king's parents,' von Streitz says.

Scott leans in conspiratorially. 'Mr McNab was. His Late Majesty commented he was the very soldier. McNab signed up when he was at Kew as a royal volunteer – when the war started. The king picked him out at the inspection.'

'Sir Walter, I swear you know everything about every one of us,' Graham smiles. 'No matter how lowly. I expect it is the novelist in you. If His Majesty wished to appoint a keeper of his subject's secrets, then you would be the man.'

Neither Scott nor von Streitz so much as shifts at this observation. Writers have been spies for the crown since Geoffrey Chaucer. Christopher Marlowe and Daniel Defoe both lost their lives in service to the monarch. It is the role in which von Streitz has been ardently endeavouring not to cast Sir Walter. Johann motions towards the piano at the other end of the drawing room. 'Does your wife play?' he asks.

Mr Graham shakes his head sadly. 'She will not take the stage in public,' he says. 'Not even for friends. She is ower shy.'

'Mrs Rocheid?' von Streitz offers.

Silently, Elizabeth gets up and crosses the gold Persian carpet. She enjoys having a sense of purpose as she sits at the piano and lifts the lid, laying her fingers on the ivory keys. Taking a breath, she plays a short Haydn piece and then the first part of a Mozart sonata from memory. Sir Walter watches Johann as his gaze lingers on her. He cannot blame the boy. Mrs Rocheid is a paragon – a thing of perfection in her fringed, pink gossamer gown and the necklace she forgot about. Scott likes her lack of show. She does not look up to check her audience's appreciation. She does not revel in her talent but concentrates upon it. She is like a bird singing on the branch.

When Elizabeth is finished, they clap. She demurely retakes her seat.

'That was lovely. Perhaps after dinner you might honour us again?' Sir Walter says.

Elizabeth smiles. 'I have not played in a while. At Inverleith House we have a harpsichord but I am not fond of the tenor. The sound resonates better on the pianoforte. It is an excellent instrument, Mr Graham.'

'My wife bought it in London,' he says proudly.

Still, he cannot help but try to bring the conversation round to the nub of his interest once more. 'How are the arrangements for the royal visit coming along?' he asks.

'We are nearly there, are we not, von Streitz?' Scott replies. 'Official portraits and so on. I have been talking to painters for the last month.'

Unlike Robert Graham, Scott would never brag, but Mr Turner has confirmed he will travel north for the visit and David Wilkie has promised to capture His Majesty's image if they can get the monarch into the kilt that has been made for him. The garb of Old Gaul, Sir Walter calls it.

The drawing room door opens again and the Inneses return with Mrs Graham and Lady Scott in tow.

'Charlotte, my dear,' Scott greets his wife. He notices that Mrs Graham casts an anxious eye at her husband, as though he might have said something embarrassing while she was out of the room.

'I am sorry to be late,' Lady Scott says in a pretty French accent.

Mrs Innes takes her seat. She has changed into a deep red frock that clashes with the ostrich feather. Mr Innes appears to have regained his composure.

'Now we are all here,' Mr Graham says, 'perhaps we should go down? I understand that Cook is making a soufflé – a dish that sadly puts diners at the convenience of the oven.'

Mrs Graham lets out a nervous giggle. Such company as this should not be held to a servant's convenience but still, they rise. Johann offers Elizabeth his arm and Sir Walter notices the lady blush. Not a high colour, but then the Grahams have lit so many candles the townhouse is practically Versailles. Downstairs the dining room glows the colour of claret beneath a gilded chandelier. The table is laid like a veritable Eden with a mound of fruit at its centre, studded with silverware buffed to a high shine. Mrs Graham is seated next to Sir Walter, Elizabeth next to Herr von Streitz.

'Perhaps we shall think of the soufflé as in your honour, Lady Charlotte,' Mr Graham says as he deposits Lady Scott to his right. 'As it is French cuisine.'

'I am quite British, Mr Graham,' Lady Charlotte replies. 'It was my mother who was French.'

'Like Mary of Guise and Mary Queen of Scots,' Graham quips.

Sir Walter is not sure that he is going to be able to stand Graham's endless royal references. But it is clear the Grahams keep an excellent table. And afterwards, over some port, he and Johann will bring Mr Graham to the matter of the seeds for Kew. He expects they will agree to split the cache – half for Edinburgh and half for the other garden. This seems fair. And perhaps, he thinks, Lady Liston will be able to inform them how many seeds the plant is likely to produce. He will write to her tomorrow. In any case he is confident that an invitation to the hunt ball being thrown in the king's honour will secure the favour he is looking for from Robert Graham – and the good graces of Kew Garden to boot.

Chapter Fifteen

Belle Brodie has indulged herself this evening. Her second gentleman has visited, though he declined to dine with her after their tryst. He prizes intense experiences – complete absorption – unlike Ruari, who likes to play. Before he disappears downstairs, she lets him push her against the painted panelling at the doorway of her boudoir and they kiss for a long time. 'Sandy,' Belle moans his name for she knows that stirs him. He likes her accent, it seems, with its soft vowels. 'Say it again,' he whispered once, and ever since she has used his name to punctuate their assignations. Sometimes it is the only word spoken. It is almost strawberry season, she notes with satisfaction, as he disappears down the stairs.

As the door to the street bangs closed, she orders the cook to make something special and claps her hands when what arrives from the kitchen is a thick slice of snowy halibut in a colourful curried sauce. The flow of herbs and spices into Belle's establishment, though secured for other reasons, has not passed Mrs Grant by and the old housekeeper has lately procured a household compendium that includes receipts for Indian dishes and even some old English combinations for meat pies using cinnamon and mace. Belle lays into the madras, pairing it with a French wine cooled on the last of a block of ice bought from a costermonger some days previously. She finishes the meal with a flaky apple pie studded with cloves and doused in melted cream. Over dinner she peruses her notes – lists of potential ingredients for her love potion. Oils that she has proven provoke warm feelings of one kind or another in gentlemen. After dinner she enlists Nellie in a game of piquet. She never plays for stakes with the staff, but the game is entertaining and Belle, tonight, is ahead.

Knowing that Ruari is dining with his wife and the second gentleman has left satisfied, Belle is surprised when the doorbell sounds some time near eleven of the clock. Nellie rises, casting her eye at the ornate fusee timepiece on the mantle by Perigal and Duterrau, who, despite their French names, ply their trade from a shop in Chelsea. 'Miss?' she says.

Belle adjusts her dressing gown and lays down her cards face up. She is holding both aces and kings. 'I can't imagine you would have taken a single trick,' she laments with her palms in the air. 'You'd better see who it is.'

'I hope you don't mind the hour,' Elizabeth says when Nellie shows her into the room. 'Oh, what a lovely gown.'

'It is for the house,' Belle replies. A social call from a lady is a new experience. Courtesans are generally shunned by society's womenfolk and as a result Belle is accustomed to being solitary. She never had a childhood friend, her governesses focused on teaching her polite behaviour rather than letting her practise it with other little ladies and gentlemen. However, she is glad to see Mrs Rocheid. 'Yellow is my favourite colour, though your own dress is quite exquisite. I like the swags at your hem.'

'Clementina chose the fabric – pink! I had it from the Royal Exchange,' Elizabeth admits. 'Mr Rocheid insisted on buying us new things. I didn't know if you'd be receiving but I noticed there was light at the shutters as I passed.'

She loiters by the door. Inside, the house is lavish, and Elizabeth feels at home. She was not sure what to expect after Clementina's judgement of the occupants of Warriston Crescent, but it appears Belle is well-provided for. That, however, is hardly the point. Both women know that Belle's house is only a short detour from the main road, but a detour nonetheless and far enough along the crescent that it cannot be seen without turning into the street. Besides which, social calls to acquaintances are usually made in the afternoon. So Elizabeth wanted to see her, Belle thinks, but doesn't feel she can admit it. It is a compliment and she is glad to be considered a friend.

'Please, sit down,' Belle encourages her. 'Where have you been?'

'Dinner at the Grahams'. I had hoped to see you there.'

Belle momentarily considers explaining why she will never be invited to dine at Mr Graham's table. She likes Elizabeth Rocheid very much. But she decides against coming clean. After all, what can she say? Being an excellent courtesan is not easy. Apart from being beautiful, wise and accomplished and knowing how to value those talents in coin, she must remain a tomb for her lovers' secrets. Her endeavours are never what people expect them to be and in the normal run of things this carves a trench between her and women like Elizabeth. Still, it feels pleasant to have unexpected company. It is a gratifying kind of intimacy to know someone respectable who is welcome out of hours. Belle tells herself that Elizabeth has not sought her out tonight to elicit what would inevitably become a confession.

'Might I offer you sherry, perhaps, or tea?' Belle says.

Elizabeth touches her stomach. 'I have never eaten as much as I ate this evening,' she replies. 'The Grahams' table was sumptuous. There was a beautiful sugar sculpture that would put Monsieur Carême to shame. I ate choux pastry for dessert.'

Belle folds her hands in her lap. She senses something is on Elizabeth's mind. 'I hope,' she says, 'that you will take me into your confidence. You seem . . . sad, I think. Has something unsettled you?'

Unmasked, Elizabeth settles on the sopha and begins to cry, softly. 'Oh dear,' she sniffs, perched on the edge of the velvet, as the gentle odour of rose petals rises in the candlelight.

Belle reaches out and squeezes Elizabeth's fingers. After a few moments' silence, she makes an offer. 'Shall I guess? Tonight you attended a grand dinner party but for some reason you feel you did not deserve to. Am I correct?'

Elizabeth nods.

'But you are a lady of good family.'

Elizabeth nods again but still doesn't speak.

'You can be honest,' Belle encourages her. 'Believe me, I know the bravery that takes. If you tell me, I will try to help.'

Here Belle's stomach turns for she knows that she has not been honest with Elizabeth herself. Still, she is accustomed to affording her lovers the courtesy of allowing their emotions to overtake her own. Why would she not afford a friend the same?

'Widows are so brave,' she continues. 'Ladies do not enter the field of battle yet they ride without qualm into something more dangerous when they embark upon a marriage. I notice you are reticent in the company of gentlemen as if you feel . . . out of place. Is that it?'

Now Elizabeth is crying more loudly into a lace-edged handkerchief she has removed from her reticule.

'I try not to think of William,' she says, her fingers like butterflies. 'I try every day. Clementina is in awe of him. She never met him when he was grown, but she remembers him as a child.'

'What was he like?'

Elizabeth has never been able to talk about it. Even in death her husband holds something over her. It is not a widow's grief, but something more difficult to put into words. It taunts her when she looks in the mirror and makes her feel both hopeless and ashamed. Now she suddenly has a flash of him, the vision she has deliberately not allowed herself to remember. William holding her down. It comes to her that she will never forget what it was like to live in that little rented house in Richmond, as though the bruises on her arms and legs are still there. On her neck. Inside her. The time he forced his fingers up her skirt when they were in the carriage and snarled that she belonged to him. Will she never heal?

'Oh God,' she lets out a mewl, like a forlorn puppy.

'He hurt you, didn't he?' Belle asks, enraged. The idea of a man taking advantage of a woman incenses her – a legacy of the situation with her parents, no doubt. 'How dare he?'

Elizabeth seems so fragile now that it's as if she is made of liquid and Belle fancies for a moment that her friend might melt altogether into the thick, blue, tasselled carpet beneath their feet.

'I'm not sorry he died,' Elizabeth bursts out. 'Clementina keeps saying what a handsome couple we must have made. But he did hurt me, Belle. I cannot put a name to what he did. After he died I was as good as penniless though in truth it was better than living with that monster, although it is wicked to say so.'

Belle's eyes flash. 'This is not your shame to own,' she says. 'I rejoice that you survived it.' She takes a breath as she considers. 'Congress can be a pleasure, you know, if the match is good. Any gentleman would be lucky to wed a lady such as yourself. I'm sorry William behaved cruelly. He was not worthy of you.'

At these words Elizabeth stops crying. It has never occurred to her that William might not have deserved her. That his behaviour was not her own fault – her lack of pride in her dress or her habit of speaking to servants with too much familiarity. Her stupidity. Her head swims. 'I was such a burden, you see.' She passes a hand over the gossamer of her gown. 'William was a worldly person . . .' her voice trails. 'A man's needs drive him and there was always friction between us because . . .' she pauses as she searches for how she might put it, 'I was not a meet mate.'

A shadow settles on Belle's face. It is not called rape inside a marriage, but she believes it should be. 'Any man who forces a woman, even his wife, is not in my view a man at all,' she says. 'That is no pleasure.'

Elizabeth suddenly feels stupid. All at once she understands that not only did William force her but that he enjoyed doing so. It is another revelation. 'He always said I was hopeless. That I held him back.' It is the most she can get out.

Belle rises. She pours two tiny glasses of sticky madeira for she recalls Elizabeth is not accustomed to spirits. 'Hopeless? What nonsense.'

Elizabeth heaves a sob.

Belle hands one of the glasses to her friend. 'This was none of your doing. He chose you and did not realize your value. I'll wager that he valued everything more highly than his marriage. His horse. His occupation. His family. Am I right?'

Elizabeth cocks her head to one side as she considers this. She does not reply.

Belle relents. 'Tell me, do you ever take a hot bath?'

A smile softens the corners of Elizabeth's mouth. 'From time to time,' she says and notes, with some surprise, that she feels better.

'Wait a moment,' Belle says and walks through the double doors to her bedchamber and the little mahogany cabinet that sits on a side table. From inside she chooses a bottle of the blend that she first concocted a couple of years ago for her monthlies. It is a dark oil containing every substance that she has been able to prove relaxing – vetiver, chamomile, clary sage, geranium, frankincense and just a touch of lavender, which, it seems, works in almost every concoction, a spike among the other oils that both wakes and soothes. Lately, in advance of making her love potion, she has been selling this oil through an apothecary's shop in London, labelling it Dr Brodie's Most Efficacious Ladies' Bathing Oil. Mr Ninian Love, the apothecary in question, has seen his business double with quite the press of ladies beating a path to his door as the fame of Belle's medicine spreads as swiftly as the Great Fire of London – mothers buying the oil for their daughters, aunts for nieces and sisters for each other. At first Mr Love would take only half a dozen bottles but he is now up to a gross monthly. Charged with making the constituent ingredients, Edzel can hardly keep up with the demand alongside his other duties – fetching, carrying and processing Miss Brodie's botanicals as she searches out the oils required for her love potion.

'Here,' Belle fetches the stoppered bottle and sits down again prettily on the sopha. 'Put a couple of teaspoonfuls of this into a bath as hot as you can bear. It will help you to feel better. And while you are bathing, try to imagine how it might have been different.'

'With William?'

'With anyone your mind cares to light its fancy upon.'

'He was a soldier,' Elizabeth adds as if this excuses her husband's brutality or perhaps explains it.

Belle brings to mind her first lover – the colonel in charge of Edinburgh Castle when she arrived in the city. He remains the most skilled practitioner of the art of love that she has ever seduced – a man who possessed and revered her in equal measure. A man who wanted her to want him. She liked him in uniform.

'He said I was cold,' Elizabeth continues sorrowfully. 'That there was something missing in me.'

'I do not see you as a cold person,' Belle says. 'And even if you were, it was up to your husband to . . . warm you. What happened tonight? What brought you here?'

Elizabeth suddenly has a flash of Johann von Streitz taking her into dinner and of sitting at the table, talking animatedly. Afterwards, she played the pianoforte again. She cannot name the myriad of feelings that this evening has prompted. Pride, passion and interest. Self-worth. 'Perhaps I am thawing,' she says.

'William is gone,' Belle replies. 'It is up to you if you allow him to continue to hurt you. There is a different path. A widow has that great opportunity – to change.'

Elizabeth nods as she considers this. She is glad she stopped on her way home, she thinks, as she opens the small brown glass bottle and sniffs. In the house where she grew up soap was made with extract of marigold, which her mother swore was good for the skin. The flowers were pretty enough but ever since, Elizabeth always found the scent, though faint, repellent. This smells far better. She feels heartened now, hopeful almost. 'You are a true friend, Belle. Thank you,' she says, as the unstopped bottle unfolds its treasures.

Chapter Sixteen

The summer days stretch. On any other year the citizens of the city would remove to their country estates for the warmer months, but this July the town quietly works itself into a Hanoverian frenzy in readiness for the royal visit. People discuss their plans for the rest of the year as either 'before' or 'after' the royal visit, the seasons abandoned as any kind of marker. It feels like a kind of madness, for George has not yet said that he will embark, and he is famously mercurial. Still, the king's missives remain peppered with questions that denote his interest and, Johann thinks, it is not until next month that the Thames reaches high stink and London becomes unpleasant, so it is his best guess that if the monarch does decide to head north, he will choose August. Last year at that time George visited Dublin for, as the king put it, he had to go somewhere.

Meanwhile, Johann finds it pleasantly light in Edinburgh. His duties are less onerous than in London, where he is constantly at the king's bidding. Successfully avoiding the intrusion of the city's keenest royalists into his diary, he finds he has time on his hands, which out of the blue provokes an unexpected rash of homesickness – a longing for childhood summers spent at the family schloss, which is currently unoccupied. He has not before given much thought to his return to Germany after his term in London and to how he might fill his home with the things he enjoys. Now he starts to ponder the possibilities.

At twenty-eight years of age Johann has never been in love, though he has always assumed he will marry. However, his dealings with ladies on behalf of His Majesty have, if anything, put him off congress with women. When George was regent, his behaviour was notorious. It was hoped that his crowning would change his behaviour, but the king has an eye for the ladies yet. Von Streitz has on more than one occasion paid off a floozy on the sovereign's behalf, and in doing so always disappoints the women for His Majesty frequently runs to extravagant promises that he has no intention of fulfilling. Thus women, in Johann's more recent experience, are generally either petitioning for access to the king or angry that they were given it.

With time on his hands, Johann attends a hastily arranged midsummer ball at the Assembly Rooms as one of Sir Walter's party, organized when it becomes clear that the ton has remained in town and requires entertainment. 'Not so bad, eh?' Scott claps the German on the back as they sip scalded brandy at North Castle Street afterwards. 'You are quite the dancer.' Johann is not sure about that. The Scotts have not been at Abbotsford since the spring and Lady Charlotte sighs that though she enjoys the sociability of town, it is a long while to go without a proper ride out, by which she means the freedom of a hack on their own land. Solitary, Johann rides out anyway, for the countryside around Edinburgh is pleasant and he has found several discreet places to bathe – a deep pool at Colinton and in the sea beyond Portobello – but it is his interest in the Garden that most surprises him. He wonders if he is drawn there because he has the excuse of being on the king's business and will not be disturbed if he chooses to read by the pond. Whatever it is, McNab is discreet and the ton have not realized the king's man's propensity for the place.

In high summer the gardeners work as long as the light holds, the day being double its winter length. More plants arrive from the Leith Garden and are dug into the soil. Two extra boys are taken on to ferry water from the well, for it has been a dry month and everything is in flower. William McNab orders a gross of wax candles on the Garden account which he ferries back to his cottage in parcels like a squirrel hoarding nuts for the winter. Robert Graham visits from time to time and takes an interest in the century plant. With Sir Walter's help he has ascertained from Lady Liston that there will be an estimated eight to ten seeds from it. McNab does not know what he is going to do. He is finding it harder and harder to sleep.

Still, he is polite when the king's man arrives on a fine bay from the royal stable and it is on one of these visits that Johann encounters Elizabeth drawing in the glasshouse with a board perched on her lap in front of the outlandish plant, the young James McNab by her side. The boy sketches his own version of the plant, and now and then she corrects his drawing with a pencil. Johann had hoped she would attend the midsummer ball and was disappointed that he did not see her amid the swirling frocks and heated discussions in the supper room. Mrs Rocheid always has something refreshing to say, like a drink of cool, clear water amid the muddy torrents and not trivial either, like so many in society. Stood behind her, he clears his throat and she turns around. Johann bows.

James slips his drawing pad into his pocket. 'I must go, Mrs Rocheid,' he says before quitting.

'I swear I can almost see it growing.' Johann indicates the aloe's stem. 'It is not quite at the roof.'

'It's exciting, is it not?' Elizabeth replies. 'Are you not tempted, Herr von Streitz, to petition the king to support the Garden?'

That old chestnut.

'My temptation does not matter. His Majesty will not thole it. Besides, we still do not have a date for the royal visit.' He is sad that he does not have more impact on the king's decisions. He would like to make Mrs Rocheid happy.

'I suppose even a king cannot enjoin a plant to grow to his time-table,' Elizabeth says with a smile. 'We must wait until the aloe is ready. Though at this rate it will burst through the glass soon enough.'

Von Streitz peers over her shoulder at the drawing. 'You are as skilled with charcoal as you are at the pianoforte. How is your pupil coming along?'

Elizabeth smiles fondly. 'At my guess he will certainly be some kind of botanist when he grows up.'

'What is this?' von Streitz asks, pointing at her drawing as he looks up at the plant. Elizabeth has captured the image accurately – one of the prongs of the aloe has been cut at an angle.

'Mr McNab has taken a cutting for Lady Liston. He hopes to propagate it and send it for her greenhouse.'

'Ah. I see.'

Elizabeth pushes a lock of hair from her face. Her hands are spotted with charcoal and frequently marked from working amid the plants. He likes that she is a little messy – it means she has been occupied. 'I must finish for today,' she says, closing the sketch pad. He reaches out and takes it from her, flicking through the pictures of Graham's flowers and McNab's carts and the drawings she makes when Belle comes to call, of her friend sitting amid banks of flowers.

'You have great talent, Mrs Rocheid. You have captured Miss Brodie perfectly.'

He hands back the notepad and helps her to pack her things. He likes that she does not offer him dinner at Inverleith House or ask him to take tea on another occasion or try to find out where he will be at a particular time. He likes that she has walked here, rather than brought a carriage, and that she is wearing the dress she wore when he first met her with its worn embroidery and mended hem. She pulls her pale peach wrap around her shoulders and points across the Garden in the opposite direction to the gate. As they walk she does not stare at him when she thinks he is not looking. She does not intrude in any way.

'We widened the gap in the holly hedge,' she explains. 'That is to say James did. He found a fissure and took the shears to it, but I am not much larger than he is and the shortcut works both ways.'

Johann squints at the hedge. There is, he sees now, a slim gap. 'How enterprising,' he says. 'Have you got your dress for the royal ball, Mrs Rocheid?'

'It is coming,' Elizabeth replies lightly.

'Should His Majesty grace us, may I have the honour of the first dance?' he asks, feeling bold.

'I should like that.' She removes the board from his grasp. 'I really must go. Mr Rocheid does not approve if I leave Clementina for long.'

As she slips through the hedge her skirt catches on a spiked leaf and he bends to detach it. 'James has taken to walking with his hands behind his back,' she adds. 'So he will not damage the plants. There was an incident with one of Mr Graham's Highland flowers.' She smiles. 'It seems a lady's attire can be as troublesome as a small boy's hands, but I think the holly will recover.'

As she moves off, he realizes that she smells like a garden but with a splash of something exotic that he cannot name. Is it frankincense? Unlike most perfumes employed by ladies, whatever Mrs Rocheid is wearing is not over-flowery. She is a mystery. A woman who does not offer herself up. He wants to follow her to the house and listen to her play the Rocheids' discordant harpsichord, but he cannot impose. Through the hedge he watches as she disappears up the hillside sensing in her a renaissance of sorts that he admires. She seems to have grown in confidence since he first met her. Or perhaps grown in radiance. Yes, that is it.

Elizabeth does not look back. She continues briskly inside, removes her bonnet and leaves her drawing things in the music room, which is now transformed. The harpsichord has been removed and a proper easel set up with a table for her paints and papers. To one side there is a small dais with a chaise longue and three lengths of red velvet draped carelessly over it. This is where Belle has been modelling for her. Clementina had the gilt mirror from her bedchamber brought down. The women have tremendous conversations during these sessions – tea is served and the discussion ranges from the refraction of the rainbow to Newton's view on reflected light.

'The end of the rainbow is where the colours swallow each other,' Belle declared last time she was here. 'It is there that colour becomes a bright and shining whole.' She spent half an hour quizzing Elizabeth about the scents she enjoys and after some questioning they discovered that for Belle smell manifests as emotion – something that is happy or relaxing or stimulating – but for Elizabeth a smell is best described by colour. Dr Brodie's Most Efficacious Ladies' Bathing Oil is a warm red, a return to the womb while the scent Belle herself wears is a mixture of orchid and lily and prompts in Elizabeth's mind's eye a cool, pale blue.

Belle was particularly interested in this idea for she is mixing a new scent which, after much conversation and a few whispered discussions out of Clementina's earshot, the women decided must be golden. Then Elizabeth spent the whole afternoon drawing her friend surrounded by yellow, which is to say plants that smell yellow, of sunshine and pancakes, the long roofscape of the New Town in the background, washed grey by contrast. Belle likes the composition of this piece – Edinburgh behind her, a glass coupe of plump strawberries and a golden plate piled with cinnamon bark at her right hand.

'What is the scent you are making for?' Elizabeth asked and Belle did not reply. How could she?

'Is that you, dear?' Clementina calls from the other room, jolting Elizabeth from her memory.

'I am putting away my things,' Elizabeth shouts back and rings the bell so that Currant Bun comes running. 'I will take a bath,' she directs. 'Could you ready it? I shall be with Lady Clementina in the drawing room.'

The maid holds back from complaint though the words 'another one?' almost cross her lips. The mistress arrived so plain and tidy. It has not gone unnoticed downstairs that in the past weeks she has spread across the house, changing everything. 'Still, Lady Clementina is less troublesome than she was,' Cook pronounces. Duncan, from his place by the kitchen fire, does not comment upon this. The old woman persists in quoting Burns at him. Cook takes a swig of the kitchen brandy. 'Mistress Rocheid will catch her death with these baths of hers,' she says.

Upstairs, later that afternoon, Elizabeth slips under the warm water in the wooden tub that Currant Bun now leaves in her dressing room rather than tidying it away. Each time she craves her bath a little hotter and today condensation drips down the windowpanes and pools on the wooden sill and the room seems to flame as she loses herself in red scent. Beyond, the garden is a blur of green grass and blue sky. She takes a deep breath and focuses on her slim, slick body rocking against the water. Of late she sleeps soundly and though she cannot remember her dreams, she has woken on two mornings laughing. She has never in her life been this happy, not even as a child. It is as if all her cares have been removed and she is getting better.

Chapter Seventeen

Belle does not mix perfume in her usual attire. Nellie stitched a plain linen gown for her mistress and procured cheap pigskin gloves that can be ruined without distress and will adequately protect Miss Brodie's lily-white skin. All this is kept in a cupboard in Edzel McBain's shed at Tanfield. Once a month Nellie helps the mistress don her uniform, binds her hair with a cotton scarf and, with Edzel banished for a few hours, Belle mixes a barrel of Most Efficacious Ladies' Bathing Oil to dispatch to Ninian Love, who bottles it as required. Mr Love's correspondence is burgeoning into quite the archive and last month a London lady visiting Edinburgh came in search of Dr Brodie at Warriston Crescent to consult the great man. Belle, thinking on her feet, declared that the good doctor had removed to Inverness, where he was tending to an established client, and would regrettably be residing for the weeks to come. Three Edinburgh ladies enquiring about where to buy the bathing oil have been directed to make postal purchases from Mr Love's shop in Piccadilly, currently Dr Brodie's only stockist. Nobody appears to have realized there is no Dr Brodie the whole city wide, a fact Belle has checked. The only medical man of any description bearing that name is a barber surgeon who pulls teeth on South Bridge. He is known as Big Sam Brodie and has a reputation for speed over skill, which is what any sensible patient would choose, if they could not have both attributes.

The money has been extraordinary. Never one to undersell her talents, Belle made clear to the apothecary early in his correspondence with Dr Brodie that the oil contained choice ingredients and was thus expensive. Mr Love declared that he was not sure that ladies would spend as much as two guineas on a bottle of any concoction. The apothecary was quickly proved wrong. There is little medical help or sympathy available for a lady's monthly pains and as no medical practitioner suffers from them (all doctors and apothecaries being gentlemen), the matter has remained little understood and even less addressed. Mr Love, at first tentative about the benefits of the product and, in truth, apologetic about the price even as women handed over their money, has since become an evangelist. It is said that the day on which a fresh barrel of the potion arrives from Edinburgh has been christened a 'Piccadilly monthly' by the waspish maids sent to procure their mistresses a bottle. Dr Brodie's Most Efficacious Ladies' Bathing Oil is now dispatched in a large barrel and if Belle could mix it, Mr Love would take two.

Belle has learned a good deal from the experience of making the bathing oil, not least that it is vital the blend stays secret. In this the concoction itself has helped her. Traditional perfumes are a mixture of one or two ingredients and are focused solely on scent, but the bathing oil being a medical mixture has made it most desirable though she is certain it is the scent that does the magic. Mr Love has no doubt been able to discern some of the ingredients, but since each oil added to the mixture changes the scent overall, in some cases dramatically, neither he nor anyone else has been able to reproduce it. This is not to say that inferior bathing oils are not now available – there has been a veritable rash of them in the wake of Belle's success, but Dr Brodie's concoction is generally recognized as the original and best. Its scarcity has worked in its favour. Belle knows for her own part that if she is made to wait for a new batch of ribbon or lace, it heightens her desire and she has decided that though she will make Mr Love the second barrel he has asked for in his previous two letters (underlining the words 'urgently required' in his latest) she will not do so immediately.

Mr Love has also petitioned the good doctor to sell him the formula, in the matter of which Dr Brodie is playing extremely hard to get. When the apothecary objected that a price of several thousand guineas was unreasonable and complained the doctor was trying to bankrupt him, Dr Brodie replied by return that he was perfectly content simply to continue to supply Mr Love on a monthly basis with as much of the oil as he has time to make. If Belle trusted Ninian Love she would probably license the receipt, but she does not.

This month, however, in addition to the bathing oil, she is also sending a smaller barrel of her citrus blend which she has told Mr Love will battle malaise and retail at a guinea and 11 shillings a bottle. She has added a dash of bergamot to her original formula, along with some tobacco and soothing thyme, to make it more elaborate and thus more difficult to make out. While her arrangement with Mr Love has yet to make as much money as taking a lover, Belle has thus far more than covered all her costs in renting the shed at Tanfield, procuring botanicals of all kinds and paying for Edzel's living costs and education. Twice a week Nellie is sent to deliver provisions for the boy – a loaf of bread, a hunk of cheese, some pies wrapped in linen and a flacon of small beer. All this is mere pocket change, but it adds up over the years. Belle's hobby has thus far taken investment and now that has been recouped, the profit can commence in earnest.

Belle is delighted that the business is proving so promising. If she is careful, betwixt Dr Brodie's Most Efficacious Ladies' Bathing Oil and the sum she hopes to make from her love concoction, she will not have to work again. This is not to say that Belle's endeavours with her gentlemen are only work (for she enjoys her occupation) but she finds that on the days when she mixes her perfumes she bounds out of bed in the morning. The love potion in particular takes up her imagination. Some nights she dreams about the ingredients but wakes unfulfilled. The orris she was waiting for was finally delivered to Edzel's shed after weeks of waiting but did not prove to have the desired effect and the receipt for the golden scent is still not complete. When it is, it will be her masterpiece. Ever-canny, Belle likes to be ahead of herself. Having money in place will mean she need not rely on anybody.

On sunnier summer days, the fumes in Edzel's shed can become overwhelming and Belle leaves the door open as she works in a pungent floral miasma. She likes being able to hear the rushing sound nearby where the Water of Leith meets one of its tributaries. Few people ever come to Tanfield so it is a surprise when today, three boys in shiny satin top hats and light coats with brass buttons pass and lean inside.

'Hallo,' one says. 'What's all this?'

Quick to her feet, Nellie makes to close the door, but the fellow inserts a well-shoed toe to stop her.

'A laboratory, is it?' He pushes into the shack. 'Whatever are you up to? It smells jolly nice.' The fellows crowd in. All three are no more than twenty years of age and rich with the confidence that goes with a lifetime of privilege. One makes for the shelves and lifts a bottle, agitating the contents as he inspects it against the bright square of the open door.

'Is this a surgeon's museum? Who is your master?'

Belle turns. She looks like a washerwoman, save that her shoes are worth three months' wages. The young gentlemen, however, do not notice this.

'Do you mind, sir,' she says harshly.

The boys stop, shocked at this tone coming from a woman whom they deem commonplace. They laugh.

'Hoity toity is it?' one of them says, lifting the stopper off a jar of orchid oil. He sniffs and his eyebrows lift before he passes it to his friend and takes another bottle off the shelf. This time rosemary. 'You're making balm? For old Graham, is it?' Receiving no reply, he puts his finger into a pot of distilled cedarwood and tastes it. His face crumples.

Nellie steps forward, her hands on her hips. 'That's none of your business,' she says firmly. 'This is private property. That jar could be poison for all you know.'

Colour drains from the man's face. 'Is it poison?' he asks nervously.

'Some of them are,' Belle says. 'You would have no way of telling. Would you?'

'We, madam, are doctors,' the young gentleman ripostes, his chin smooth as Belle's smooth white bottom.

Now it is time for Belle and Nellie to laugh.

'You're not doctors,' Nellie says. 'You're students, and lacking in sense at that.'

The words hit home.

'Well . . . I . . .' None of the young gentlemen manages to finish this sentence and instead they shuffle uncomfortably.

Nellie is hitting her stride. 'I suppose you're on your way to the Botanic Garden. You folk are always hanging about there, though there are no lectures at present, what with the move. You know that, don't you?'

'We know.'

Belle notes with pride how far the girl has come. When she first arrived at Warriston Crescent she would not have said boo to a goose.

'We're looking for the blind girl,' the first student admits.

'What blind girl?' Belle asks.

'She mixes whisky for Mr Stein,' the boy says.

'And what would you be wanting with poor Mhairi MacDonald?' Nellie challenges him.

The gentlemen look sheepish. They certainly want to bolt now, and only require a way to do so that will leave them a scrap of dignity.

Belle has never met Mhairi but it's clear Nellie knows the girl. In any case she feels outraged on her behalf. 'Is it a freakshow you're after? Come to bait a poor blind woman. Shame on you,' she snaps.

'They say she can tell fortunes,' the young man protests. 'We're going to pay her.'

Belle looks at Nellie to confirm this.

'She's not a seer. Nor a witch. But without her sight she can tell things,' the girl confirms.

'What things?'

Nellie shrugs. 'Where you've been. What you've been up to. They say she's improved Mr Stein's whisky tenfold. Gentlemen now clamour for the stuff.'

Belle's eyes widen. Improving Mr Stein's blend is no mean feat. For a long time the distillery was famed for spirit so rough it could be used to clean the foot scrapers at New Town front doors. If the girl has made such a change, it is impressive.

'She'll be working now, anyway,' the girl says. 'You wouldnae catch her till the end of the day.'

The gentlemen nod. As they make for the door one tips his hat. 'Jolly nice smell,' he says. 'There was no need to be cheeky.' It is fascinating, Belle thinks, how much a person's appearance defines what is thought of them. If these young gentlemen had met Nellie in the park on one of her undercover scent missions, or Belle herself at the Assembly Rooms, they would be more circumspect. Working women, she notes, have an insight into how people really are.

As the boys disappear, she stoppers the barrel beside the workbench and hoists herself onto the stool Edzel uses to study.

'How does this blind girl know where people have been?' she asks.

Nellie shrugs. 'It's like she can smell it aff you,' she declares. 'They say when you lose one sense, others heighten. She can tell where the barley's been grown, for the whisky. She sends it back if it's the wrong kind of earth, whatever that means.'

Belle considers the shelves round the shack's walls. She has been wondering how to complete the concoction of her love scent. She has a start in the strawberries and in cinnamon, the effect of which, she notices, puts men at their ease. Star anise will lend richness and a dash of one of the blonde woods will be required – pine perhaps.

Pine heightens the awareness, making someone more alert – an important ingredient in bringing on feelings of love and one that took a while to pin into this spectrum of gold, as Elizabeth would have it. Belle has procured ambergris to ensure the scent lingers and has tested the quantity required when combined with different solutions on her own skin. But the receipt for this, the scent upon which her reputation depends and her fortune will be made, will need to be more complex than a simple five ingredients to merit the money she intends to charge, and to make it impossible to copy.

It is this that has fired Belle's interest in the American aloe. If she extracts the scent from the flowers about to bloom, that is all there will be of it on this side of the Atlantic. It is the perfect secret ingredient. From what she understands, the stem of the aloe grows tall, but it supports only a few flowers. If she can make even half a gill of absolute she will be lucky, which will in turn define how much of the scent she can produce. Though how she might get her hands on the blooms is quite another matter. Still, she thinks, it would give her a bottle to sell in Edinburgh, a bottle for London and after that money is made a bottle for Paris and perhaps Rome, now it is safe to travel to the continent. Her freedom and fortune are in sight.

Unlike the bathing oil, however, it is not proving easy to mix. Belle knows her talents but although she loves her work she also knows her limitations. She has a good nose but not a great one. If this girl is as skilled as Nellie says, then the fact she is blind is a blessing. Mhairi MacDonald might be able to smell the concoction but she will not be able to see how much of each ingredient she is putting into the mixture or, indeed, tell how those ingredients are made. Someone working from scent alone cannot write down a receipt – not one that can be copied. It is an intriguing idea, and one that might solve Belle's problem.

'Nellie, go to the distillery please and tell Miss MacDonald that I desire to speak with her.'

'I dinnae expect those gentlemen meant any real harm,' Nellie objects. 'They're only students.'

'Tell her it will be to her advantage,' Belle adds. 'Then have Edzel dispatch that barrel, would you?'

She hands Nellie the key to the shack and pulls off her heads-quare, shaking out her hair, emerging from her over-dress and laying her gloves on the bench in one smooth movement. Perhaps today will be a lucky day, she thinks, a golden one.

Chapter Eighteen

Robert Graham is bursting at the prospect of an invitation to one of the royal balls. As a result, he is keeping a close eye on the century plant and passes Warriston Crescent several times a week more than he used to. Upon occasion he cannot resist the temptation to visit.

He brings Belle books, including botanical treatises and an illustrated account of the function of the nasal passages, for he has gathered that she is highly intelligent, and interested in perfume. He likes it when she questions him for it means she is paying attention. Ever on the lookout for ways to improve his standing, Mr Graham has taken Belle's advice on which scent to procure for his home and all eighteen rooms at 62 Great King Street now sing with the sweet smell of geranium leaves warmed by exotic ginger. In keeping with his belief that the more difficult something is to obtain, the higher its value, he went to the trouble of procuring an absolute of geranium from the south of France and a distillation of finest ginger root from a wholesaler in Bombay. When they arrived he put his laboratory to its first use in a long while and mixed the scent himself. His wife has taken to dabbing this fragrant treasure in a salve onto her skin before she goes out. When Lady Charlotte Scott remarked on it, Mrs Graham sent her a tiny flacon as a gift. Everything is going well.

When Belle arrives home, Graham is waiting for her. She sighs. Anyone can see he is a snob and a social climber, so she does not entirely understand what he wants of her, though she cannot deny he is proving useful.

'Nellie did not answer the door,' he says.

'She is running an errand,' Belle explains. 'Are you on your way to the Garden?'

Graham nods. 'I cannot stop for long.'

'Mrs Grant will send up tea.'

'That won't be necessary. Not for me at any rate.'

Belle thinks that if she does not ring for tea he will probably go more quickly. She would enjoy a cup, but she will wait. 'It's a lovely day,' she sits down. 'I met some of your students this morning at the Water of Leith.'

'My students?' Graham delivers a few lectures a year at the university, but he does not engage with students as a rule.

'They mentioned you when I asked them why they were there.'

Graham looks uncomfortable about being name-dropped by undergraduates and he changes the subject, giving Belle an update on the aloe's progress.

'When do you expect the plant to flower?' Belle enquires.

Graham, Belle has learned, dislikes saying that he doesn't know something. 'It's impossible to predict the date, my dear Miss Brodie, but the stem is now well in excess of eighteen feet in height,' he says. 'McNab has removed the pane of glass directly above it for it would have gone through the roof. It is expected to grow considerably higher. Every time I visit it is taller.'

Belle smiles indulgently. 'I long to see it,' she says.

'You will be the first to know when it blooms,' Graham promises.

Belle has been wary of asking for what she wants, but today she has a feeling that things are falling into place and cannot resist. He has called now, after all, on several occasions. 'I have a fancy, Mr Graham,' she says flirtatiously. 'Will you indulge me?'

He motions her to go ahead.

'Might it be possible to pick the flowers of the *Agave americana*?'

Graham suppresses a cough. 'Pick the flowers? As if they were roses . . . or lilies?'

'Exactly,' she says, clapping her hands. 'I thought to myself, what a luxury they would be. So unusual.'

Graham stands. 'Miss Brodie,' he says, taking a deep breath as if he is about to commence a lecture, 'the *Agave americana* is a treasure. Its value does not reside in its blooms. You cannot pick them. For then there would be no seeds, do you see? To pick the flowers would squander the whole exercise.'

'Ah. Yes,' Belle replies, as if she did not already know.

'The plant is vital to science, dear lady. McNab will nurture half its seedlings and the rest will go to His Majesty's garden at Kew. It is all arranged.'

'Of course. Silly me. Ladies sometimes take a whim,' she says. 'When I have a desire, I'd do almost anything to bring it off.' She leans forward, knowing that if Robert Graham were ever to press his advantage he would do so now. She stares at him steadily, with absolute frankness.

'Absolutely impossible,' he pronounces crisply. 'I really must be off.' He bows formally and takes his leave.

Belle watches from the window as he mounts his fine grey and sets off at a trot towards the main road. In truth she is glad that he did not try to kiss her. While the lovers she has taken both wish to please her, it is evident that Mr Graham cares less about that kind of thing. He seems uninterested in sensory pleasure and she wonders, once again, why, if this is the case, he calls with such regularity. In any regard she will have to think of another way. With a shrug she rings for tea, which Nellie brings up on a tray.

'Mhairi is in the kitchen. Mrs Grant has cut her some ham,' she says.

'Send her up, would you?'

The first thing that occurs to Belle when Mhairi appears is that the blind girl is the most attractive young woman she has ever seen. Her hair is golden, her eyes are green as a whisky bottle and she has a sweet snub nose that would not mark her out as a classical beauty but is nonetheless enchanting. The girl's deportment is unexpectedly elegant. She stands straight as a Lombardy poplar, as if she has been planted in the doorway. It crosses Belle's mind that if you dressed this paragon properly you could pass her off as anything from a duchess to a lady of the queen's chamber – that is, until she opens her mouth.

'You wanted to see me, Miss Brodie.' Her accent is a sudden shock, wide as a gaping doorway.

'Come in,' Belle says.

Mhairi lifts her chin as she follows Belle's voice and uses her stick to guide herself round the sopha.

'Here?'

'Yes,' Belle regards her. 'You may sit down.'

There is a momentary silence. It is unusual, Belle thinks, for her to not be able to read a new person. In general she prides herself that she has a feel for what everybody wants, but this girl not being able to meet her eye (of course not) makes that impossible.

'You asked for me?' Mhairi says.

'You came promptly.'

'I had done for a while. I will return.'

'What is it you do exactly for Mr Stein?'

Mhairi considers this question seriously. 'I inspect the ingredients.'

'There are only three ingredients to whisky, as I understand it.'

'Aye,' Mhairi says enthusiastically, 'so if one of them isnae right, it's important.'

'What else?'

'I oversee the processing. The men can be gey careless. The sprouting of the barley and that. The taking of the water – we draw from the river but some days it can be bitter. Then we use water from the well. Mr Stein has installed a bigger smoking room so we can make peated batches. And then there's the barrels . . .'

Here she stops, realizing that she has perhaps been indiscreet – what happens behind the gates of the distillery is a trade secret. Mr Haig would give his eye teeth to know Mr Stein's methods.

'I understand that you blend the spirits,' Belle prompts her.

'Aye. Mr Stein makes single malts, too, but a blend is more regular. Some folk prefer it.'

Belle rises and crosses to the set of crystal decanters beside the fire. She turns over a glass and pours a measure of the whisky that the second gentleman prefers. It comes from Orkney. He has it sent to Warriston Crescent directly from the island, where she believes he once lived. He likes a glassful sometimes before he tups her. 'Here,' she says. 'Tell me what you think.'

Mhairi breathes in deeply and sips. A smile breaks across her face. 'Seaweed,' she says. 'Aye, and the best of peats. This is a proper island uisque. We canna make this here. The water is not right.'

Belle disappears into her bedroom. She pours a tot from the breakfast bottle beside her bed and returns, snatching the first glass from Mhairi's hand and replacing it with the second. The girl sniffs again.

'Mmm,' she says. 'This is Doric dram. It reminds me of home, though I'd say the barley has been left a wee bit long at the malting stage.' Her nose crinkles.

Belle sinks onto the chair beside the fire. The prospect of being able to make four bottles of perfume worth perhaps three thousand guineas each is suddenly becoming more viable. She scents her absolute freedom. 'I want to engage you, Miss MacDonald,' she says.

'Oh, I cannae, miss,' Mhairi replies. 'I gave my word to Mr Stein that I would not make whisky for anybody else.'

'Did Nellie tell you that we encountered some gentlemen today who wanted you to tell their fortunes?'

'Young gentlemen seek me out for that often.'

'And what do you charge them?'

'Just the twa shillings, miss.'

'And you tell their fortunes?'

'No exactly. I tell them where they have been and surmise where I think they are going.'

'Tell mine,' Belle says coming to sit next to her.

'It is only a trick, miss.'

'I know. I will pay you to see it.' She presses two shillings into the girl's palm.

Mhairi sighs and slips the coins into the fold of her belt. She brings up her fingers and passes them lightly over Belle's face. She smells faintly, Belle notices, of the smoking room.

'You've been at the river today, but you do not go often. Mr Graham was with you lately and another man, who smells like a manse. But you do not love either of them. Without all the perfumes around you, you smell of the air, miss. Like a cloud. I think you'd fly away if you could. Your spirit is pure gallus.'

Belle gasps.

Mhairi's lips purse. 'I'm sorry if I overstepped the mark,' she says. 'But that's what I get.'

'Can you smell people's desire? Their secret experience? What does a virgin smell like?'

Belle is animated now.

Mhairi's face betrays only a hint of amusement. 'A virgin? I dinnae ken that,' she says with a chortle before adding, more seriously, 'but attraction is a warm smell, rich and musky. It is unmistakable. Women give it out as much as men when they see what they want, though it is not commonly thought so.'

Belle rises to her feet. 'It's not whisky I need your help with. I will pay you for a portion of your free time. Mr Stein need never know.'

'And what would I be doing?' Mhairi sounds suspicious. Belle is not a fool. She realizes the girl knows her occupation, though she suspects she would not judge it. For someone so young and disadvantaged, Mhairi is unexpectedly worldly.

'I am mixing a scent, Miss MacDonald.'

'Are you aye?'

'It is something special. I do not have all the ingredients I need yet, but I am making ready. Will you meet me on Sunday at the shed at Tanfield where Edzel McBain stays?'

'Is he the young lad who smells of pork pies and foosty books?'

Belle laughs. 'I expect he is,' she says.

'I go to Saint Giles on Sunday in the morning,' Mhairi replies. 'But I can come after.'

'Let us say two of the clock,' Belle suggests.

'Mr Stein pays me very well, miss.'

'I will pay you likewise. Ten shillings each time you come and another ten shillings for your discretion, which is a pound. And if I am satisfied with your work there will be a bonus of ten pounds at the end.'

'Make it a flat guinea each visit and a bonus of a dozen more and you have your deal. I will not tell a soul.' Mhairi holds out her hand. Belle considers for a moment and shakes it.

Downstairs, Mrs Grant provides Mhairi with a cup of milk before she leaves.

'All right, lass? What was the mistress after?'

'She's buying a barrel of whisky,' Mhairi lies smoothly, as good as her word as she downs the milk and wipes the snowy vestiges from her lips. The money Belle pays her will boost the savings she keeps in a tin box behind the wainscot in her bedroom. One day she will use this stash to buy a plot of ground where she can live and work – somewhere she will not be at the beck and call of Mr Stein or anybody else.

Nellie shows her up the stairs from the basement door. 'I can take you along, if you'd like,' she offers.

'I'll be grand.' Mhairi lowers her voice so that nobody inside will hear. 'I didnae tell her about you, Nellie, but your mistress is no fool. You maun be careful.'

Nellie blushes. Not that Mhairi can see that.

The streets are deserted as she makes her way back. Mhairi stands on the bridge, listening to the rushing of the water punctuated by birdsong and the smell of summer sweetness on the air, the banks of the river bounded by wild flowers. Further along, almost back at the distillery, she senses him. He has taken to waiting for her when he is at his leisure. She suspects there are days when he stands outside the gate for a long time to no avail.

'Duncan,' she calls.

'Where have you been?' Duncan steps forward. He smells reassuringly of leather tack and hay from the loft and the smell Mhairi has just described to Belle Brodie – the warmth of attraction.

'What's it to you, where I've been?' she replies.

'Mhairi . . .' He almost sounds offended.

She laughs. His attentions are growing on her. Men often form a fascination with her, not only because of her looks (which are almost the only thing of which Mhairi is unaware) but because of her air. Her father used to say it was well she would always have to carry a stick. Duncan, though, is proving more mannerly than most prospective suitors. She cannot sense any other women around him and he has never tried to lay hands on her, except once, walking her home, when he helped her ford the Water of Leith on a day when the water was high and she let him take her hand. Sometimes, when she sits by the lavender at the cusp of the Rocheid estate, he arrives, as he did that first day, as if he knows she will be there. They talk as she runs her fingers through the blooms, and they breathe in the scent together.

'Miss Brodie asked to see me,' she tells him.

'Miss Brodie? Do you not know what she is?'

'Rich is what she is,' Mhairi retorts.

'Is she after whisky?'

'Aye,' she lies. Mhairi is discreet.

She turns towards the distillery gate. 'I need to get back.'

He shifts behind her. 'I brought you this,' he says and pulls a linen napkin from his pocket. As he opens its folds, a sweet smell wafts in her direction, something unknown and exotic.

'What is that?'

'A slice of pineapple. The groom at the Fettes estate got it from the gardener. I helped him restore a saddle. I thought you'd like to taste it.'

Mhairi takes the slice and brings it to her lips. It is unlike anything she has ever eaten.

'Oh,' she breathes, 'Duncan, this is fantoosh.'

His smile is so broad she can almost hear it. 'I knew you'd like it,' he says.

'Do you like it too?'

'I havenae tasted the thing.'

She hands the slice back and gingerly he sinks his teeth into it. 'Oh,' he says, 'aye.'

They stand in the laneway, sweet-breathed, letting the rush from the pineapple settle. 'I thought you should try it,' he says awkwardly. 'I knew you'd be curious.'

'You're very kind.'

This is the greatest success Duncan has ever had with Mhairi and, fired by it, he blurts, 'Would you come with me to the High Street? There's going to be a flogging.'

Mhairi has heard of this. The capital has been scandalized by the story of a young man arrested for breaking into the house of his fiancé's parents in the Old Town and stealing their best candlesticks and two portraits said to have been painted by Anne Forbes. Though the thief was masked, his mother-in-law-to-be recognized the scoundrel's gait as he retreated down the darkened close. Needless to say, the engagement has been called off.

'Oh, aye,' she says. 'When is it?'

'Friday at noon. I can borrow the trap from the stable. They'll no be needing it.'

'I wouldnae mind at aw.'

Duncan's face lights. 'I didnae ken if you'd be able. I thought we could go to Deacon Brodie's for a glass of ale. After it's done.'

'It's a scandal they named that auld howff after a criminal,' Mhairi chortles. 'But I'd like to come. I'll see what I can do about getting off.'

Chapter Nineteen

Some days when the High Street is busy, if he has the leisure, Johann dons a cape, pulls his hat low and escapes the incessant banging of the palace's workmen, slipping past the debtors from the jail behind the palace and proceeding up the cobbled highway into the crowd. It is said that Mary Queen of Scots left the palace the same way and, like her, Johann believes these excursions give him a feel for the people of the city, who have turned out in force for the flogging of the unfortunate thief. He hears that there is talk that the law lords of Scotland will ban public whipping soon, a forward-thinking notion that would yet be considered too liberal in London. Johann wonders where everybody has come from. He has seen the place busy before, but today, the Mile is thronged to bursting. Crowds of high-spirited students from the university have abandoned their lectures. Ahead, past the Tron Kirk, jeering gentlemen hang out of first-floor windows precariously holding glasses of brandy, and huddles of barefoot children fetch trays of pies from gloomy subterranean bakeries on the Cowgate and ferry them up the hill to sell for tuppence a time.

The sky is blue without a hint of cloud and Johann feels as if he is not so much diving into a crowd as diving into a language. In polite company in this city, everybody speaks English but the Scots words Johann picks up from the streets are like salt in a bland dish. When he was twelve his father sent him to a cousin in Denmark for a year where he was presented at court in Copenhagen at the peak of Christian VII's reign. Johann played with the king's young grandson in the royal nursery at Christiansborg Palace and his ear became attuned to the language. Now, in Edinburgh, familiar words shoot at him from passing conversations – braw and bricht and bletherin, dreich and drookit and dauner. Sonsie dames and canny laddies. The language feels part Danish, part French and part English. He is surprised he can understand it with such ease, but he can, and it feels like some kind of comfort.

He walks up the hill in the direction of the flogging but does not jostle to gain a place, for the punishment does not interest him. Instead he loiters in a sunny spot at the Tron, soaking in the atmosphere. The air is so warm and dry that the shit on the street has turned to dust. You can almost imagine decent people living on this side of town. A gentleman emerging from a close further up recognizes him and Johann waves at his cheery call but turns away – he is not so lonely as to pass his time with fools. Ahead, a young lad is calling to his girl. 'Fanny! Will ye no come down and see the rogue skelpt?' It is most amusing. Johann turns to look at the crowd in the other direction. Through the confusion he sees the Rocheids' coachman, Duncan, accompanied by a pretty blonde, tie up a horse and trap along South Bridge and dive in to the mass of good cheer. Edinburgh feels as if some kind of festival were underway – the normal bounds overrun.

'Duncan,' Johann hails the coachman as he approaches. The man does not have the air of a servant, he realizes. 'Have you come to see the flogging?'

Duncan shifts from foot to foot. 'Herr von Streitz. Aye. We have.'

'And who is this?'

'Mhairi MacDonald, sir.' Mhairi bobs a curtsy.

'Is this your sweetheart, Duncan?' Johann grins. 'You were bound to choose a beauty. Your father had quite a reputation with the ladies, I understand.'

If Duncan were a dog, he would growl.

'What do you mean, sir?' Mhairi asks, her voice sweet as cherry juice.

Johann catches the coachman's eye. 'I'm sorry,' he says, realizing he has spoken out of turn for perhaps the first time since he was a child – the consequence of him relaxing, perhaps. He looks apologetic as it comes to him too late exactly how Mhairi has managed not to partake of the gossip that has gripped the entire city. 'Sometimes I talk nonsense,' he says. 'It was said only in jest.' He feels bad that he has outed Duncan to his sweetheart. 'Please, let me buy you something to eat at the oyster house,' he offers, motioning back along the bridge where a sign advertises beer and seafood. A gentleman taking another man's servant for a drink is unusual, but Johann is accustomed to talking to the staff wherever he goes. He hopes Duncan doesn't assume he is trying to bribe him for information about the Rocheids or the nearby Botanic Garden. He genuinely wants to apologize – that and pass a little time.

'The fare is good, I'm told,' he adds.

'Who said that? More gossip, is it?' Duncan replies, clearly holding a grudge.

'One of the footmen at the palace told me,' Johann admits stoutly. He likes that the man is not easily bought. 'Please, let me make it up to you. It's a sunny day. You must be thirsty. I am.'

Inside, the air smells of polish and dripping beer taps and tallow from the candles. The light is low. Johann hands over a coin at the bar and a woman brings three clay cups of perl and a bashed pewter plate of shucked oysters. He watches as Mhairi downs an oyster from the shell and takes a sip of the beer. She licks her lips. 'Do they make this here?' she asks. 'There's a taste o rock from it.'

Johann smiles. The girl is perceptive. 'They brew it in the outhouse. Edinburgh is built on a dead volcano so it is a fair guess that the city's water might rise through rock. They say the geology is unique. Many scholars are engaged in the study of it.'

Mhairi sips again. 'I have heard that said,' she confirms. 'Yes. The ghost o hot ash.' She picks another oyster off the plate and chuckles.

'You could make something grand out o that. At the distillery where I work, we take water from the river, but it is of a different character. It rises in the Pentlands, and tastes green, like the hills.'

'Do you brew?' Duncan asks her. 'My mother was an ale-wife. She used the barley from my father's farm.'

'Not here,' Mhairi declares. 'But at home I did. I always thought I might do it for my living,' she adds, as if that isn't what she's been saving all her money towards. She can hardly tell him of her plans here, with this gentleman in tow. Besides, her mother gave her little advice when she left home, save this: *Let a fellow tell you his dreams, before you trust him with yours.*

Johann sits back. He finds ordinary people fascinating – they understand how everything works. From the luxury of his palace the king often declares how he would like things to be, but he has little notion of the labour involved in making it so. The sheer knowledge of women who bake or brew and men who carve stone or work metal always astounds him. He likes the making of things. The world this blind woman inhabits may be dark, but it is luxuriously sentient. He motions to the landlord.

'Do you make any other beer?' he asks.

'Aye, sir. We brew a pale ale.'

Johann orders a jug and Mhairi tastes it carefully, the men hanging on her pronouncement.

'These hops are braw,' she proclaims.

Johann laughs. 'I should like to taste your ale, Miss MacDonald,' he says.

Twenty minutes later, the plates empty and the beers quaffed, they emerge into the sunshine and turn back towards the Tron. There is a roar from the High Street.

'That'll be the flogging,' Duncan says.

'If you hurry you may still catch it,' Johann replies.

Duncan shakes his hand. 'You will not come with us, sir?' It is kind of him, but it is time to go.

'I have not the stomach,' Johann admits.

Mhairi looks surprised but says nothing. He waves the young couple off as they disappear into the crowd.

As he turns down the Canongate, mourners are leaving the church and Johann recalls that today are the funerals of three men killed in an accident on Picardy Place. The week before, the first floor of one of the new houses collapsed on account of the people crowded to attend an auction. It is quite the day at the Old Town, no wonder it seems so busy. Two women cry quietly into their handkerchiefs as they are handed into a carriage with painted wheels. He slips past them, through the gates into the graveyard where a digger is already filling one of the holes. A blackthorn bush cascades its pale petals onto the pathway. The clean lines of the church feel like a relief after the dark, showy buttresses and ornate Gothic crown of the High Kirk up the hill and the tiny chapel inside the palace dedicated by the Comte d'Artois, a fleeing Bourbon noble who briefly took respite at Holyrood after the French Revolution.

In the wake of the funerals, a minister is laying a branch of hawthorn onto a grave on the far side. His hair is peppered with grey, though his eyes look too young for such a dusting. Johann nods a greeting and the priest touches the headstone fondly before turning back onto the path.

'Hello,' he says. 'I'm Reverend Brunton. Can I help you?'

Johann introduces himself. 'Johann von Streitz. I was just taking a walk,' he explains.

'Is that a German name? I spotted you for a traveller, sir.' The reverend smiles and quotes from the book of Luke in Johann's mother tongue. ' "Und Reisende werden aus Ost und West sowie aus Nord und Süd kommen und sich am Tisch im Reich Gottes zurücklehnen." I learned German as a boy,' he adds.

It is the habit of the king's German staff never to speak their own language. Such was British antipathy to the Hanoverians when George I arrived in London and it was realized that he was unable to speak English that the utterance of German has been banned among

His Majesty's personal attendants for more than a century. Johann finds he is laughing. These words about people coming from the four points of the compass to sit at the table of God sound guttural to him now – not as smooth as English nor as warm as Scots.

'It has been a while,' he says.

'You must miss home.'

Unsure how to reply, he falls back on his manners. 'A place is its people and there are some people I miss. But then, when I go back, I'm sure there are those from here that I will want to bring with me.' He hasn't realized how true this is until he has said it.

'All life is so,' the reverend replies sagely. 'The company of men and the kindness of women are the true gifts of God.'

'Are you the minister here?'

Brunton shakes his head.

'You came to the funeral?'

'I did. Though in truth, I come daily. My wife is buried here.'

'I'm sorry.'

The minister motions along the pathway. He gives an apologetic smile. 'It is four years since she departed. I will never marry again,' he says.

'I'm sure your parishioners hope it for you, sir,' Johann replies. 'You are yet young.'

Reverend Brunton eyes him. 'I no longer lead a congregation. I am the librarian at the university and a zoologist.'

'A man of letters, then.'

'My dear Mary was the same. You have perhaps heard of her? She wrote novels. Her work has appeared in translation . . .'

'I read mostly classics and poetry,' Johann admits.

'Are you married, Herr von Streitz?' the reverend asks. 'Is your Frau travelling with you?'

A minister will always have the authority to ask a personal question. Normally Johann simply bats off this kind of enquiry but today he is touched by the fact that this man has used a funeral as an excuse to visit his wife's grave – as if he might need one. Or perhaps it is the way Duncan stared nakedly at Mhairi as she downed the oysters. As if he wanted to consume her.

'I am not married . . .' he says, the stretch of lawn that runs from the family schloss down to the river coming into his mind. 'Though I have lately been considering my future.' It feels like an outrageous admission, but it is a strange relief to say it out loud.

The men are now back on the street. The remnants of the crowd dispersing further up the hill pass in dribs and drabs. A man sings a drunken ditty and several rag-taggle voices join him in the chorus. Reverend Brunton turns towards Holyrood. He touches his hair as if to tidy it, his finger sporting a signet ring with a lion rampant carved into a pale blue cabochon. He is moneyed for a minister, Johann notes. His faith is not born of the need of a younger son for a living. And yet he does not seem stuffy, which is unusual for a man of conviction. Brunton pauses for a moment, also sizing up his new companion. Then he issues an invitation.'I believe today they are moving the copper beeches from the old Botanic Garden in Leith to the new site,' he says. 'I have heard it is a wonder to see the trees in motion. I plan to walk over. Would you care to join me?'

As a rule Johann would normally refuse this kind of offer, but there is something about the minister that holds him. Besides, although he has seen the sketches Elizabeth has made of McNab's trees being moved, he has not witnessed the endeavour.

'Indeed,' he says. 'I have heard of it and I am most curious.'

The men set off down the hill.

'If I might give you some advice,' the reverend lowers his voice conspiratorially. 'I hope you do not consider this rude of me, but I will be frank. Do not tarry in making your plans, sir. Find a woman and be happy. I, for one, sincerely hope that you will marry for love, Herr von Streitz. It is, in the end, the only thing that matters.'

Johann's face betrays his surprise at such honesty. Reverend Brunton laughs.

'I am an evangelist,' he admits. 'Though not for the Almighty. My wife and I eloped in a rowing boat. Her family were Catholic. I fear we loved each other more than either of us loved God. It is a terrible thing for a minister to admit, but it is true. I am fortunate indeed that I was allowed a few years with both Our Lord and Mary in my life. I highly recommend marriage. And love too, of course, for that is what it comes down to.'

The men veer off at the gates of the palace. They ignore a debtor standing at Abbey Strand with a fine embroidered jacket for sale. It is at least four decades out of fashion, expensive in its day, with beautifully worked pansies round the collar. Anyone who frequents this part of the city becomes used to bypassing such desperation. They continue past the bathhouse and up the slope towards Royal Terrace. The sound of building work on the new tenements wafts towards them as they crest the hill.

'Might you settle here? In Edinburgh, do you think?'

'I am in service in London,' Johann admits. 'Though if I make a marriage, in a year or two, I will return home.'

'And where is that? Bavaria, by your accent?'

Johann is impressed. Reverend Brunton is not far off. 'Saxony,' he says. 'Near Leipzig.'

'Ah – well, I have been a fool for love and all I can say is that it was worth it.' The man's tone is cheerful. 'I knew when we left Orkney that I loved Mary, but it grew to be more than that. I miss her so deeply that to feel her presence I have found I would commit any sin. Which is a sin in itself, of course.' Here he pauses to compose himself. 'So, I implore you, find a woman you love, Herr von Streitz,' he repeats. 'You will never know yourself if you do not, and you will never know God, either.'

Johann considers this. He knows it is not so simple, but perhaps it should be. 'Thank you,' he says.

Ahead, a procession of five carts proceeds up the road from Leith. A steady stream of youngsters runs alongside it, jumping to touch the low branches of the copper beeches as they turn into Picardy Place and down Broughton Loan where householders make the now familiar scramble onto the pavement and windows are thrown open so that children can reach the passing branches with their plump fingers and tear off a memento. 'Good Lord,' Brunton exclaims, 'I had not realized they were moving trees of such height. How extraordinary. They must have been terrified, do you not think, the first time they hoisted one of these huge plants onto such a little cart? It could fell a house. It could kill a man. And yet they held it there.' He stares in awe. 'The only bravery is not in battle,' he adds.

Johann thinks this is something Lord Nelson said or perhaps the Duke of Wellington. He cannot remember. But the minister has inspired him. Suddenly he feels nervous and determined and full of hope all at once, swept along by the excitement on the street. 'I am glad I ran into you,' he says.

'God wishes you happiness. I am sure of it,' Brunton replies earnestly. 'And so do I.'

Chapter Twenty

Elizabeth and Belle walk amiably arm in arm to the bookshop at the far end of George Street. Belle has tempted her friend away from an expedition to the Garden, convincing Elizabeth that this is a better use of her time. Jamie pulled up Belle's carriage outside the Assembly Rooms and saw to the horses while the ladies browsed sheet music at Mr Ferguson's on the first floor of Number 46. They then moved to a booth at the Assembly Rooms, to buy tortoiseshell hair ornaments and a yard of gold silk ribbon as a present for Clementina. Now outside, Belle holds her hanway aloft, providing extra shade from the sunshine as they glide towards the bookshop, gossiping and intermittently stopping to glance at the wares on display in the windows and enjoy the additional shade of the canopies. The delicious smell of baking hangs in the air. In the front rooms of George Street's private houses, they discreetly notice the chandeliers and the fashionable oriental wallpapers, but it is the prospect of the new edition of *The Liberal*, containing a contribution by Lord Byron that they are most excited about.

'I like to borrow periodicals from the library but there are some publications it is simply better to own,' Belle opines. 'I am accustomed to write notes in the margins,' she whispers. 'On poetry especially.'

"Be thou the rainbow in the storms of life. The evening beam that smiles the clouds away and tints tomorrow with prophetic ray,"

Elizabeth adds, quoting England's most wicked poet, who is currently residing in Greece.

'Oh, that is very good,' Belle says breathlessly.

They have crossed Frederick Street when Elizabeth spots the old woman with a basket over her arm, coming out of the apothecary's shop. Under her mop cap her white hair is distinctive and, Elizabeth notices, she is wearing sturdy boots – a contrast to the thick, gold chain clasped around her neck, which she did not notice before, being at a greater distance the night she spied the Garden through the holly bushes. Closer now she can see the woman is not elegant, but neither is she living in poverty. 'That lady,' she indicates, 'do you know her? I saw her visiting Mr McNab. Her name is Dickson, I think.'

Belle shakes her head. 'I do not recognize her,' she says. Then, with a sly smile, 'We must find out. Of course we must. What fun.'

She pulls Elizabeth on and though Elizabeth objects she does not do so with vigour.

'Excuse me,' Belle hails the woman politely. The woman turns. 'I'm sure we have a mutual acquaintance in Mr William McNab, madam? Am I right? My name is Isabel Brodie, I wonder if I might enquire as to yours?'

The old woman pauses, her pale stare unforgiving. 'I ken who you are,' she says.

'But who are *you*?' Belle pushes her.

'I am Mrs Dickson of Dickson and Sons,' she announces in a business-like manner. 'I run the largest nursery garden in the city.'

'Ah – no wonder my friend has seen you at the Botanic Garden then. She thought that was your name, and I have seen your catalogue. It is quite excellent.'

The woman bobs a reluctant half-curtsy as if the exchange is complete, but Belle is enjoying herself. 'I am in need of seeds,' she says.

This is not true. Belle does not grow any of her ingredients. It would take additional expertise and besides, many of the things she needs are exotic and she would require an acre of greenhouses to nurture them. Her passion is in the experimentation, the mixing of different scents and the observation of their effects.

'I wonder you have seen my catalogue, miss,' Mrs Dickson offers, 'there is not much garden ground along Warriston Crescent.'

Belle stops abruptly but Elizabeth, encouraged by her friend's spirited enquiry and emboldened by what she knows is a lie on Belle's part, chimes on. She remains curious about the old woman's visit to the Garden that evening in the dark.

'Mrs Dickson, have you seen Mr McNab's century plant?' The words sound discordant suddenly as she senses Belle's unease, or perhaps it is because she need not ask the question – she knows Mrs Dickson has seen it.

'Aye, ma'am.'

'We are agog at when it will flower,' she continues. 'You are a seedswoman. Do you have a view?'

The old woman's expression makes it plain that she is not someone who routinely indulges in casual conversation or makes fanciful predictions. 'I would not like to say,' she replies.

There is an awkward silence.

'Well,' Belle cuts in hurriedly, 'it was as well to make your acquaintance.'

Mrs Dickson nods.

'Are you all right?' Elizabeth enquires as the women proceed to the bookshop.

Belle takes her arm. 'I'm fine,' she says, opening the door. *The Liberal* is in stock and Belle, back in sorts, buys two copies, presenting one to Elizabeth as a gift. 'Of course, Lord Byron is not the kind of gentleman ladies should put themselves in the way of,' she comments. 'But his poetry is divine. What do you think of Mr Shelley's work, Elizabeth?'

'Mr Shelley? Yes,' Elizabeth enthuses. 'It is a tragedy, is it not, that Mr Keats died so young? His work is also inspired, and we will know no more of him.'

The bookseller ventures that Mr Shelley's *Hellas* will be in stock before the summer is out and adds that there is quite the vogue for all things Greek just now.

'You could go to Greece, Belle,' Elizabeth ventures fondly as the man rolls each copy of *The Liberal* separately in brown paper tied with string.

'I could, I suppose. And see the actual Parthenon,' Belle agrees, 'rather than the copy they are building on Calton Hill.' She sighs. 'It is taking an age. In any case, we should make our own monuments – something of our own history rather than copying everybody else's.'

'Like Sir Walter bringing back tartan, you mean?'

Belle pauses to consider this. It is not exactly what she meant for tartan does not come from Edinburgh or even Perthshire, where Belle was raised. But still.

The women leave. As they step back into the sun, Mrs Dickson is still hovering along the street, outside a cobbler's premises in the basement.

'I have heard that if you ask at the Assembly, they sometimes have sherbet. Let's see if they can accommodate us. I, for one, would like to be refreshed,' Belle declares.

The women move in the shade from canopy to canopy but as they pass the cobbler's Belle pulls her friend almost to the kerb to avoid the old woman. Elizabeth does not like to be rude. It is not in her nature to snub anybody. Besides she has an idea. Clementina's birthday falls next month and she would like to buy her something.

'Mrs Dickson,' she hails the older woman. 'Have you heard tell of the new garden that will be established at Inverleith? The Royal Caledonian Horticultural Society will be in charge of it. My cousin, Mr James Rocheid, has ceded land to the government who will, I understand, in turn, lease it to the benefit of this worthy project. I wonder what you might know of the species the garden intends to propagate? The aim is to increase the yield of crops, as I understand it, and my cousin, Lady Clementina Rocheid, is most interested in the matter. For our family farm.'

'I know the Royal Caledonian, ma'am. Several of its gentlemen are customers of Dickson and Sons.'

'I have a fancy to buy some seeds for my cousin. She would be most interested in increasing our yield. I'm sure our own gardeners are aware of most innovations, but if there was anything in particular you might recommend . . .'

'There may be some advances in fruit trees . . .' Mrs Dickson starts. 'There is a new grafting technique . . .'

Belle tugs at Elizabeth's arm.

'I would not hold you up, madam,' Mrs Dickson says coldly.

Elizabeth casts her friend a glance. They talked about planting for hours at Lady Liston's and all the way home in the carriage. It is not like Belle not to be interested in botanical matters. Or, for that matter, in the best choice of a present.

'Are you all right?' she asks her friend.

'The sun . . .' Belle gesticulates. 'It is terribly hot.'

'I am at Inverleith House, Mrs Dickson,' Elizabeth says. 'Perhaps you might contact me discreetly so my cousin will not hear of the matter? I should like to surprise her. I will buy what you recommend to a value of two pounds English.'

Mrs Dickson bobs another half curtsy and Belle turns, her nose in the air, ready to move on. Her discourtesy is pointed.

'Hoity toity,' the old woman murmurs under her breath.

Perhaps if the students had not said the same only a few days previously at Tanfield, Belle might have let this pass. Perhaps if she did not feel as she does today, on the tired side, or had not been frustrated in her desire to pluck the aloe's blooms by Mr Graham. Perhaps if she had succeeded by now in the receipt for her love potion or if Mrs Dickson had not stared quite so contemptuously down her nose, Belle would have continued along the street. In any case, she turns back.

'What did you say?'

Mrs Dickson demurs momentarily. 'I did not mean you to hear me, ma'am.'

'I am the great-granddaughter of a duke,' Belle says bluntly. 'And you cannot match your shoes to your aspirations,' she gestures, 'old woman.'

Mrs Dickson purses her lips in quiet fury. 'I'll not take that,' she says with determination. 'Not from the likes of you.'

Belle sets her jaw. 'How dare you?'

'There are some who would ask how *you* dare, Miss Brodie. Granddaughter of a duke, aye? And whore to whichever man will pay your bills. It's as well you bide beyond the city limits or the magistrate would have you up.'

Elizabeth blanches but Belle does not even notice. Her temper is roused. 'Whichever man? Whichever man?' she snaps. 'They did not say that to Lady Hamilton when Lord Nelson was her lover.'

When Mrs Dickson laughs, the sound comes from her ample belly. 'Lord Nelson, is it? How many men have you entertained this week, my fine lassie? This month, even? You sell your quim for coin to the highest bidder. It's to hell you're headed. Your grandpa's title will no save you God's judgement. So don't come fancy with me.'

The old woman turns on her heel and disappears towards Princes Street before Belle can riposte. She spins round. Two shopkeepers have appeared in their doorways and a stableman has climbed down from his box to watch the exchange. In one of the houses a woman in a powder blue spencer loiters by her open window, examining one of the curtains, quite unnecessarily.

Belle comes to her senses suddenly realizing that she is standing on the city's main thoroughfare airing her private business for the world to see – fighting with a common gardening woman, a thousand times her social inferior. Flustered, she turns towards Elizabeth but cannot meet her friend's gaze.

'Is that true?' Elizabeth's eyes fill with tears.

'I have two lovers,' Belle admits quietly. 'What business is it of anybody else? Many women in London . . .'

Elizabeth, however, has spent time in London and is not diverted by Belle's suggestion of the capital city as a place that is morally superior or more sophisticated.

'And you do this for money?'

Belle does not reply. As it sinks in, Elizabeth feels as if the paving stones along George Street have fallen away and she is tumbling. As if her life in Edinburgh were somehow temporary, James Craig's sandstone design swaying in the breeze like a stage set and she once more standing outside the cottage in Richmond with the last of her things packed, not knowing what lies ahead of her. If James Rocheid finds out she has befriended a strumpet, he could throw her onto the street.

She puts up a hand to stop Belle speaking, for in her panic she cannot properly follow what is being said. Something about unjust judgements and ignorance and the art of love. How men can do what they like so why shouldn't women? Madness. All Elizabeth can think is that she has the sum total of forty pounds hidden in her travelling case and a few dresses besides, and if her place at Inverleith House is denied, she will have to live off that for the rest of her life and William's tiny army pension, which would not keep a mouse in fresh cheese. Her mind is racing through instances of her own stupidity. There must have been signs of this that she could have read. What will people think?

'We should go back to the carriage,' Belle says.

Elizabeth shakes her head. She finds she cannot speak. Belle's carriage being to the east she turns decisively westwards, pushing off Belle's arm as her friend reaches out.

'Elizabeth!' Belle calls after her in distress as Elizabeth barrels along George Street and turns north at the junction, down the hill past Sir Walter Scott's residence – oh, the shame – and onto Queen Street. How did she not realize? How could she have missed this? She searches her memory for some indication but comes up with nothing except her own naivety – exactly what William always levelled as her greatest fault – stupidity. She does not understand the world. She never has. She is a fool.

As she comes to the junction down to Pitt Street a man's voice cuts through the hurly-burly of her confusion.

'Mrs Rocheid,' Johann says delightedly. 'Have you been shopping?' He bows.

'What?'

'Shopping,' he indicates the package in her hand. The poetry.

'I went to the bookshop,' she stutters distractedly.

Von Streitz offers his arm. 'This is a most fortuitous encounter,' he says. 'Perhaps you will allow me to accompany you? Are you walking home?'

She nods.

'It is a lovely day,' he says, and makes to take the parcel, but she snatches it away, and over his shoulder her eyes follow Belle's carriage as it disappears down the hill. Damn her.

'How did you know I was here?' she asks. It suddenly feels as if the whole world is watching.

'I did not know,' Johann frowns. 'I am headed to call on Sir Walter. I have come from the other end of town where the trees are again in transit. A copse of copper beeches today. It was quite the sight. If you don't mind me saying so, I think you should draw more pictures of the process. The ones I have seen show the mode of transport clearly, but it seems to me if you set that image against a sketch of the street a viewer will understand more easily how extraordinary Mr McNab's method is. The scale of it. I myself would like to see such a picture.'

His words barely register, but she allows him to walk with her past the railings of the private park where well-dressed children are playing a game of catch on the half-laid lawn, a hapless nanny chasing a little boy who is rolling around on the ground with the family dog. Gradually Elizabeth manages to arrange her features calmly as they continue down the hill, Herr von Streitz commenting first on the charming view of Fife in the distance and then on the presence of seagulls nesting among the chimneys. 'I fell into conversation with a zoologist today who commented on the natural aggression of the species,' he says. 'They have been known to attack.'

As they cross Great King Street his conversation turns to the Grahams' dinner party. 'I thought you played beautifully. Haydn is a favourite of mine.' He pauses, considering Reverend Brunton's advice about love and regret. About taking chances. He pictures Mrs Rocheid at the schloss's gilded dining table. They walk a further block in silence as he decides to simply say it, for there is nobody around to hear. At the trees at the bottom of the hill, he pulls her to one side. 'When you were sitting at the pianoforte that evening, you brought to mind my family home in Saxony. Mrs Rocheid, I hope you do not object to me saying that I cannot help but imagine you singing there. A songbird for my guests, rather than Mr Graham's. It is mere fancy, I know, but having luckily run into you, I must take the opportunity to admit I find myself drawn to you. I find my heart open. As a woman who has been married, you have more experience than I in such matters, but if you were able to entertain my ardent attentions, I hope I might call on you not only as a family friend but as an admirer.'

Elizabeth's cheeks burn. Her blushes are close to the surface after what has happened with Belle. Her eyes fill with tears. She stares. Has he just asked if she will receive him as a lover? Has he just insulted her? 'It seems, sir, that there are many women in Edinburgh who accommodate gentlemen's ardent attentions. I am not one of them,' she manages to get out.

It is now Johann's turn to blush. 'I apologize if I have offended you. I am not schooled in the ways of courtship. I spend my time with His Majesty in proximity . . .' he starts.

'I know about His Majesty,' Elizabeth cuts him off. 'I know what his interests are. I have read the broadsheets. It seems to me that Miss Austen was quite right about the king.'

Johann mumbles. He can see what she means. Perhaps undertaking the king's business has given him too transactional a view of relationships. There is no question that His Majesty lacks poetry in this regard. George has been known to pay cartoonists not to print their drawings of him, fat and pawing a succession of lovers.

When Johann was appointed to the job, the retiring gentleman – a distant cousin from Hanover – briefed him frankly in his duties. Among them were ascertaining which of the illegitimate children credited to the king's pleasure were in fact his. 'You must see to it that this information remains secret. This is not France,' the man said. 'And it is our job to ensure it does not become so.' During the king's visit to Ireland the previous summer, Johann had to resort to threats to discourage a number of Dublin's more vociferous ladies from starting a petition to censure George's behaviour. Almost the moment the king set foot on Irish soil at Howth, he embarked on an amorous spree that would put a fitter, younger man to shame. He had only just been happily bereaved of his wife before he set sail and, as one of his courtiers observed wryly, the sovereign clearly felt he deserved an orgy of celebration. His Majesty, in truth, is in the habit of retiring to Windsor when public attention becomes piqued and leaves it to others – which is to say Johann von Streitz – to pour oil on his troubled waters. In private Johann knows that some in the royal household refer to him as Keeper of the King's Bastards.

Johann is shocked that Elizabeth would think this is what he meant.

'Madam, I am not George,' he says. It is the most he can say, for spelling it out would be tantamount to treason. 'None of us is the sum of the company we keep,' he adds.

Elizabeth's temper rises. 'What do you mean by that?' she snaps.

'I cannot say.' Again, it would be treasonous.

Elizabeth does not understand. A single tear of humiliation slips down her cheek. Belle has ruined her. 'I will thank you not to spread gossip. I have been foolish and too trusting and did not understand . . .'

'But that is precisely what I admire about you most, Mrs Rocheid,' Johann interrupts, raising a hand. 'You know so naturally how things ought to be done. Ladies such as yourself and Miss Brodie are paragons of your sex.'

Elizabeth has to restrain herself from slapping him. She has pulled away. They are, by now, across the bridge at the head of Warriston Crescent. The thought that only a short time ago she had gone to Belle's house in the middle of the night and that Belle had encouraged her to loosen her morals . . . She feels insulted and thinks she might burst into tears.

Johann persists. 'It is what I most admire about the working class, do you see? Their pragmatism. That polite society venerates keeping people, especially women, in ignorance of the workings of the world, seems to me foolish. Why should you not know everything? You, Mrs Rocheid, are good at so many things – drawing and painting and music. It would take me a long time to list your skills, madam. You cannot conceive of the joy you would bring by allowing me . . .'

'Joy!' she snaps, horrified. 'Certainly not.'

'You may talk yourself down, but, Mrs Rocheid, I am inspired by you. By your very person.' His voice is pleading now.

Elizabeth decides to take the shortcut through the Garden. She must get away from him. She marches down the laneway with Herr von Streitz in her wake, pushing past two students, one of whom is giving the other a piggyback.

'I did not mean to offend you, dear lady,' he says once the boys are out of earshot. 'I felt, when I took you into dinner the other evening, a certain music between us.' He looks into her eyes. 'I'm sure of it. But I may have been mistaken.'

'Sir,' Elizabeth manages to get out through her outrage. 'I am not equal to the attention of gentlemen. My late husband would not like it.'

Johann does not avert his gaze. 'You did not feel it then?'

She stops. Her face is flushed, and she does not trust herself to speak. 'I am going home,' she manages to get out and promptly disappears up the slope and through the gap in the holly hedge.

Johann stands winded, staring after her. Turning, he lays his palm on the rough bark of a nearby oak tree. What has just happened? He cannot decipher it. Why on earth is she so angry? He feels entirely deflated. Mrs Rocheid, he has realized, is the perfect woman. He cannot understand why he did not see it before. She is unimpressed by his position, and so talented. He admires her for a dozen reasons, among them her experience. She is a woman of the world. He feels suddenly bereft, his chest empty. This is what they must mean when they talk of gentlemen losing their heart to a lady. He considers climbing the oak's sturdy branches to catch a final glimpse of her but before he can do so, he hears someone shouting his name.

'Herr von Streitz,' Mr McNab calls from a distance, spotting the king's man standing alone on the fringes of the arboretum. 'Can I help you?'

Johann shakes his head.

'It has not flowered yet,' McNab adds, assuming that the aloe is the reason for Johann's visit.

Johann cannot think of that now. 'You are married, are you not?' he asks, dejectedly.

'Yes, sir.'

'And you are happy?'

'Very happy.'

'It was a love match, then?'

'Truth be told, sir, I was not sure that she would have me. But I knew I had to try,' McNab smiles.

'What happened?' Johann asks, genuinely curious.

'I asked her twice. Mrs McNab that is. Miss Whiteman as she was. She seemed shocked the first time, but I waited for her to see the sense in my proposal. I had not yet been offered this position, although I had prospects.' He pauses at the irony of this now. 'Anyway,' he continues, his smile returning. 'I believe we were meant for each other.'

'But how did you know, Mr McNab?' Johann's enquiry is urgent. He is unaccustomed to asking for counsel. He is usually the one giving it.

The gardener shrugs. 'It was natural somehow. A call to attention. Like the budding of a flower. You know how the petals unfurl quite suddenly and all is revealed. I admired her a great deal. I only had to wait and hope she felt it too.'

'Yes,' Johann says, deciding in the wake of this information that marrying Elizabeth Rocheid is his destiny. 'That is what I will hope for.'

Inside Inverleith House Elizabeth hands her coat and bonnet to Margaret and joins Clementina in the drawing room. The interior of the house feels cool after the long walk home in the baking sunshine.

'A hand of cards, my dear?' the old woman offers.

Elizabeth nods. Still trembling from this afternoon's events, she lays her copy of *The Liberal* on the side table and hands over the little parcel.

'I thought you'd like this,' she says.

'You are very good to me,' Clementina kisses her on the cheek, pulling the golden ribbon out of its wrapping. 'In my younger days I would have worn this tied round my neck, but today I fancy it for my hair. Can you help? It seems a lot of bother to call the girl.'

Elizabeth winds the ribbon through Clementina's powdered grey tresses artfully and the old lady stands to check herself in the mirror on the mantle.

'Oh yes,' she pronounces. 'I like that. You are a treasure, my dear. I could never let you go.' She reaches for the deck of cards. 'Piquet?' she offers. It is her favourite.

Elizabeth sits at the table. She wonders whether what Clementina has said is true or if the old woman would abandon her if she knew the truth of the company she has been keeping or the disgraceful suggestion Johann von Streitz has just made. She knows it is easy to lose everything – she has no absolute right to be here, it is a courtesy extended to her, is all.

'You deal,' she says.

'Och yes,' Clementina shuffles the pack. 'Let's have a hand or two and then we can call for refreshment.'

Chapter Twenty-One

That night Clementina is long abed but Elizabeth cannot conceive of sleep. Instead, late, with only two candles alight, she sits alone in the drawing room by the window and watches the city as one by one the flames of the far windows dim beneath the stark white lamp of the moon. The air outside is cool and fresh. She has become accustomed to the smell of lilac at night on this side of the house but this evening the scent is laced with honeysuckle as if a bough was creeping along the façade and over the window frame. Around her, the rooms are absolutely silent except for the ticking of the clock on the mantle. One of the clock strikes and then two, as Elizabeth goes over and over what happened.

She did not eat dinner, but she managed to show no other sign of her distress until Clementina retired. Then she dismissed the staff and sat crying for an hour in a high-backed chair by the fire. Howling. Gasping to catch her breath. Belle is a liar and a whore and Herr von Streitz is like every other man – what must he think of her, to have made such a proposition in that way, in the street? How will the world judge her, seeing her arm in arm with a courtesan along George Street? A kept woman. A whore. A lady's reputation is as frail as a butterfly's wing. She crumples the drawings she made of Belle and throws them to the ground. As the tears subside, she rubs her eyes. Her appetite stirs, longing for sweetness – a choux bun or a shortbread biscuit or a soft slice of bread spread with butter and honey. Some comfort. There is, she knows, no hope of any such thing at Inverleith House for the pantry contains only Cook's bread, which is as good as a brick, and no cake at all. Still, the desire is overwhelming. It has been hours since she ate. At dinner she only picked at the fish on her plate. So, without as much as debating the matter, on a whim, she lifts a candle and leaves the room, moving into the darkened hallway and down the servants' staircase concealed behind a door backed with green baize to muffle its opening and closing. Tiptoeing as she makes her way into the service part of the house, the bowels of the place.

She has never before made the descent to the kitchen, but she is guided by her nose – the smell of roasting meat and simmering broth. The room is warm as she enters, for the stove is always alight. Nobody is up. The table lies ready for the morning's breakfast. A cat sits curled in a chair at its head, sleeping. In Richmond Elizabeth had only a single maid – a thin slip of a fifteen-year-old who mostly kept things clean and did the shopping. Elizabeth shifted for both of them in the kitchen, though she has never admitted to anyone that she fell so low. Still, the lure of baked apples in pastry is almost overwhelming now. And why should she not be satisfied? The food at Inverleith House is plentiful but she has, she realizes, felt deprived of the comfort of sweetness. The indulgence of it.

Lifting the candle to peruse the pantry shelves she finds buttermilk and honey and a bag of strong white flour. The yeast does not smell right but she grates apple into it, and, donning an apron discarded on a chair, she sets to work, measuring and stirring, the familiar smell egging her on as she rolls up her sleeves and kneads the mixture. It feels good to make something with her hands. Once the rolls are baking in the oven, she melts butter and adds it to a mixture of wheat flour, coarse ground oats and sugar that she grates from the cone. A tiny pinch of salt and a spoonful of ground cinnamon completes the receipt and with two teaspoons she fashions slick, yellow quenelles that glisten in the candlelight as she slips this second tray of biscuits into the oven and removes the rolls.

Her mouth is watering now, and she is so bent to her task that she does not see the shadowy figure of Currant Bun hovering in the doorway, staring at her slack-mouthed. It is only when the girl steps backwards, trying to melt into the darkness, that she comes to Elizabeth's attention.

'Margaret,' she exclaims, surprised.

Currant Bun does not know where to look. 'I came for a glass of milk,' she says. 'I could not settle.'

Elizabeth motions her to enter. 'I couldn't sleep either,' she admits.

Currant Bun allows herself an awkward glance at the rolls. 'They smell nice. Where did you . . .?' she stops. It's none of her business.

'London,' Elizabeth says, as if it is usual for upper-class ladies in the capital to bake their own bread.

'There's blackberry jam in the pantry,' Margaret offers.

Conspirators now, the women spread a roll each with butter and jam. Margaret pours two cups of milk and they eat in silence, sitting at the table with the lone candle flickering. Elizabeth fetches the shortbread from the oven, and they do not let the biscuits cool, eating them quickly with spoons, like children, before the hot dough can harden. Margaret laughs as the sweet, buttery mixture melts on her tongue.

'These are like my mother's syrup rounds,' she says.

'You cannot tell anybody,' Elizabeth begs. 'You won't, will you?'

'Cook would be ragin, madam,' the maid replies. 'No one likes it when their job is owertaken. It is a shame, though,' she smirks, 'that you cannae gie her instruction.'

The very idea makes Elizabeth giggle. 'I mean it,' she says, suddenly serious. 'Nobody must know.'

'Yes ma'am,' she nods. 'Lady Clementina says that it is a maid's duty to keep her mistress's confidences.'

What Clementina had in mind is no doubt the details of a dalliance with a gentleman, Elizabeth thinks, and remembers what prompted her into the kitchen in the first place. She stares out of the dark window in the direction of the river and wonders where Belle is. Her temper stirs. Belle, she thinks, is no doubt in the throes of ecstasy with some gentleman. Any gentleman. For money. The harlot. Congress can be a pleasure, is that not what she said the other night? She should have drawn her as Theodora, the whore Empress of Babylon, not surrounded by her damn flowers. How could she not have realized that Belle was a molly-cat? The thought makes the last of the biscuits rise in her stomach.

'Ma'am?'

'I'm all right,' she waves around the room, her forearm pale with flour. 'Would you . . .?'

'I'll clear it, ma'am.' The girl's eyes are bright at the idea of the mistress of the house not only putting her hand to bread making and biscuit baking but also washing the dishes. Even Cook doesn't stoop that low.

'Thank you,' Elizabeth rises. 'I'll leave you the candle. I can see myself to bed.'

The hallway is striped with moonlight and shade as she emerges into the upper house and climbs the stairs. Currant Bun turned down the bedcovers hours before, and the sheets are smooth and cool. Outside, an owl hoots in the trees. Elizabeth slips off her shoes and removes her dress, falling into bed in her petticoats and staring at the ceiling fretfully. Belle Brodie was only half the humiliation of the day and now it is the other half that occupies her. Herr von Streitz and his . . . she can scarcely put a word to it . . . suggestions. She feels embarrassed that she was fool enough to lay herself open to such danger. Everyone must be laughing at her. Robert Graham at his dinner party and, she remembers with a sting, Sir Walter Scott. The way she babbled about Belle that night – no wonder Herr von Streitz assumed what he did. If he could have seen her in the kitchen this evening he'd have laughed. Some fine lady, with floury fingers, eating below stairs in the company of a maid.

She vows silently never to leave the Rocheid house and grounds again. She will send Mr McNab his drawings – James can take them.

She will refuse Clementina when she suggests an outing to the Exchange. She will not take up her invitation to the royal ball. She will be good and always remember how lucky she has been. She will not wish for anything more than to retain her place. She has no idea how she will ever sleep, but in the end, almost at dawn, the tiredness in her limbs and the comfort of the bed overtake her as she slips unconscious into the last vestiges of darkness. She survived William, she will survive this. The shame of it. She must only make herself small and quiet. Yes, she thinks, I shall simply disappear. As sleep finally comes, she smells the tantalizing scent of baking cake, warm and soft and delicious. With her last sliver of awareness, she melts into an imagined flood of hot raspberry and vanilla, where everything will be all right.

Chapter Twenty-Two

Belle also decided to forgo her dinner. She had Nellie draw a bath, snapping as she stepped into it that the water was too hot though within five minutes she was ringing for more jugs of warm and fussing over the towels being laid out incorrectly, as if such a thing were possible.

'She's in some mood this evening,' Nellie reports in the kitchen as Mrs Grant heats more water on the stove. 'I can't imagine what has got into her.'

After two hours, her fingertips like raisins, Belle dries her skin and pulls on a plain white nightdress. Barefoot, she calls for her pennyroyal tisane and sips it by the window, staring across the fields opposite the terrace, over Wardie land in the direction of Inverleith House. She feels bereft, which in truth makes no sense. She has enjoyed Elizabeth's acquaintance these last few weeks but, when it comes down to it, it is not the loss of a new friend that troubles her most. The public humiliation administered by Mrs Dickson is far worse. As darkness falls, Belle runs over and over what happened on George Street . . . the lady by the window, the coachman loitering nearby and the hate on the old woman's face as she snarled her accusations. Belle hates the fact that she has to hide. Why must it be women who shoulder the shame and not men? Why is it so shocking that she might choose her own path and be perfectly happy along it?

How many married ladies have made their matches for a fiscal consideration and are feted rather than condemned? The fact there is no justice frustrates her.

This is how Alexander Brunton discovers her when he comes to call, past ten of the clock, much later than his usual visits. 'Oh,' he says, for he has never seen his mistress wear an item of clothing so plain. She looks like a girl – younger and more innocent. In white like this with her hair round her shoulders, she could be an angel.

'I am in ill humour,' she admits.

'Your courses?'

She shakes her head. If only it were the matter of a little blood. 'I lost a friend today,' she says, for she cannot tell him that she was unmasked in public.

'I do not expect I am going to make things better,' he says.

Belle regards him as he sits on the sopha. She cannot recall that he has ever sat down like this in the three years she has known him. He, her second man, is usually silent and does not stay to eat or play cards or converse.

'Would you like a whisky?' she asks.

He shakes his head. 'Thank you. No.'

'You will not stay then?'

He draws from his jacket a sealed paper and with it, lays a leather pouch on the satinwood side table. It lands with a clink. 'I have been offered an opportunity,' he says.

'You are leaving?' she asks.

'Not Edinburgh.'

She pauses, understanding. 'Only me?'

He nods and indicates the items he has deposited on the table. 'This is to thank you.'

'Thank me?'

'You saved me, Isabel. My sin with you shielded me from the full force of my grief. I can say no more than that, but you have been a godsend, if it is not a further sin to call what we have done, that. To believe our affair was somehow divine.'

She studies his face. She does not understand what he means, but she thinks that perhaps it does not matter.

'I'm sure there will be times I will miss . . .' his gaze lands frankly on her body.

'And this?' she gestures to the offering.

'The paper is a deed. It's the plot for a new house, which you can build for yourself or sell on, as you wish.'

'Where?'

He gestures out of the window. 'Halfway up the road. If you choose to build a house there, it will overlook the new Garden. The plot can accommodate a larger dwelling than this. It runs east to west, which is better, I think, for the light and you could have a proper garden – a small one but a garden nonetheless. I know you are interested in plants.'

'And the pouch is money?'

'Fifty guineas,' he confirms, 'in coin and a banker's draft for five hundred more upon which you can draw. Mr MacPherson on George Street has been notified. I know he is your man in such matters.'

'Ae fond kiss,' Belle says.

'Ae fond farewell,' he counters.

She finds herself curious. 'Might I know the reason?' she asks. 'This grief of yours?'

Alexander finds himself almost moved to tears. He cannot tell her about the loss of his wife any more than he has been able to speak of it all along. It simply is not possible. Nor can he say exactly why today is the day he has chosen to break with her. Perhaps it was his conversation with Johann von Streitz – such an upstanding young man with the prospect of true love ahead, the love Brunton had for Mary when he met her in Stromness. 'It is simply . . .' he starts, but he cannot get the words out. 'I am ready to move on,' he manages at last.

Belle does not press him. It does not worry her that she has misread Mr Brunton. Instead she turns her attention to the practicalities. 'The opportunity you have been offered – what does that entail?'

He sighs. 'I did not seek it, but I am to be moderator.'

Belle leans forward. 'Of the church? You are a clergyman?'

He nods.

She giggles. He is the more passionate of her lovers. This need not preclude him from being a man of faith, but still it is amusing.

'The post will commence next year,' he continues, 'but notice of it will be mooted at the time of the royal visit. And for that reason I must give you up, my dear, if I am to take it. I have swithered, but I believe it is time to end our arrangement. It would not be honest of me to continue, now my decision is made. I will take the moderatorship. It is God's will. I believe that.'

Belle can hardly take it in. 'I thought you made your money in property.'

'I do. I have several investments in land and with two builders whose businesses I own in part. My position as a man of God does not preclude my making money. I do not regularly practise as a minister. In fact, I am a librarian now and a zoologist at the university. But I have a chair at the General Assembly and from next year I may lead it. As I understand things, the assembly is interested in my nomination on account of my academic endeavours. Because I do not have a flock of parishioners, you see.'

Belle tries to square this with the man she has met with regularly for the past three years. 'I have not known you properly,' she says.

Brunton's expression is gentle. 'You have known the heart of me.'

'But not the detail.'

'No,' he agrees.

'Thank you for coming to tell me.' She sounds graceful, she realizes. More graceful than she feels, for, despite her amusement at his being a clergyman, he has wrongfooted her. But that is for the best. 'It is kind of you to provide this compensation.'

'You are not upset?'

'It is never flattering for a woman to be left . . . but I understand.'

Brunton stands. 'If there is ever anything . . .?'

'You will not hear from me again. I promise,' Belle says calmly.

He bends his head and kisses her hand gently. 'I will never forget you.'

It would never occur to Belle that he might. 'Nor I you,' she adds.

As he leaves, Belle listens to his steps recede in the hallway. The door to the street clicks open and closed. She does not pick up the money or the papers to examine them. It is a generous settlement though not enough to keep a lady lifelong. That has always been the trouble, she thinks, trying to make a life's fortune in the brief years of her flowering. Her father did so by enslaving others. Had he failed, the Brodies would have considered him a gentleman still. She has no such safety net – a room in her brother's house, perhaps, if she is lucky and her sister-in-law has no say in the matter. She could never bear it in any case. Still, this money is a welcome addition.

The decanter of his whisky catches her eye, and she gets up to pour a dram. It occurs to her that she was wise to take two lovers, for the departure of one now leaves a vacancy not a void. It is not a vacancy she is immediately minded to fill, for if her plan comes off she will not need to do so. As she savours the peated malt she thinks it will be the last taste she has of Alexander Brunton and she wonders if there is a particular alignment of stars that has caused the ructions of today. It seemed, she notes, a perfectly normal day when she woke in the morning. But perhaps that is how change occurs.

Laying down the glass, she lies on the sopha and stares at the ceiling with its gilt and crystal chandelier and ornate ceiling rose with the plaster fleur-de-lis – lilies of peace. Momentarily, she wonders how in the world she might find a place where a lady can please herself as a gentleman does. Ultimately her love potion will save her. She has not thought of it like this before, focusing as she has on the money the scent will bring. But perhaps it is not only money she desires, she thinks, but tolerance. She will not marry, for that is a step too far and has never been her interest, but if her plan comes off she will be admired for her skill and innovation, traits that are universally praised. She reinvented herself once and now she will do so again. The perfume is coming. Mhairi MacDonald has already started to mix it.

The girl spent all Sunday afternoon in the shed, swathed in an apron, with her blonde hair tied up, adding cinnamon drop by drop to a small pool of strawberry oil. She hummed as she sniffed her way through every jar on the shelf, taking breaks to revive her senses in the fresh air, dipping bare feet into the Water of Leith as it swirled between the rushes. Her receipt so far has not included the pine oil that Belle expected, but she has added a single drop of pink peppercorn and a few drops of star anise and of gorse. 'A Highland ingredient,' she smiled. 'It reminds me of home.' Belle did not say that the gorse was gathered from the Braid Hills, to the south of the city, where she scented its flowers on the air while out riding two years before. She is a formidable collector – the shelves of Edzel's shed house the most diverse perfume library in the world, though she does not know it for she has nothing with which to compare her collection. The gorse is an intriguing choice, inspired even, though the resulting perfume is on the sweet side. Still, as Belle sniffed it, she flooded with a sense of well-being before agreeing with Mhairi's final pronouncement. 'It needs something else, miss, a good stock. Like soup – something to add depth.'

Now Belle walks barefoot to her bedchamber, which smells today of nothing other than the remnants of her bath. She climbs into bed and tries to bring Mr Lunardi's candy-coloured air balloon to mind. 'All life is uncertain,' she murmurs as she drifts off. 'I will play my best shot at it. I must finish the scent, is all.'

When Nellie opens the curtains the next morning and light seeps into the room on the first day of the new month, Belle opens her eyes. The oysters are on the side as usual and the smoky scent of tea snakes towards her. The girl draws a note from the pocket of her apron. Belle sits up and yawns. She snaps the seal. Inside, in Robert Graham's tidy hand, there is a single line of script that prompts a grin across Belle's face so wide it makes her cheeks sting. *The aloe has flowered*, it says. *I will come for you at ten o'clock.*

Chapter Twenty-Three

1 August 1822

Like Belle, Elizabeth had imagined it would be a sunny day when the aloe flowered, but the weather is cool when the blooms finally come. The sky is overcast and a band of haar slips off the Forth and over the city. It is difficult to believe that it's still summer when the air feels chill and the place smells green and there are no views to Fife or anywhere else.

When Margaret pulls back Elizabeth's curtain the lawn is completely obscured. 'A note for you, ma'am,' she says, handing over a piece of paper from her pocket.

Elizabeth sits up. It is still early. She struggles to focus on the handwriting as Margaret helps plump her pillows. Then she makes out the news. 'Quick,' she says. 'Wake Lady Clementina and tell her we are going out.'

'Out?' Margaret repeats.

'The aloe has bloomed. Tell her,' Elizabeth says and throws back the covers. There is no doubt that the old lady will want to be roused to visit the greenhouses for this great event. Margaret bustles off and Elizabeth, remembering the disgrace of the day before, fumbles with the dress laid out for her. She does not want to face the world but how will she draw the flowers if she has not seen them? Reasoning that the earlier she visits the Garden, the fewer people are likely to be there, she pulls on the worn Empire line and a plain spencer and when Margaret returns, Elizabeth instructs her to fetch her new bonnet. Downstairs, she waits for Clementina, as the corseting on the old woman's frocks takes a good twenty minutes to secure. Elizabeth paces the music room as Clementina swithers over whether to fix a feather to her hat or wear her fancy brooch. Rushing the old lady in the past has provided diminishing returns, so Elizabeth passes the time inspecting the sketches she has made of the *Agave* as it has grown and one, lying on her table, that James attempted. The boy is becoming skilled at flowers, but cannot capture the texture of bark or the unexpected shapes of cacti. His drawing of the aloe looks rather more like a large green sea creature with flailing tentacles than a static succulent rooted in the earth.

'Come along,' Clementina says when she finally comes downstairs, as if she is the one who has been waiting. 'We shall breakfast on our return. Or you can walk if you like,' she adds, pulling on her gloves.

Elizabeth shakes her head. 'I will come with you in the carriage,' she says and ties on the bonnet.

The gardeners have been working since the sun came up. Since the stem burst through the skylight like a flagpole more than a week ago, Mr McNab has arrived every day at six, when he inspects the plant before anything else. He even walked down to the Garden on Sunday to see if the flowers were out yet. He knows he cannot hide the blooms, and watches with a sense of dread as the aloe prepares for its swan song. Mr McNab has laid down the law with the working men that he will inform the relevant people when the time comes, though one of his gardeners, Edward, has been offered a tanner to tip off Edinburgh's newest publication, the *Scotsman* newspaper, for the story of the century plant has captured the interest of several amateur botanists. Searching for an excuse to leave the grounds, Edward has already offered to deliver McNab's notification to Mr Graham and to Inverleith House but was refused and James

McNab engaged for the purpose. Instead the young gardener has taken himself off to work at the bottom end where he will slip across the boundary and over the staked-out plot of the house that will become Number 11 Inverleith Row. If he hurries, he will be at the *Scotsman* offices in time to make this week's edition and the editor might give him something extra for taking the risk.

McNab is distracted. The flower will be the focus of attention now. He is a man listening to a bell tolling, half-deafened but unable to make it stop. 'Are you all right, sir?' Donald, his most recent recruit, asks as McNab emerges for the third time this morning from the latrine beside the compost heap.

'I must have eaten a bad egg,' McNab replies. But he has not eaten any egg, good or bad.

'There will be crowds today,' the young lad adds.

McNab nods gruffly. He imagines most of his time will be taken up with the aloe's flowering. Mr Graham will bring students to view it, though to date the Regius Keeper has shown little interest in the kind of lectures Mr Rutherford gave regularly to the crowds of young men who packed into the upper floor of the cottage at the old Garden. He sighs. While there are a good many serious students there are also among them clowns who must be kept in check or they may horse about and damage the planting. Two drunk students trampled a nursery bed last month before they could be contained. Those young gentlemen will be doctors in only a few months, he thinks, and checks himself for finding the idea harrowing. Just because they indulge in high spirits does not mean they will not be able to physick.

When Robert Graham's carriage pulls up, William McNab loiters in the shed before opening the door to greet him. Graham bounds down, launching himself into the muddy yard. 'Well, well,' he says. 'What a day!' He turns to hand down Belle, who has pulled herself together admirably for the occasion, dressed immaculately in a gold-threaded frock with a matching hat ornamented with a pale blue ostrich feather. She looks as if she has stepped straight out of a fine

Sara Sheridan

piece of porcelain. 'Good morning, Mr McNab,' she greets him. 'And congratulations – this is quite the achievement.'

She hardly gets this out before Graham begins to animatedly talk over her. 'I have written to Sir William Hooker in Glasgow. He may wish to view the plant.' His tone is one of a man issuing instructions. 'We must celebrate, of course. I have told my cook to send down a couple of hampers – pies to be served to visitors and half a case of Rhenish for special guests. You will lay them aside.'

'Yes, sir,' McNab says. It is clear that sight of the aloe's flowers is to be in Mr Graham's gift.

'They will be delighted at Kew,' Graham gushes. 'I will write later today to inform them. This is great progress, McNab. Great progress.'

McNab feels his bowels turn but manages to control himself. There will be a week of this at least. Nobody is entirely sure how long the aloe will flower before it produces seeds. It may depend on the weather. 'Well, we must see it. Come along,' Graham offers Belle his arm and she lifts her skirt an inch to save the hem of her dress as they turn in the direction of the glasshouses.

As they move off, the mulberry carriage with the Rocheid crest rumbles into the yard. Duncan jumps down to open the door and Lady Clementina peers out. 'Mr Graham,' she cries out, ever sprightly, descending without help and making her way towards the party. 'Belle my dear,' she kisses the girl on the cheek. 'I am tremendously invigorated to see these flowers!'

Elizabeth lets Duncan hand her down. 'Mr McNab,' she says and, her stomach sinking, adds a more general 'good morning' in the direction of the others, which on account of the general excitement, is not recognized as a snub.

'Elizabeth!' Belle says, steeling herself to brazen it out. 'How lovely to see you.'

Elizabeth nods but does not smile. 'Clementina, let me help you.' She offers her arm, as a way of distracting attention from her coldness. This is uncomfortable, but she will examine the bloom and be home in twenty minutes. It will be easy to entice Clementina

206

back to Inverleith House for breakfast. Meals are the old woman's measure.

'Who else have you informed?' Graham asks McNab as the party moves eagerly in the direction of the greenhouses.

'Only yourself and Mrs Rocheid. She has been sketching the plant's progress as the stem has grown and can now draw the flower. It will be a valuable record. I am not aware of a drawing in existence of the *Agave americana* in bloom.'

Graham nods and makes a gruff noise. He can hardly object. It is in his interest as well as the Garden's that there be pictures for publication and he wrote a couple of notes before he left Great King Street himself. 'I will see to it that the Edinburgh monthly magazine takes your sketches, Mrs Rocheid,' he announces. 'Leave it to me.'

Clementina beams like an ingenue. 'The maga,' she says. 'Marvellous.'

One of the garden boys is frozen like a statue at the bottom of the path, staring in awe at the towering aloe ahead. McNab shoos the lad away as the party stops in silence to take in the crown of the stem, craning their necks to see it. A wide smile spreads across Mr Graham's face. The shoot has thickened over the last few days and sprouting on either side are clusters of small, yellow flowers with vertical fronds. They are striking and delicate, entirely out of keeping with the plant's bulky stem. Belle claps her hands with delight at this long awaited flowering and Clementina lets out a low laugh. 'It's beautiful,' Elizabeth breathes.

'It is, ma'am,' McNab agrees. The group moves forward slowly, their eyes not moving from the yellow flowers bright against the flat white sky as if to highlight the plant as God's own creation.

'One day we will have glasshouses in the Garden tall enough to accommodate this species,' Graham says. 'Have you measured it, McNab? It must be twenty-five feet?'

'Not quite, sir. Twenty-three.'

'Twenty-three feet,' Clementina repeats in wonder. 'And half of that grown in the last few weeks. It is an amazement,' she pronounces. 'After perusing Elizabeth's drawings, I am most excited to see it in the flesh.'

McNab opens the door of the glasshouse. Condensation drips on one side and the air smells musty. Clementina draws a lace handkerchief to her nose. 'Eugh,' she says as she stares upwards at the marvel.

Belle steps inside and breathes in deeply. Mr Graham pushes forward, taken aback at the physical nature of his guest's enjoyment. 'Move up a little,' he prompts her.

Belle opens her eyes as if she has just awoken from a tranquil sleep. 'Oh yes,' she says.

'What would you say it smells of, Miss Brodie?' McNab cuts in. 'You're the one with the interest in such matters.'

Much to Mr Graham's chagrin, Belle answers with poise as if this is the most interesting question in a day, which in his opinion, at least, will be full of far better questions. 'There is grass in it and naphtha and a smell of the earth, like clay,' she says, dreamily. 'Almost like fungi.'

'Pah!' Clementina exclaims, craning her neck. 'It smells like a rotten woollen sock to me but my, what a beauty. What a size! The flowers are striking. Yellow flowers are most fashionable.'

'The interest is in the seeds,' Mr Graham cuts in. 'For the real treasure we must wait a little longer.'

'There are nine clusters of flowers,' Elizabeth counts in wonder. 'How extraordinary!'

McNab notes that probably means nine seeds. He might get away with telling Mrs Dickson that there are only eight, he reckons, and wonders if Kew will be content if he sends them one.

'Mr Graham,' Elizabeth continues. 'I wonder, might I pick a flower from one of the clusters in order to draw it at Inverleith House?'

Belle laughs. 'I don't know how you'll get up there, Elizabeth. It's a good eighteen feet to the first bloom.'

Elizabeth ignores her.

'I can fetch a ladder,' McNab offers and gestures towards one of the gardeners working beyond the greenhouse to help.

Mr Graham makes a face. 'I don't know,' he says. 'I'm not sure it's wise.'

'I'll need to examine it closely,' Elizabeth presses. 'I cannot draw from a ladder. I must have the flower before me.'

Clementina chortles. 'Girls today . . .' she mutters as if in her youth young ladies were perpetually balancing their sketchpads on the rungs of ladders and making no fuss about it.

McNab secures the ladder and waits for Mr Graham to give him the go ahead.

'Of course, it would be excellent to get a transverse section of the stem,' Graham says, 'but that will certainly have to wait. Up you go, McNab!'

The gardener pulls a penknife from his pocket and flicks it open as he proficiently climbs past the roofline, where he expertly cuts a single flower for Mrs Rocheid's use and comes back down. He places the bloom on Elizabeth's outstretched palm. Belle peers at the small yellow beauty balanced like an intricate ornament on Elizabeth's hand, all ochre petals and upright stamen.

'How pretty,' she says. 'When you get close it is a little like honey-suckle except for the colour.'

'The placement on the stem is quite different from honeysuckle,' Mr Graham corrects her.

'I am so glad to have seen it,' Belle says with enthusiasm, turning in Graham's direction. 'Thank you for bringing me. Now, perhaps we might leave you and Mr McNab to discuss your business. I'm sure we ladies would like to promenade.' She reaches for Elizabeth's arm, but it is snatched away.

'Clementina and I must return to Inverleith House. We have not yet broken our fast and I want to get started on the drawing. The flower will wilt in no time,' Elizabeth babbles.

'Would you like to accompany us, my dear?' Clementina asks Belle.

Elizabeth sets her jaw. 'Miss Brodie has other business, I'm sure,' she says. 'I must concentrate on my work.'

Belle lets a long silence hang over the party. Elizabeth blushes. 'Thank you, Lady Clementina, but I shall return to Warriston Crescent,' Belle says at last.

Graham can see tempers are fraying but assumes it is on account of excitement. He is a man almost entirely without empathy, who believes the emotions he feels to be the universal experience. However, when Johann von Streitz arrives, he reads the situation straight away. Elizabeth shifts as though wishing the ground would swallow her up, while Belle preens herself like an unrepentant pussy cat who has tipped over the milk. Johann stares in wonder at the bright flower heads, like golden fireworks against the blanket of cloud. 'Good heavens,' he says. 'How long will the flowers last?' But even as he asks the question, he can barely tear his eyes away from Elizabeth, who keeps her gaze firmly fixed on the ground.

'I don't know how long the flowers will bloom or when it will seed. It is the first in the country. On the continent, in fact. We will have to simply observe,' McNab pronounces.

'Do you know yet the date of His Majesty's visit?' Graham interrupts.

Johann shakes his head. 'I do not.'

'We must go, cousin,' Elizabeth surprises herself. Normally she would wait for Clementina to make the decision, for someone else to act, but now both her tormentors are here, she cannot bear it.

'I had hoped to talk to you about your illustration, madam,' von Streitz says. 'I am sure Kew would be most interested to have a copy of whatever you produce. For the library. My goodness it is a beauty, is it not?'

'Mrs Rocheid's illustration will appear in the Edinburgh monthly magazine,' Graham says. 'Kew takes it, I should imagine.'

Johann does not hesitate. 'Sir William Hooker always sends a copy of any innovation at Glasgow to Kew by express,' he says. 'An original – not a print.'

Graham wavers. 'We shall see. Of course. We shall see.'

'Two drawings then,' Elizabeth notes. 'I had best get on.'

The women walk back towards the yard. Elizabeth moves to assist Clementina to mount the carriage and does not object when Belle offers her arm to help the old woman, though she does not meet Belle's eye. Lady Clementina safely stowed, Belle lays a hand on Elizabeth's shoulder.

'There is no reason not to be civil,' she says.

Eyes blazing, Elizabeth turns on her. The gentlemen are tarrying down the path, talking about seed heads and storage in transit. 'There is every reason,' she hisses, a dangerous fire in her eyes. She is not sorry she came, for the aloe is extraordinary, but she will not loiter. Instead she mounts and closes the door, knocking on the box to signal Duncan to go.

Belle stands, as if abandoned, watching the carriage trundle down the lane and turn left onto the highway just as three young gentlemen arrive in a cab, jump down eagerly and walk through the gate. 'Madam,' one greets her, as they tip their hats and pass, a shiver of laughter, a kind of bravado, running through them. Belle hopes that if she pays for Edzel's education he will not become an unmannerly fool. Her eyes mist with tears. It was an insult and unkind of Elizabeth not to allow her the opportunity to explain.

'Miss Brodie,' Johann catches up. 'Mr Graham says to take his carriage home and send it back for him. He may be a while.'

Belle turns towards von Streitz, releasing the lingering scent of clove oil, bay leaves and berries onto the damp air. It feels as if it is autumn today – which is what inspired her to choose that bottle, which she has not opened for weeks, since the sharp, cold days of February when the air felt as if it had been scented with woodsmoke for months on end. 'Thank you, Herr von Streitz.'

He offers her his arm. 'Are you all right?' he asks with concern as he catches sight of her expression.

'Mrs Rocheid and I had a disagreement yesterday,' Belle admits. 'I hoped she might have forgiven me. But she has not.'

Johann's expression does not waver. He is adept at the art of listening. 'She seemed out of sorts when I met her yesterday as well,' he admits. 'Is there anything I can do?'

Belle shakes her head. 'I shall go home. I have a busy day.' She does not add that this entails working out how to get her hands on the mystery perfume ingredient, her stock of sorts, now being so ardently admired by Mr Graham as he quizzes the students on how they heard that the century plant had bloomed.

Johann hands her into the carriage. 'Warriston Crescent, then back here, John,' he instructs Graham's coachman and steps back to watch it retreat.

'I heard at the *Scotsman* offices,' one young doctor says, behind him. 'I dropped in to have a porter. The town is ablaze with the news. Everyone will want to see it. Does it have properties, sir? Do we know yet?'

Robert Graham makes a noise like a disgruntled carthorse. 'Perhaps we ought to sell tickets,' he spits, furious that news of the flowers has escaped. 'You should not have come without an invitation,' he complains. But it is too late, of course, for that.

Chapter Twenty-Four

Belle closes the front door behind her and quietly climbs the stairs. She is someone who usually clatters about the house when she returns, casting off her bonnet and gloves and making demands as she settles – 'Fetch me a glass of rum and marmalade' or 'Where is my cashmere stole?' or 'I cannot for the life of me find the book I was reading'. Her silent entrance into the boudoir thus surprises Nellie, who is sitting on the chaise, sipping from a porcelain cup with her ankles tucked prettily underneath her and her top button undone. The girl springs to her feet and tips her drink to the floor.

'Nellie?' Belle's voice is measured but there is no question that she is shocked at this presumption.

'Sorry, miss,' Nellie says and neatly turns the cup upside down on its saucer, to take it away. 'I'll clear the mess.'

'What are you drinking?' Belle casts her eyes to the whisky decanters, but they are perfectly in place.

'Only a cup of tisane,' Nellie says.

Belle sniffs. There is the faintest tinge of peppermint on the air. Pennyroyal.

'Nellie? What have you done?'

Nellie stands tall as if this question is an outrage. 'Nothing, miss. I like the taste,' she says.

Belle takes off her bonnet and gloves and strips herself of her spencer. 'Put these away, would you?'

'Yes, miss,' the girl curtsies. 'Shall I bring you something from the kitchen?'

'I am quite all right, thank you.' Belle perches on the sopha, pretty as an ornament though she is vexed. It has been a trying morning.

Normally Nellie would ask what is wrong, but today she scoops up her mistress's things without another word. As she leaves, Belle sits back and stares round the room as if checking that the boundaries of her world are still in place. Slowly her eyes move towards the window and she focuses on the sky. Across the street the sodden leaves of the sycamore trees dance in the light breeze like figures on a music box against the blank canvas of cloud. It feels relaxing and yet Belle is troubled. She had hoped Elizabeth would reconsider. She wishes she could speak to her friend, but she cannot see how that will be possible. She briefly considers throwing herself on the mercy of Johann von Streitz, asking him to talk to Elizabeth on her behalf. She wonders how courtesans are viewed in Germany. Belle's profession was certainly revered in France during the reign of the Bourbons and Napoleon's fleeting empire. French kings were known for their lovers until the masses killed Louis. Belle imagines being a royal courtesan, writing poetry, hosting salons and setting the fashion of the day. It sounds exhausting.

Nellie comes back with a wet cloth and dabs the carpet. Her button is now fastened and she has also tidied her hair. Something is amiss and yet Belle cannot quite put her finger upon it. Perhaps it is because there is more than one thing wrong. Quite sensibly, she decides that she can only address matters individually.

She had intended to bring Nellie with her on her mission but now, without being able to articulate why, Belle decides against it. 'I will change,' she announces. 'Would you lay out the navy linen?'

'But miss, your dress today is beautiful. You look like a picture.'

'I'm going out again,' Belle continues. 'I shall require proper boots.'

Striding along Warriston Crescent half an hour later, Belle casts only the merest glance up the highway towards the Garden and the turn for Inverleith House. At Tanfield, Edzel is not expecting her but he is not exactly lounging about sipping tea. He has taken off his top and is energetically making a mash of rose heads for distillation. The air is filled with the scent of the bruised petals, pink and red in the copper pot. His skin, white as milk, gleams as he works. 'Miss Brodie,' he turns away from the still and catches his breath. 'Is everything all right?'

Belle nods curtly. She sits on the high stool at his desk and motions him forward. 'Are you still interested in becoming a doctor, Edzel?'

'Yes, miss.'

'Reverend Mathieson says your studies are proceeding well.'

'Thank you, miss.'

'Do you consider yourself ready to sit the matriculation examination?'

Edzel has no idea. His eyes widen in lieu of reply.

'How old are you now?' Belle continues.

'Fifteen.'

Belle takes this in. Fifteen is young for a boy to be admitted to the university, and in the usual run of things, most will be older. 'There are new regulations in place, as I understand it – apothecary classes are required for graduation though with the experience you have gained here you will find those easy, I should think. Would you like to try the written exam? The new intake will be in the autumn.'

The medical school has instituted a change in the annual timetable because bodies for dissection fester in the summer, even this far north. These days the dissection rooms lie empty during June, July and August with fresh corpses procured for use in late September. The faculty's year has come to be defined by this arrangement. The stench of corpses rotting as the students strip them to the bone is bad enough without adding heat to it.

A cautious grin opens across Edzel's face. 'What about my job here, miss?'

'Don't worry about that,' Belle says. 'You'll work for me over the summer and if you pass the examination I will pay your lecture fees and the cost of a room near Old College to accommodate you. Nothing fancy, mind. You will have a small allowance for books and food. I expect they will put you to work in the Infirmary.'

A flush blooms on Edzel's face. This is a huge opportunity. The lectures will cost more than his father makes in a year, never mind the rest of it. 'Thank you, miss.'

'In time, I expect you will be my doctor,' Belle adds wistfully. 'Dr Morton is getting old.'

'Yes, miss.' He finds this difficult to imagine but is willing to try.

Belle approaches the shelves and opens the bottle Mhairi has been trying to mix. The century plant's low, musky scent will be the perfect addition to this fledgling. It will make it fly.

'When did you last see my maid?' Belle asks Edzel.

'She brought a basket two days since,' the boy answers.

Belle regards him. There is no hint of shame in his voice – whatever Nellie is hiding, it isn't him. 'Well,' she says, closing the stopper on Mhairi's concoction, 'I have a job for you, Edzel. And if you succeed in it, you will have your place, if the college will take you.'

'Yes, miss.'

'Be ready tonight.' She says this as if Edzel might have other plans, attending a recital or going out for dinner. 'I shall require your assistance.'

'Yes, miss.'

That night the moon is only a sliver and the clouds obscure its light anyway. It is the perfect weather. Belle drinks her pennyroyal tisane and dismisses Nellie, pretending to go to bed early. She then waits an hour until the low light from the kitchen lamps no longer casts yellow squares onto the muddy back yard, and, sneaking into the dressing room, she pulls on a pair of dark britches and a brown woollen jacket she procured earlier from her brother under the guise of charity. 'Some boy you've found?' Joseph mocked her. 'You cannot help every stray dog, you know.' The clothes fit well enough and sitting in front of her gilded mirror she hides her hair under a green knitted cap, casting a curious eye over herself as she does so. She makes a strange kind of boy, but she will pass in the dark.

Next, she pulls open the bottom drawer of her chiffonier. She sent Jamie that afternoon to the second-hand clothes shop wedged between a papermaker and a butcher down a vennel off the High Street. She told him to buy clothes – not too worn – to suit Edzel. 'Something a young gentleman might wear,' she asked nonchalantly, 'respectable enough. Nothing too showy. The kind of thing a student might have use for. Two sets of britches and a cravat, a waistcoat and a topcoat or a cape.' And, most important of all, a hat. 'Get him a topper – why not? Buy two,' she adds, as if it is a whim.

Now she takes one of the black top hats from the box that Jamie delivered. Almost entirely generic, its silk is slightly worn. It smells dusty. She cuts out the maker's label with the small pair of scissors on her dressing table and burns it, allowing the ashes to drop into the grate. Then she tucks the hat under her arm, slips an empty bottle of brandy into her pocket, and sneaks downstairs into the night.

It is always quiet along Warriston Crescent but tonight it is as if the houses are derelict with their glossy black windows. Not a single chimney is smoking for it is still too warm to light a fire and everyone is abed. She can hear the rushing of the water from the row of gardens behind as the Water of Leith flows eastwards to the sea. At Tanfield she pauses outside Edzel's shed, also in darkness. She hopes the boy has not forgotten. She raps insistently on the door and waits. An owl hoots and a moment later the lock slides back. Edzel's hair is tousled. 'I fell asleep,' he admits. His eyes widen at Belle's attire. 'Miss?' he squints into the darkness.

'Tonight you will call me Tommy. And I shall call you John,' she says.

'John,' Edzel repeats, mystified. 'Miss, are we going to do something . . . that we shouldnae?'

'We are,' Belle says in a whisper. 'But I will look after you. Hurry.'

Belle suddenly sees that Edzel's character as a man will spring from this moment. If tonight goes well, he will always like to transgress. She blushes, seeing a flash of maturity in such a child and it crosses her mind that Mhairi's gifts have given her airs. As if you could see a fellow's future in the events of his childhood.

'We will be up before the magistrate if we are caught. If anything happens, Edzel, you must allow me to organize everything. You will say nothing. Do you promise me? I will see to your interests.'

Edzel shifts his weight slightly. 'Miss?' he says.

'Come along. If everything goes as I hope, you will earn your place at the most prestigious medical school in the world. It is tonight that you start your journey to becoming a doctor. To becoming a man.'

Edzel's face remains sceptical, but he nods at the certainty in Belle's voice. He thought he was to earn his place by sitting the matriculation paper, but Miss Brodie sounds certain. 'Yes, miss,' he says.

Belle eyes him.

'Tommy,' he corrects himself.

'Bring your knife – the one you use for preparing roots for the mash.'

He disappears into the shed and comes back holding the blade.

'Come on then . . .'

They walk in absolute silence. The road is deserted though there is the faintest whinnying of horses in the field opposite the laneway to the Garden, where Belle pauses momentarily. The Wardies keep a fine stable and in the summer their steeds have the run of the top two fields. Edzel is distracted by the sound of the animals and is nervous that they are going to hurt them. 'We're not going onto Wardie land, are we?' he asks. He is relieved when Belle cuts to the left, along the lane with a tip of her head and a swift 'This way.'

When they reach their destination, Edzel pauses. 'Is this the . . .?'

'It's the Botanic Garden,' Belle whispers as she hoists herself over the top of the locked gate and drops into the yard. Edzel follows her and surveys the main area of planting with the arboretum behind as he finds his feet.

'Do all these plants have medicinal uses?'

'Most of them. You shall come to learn them, I imagine.'

Belle drops the top hat on the path. She stamps on it and birds stir in the trees at the unexpected bang as it breaks. Then she lays the empty brandy bottle at a jaunty angle. It is of a common sort, although too expensive for a working man.

'There,' she says.

Edzel giggles. 'What was that?' he asks.

'Nothing,' Belle says. There is no point in explaining she is planting evidence to direct attention towards the mass of students at Old College. This, she knows, is how it will seem when Robert Graham bustles through the gate to investigate the matter tomorrow, or rather later this morning, for it must be now almost two of the clock. She wore her most delicate dress earlier to imprint upon Graham's mind the vision of her as a woman too refined to venture out in the night to scale gates and ladders, and indeed, anything else that may be required. It was more important that she looked the very lady this morning than at any time in her career.

The ladder is next, she thinks. It has been returned to the store but she leads Edzel straight to it – just as she saw the gardener at McNab's behest pick it up earlier. Together they prop it against the greenhouse's frame.

'What is it?' Edzel squints upwards at the strange stem protruding through the roof. In the darkness the aloe is a looming, alien, dark presence.

'It's no matter,' Belle hisses. 'Give me the knife and hold the steps.'

Edzel complies and grasps the ladder firmly as she ascends, pulling a gauzy pouch from her waistband as she reaches the top and efficiently culls the flowers. She sniffs the blooms in her palm and closes her fingers over one to crush the petals a little. Edzel looks over his shoulder. The Garden is absolutely still – the only light in the distance, up the hill in the city, where one or two night-owls are still playing canasta and drinking port amid the flickering candles. Belle fills the bag efficiently and leaves one head of flowers on the plant – only one and that for Mr McNab, who she very much likes. He will be able to propagate a new *Agave americana* with the single seed it will produce. Efficiently she climbs back down the ladder.

'Leave it on the side,' she instructs Edzel.

'What is it?' he asks with a nod towards the bag in her hand as he lays the ladder on the ground.

'You will make oil from it.'

Edzel opens his mouth to protest. 'But there is hardly enough . . .' he starts. They order bushels of rosemary and crates of lilacs. The rose petals he has been processing came in a shipment of four large baskets woven from rushes. This little bag will not produce a table-spoon of oil, perhaps not even a teaspoon.

Belle interrupts him. 'You must do your best. It is very precious.'

As Belle turns, she miscalculates her step in the darkness. The ground is uneven, and she lets out a squeal as she goes over on her ankle. 'Damn,' she says, 'I shouldn't have rushed.' Edzel helps her up. She takes in a breath sharply for it hurts badly when she leans on her right leg and she feels nauseous. 'Damn,' she curses again and tries to bring her emotions under control. Her leg is shaking invol-untarily. She thrusts the bag towards Edzel's outstretched fingers and puts her arm around him for support.

'Are you all right?' he whispers. 'I can fetch help.'

Belle shakes her head. 'I'll be fine,' she says. 'We must walk back.'

'I could get Jamie with the carriage,' the boy offers helpfully.

'No.' Belle does not waste energy explaining. Nobody else must know. She wonders if Edzel is strong enough to carry her, but judges Warriston Crescent too far for him to manage.

'Help me,' she says. 'We must go slowly.'

'It's a shame I am not a doctor already,' Edzel smiles and helps her hobble towards the gate.

'I wonder they do not have a watchman.'

Silently, Belle thanks Robert Graham for his corner-cutting. Scaling the gate is agony for she must put all her weight on one foot and raise the other to clamber over. With effort, she makes it, though she feels woozy from the pain. Edzel is patient and slowly they make their way back down the highway and turn into Warriston Crescent. He helps her mount the front steps. She steadies herself using the door knob and nods towards the gauze bag now protruding from his pocket. 'Go on,' she hisses. 'Get what you can from it. I will come in a day or two. Don't let in anybody except Mhairi. No one, do you understand?'

'Do you not still require assistance, miss?'

'They will help me inside,' she lies. Getting up the stairs and out of these clothes will be a gargantuan task but at least the staff will ignore the front door opening and any noise she might make on the stair. Accustomed to comings and goings in the night as they are, they know better than to investigate.

She watches Edzel's frame in the darkness as he hurries along the curve of the crescent and disappears in the direction of the bridge. As she takes a breath to steel herself she is distracted from the throbbing of her ankle by something moving amid the sycamores on the other side of the road. 'Hello,' she calls out tentatively, but there is no reply. It is probably a fox, she thinks, for who would be abroad at this time of the night here, beyond the city limits, loitering among the trees? Judging by the windows, the Wardies are early abed and Clementina and Elizabeth have no business on Warriston Crescent. She squints into the darkness – the lack of moon has covered her well, but it also stops her seeing potential danger. Still, there is no more movement, so she turns and slips inside.

The britches make it easy to sit on the stairs and go up backwards using her left leg to propel her, like a toddler learning to walk. Her right ankle, she notices, is swelling. At the top she gets onto her knees and carefully makes it to the dressing room, stripping off the clothes, stuffing them into the drawer and pulling on her nightdress again. She removes the hat and her hair flops to her shoulders. She should send for a doctor, she knows. People can die of such injuries. Back on her knees she trundles through to the hall and back down the stairs on her bottom, where she lies at the foot and pauses to check there is nothing she needs to further consider before screaming. There is not. So she screams, 'Help me. Help!'

The house remains silent. 'Come quickly!' she tries again.

Mrs Grant is the first to appear, her hair tied with strips of frayed cotton and her nightdress with a faded stain at the hem. 'Miss Brodie!' she exclaims. 'Whatever has happened?'

Jamie appears behind the old woman. 'Stand back, Mrs Grant. I'll lift her. Hold still, miss,' he says, scooping Belle into his arms.

'You must send for the doctor. My ankle,' Belle points. 'I tripped up the stairs after bidding my gentleman farewell. I quite lost my balance.'

Jamie lays her carefully on the bed, which she realizes she should have tumbled if it is the pretence that a gentleman has visited. Perhaps, she decides, the tryst might have been on the chaise longue. In any case, neither Mrs Grant nor Jamie appear to notice its tidiness, nor Nellie when she arrives and hastens to find some cotton to bind the injury. Jamie disappears and Mrs Grant says she will steep some chamomile. 'It will calm you,' she says, and has no sooner disappeared than she reappears again to also offer a jug of beef broth 'to keep up your strength, miss.'

Belle replies that the chamomile will do fine. Claire the under-stairs maid is set to lighting the fire.

'Aw, miss,' says Nellie, 'it looks awfy sore.'

Belle leans back on the pillows. It has been bad luck, but worth it. Quite the evening adventure. 'I'm sure the doctor will bring laudanum,' she says. 'Then I can sleep. You must tell nobody about this, Nellie. No one.'

Nellie looks up. 'Of course not, Miss Brodie.'

'Nor you, Claire.'

Claire looks startled. Miss Brodie has never spoken to her before. 'Yes, miss,' she says quietly as if the admonishment is an honour.

'It is comical,' Belle adds. 'A lady so excited to get back to bed that she injures herself. I feel foolish.'

A slim smile plays at the corners of Nellie's mouth. If she does tell anybody, that the lie is amusing will make it play. 'The gentlemen always appreciate your enthusiasm, miss,' she says drily.

Belle watches as the girl ties the cotton. There is no question that something has changed.

'Jamie is strong,' Belle drops casually. 'He lifted me as if I were a feather.'

'There you are, miss,' Nellie says. Not a blush. Not a gleam of interest. Not Jamie, then, Belle thinks. Nor Edzel. What is Nellie up to? She will set herself to this thorny problem tomorrow, she decides, as Mrs Grant returns with a tray of chamomile tisane and thin slices of white bread smeared with butter and blackcurrant conserve, just in case the mistress has an appetite after all.

'I'm sure the doctor will not be long,' the housekeeper says.

'You may go back to bed, Nellie,' Belle adds. 'Mrs Grant will sit with me.'

'Yes, Nellie,' Mrs Grant adds with a tinge of pride. 'Go down with Claire. I will see to this.'

Outside, still under the sycamores, Duncan wonders what it is that he has seen. Inside was all darkness but now there is candlelight at the edges of the shutters on the first floor. He was coming back from Mhairi's lodgings when he noticed the two men acting suspiciously as they turned into Warriston Crescent, the one helping the other hirple along. He quickly recognized Edzel but not the other man and, intrigued, he used the cover of the thicket to follow them. They seemed unlikely burglars for how would the crippled one ever ply his trade? His interest was piqued when they stopped at Number 17, for he knows that is where Miss Brodie resides. But he still does not understand the meaning of what he has witnessed.

He waits for a while and is just turning to leave as Jamie shoots up the stairs from the basement and starts running along the road to fetch the horse from the mews off Rodney Street where it is stabled. 'Hey!' he calls. Jamie turns. He recognizes Duncan. 'Everything all right?' Duncan asks.

The mistress took a tumble down the stairs,' Jamie says. 'I am to fetch the doctor.'

'Which doctor?'

'Dr Morton on Queen Street.'

'Is Mr Graham not closer? I am sure he would help.'

'Miss Brodie sees Dr Morton,' Jamie replies stoutly. The mistress trusts Morton, who does not judge her activities. He's known for being good with women, never checking with a husband whether he'd prefer his wife or his child to survive a birth. Not half a century from now the University of Edinburgh will admit female students to its medical school, a move that will split opinion for three decades and cause at least one riot. It will also advance the care offered to women exponentially. But not yet.

Duncan shrugs. 'I hope the lady gets better soon,' he says. Jamie sprints away, without, Duncan realizes, asking him what he is doing here. He would love to stay with Mhairi – not in the way that people might presume, just to sleep on the floor at her door, though she will have none of that nonsense. In the end he prefers it that way. He will wed her, if she will have him. He has known it from the beginning. With a shrug he turns in the direction of Inverleith House, taking the most direct route. In doing so he will cross many boundaries, through Wardie land, cutting across the field where the horses sleep, over the highway through the Garden and back onto the Rocheid estate, where he will slumber among the hay bales over the stables and dream, as he does every night, of a life with Mhairi MacDonald at its heart.

Chapter Twenty-Five

Clementina wakes to the sound of her own screams about two hours before dawn. She bounds out of bed with the enthusiasm of a younger woman and pulls open the curtains so sharply that the swagging almost rips. Outside, clouds obscure the moon making the darkness practically absolute. Apart from a flaming torch on the castle esplanade, the city is all black shadow, the rakes abed at last. Her bedroom door bursts open.

'What?' Clementina starts, forgetting that she cried out as Elizabeth and one of the maids enter barefoot, clutching candles.

'What's wrong? What happened?' Elizabeth gasps.

Clementina squints at her. 'What do you mean?'

'You screamed. You scared us half to death.' She lights her candle to the wick beside Clementina's bed and motions to the maid to tidy the sheets.

'I had the feeling that something awful was happening,' Clementina says. 'Something wicked.'

Elizabeth helps the old woman back into bed and the maid closes the curtains. She worries that the old lady is getting worse.

'I have a second sense,' Clementina says. 'I always know when something is wrong.'

Elizabeth does not point out to her cousin that earlier this week she was bereft after the revelations about Belle, and Johann's uncalled-for advances, and that Clementina noticed nothing at all. Or that frequently Clementina exercises herself over the least likely of possibilities including mass starvation across the capital, despite the modern advances that boost the yield of crops year on year. Or that she didn't notice that yesterday, fruit tarts were served that surpassed Cook's ability to make pastry (for an accommodation has been reached).

'Someone is prowling in the night,' Clementina insists. 'Check the shutters and the doors downstairs,' she directs the maid, who disappears obediently.

Elizabeth turns the tapestry-work chair by the fire so it is facing the bed. 'I will sit with you till you get to sleep,' she says. But there is no need to wait long. No sooner has Elizabeth made herself comfortable than Clementina has clambered back into bed and promptly started to snore. Elizabeth sighs. She gets up and pulls aside the curtain. The figure of a man cuts across the lawn in the darkness but, she reassures herself, it is only Duncan. She wonders where he might have been, for it is not his half day, but then a household such as this with only two women does not place many demands on the staff. She watches as he disappears in the direction of the stables and wonders if this is what Clementina sensed. But why would she?

The next morning Elizabeth wakes later than usual, bright sunshine like pins round the edges of the curtains. Currant Bun bustles in and lays a cup of tea on the bedside before drawing the drapes. Elizabeth squints. 'What time is it?'

The girl does not know exactly. 'I thought it was best to let you sleep, miss. After the disturbance last night. Though it is not yet ten of the clock,' she adds. At ten sharp, Cook lays out wheaten bread and butter in the kitchen for those who have been working since six. The bread is leaden, but everybody eats it.

'Is Clementina all right?' Elizabeth enquires.

'Her maid is waking her now. Her ladyship is perfectly well.'

Elizabeth takes a sip of tea. She has been considering making croissants if only she can find a receipt. She wonders if she might dispatch Margaret to the library. It would certainly cheer her. It has been settled that any evening, should she wish it, the kitchen will be cleared by ten and she can bake to her heart's content. Cook will claim the resulting fancies as her own.

'Can you read?' Elizabeth asks the girl.

'Yes, ma'am,' Margaret confirms proudly. 'Everyone learned in my family, even the girls. All of us must be able to read the lord's word to save our souls.'

Ah yes, Elizabeth thinks. Of course. You don't even need to check here.

'I will write you a note to deliver to the librarian on the High Street,' she says. 'We need a household book – something French. I have a fancy for pastry . . .'

Margaret looks enthusiastic. 'French pastry, ma'am?' she says breathlessly.

'The kind they eat at breakfast. I had one at Richmond when some French ladies invited me to take morning coffee.'

Margaret is unsure how to respond to the notion of French ladies. The whole idea seems unbearably glamorous. 'Oh, ma'am,' she mouths.

'I will write down the name of what I am looking for,' Elizabeth says. 'We will need extra butter churned at the farm.'

There is a knock at the bedroom door, which opens to reveal a maid holding a note. 'I'll take that, thank you,' Margaret snaps. She is still new to her position and guards her privilege fiercely, closing the door on the girl without compunction and handing Elizabeth the paper. She turns to tidy the dressing table with half an eye still to the mistress.

Elizabeth puts down her cup and reads slowly. 'Oh,' she says. Clementina, it seems, was right. Something dreadful did happen last night. She jumps out of bed and snatches up her day dress. 'Quick,' she says. 'Help me! Poor Mr McNab!'

It is Michael O'Halloran who notices the theft. A grave Irishman from Donegal, he considers himself lucky to be employed by the

Garden rather than on a building site, but his uncle is head gardener at a big house near Stranraer and managed to secure him the position. After McNab unlocks the gate as usual just after six, Michael comes running. Mr McNab,' he cries, his voice fired by unaccustomed urgency. 'It's the aloe, sir.'

McNab's stomach turns. The minute the plant seeds his options are contained. It seems too soon for this to have happened, but nobody knows how long the plant will take to do anything – seed, flower or die. His palms begin to sweat but he turns bravely towards his fate, his senses heightening. He is aware suddenly of the sun on his face and the fresh smell of the Garden this morning as if this is a dream he is trying to remember. McNab cuts down the uneven path towards the greenhouses, followed by his men.

When they get there, a murmur ripples across the group like a tide. McNab is anchored to the spot, barely able to take in the sight before him. The flowers are gone. The stems have not been pared by an expert – the angle of the cuts are wrong – but there is no denying what has happened. 'There's one left,' somebody says and the group bursts into a low chorus of unanswerable questions, for why would anybody take the flowers of the aloe? McNab realizes his breath has become shallow. He lets out a gasp and falls to his knees. The men part to give him space and Michael O'Halloran offers the head gardener his hand in sympathy. Confused, McNab allows himself just one moment of prayer before he permits O'Halloran to help him to his feet. The group shuffles uncomfortably at the boss showing such emotion. He is not a man known for sentimental displays but McNab has himself under control now. He opens the door of the greenhouse to make sure there is no other damage.

From the back, Jack – one of the water boys who has been kept on because he is a good worker – gives a shout. 'Look!' he says, pointing at the damaged top hat and the abandoned brandy bottle lying off the path among a patch of assorted Asteraceae from which a salve is made to heal wounds. McNab inspects the discovery. 'They will have left no footprints,' he says. 'The ground is too dry.' He picks up the top hat and inspects it for any distinguishing feature, but he finds none. It is the most standard hat he has ever seen – silk and felt of a medium quality and black like almost all other hats.

'A gentleman did this,' O'Halloran pronounces, his tone disbelieving.

McNab picks up the brandy bottle and sniffs it. Will this theft let him off the hook? And how would he behave if he were not in the position in which he finds himself? 'You will say nothing of this to anyone, do you hear me?' he snaps at the men. 'I will write to Mr Graham immediately. He must direct our actions. Everyone back to work!' McNab motions to Jack. 'You'll deliver the note.'

Back in the shed he pulls the small writing box from the shelf and scribbles the barest of details onto a sheet of paper.

Dear Mr Graham – this morning we have discovered the theft of all but one of the flower heads from the aloe. I have reason to believe that this outrage may have been perpetrated by a gentleman. By grace I hope the single remaining flower head will produce a seed that can be used to propagate a new aloe for the Garden's collection. I send this immediately by hand and await your instruction. I am mindful that you may prefer to inform the magistrate of the crime yourself. I shall hold all evidence in readiness here. W McN.

With no ceremony Jack is dispatched to Great King Street. Next, McNab seeks out the errant, Edward, in the arboretum. 'If news of this morning's tragedy reaches the *Scotsman*'s pages before Mr Graham expects it to do so, I will send you home and you will not return,' he says. He is no fool. He knows what happened yesterday. Edward shifts, leaning on the shovel he has been using to prepare a place for the Garden's latest arrivals – the copper beeches. 'Yes, sir,' he says sheepishly. He cannot bring himself to meet McNab's eye.

The head gardener returns to the shed. It is only seven of the clock, the light is fresh and the world once more feels full of possibility after weeks of a dead end. He closes the door and finally allows himself to fully take in what has happened. He will have to explain to Mrs Dickson and come to an accommodation with the seeds-woman, he decides nervously. But if he can remain useful, surely he will be able to work off his debt to her. He casts an eye on the heating kettle and thinks this is an occasion for more than a cup of warm milk so he fumbles in the cupboard and finds the remains of a naggin of Mr Stein's whisky – and not one of the cheap ones either. He pours a tot into a cup and toasts his good fortune. Then he picks up his pen again and addresses a sheet to Dickson and Sons on London Road in which he explains the situation and speaks frankly. Mrs Dickson would never forgive him for favouring Kew over the deal he is promised to but there is no favouritism implied by a robbery. 'Might I offer you the opportunity to take some cuttings from the aloe? I have so far not been successful in propagating these, but with your particular skills, you may fare better. I know this will not entirely ameliorate my debt to you, but it may go some way towards it.' He signs and folds the note.

In Great King Street Mr Graham's man enters the bedroom and wakes the master. The Grahams keep separate rooms, with the lady housed in larger accommodation to the rear where a mahogany four-poster is upholstered in sky-blue, fringed damask. Mr Graham sleeps in his dressing room on a single bed with a window to the street. He visits Mrs Graham once a month for they have been married for many years and he does not like to impose. This arrangement is of his choosing and entirely acceptable to him. The Regius Keeper often falls asleep imagining himself camping upon some great botanical adventure – up the Amazon or deep in the forbidden interior of China. Many mornings he opens his eyes with mixed feelings – relief that he is here, in Great King Street, where breakfast will be served, and disappointment that he will never venture abroad for, unlike his cousin Thomas, the naval captain, he is not the adventuring sort.

'What is it?' he asks sleepily.

His man opens the curtains and Graham squints into the early morning light. The shadowy figure of his valet offers the letter, folded but with no seal. Graham sits up and, fumbling, takes it, recognizing McNab's hand. He opens the page and reads with an increasing sense of horror. The valet waits.

'What are you hanging about for?' Graham snaps. 'Fetch my clothes.'

'The boy is downstairs, if you wish to send a reply, sir,' the man says steadily.

'That won't be necessary. I must go myself. I must go immediately!'

Graham pulls aside the gold taffeta quilt and dark woollen blanket and gets to his feet unsteadily. 'This is unexpected. Most unexpected,' he mutters to himself, panic rising in his voice. He whips McNab's letter open again. The rogue left one flower. Which means there will be one seed to send to Kew at least. As he pulls on his undershirt he curses his fate. Why could this not have happened to one of the other plants? Why must it be the aloe? And what does McNab mean about the thief being a gentleman? What gentleman would perpetrate such an act of wanton destruction? 'Have my horse brought round,' he barks at the unfortunate valet who abandons his master's cravat on the chair, only too glad of an excuse to leave.

At the Garden the atmosphere is subdued. McNab's expression is grave as he emerges to greet the keeper.

'How did this happen?' Graham rages as he dismounts. There is no question that he holds McNab responsible.

McNab holds firm. 'I do not know, sir, but we must thole it,' he says. He shows Graham the hat and the empty bottle.

'Brandy!' Graham spits. 'Oh, this is has all the marks of one of those idiot lads.'

'Lads, sir?' McNab echoes.

'Students. These bottles are available at drinking clubs near the university,' he snaps with disdain. 'They are commonly left empty about the setts.'

McNab nods. 'But why would they want . . .?'

'There's no sense to it! No sense at all,' Graham snaps angrily. 'High spirits they call it. You wouldn't believe some of the things young gentlemen get up to. The Chancellor calls them immoral but it's worse than that – they are animals, McNab. Make no mistake about it. It only takes one to challenge another to a wager. Who can hold their breath the longest? Who can climb the façade of Old College? Who can, I don't know . . . I shall report this to the University Court straight away. Do you think the remaining flower will seed?'

'I hope so, sir. I expect so.'

'We must guard it. We must have a watchman installed.'

McNab nods steadily. 'A shilling and tuppence a night,' he says.

'Fourteen pennies!' Graham repeats as if he cannot believe he did not insist this money was spent. 'We have squandered thirty years of nurturing this plant and have lost all our industry for want of four-teen pennies!'

McNab controls his features carefully. Mr Graham has not yet replied to the letter that he sent in the matter of the promised wage rise.

'I will inform the magistrate,' Graham says. 'We must endeavour to bring the rogues that stole our flowers to justice.'

McNab agrees although it is obvious there is no mending the offence and with no further clue than the battered hat and the empty bottle it will be difficult to trace the culprits. 'I can't see how the young gentlemen might be discovered, unless they give themselves up. It is possible if there was drink taken, they might do so.' He imagines a young man waking, hazy, to a bunch of poorly pared yellow flowers in his rooms and a sense of overwhelming guilt. Might he realize what he has done and return the flowers and if so will they still be able to induce the blooms to seed? He judges it unlikely. The flowers will fade fast on the stem. 'As you say,' he continues, 'there is no mending this. It would be better if it had not happened.'

Graham hears only the last sentence. For a moment the keeper considers whether McNab has made a helpful suggestion. Might he be able to cover up the robbery? It would save him face. There must be a dozen gardeners here but working men might be bought off.

'Do we know the appearance of the seeds, McNab?' he asks.

McNab shakes his head. 'One might assume a large specimen but then from acorns do mighty oaks grow. Why, sir?'

'These men,' Graham gestures, 'do we have their loyalty?'

'I am certain that none of the gardeners cut the flowers, sir.' If Graham is hoping to blame one of his men, it is a serious allegation. Edward might be a snitch, but he is no thief and certainly not when there is no profit in it. Working men can be hanged for stealing from their employers. The least they can expect is to be deported. It is precisely what has been keeping him awake these last several nights.

'The hat, sir,' McNab adds, 'and the bottle, would indicate that it was not one of the gardeners . . .'

'Of course not,' Graham waves off the suggestion. 'I mean, will the men keep news of the robbery to themselves?'

'I have told them to, sir.'

The invitation to the king's ball in the balance, Graham now considers the possibility that they could supply other seeds to Kew. Surely the mistake would not be uncovered for months. Perhaps even a year or two. One seedling looks much like another. He sighs. It is impossible though – a step too far. Still, he did so want to dance with his wife in the presence of His Majesty.

'I shall write to the magistrate and to the University Court straight away,' he says, resignedly.

'I shall invoke the men not to gossip.'

'Quite right,' Graham agrees. 'And McNab?'

'Yes, sir.'

'Leave Herr von Streitz and Sir Walter to me. They are going to be terribly disappointed.'

Later, Mrs Dickson has replied by return that she will come, and now, ensconced in his hut, McNab is endeavouring to find a trustworthy watchman. Someone who will guard the aloe's one remaining bloom but not give him up to Mr Graham should he see Mrs Dickson taking cuttings. He settles upon old Richard Eyre, who worked for many years at the old Garden. Now retired, he could use the money, but will understand the need for discretion. Eyre's wife is dead, and he lives alone in a tumbledown cottage on the fringes of the Gayfield estate. As the old man cannot read or write, McNab decides he will walk over and engage him personally. But he is stopped in his tracks by Elizabeth, who almost trips as she rushes down the hill through the trees.

Her hair is scarcely combed beneath her bonnet, and her hands are scratched from pushing her way through the holly hedge. 'Mr McNab!' she calls.

McNab looks up. 'Mrs Rocheid.'

'I just got your note,' Elizabeth sounds out of breath. She takes a moment to compose herself. 'How terrible!'

'There is one flower head remaining,' McNab says, focusing on what most people would consider the most positive aspect of what has happened.

'Is there anything I can do?' Elizabeth asks.

McNab smiles. He is sure that as many people will come to gawp at the denuded plant as would have come to see it in flower though none of them will be as useful as Mrs Rocheid.

'The drawing you were to make of the plant's appearance in bloom will be important but perhaps you might also sketch the damage?'

Elizabeth raises her empty hands. 'Of course,' she says. 'I should have brought my things. I will go back for them.'

'James can fetch them for you,' he says, and calls his son. The boy dispatched to Inverleith House, McNab offers to show her the vandalized stems. In the greenhouse, Elizabeth squints upwards. 'Would it not have been usual to cut the flowers at an angle of forty-five degrees?' she asks.

'It would seem the gentleman who took the flowers was inebriated,' McNab says. 'We found a brandy bottle.'

'A gentleman?' Elizabeth repeats.

McNab nods but does not elaborate.

'Do you know when the theft occurred?'

'Last night,' McNab says simply. 'We cannot tell the time.'

Elizabeth recalls Duncan crossing the lawn towards the stables in the darkness.

'Why do you believe it was a gentleman?' she asks.

'We found a top hat, rather battered, over there.'

Elizabeth considers this. A working man might, at a push, treat himself to brandy, but the top hat seems conclusive. Not Duncan, then. But there is no saying that he did not see something. 'And you have no notion of the hour at which the crime was committed?'

McNab shakes his head. 'I went home at nine last evening,' he says. 'The plant was in perfect condition.'

'You went home late,' Elizabeth comments.

'We work as long as the light holds. I reopened the gate at six this morning.'

Elizabeth lays her hand on the aloe's fleshy protrusion. 'If only the plant could tell us,' she says wistfully. 'You are taking it bravely, sir.'

'Tis done,' McNab shrugs.

Rosy-cheeked from running, James arrives with Elizabeth's things and lays her box on top of the stool at the other end of the greenhouse. A half-finished line drawing of the plant from the day before is open on the front page, the clusters of yellow flowers drawn in detail and a close view of one bloom boxed at the edge of the paper.

'Mr Graham, I'm sure, will want something for the newspaper,' McNab says. 'In black and white, if you can. They are bound to report it.'

'I'm glad I can be useful,' Elizabeth replies. As she unpacks her lead and charcoal, McNab bustles off to engage the watchman.

The sun is out, its light changeable as clouds pass overhead. She will need to pay attention to the shadows today. The memory of Clementina's late-night vision crosses her mind. She feels as if she ought to be able to tell who has done this, yet the crime is inexplicable. Why would anybody want to steal such ordinary-looking flowers? She dismisses the vague suspicions she has about Belle as uncharitable, for the aloe's scent was agreed by all to be most unpleasant. She must steel herself against thinking the worst simply because they are no longer friends. And as for Duncan – well, the top hat makes that impossible.

At lunchtime, while she carefully sketches the outline of the plant where it has been torn, she hears McNab talking to two men sent by the magistrate. He hands over the evidence and patiently answers their questions before bringing them to see the aloe. 'Mrs Rocheid is making a sketch for the newspaper,' he says.

The men are both stocky and one of them wears a moustache. They tip their hats. Elizabeth holds up her drawing for them to see.

'It'll be difficult to find the rogue out,' says the barefaced fellow. 'We can ask the hatmakers about town if anybody recognizes their handiwork and see if householders up Pitt Street or past the toll were roused by somebody passing.'

'It was uncommonly dark last night,' the moustached man adds. 'Even if the thief was noisy and someone looked into the street, it seems unlikely they could give a useful description, though they might tell us if it was one felon or more.'

'Mr Graham guesses it was a student,' McNab adds.

The men nod sagely. 'We will ask in the howffs around the university and the landladies if anybody has seen . . .' Here the clean-shaven man hesitates for it sounds ridiculous, 'a fellow with a bunch of yellow flowers.'

Elizabeth lowers her drawing board and gets back to work. When she has finished, she will question Duncan, just in case he knows something. Anything at all.

Chapter Twenty-Six

In her drawing room in Warriston Crescent, Belle Brodie is ensconced on the sopha, her injured leg raised on a stool and a profusion of colourful cashmere shawls wrapped around her frame. Dr Morton has declared that her ankle is only sprained, not broken. He has prescribed laudanum to dull the pain and green tea to bring down the swelling. 'You will need to rest it, though a turn now and then to help strengthen the muscle is in order. You'll be right as rain in a few days, Miss Brodie,' he says before praising Nellie's work in binding the ankle. Nellie takes little pride in Dr Morton's endorsement, Belle notices. The girl has not been attentive this morning. Belle has had to ring the bell twice to summon her. She cannot recall when she last had to do this, for in the usual run of things Nellie shows the devotion of a lapdog, ever at her mistress's heel.

To determine what is going on, she summons Jamie to the drawing room. The coachman arrives nervous. 'Yes, miss,' he says, passing a hand over his hair. He is not usually admitted to the upper chambers of the house, Belle's orders being more generally relayed through Nellie or given during outings when Jamie is driving the horses. However, he has known Belle since he was a teenager and she a child, for he was in service at the house where she was raised. When she left, he drove the carriage from Perthshire to her brother's place and when she emerged with her stake money, she asked if he would like to stay in her service. It did not take him long to consider this proposition. He knew that Miss Brodie would be a more generous employer than the sour-faced housekeeper left in charge of the Brodies' country mansion. He has never regretted his decision.

'I need your help,' Belle says frankly. 'You are aware of the latitude I give my staff.'

Jamie nods curtly.

'I am concerned that Nellie is . . . up to something. I would like to know what.'

'Miss, should you not enquire of Mrs Grant?' Jamie says.

It is clear that he sees this matter as women's business.

'I considered that,' Belle admits. 'But you will do better. I want you to keep an eye on her. Follow her. Tell me where she has been.'

'I'm sure Nellie only does your bidding, miss.'

'If you are equal to the task, I will give you an extra half day each week for the next month.'

Jamie pauses. She knows that if she offers him money he will not succumb for that would feel like klyping on Nellie. But Jamie likes the horse races and there will be a meeting or two in the coming weeks, what with the light nights. And he is also partial to a barek-nuckle fight. He is not a man for a wager, but he likes to watch.

'I would consider it a personal favour,' Belle continues smoothly, 'if you could start immediately.'

When Jamie takes his leave, she settles on the cushions. There is nothing to do now but wait for Edzel to get on with the job. The flowers will be laid on a tray smeared with clarified lard to infuse the scent and then Edzel will process the fat. Sometimes he uses tallow, but the lard is finer. In warm weather the infusion will complete more quickly than during winter, but still, she must be patient. To enliven her time, she finds herself tempted by another project. In her latest foray of borrowing from the Assembly Rooms' library, Belle has discovered that the great Élisabeth Vigée Le Brun painted Britain's most famous courtesan of the Georgian age, Lady Emma Hamilton, three times when she was in Naples. Inspired, Belle has decided that she would like to have her portrait painted too. She enjoyed posing for Elizabeth's sketches at Inverleith House and she has decided it is time to address posterity. There are, after all, limited ways in which a lady's memory can endure. Belle will not have a stained-glass window in a church or a pew in her name, and it's evident that Elizabeth will sketch her no more.

Belle's preference is for a female artist, for it strikes her that a woman painting a woman will be more notable over time. Contacted yesterday, Miss Barbara Nasmyth, daughter of the great painter Alexander Nasmyth, expressed an interest in Belle's commission in a rather off-hand note in which she declared that at present she (and her sisters) are busy at work in their father's Princes Street studio like every other artistic soul in the country – preparing canvases and pre-painting backgrounds lest they be called upon to paint the king. Belle, however, is adamant that she will find somebody. If she is to merit more than one painting over the course of her life (and in her new social position she will certainly do so) she has to get on with it. While Le Brun's rococo style is now passing out of vogue, Belle plans to be captured in a neoclassical pose, on her sopha. She is also considering a little joke, the one started by Elizabeth in her botanical sketches. She will have blooms near her that will include the ingredients of Dr Brodie's Most Efficacious Ladies' Bathing Oil and some of the flowers from the scent Mhairi is developing. On a walnut side table will be a plate of strawberries and another of cinnamon.

Downstairs, when Nellie finishes her tasks she announces that she has to buy a set of buttons. Jamie feels a twist of guilt that he will follow her, but if he doesn't, the mistress will surely find somebody else to oblige. So, when Nellie pulls on her jacket and disappears along the crescent with the lace edges of her cloth cap bouncing, he tails her at a distance as she crosses the bridge and disappears down the pathway along the Water of Leith. This, he notes, is not the way to the haberdasher's and from her pace he ascertains that she is in a hurry. He skulks at the corner as Nellie passes the distillery and continues along the path, which is dappled with sycamore shadows. The mistress is not wrong. The girl is up to something. At the crossing, he loiters behind an ash as Nellie carefully lifts her skirts to ford the river and on the other side stops at the gate of a pleasant, double-fronted stone house. He wonders what on earth she is doing. Is this an assignation?

Having bustled along the muddy path as fast as she can, Nellie is calm now. Jamie watches the girl lean against the wall and from inside the house, through what he assumes is an open window, the sound of someone playing the pianoforte emerges onto the street. The musician runs through some Beethoven pieces, which Jamie recognizes, and those of another composer, which he does not. Nellie closes her eyes. She has been here before, he thinks. It is as if she is in a trance.

When the music stops, she walks on, Jamie keeping his distance as she emerges onto the main street and across the river again, over the Stock Bridge. She is no longer rushing. It is busy here, three costermongers shouting their wares and maids in and out of the shops at the top of the road. He is certain that she has not spotted him. A paperboy shouts the headline of the evening edition, a theft from the Royal Botanic Garden. Several people buy copies. Jamie wonders what kind of flowers might be worth stealing, theft being a capital offence. He waits as Nellie disappears inside the general merchants and emerges clasping a small packet tied with string. The buttons, he notes, and then he follows her as she makes her way back along the Circus and turns into Great King Street, pausing only momentarily to cast her eyes over Robert Graham's grand house in the middle of the terrace, where John the coachman waits at the door, his cab ready. She says something to him as she loiters, playful as a kitten in the sun.

Jamie squints from the cover of the trees overhanging the railings at the Circus. John answers Nellie and she frowns at his reply. Jamie smiles at this. John is well known for showing little interest in the lassies. He prefers other delights and goes drinking with his stable lad ower often. Whatever Mr Graham's coachman has said to Nellie it has not pleased her and she turns on her heel and sweeps around the corner, making her way back down Pitt Street, towards home.

'John,' he greets the man as he passes in Nellie's wake once she has turned the corner.

'Jamie,' John replies and turns to open the door of the carriage as Mrs Graham emerges from her front door.

The mistress will be disappointed, Jamie thinks. The most Nellie might be accused of is dawdling, for she is not a block ahead of him any longer and is returning to Warriston Crescent more slowly than she left it.

Chapter Twenty-Seven

Making the oil takes three days, and during this time Edzel does not sleep more than two hours together, and those snatched in the middle of the night. The work is not difficult, but he is terrified he will be caught. The magistrate's officers, fired by the seriousness of the crime at the Garden and the quantity of eminent persons making enquiries about it have efficiently contacted householders nearby as to any disturbance on the night of the robbery. On the first afternoon this leads them to Edzel's door. When they ask him what he is doing in the shed, he claims it is a soap manufactory and he the only employee. 'That accounts for the smell,' the moustached officer says, wrinkling his nose. Edzel does not elucidate further. Yes, he admits, he sleeps here. But no, he heard nothing on the night of the robbery. When they ask the name of someone to vouch for his character, he directs them to Reverend Mathieson, the minister who tutors him. This is not what Miss Brodie told him to do and upon closing the door of the shed, Edzel finds that he is shaking and guilt-ridden, although also in a state of some excitement.

While he finds he cannot stomach the pies that Nellie delivered a couple of days before, he can face the beer, and he finishes his week's allowance in half the allotted time before venturing up the hill to O'Brien's to have his jug filled from his savings. For the first time in years, unable to concentrate, he does not study at night, instead slowly sipping his ale as he considers his position and checks and rechecks the blooms on the larded wooden sheet. The quicker he can process them into something unrecognizable, the better. He has considered using warm fat to remove the scent, which is faster, but there is no saying that this would not destroy the flowers' precious oils, for not every plant takes heat well and Edzel can take no chances.

On the third day he judges the petals to have given up their scent. As he sniffs he finds himself mystified as to why Miss Brodie went to such lengths to procure these flowers, for the smell is not attractive. Still, he must do as he is told and he starts to process the fat, meticulously removing the petals, shredding them and putting them into a bucket of brown dye, which was left in the shed upon the tanners' departure. Immediately they become a shitty dull sludge. Well past midnight he ventures out and casts them into the river, a ladle at a time. Once they've floated away he sits on the riverbank, smoking a pipe and watching the dawn rise. It is a beautiful morning. A sudden movement nearby makes him jump.

'Edzel,' says a familiar voice.

'Mhairi.' His relief is palpable.

'What are you doing up so early?' she asks.

'I could ask you the same.'

Mhairi cocks her head. 'I am always up early. For the air,' she says, cocking her head. There is a change in Edzel. He does not normally smell of pipe smoke, but it is not only that. Usually she senses him as a boy but today it is clear that he has matured. When she imagines him in her mind's eye, he is not a child any longer but a man and he has lost his keenness, somehow, perhaps even his innocence.

Edzel knocks out his pipe. 'Can I offer you some pie? I have an appetite.'

'Ta. But naw.' Mhairi has broken her fast with a bowl of porridge, a dollop of cream and two glasses of milk. The landlady at her boarding house near the Stock Bridge serves breakfast from five-thirty at her kitchen table as the hens peck the ground. Some days Mhairi does not eat until after seven, though this morning, like the hens, she was an early bird. She gestures towards the shed and they go inside, leaving the door open. A curious noise escapes Mhairi's lips. 'What have you been up to?' she asks.

Edzel chooses a pie from his basket and takes a bite.

'Making oil for Miss Brodie,' he says. The clarified lard is now in a copper pot, ready for gentle heating and combination with a small amount of the pure alcohol Edzel distils.

Mhairi sniffs her way to his workbench and lifts the copper to her nose. She makes another noise – like a curious cat. 'Och, that's gey unusual. It imparts a heat, does it not?' she says.

Edzel puts down the pork pie and takes the copper to sniff it. 'Miss Brodie has a nose all right,' he agrees.

Mhairi sinks onto Edzel's stool. The scent reminds her of the lady's bedstraw her mother uses to curdle the milk, only more potent. It is the very stock that she had been hoping for. 'It'll be perfect,' she says. 'If I'd time, I'd stay to help. When will it be ready for mixing?'

'Soon,' he promises and then adds, 'Miss Brodie usually makes her own scents. Will she be giving you my job, Mhairi, when I go to the university? Is that why you're here?'

Mhairi smiles. 'Who knows what the lady has in mind, but I can tell you that I have no desire to take your job, son.' She considers adding that she is being paid, for her Sunday afternoon and various hours, more than Edzel earns in a sixmonth, but she decides against it. 'I'll be back later,' she says.

But it is Belle who arrives later that morning with a silver-topped cane in her neatly gloved hand to support her limp.

'Well?' she asks, straight to the point when Edzel lets her in.

'It made a tablespoon almost. I've just finished it,' he says and beckons her to the bench. 'Miss MacDonald came by.' He steps back to reveal a single, small dark brown bottle that has just been filled. 'She seemed to like it.'

'And it is clarified properly? It will keep?'

'Yes, miss.'

Belle opens the lid and breathes in the scent. A look of concentration settles on her face. She uses her pinkie to take a single drop and smooths it onto her skin, then she breathes in again as the perfume opens – a sniff of straw that deepens into something more exotic. It is exactly what she hoped for – fresh mushroom and yeast. A sense of possibility. A smile breaks across Belle's lips like a curtain being drawn back on a tableau. 'That's good,' she says. 'Very good.'

Edzel hangs on her words, his relief palpable. He opens his mouth to ask a question when there is a knock on the door. Belle puts down the bottle guiltily and interposes her body between the entrance and the bench. She nods at Edzel, who pulls back the lock.

Outside, in the sunshine, the two magistrate's officers have returned. They peer inside, past Edzel, at Miss Brodie.

'Mr McBain,' one says, as if asking a question he is not able to properly form, 'who is this lady?'

Belle steps forward cool as a glass chilled, ready for the wine to be served. 'I am Miss Isabel Brodie. Edzel's employer.'

'Ah . . . yes . . . Soap, isn't it?'

Belle ignores this. 'What is your business?' she asks. 'Edzel has work to do. There will be a smell, I'm afraid.'

'We are investigating the theft of the aloe flowers from the Botanic Garden. You may have heard of it.' The man takes a two-day-old copy of the newspaper from his pocket and shows her the picture that Elizabeth Rocheid drew, her neat initials at the foot.

Belle does not look at it. 'I am acquainted with Robert Graham, the Regius Keeper of the Botanic Garden. I visited the aloe with him the day before the theft. It is a terrible business. Have you made any progress?'

The man shifts. It has been three days and they have turned over student accommodation across the Old Town. It seems the city's householders saw nothing that night – not anywhere on the route from the Garden into town. The officers even questioned people along Warriston Crescent though at Number 17 it was Mrs Grant they spoke to. The old housekeeper swore everyone was abed and only remembered later that was the night the mistress hurt her ankle bidding an overenthusiastic farewell to one of her gentlemen. Not that Mrs Grant would risk her annual bonus by telling the magistrate's men about that. The trail is so cold that the night before the two investigators were reduced to asking prostitutes around the Old Town if they had seen or heard anything. Which they had not. Interrogating ladies of the night is both a tiresome occupation and a stimulating one. Both men ended up paying a tanner each for an upright along one of the pends that run down to the Cowgate.

'Nothing,' the man says. It feels as if the flowers have been stolen by a ghost.

Belle shrugs. 'What a shame,' she replies. 'Not that the return of the flowers might make it right.'

'What do you mean, miss?'

'Mr Graham hoped the blooms would seed. Even if you recover them, they will have withered by now.'

'What are you up to?' the man asks, trying to look round her at the workbench and the shelves.

'We are making soap,' Edzel cuts in.

Neither of the men is familiar with soap production.

'Is there much money in that?' the moustached one enquires.

'It is a hobby of mine, as well as a business,' Belle says. 'I like the smell.'

'Miss Brodie,' the man ponders, as if running through a list of names. 'Oh,' he lets out as he remembers why he has heard of her, 'Miss Belle Brodie, is it? Ha!' He laughs though from his lips it sounds more like a dog barking than a sign of amusement. 'Well, I didnae ken that was you. You are a cut above the usual doxy.'

Belle draws herself up. 'I am the great-granddaughter of a duke and a lady,' she says. 'I will thank you to remember it.'

'Takes four generations, does it, for the mighty to fall? What exactly is the smell in here? It is gey unusual.'

'None of your business,' Belle snarls. 'It is a scent we are working on, is all.'

'Everything is our business, miss. That is the nature of magistrate's men.' The officer pushes past her. He opens a sack of cinnamon bark lying on the lowest shelf and picks out a shard.

'What is this?'

'Edzel will make scent of it,' Belle retorts. 'That is what he does.'

'And do you make scent of flowers, my lad?'

Edzel nods. 'Roses,' he says. 'Rose soap for the ladies. And lilac. I can show you, if you like?'

The officer nods curtly and Edzel pulls a bottle of rose oil from the shelf. The man looks nonplussed. 'Flowers?' he says, as if this a mystery quite beyond him.

'I make the flowers into oil,' Edzel explains.

The officer takes a reluctant sniff and then coughs.

'That one is rose. This is lilac,' Edzel says helpfully and reaches for another bottle.

'And these flowers that were taken . . .' the officer starts.

Edzel and Belle look at each other and laugh.

'What's so funny?' the officer cuts in.

'That bottle of rose oil contains the scent of several hundred flowers. Our raw ingredients arrive by the stone, sir, not the handful. A wee posy will not make enough for much in our business. Besides, the flowers did not have an appealing smell. I commented on that particularly when I visited. You may check with Mr Graham, if you wish.'

The officers look abashed. 'So you did not see anything. You did not hear anything. And the stolen flowers would be of no use to you,' the clean-shaven man surmises.

'No lady would want to smell like an aloe, I assure you,' Belle says smoothly.

'And you, lad?'

Belle steps in to defend her boy. 'I shall be sure to tell Mr Graham that you have been wasting time interrogating lads engaged in making household goods. No wonder the trail has gone cold. Now, if you don't mind, I shall return to giving Edzel my instructions.'

The men leave, disgruntled. Belle and Edzel listen to their footsteps. Belle regards Edzel – he dissembled extremely well, better than she would have expected. She picks up the new glass bottle and puts it on the shelf with the others. It is notable only in that it is the smallest.

'Hiding a tree in the woods,' she remarks. 'What's wrong?' she asks Edzel, whose face now shows signs of dismay.

'It does not do well to rile such men.'

Belle shrugs. 'We could not defer to them. That would be suspicious.'

Edzel does not argue. There is little evidence to hide now in any case. Only the small brown bottle. Once the perfume is mixed nobody will be able to discern it separately.

Belle turns to go. 'Mhairi will come,' she says. 'Stay here till she does.'

'Yes, miss,' Edzel replies as his mistress limps into the sunshine and heads back towards the bridge.

Belle is considering keeping the cane. There is something distinguished about the tapping sound it makes. At Warriston Crescent she calls for her carriage and decides to make her way to the glassworks at Fountain Bridge. She has a fancy to buy bottles for her new creation now its advent is so close. On a serpentine-backed mahogany chair in her hallway, she waits for Jamie to bring the horses from the mews and ponders. In fairy tales, the treasure comes in a plain package. Cinderella's worth is, after all, in her soul, not her outward appearance. On George Street the apothecary sells French perfume in sculpted bottles, latticed with gilding – splendid and flashy but Belle decides that she will speak to a different aesthetic. Still, she wants more than a workaday dark brown. The perfume must look like magic, not medicine.

She settles on unadorned ruby glass and resolves to have four plain walnut boxes made with fitted horsehair cushions, each finished in a different colour. One purple velvet, another midnight blue taffeta, a third of ochre silk and the last one green damask. This will

make each bottle unique – in its own box with a tiny Bramah lock
and a key with a matching tassel. She imagines the delight of a young
lady having such a secret – a love potion to unlock at will. The yes to
a young lady's most important question.

When the carriage arrives, the magistrate's officers are talking to
one of Belle's neighbours outside: a Black woman married to a
customs officer, who moved onto the street the year before. The
gossip around the doors was that he discovered her stowed in a shipment of tobacco, escaped from the West Indies. The truth, however,
is that she was born in Bathgate. The moustached man is interrogating the woman loudly. Belle pauses and waves at Jamie to wait there,
walking along the façade of the terrace, tap, tap, tapping her cane.
Further up, Duncan is delivering a wheelbarrow of manure to the
first house on the street. He stops to watch her.

'Madam,' Belle hails the woman. 'Are these men bothering you?'

'It is something about a flower . . .' the woman replies nervously.
'But I have told them I know nothing.'

'We have all told them that,' Belle assures her.

'Stand aside, Miss Brodie,' the officer says, waving his copy of the
old newspaper. 'We have the right to ask questions.'

'I imagine the magistrate would want you to ask questions that
are helpful,' Belle retorts, 'not harass women whose days are busy
enough. This lady is my neighbour.'

The officer mutters under his breath. Belle thinks she discerns the
word 'nosy'. 'As I understand it there was evidence found in the
Garden. A top hat and some brandy,' she snaps. 'Should you not be
asking these questions of gentlemen rather than ladies?'

The officer turns on her. 'We are pursuing our enquiries, madam,'
he growls. 'Not yours.'

But Belle has a point, and the men walk away.

'I hope they didn't trouble you,' Belle says once they are out of
sight.

'I'm all right thank you, Miss Brodie. You hurt your leg,' her
neighbour remarks.

'I tripped upon the stair three nights ago,' Belle says lightly. 'The injury is healing.'

On the corner of the street, Duncan hears the two women bid their goodbyes. Carefully, he counts back. It was three nights ago he saw the figures on Belle's doorstep. He glances in the direction of the magistrate's men. Well, well, he thinks. She looked quite different in breeches, the sonsie dame. But he says nothing.

Chapter Twenty-Eight

The magistrate's men are frustrated. Their enquiries seldom take them far into the orbit of upper-class women and even more seldom do those women refuse to cooperate. Ladies generally answer questions without reservation. They have remarked before that working-class women tell the truth with economy, while upper-class women feel the need to explain.

'She'd appoint herself judge and jury that quine,' the moustached officer says as they turn away from the head of the crescent.

It is somehow more annoying that Belle is probably right and that there was no measure in questioning the Black lassie. After all, the rogues most likely came back into Edinburgh by the highway and would have no reason to turn off at Warriston Crescent. As she said, the thief is a gentleman, probably a student and almost all of those are housed in the warren of streets near Old College or with relations in the New Town. But their enquiries are coming to nothing.

'Let's try the lad again,' says the clean-shaven fellow and the men turn into Tanfield, where Edzel, with no particular work to do and having drunk a sufficiency of ale, is sitting by the river next to a bank of rushes with only the sunny afternoon ahead of him. James McNab is by his side, drawing the plants in the water. He likes to visit Tanfield though he has not seen Edzel in his cups before. Edzel gets to his feet too swiftly, like a puppet whose strings have been jerked. He never normally drinks so much. It reminds him of his Pa.

'What is it now?' he says impatiently, swaying a little.

'Who's this young fellow?' the men ask, indicating James.

James introduces himself as he has been taught. He holds out his hand and gives his full name, telling them who his father is.

The moustached officer laughs. 'The very gentleman, isn't he? What have you got there?'

James shows them his pictures. The notebook is filled with sketches of plants. Trees in barrels and summer flowers. When he gets to the aloe, the officer takes the newspaper from his pocket. 'That's the aloe that was stolen,' he says.

'Only the flowers were stolen, sir,' James corrects him. 'The aloe remains in the greenhouse.'

The man ignores this comment. It seems everybody down here at Canonmills has a bone to pick.

'Why do you have a picture of it?'

'Mrs Rocheid is teaching me to illustrate.'

The men loiter. One of them sniffs. 'It's a strange smell,' he says. 'I thought you were making soap with roses.'

'I will get back to it. They are steeping,' says Edzel.

'Where do you sell this soap?'

'There is an arrangement with an apothecary.' Edzel is glib, not a word of a lie.

The barefaced fellow's expression turns spiteful. 'Your mistress is a doxy. A jade. You know that, don't you?'

Edzel will not have this. When he lived on Thistle Street there was a working girl who plied her trade from the doorway of Number 45. As a child he would watch her out of the window. Miss Brodie owns a house and employs staff. She is his benefactor.

'Take that back,' he demands.

The ferocity of the officer's response takes him by surprise. The man is quicker than Edzel's father, who would only become violent when he was drunk. Once provoked, however, Edzel launches himself into the affray. The work at Tanfield has made him strong and as he unleashes his fury – something he never had the nerve to do when his father used to beat him – he knocks over the moustached man. 'She is not a doxy! She is not a jade!' he shouts. 'She is a gentlewoman!' When the other officer pulls him off, Edzel kicks him in the stomach and it is with difficulty that the two of them manage to finally subdue the boy.

'It's the gaol for you,' the man says. 'You cannae attack a magistrate's man.' They cuff him to the branch of a tree that overhangs the water while they search the hut.

Edzel hisses to James, who is standing, shamefaced nearby. 'Come here,' he motions with his head.

James stares at the door of the shed, rooted to the spot.

'Come here,' Edzel hisses again.

James edges closer.

'Will you do a service for Miss Brodie?'

James looks worried. He is too young to know what a doxy or a jade is, but he knows it is not good.

'For Mrs Rocheid's friend?' Edzel adds for good measure.

James nods slowly. That is more acceptable.

'They will take me away. When we have gone you will go into the shed and on the shelf you will find the smallest brown bottle. The smallest one, mind. It has no writing on it and it is at the front.'

James's eyes are wide.

'You will take that and you will hide it somewhere safe. Not in the Garden. Not with your Pa. Not,' he adds, thinking on his feet, 'at Miss Brodie's. Put it somewhere safe and I will come to fetch it later, all right?'

The sound of something banging emanates from the shed. The magistrate's men are messing about with the still.

'Don't mind them. There's a coin in it for you, James. Miss Brodie will be pleased. Mrs Rocheid too,' he adds.

James hesitates. He would like a coin.

'Tell nobody. Only wait for me. You're a clever lad, you'll think of somewhere to put it.'

Five minutes later, as they take him away, Edzel entreats the magistrate's men to send word to Miss Brodie, which in time they will do, but slower than he would like. James loiters by the shed's closed door. He waits a good ten minutes before he turns the handle. The men have tussled Edzel's bed, they have opened the still and shifted the books. The tallow lamps lie to one side with their glass cracked. He takes this in as he makes his way to the shelf where he easily finds what he is looking for. Slipping the smallest bottle into his inside pocket, he takes off, over the bridge, up the road and through the holly hedge.

By dint of chance it is this very afternoon that Elizabeth Rocheid asks Duncan about his movements on the night the flowers were taken. It has been a busy few days, for her illustrations are proving much in demand and Clementina has required attention. There is no question the old lady is getting more erratic. She cannot always recall what she has said, and simple matters like whether lunch has been served have started to slip her mind. Nonetheless, today she has taken it upon herself to visit the farm and discuss the matter of the fruit harvest, leaving Elizabeth at a loose end. She spots Duncan, who has returned from his trip to deliver the manure, and taps upon the drawing room window, beckoning him inside.

The room is strewn with drawings across every surface. A dusty pile of charcoal sits on a fancy cherrywood side table. The last time Duncan was here, he is sure it was far tidier. He sniffs, uncomfortably aware that he smells faintly of manure.

'I will not beat about the bush,' Elizabeth says, 'I saw you coming home late the night the Garden was robbed. Can you tell me where you had been?'

Duncan dislikes being put on the spot as if he were a child in the schoolroom, but Mrs Rocheid has the right to ask him. 'I was visiting my sweetheart,' he mumbles.

'At three of the clock?'

'We talked till late.'

'Where?'

'In her lodgings near the Stock Bridge.'

Elizabeth cannot help but show her disapproval. 'It seems late, Duncan. What are your intentions towards this sweetheart of yours?' she asks more gently.

Duncan meets her gaze. 'That's none of your business, ma'am,' he says coldly.

Elizabeth has not the heart to fight with him. 'You were abroad the same time as the thief who stole the flowers. It is unlikely, I know, but did you see anything at all?'

Duncan remains evasive. 'They say the robbery was perpetrated by gentlemen from the university,' he replies.

Elizabeth accepts this as an answer though it is not the answer to the question that she asked. The route from the Stock Bridge to the hayloft, however, would not normally take Duncan past the Garden or even up the main road. She regards him for a moment. 'Nothing?' she checks.

Duncan holds fast and she dismisses him for outside she can see Clementina returning and there is no measure in troubling the old woman about the staff.

Inside, Clementina collapses into a cushion-strewn chair at the fireside. 'My God,' she says, 'the plum trees are marvellous. We shall have such a crop!'

Elizabeth professes herself glad of it.

'There is mischief afoot,' Clementina continues. 'You will never guess in a hundred years whose carriage was stopped on the other side of the tattie fields.'

Elizabeth does not care for gossip and refuses to encourage her by asking who.

'Just up from the Stock Bridge,' Clementina says to tempt her cousin.

'Shall I have tea brought?' Elizabeth asks, in the hope that this will distract the old woman.

'Ah yes,' Clementina says. 'Tea and some of those biscuits.'

Elizabeth's smile is slim as she rings the bell and gives the order. The biscuits are made with syrup and cardamom, and she now bakes two batches a week. They are Margaret's mother's receipt and a new favourite with the household. 'I must go upstairs,' she says. 'To my closet.'

Clementina lets out a harrumphing noise but Elizabeth disappears up the stairs nonetheless. The old woman looks round. Next door there is the sound of movement. When she calls out 'Who's there?' James McNab appears in the connecting doorway to the old music room, now arrayed with Elizabeth's art materials.

'Good day Master McNab,' says Clementina. 'Are you here for your lesson?'

James cannot lie. He has not been brought up to it. 'I was hoping to secrete this,' he says, pulling the small bottle from his pocket.

Clementina, ever the grand lady, motions him forward with an hauteur emanating from decades of being in charge. 'What is it?'

James shrugs. 'It belongs to Miss Brodie,' he says. 'Her boy will come for it.'

The old woman does not ask any questions, only holds out her hand. She opens the brown bottle. The smell is familiar, but she cannot recall why. It reminds her of picnicking in her youth, in May, when the weather was generally fine. Of tarrying out of her mother's sight.

'I have my own business with Miss Brodie,' she declares. 'James, would you fetch my writing slope?'

The boy hesitates, his eyes still on the bottle.

'I will look after it,' Clementina promises, her fingers closed over the brown glass. 'The desk is over there.'

James carries the writing box carefully for it is worth a fortune. He lays it on the side table. The old woman opens the box. 'You had best get on with your lesson,' she says. 'What are you drawing today?'

'Water rushes,' James replies. '*Butomus ambellatus*. The flowers are pink.' He disappears back into the music room for he needs coloured chalk to finish his sketch. Clementina withdraws a piece of paper and a quill. She flips open the inkwell and contemplates for a moment before deciding that, regardless of whether Elizabeth is interested or not, she should tell Belle Brodie what she has seen.

My dear Belle [she writes], *I must tell you what I witnessed today for it concerns your household. This morning whilst engaged in inspecting our home farm, I saw your serving girl, Nellie Patterson. She was abroad between our estate and the Fettes' and I was surprised to see her get into a carriage that was stopped. It belongs, I believe, to Mr Graham, though I cannot say who was inside. She stayed for almost half an hour before the carriage moved off. Should a maid in my employ be seen in such a fashion I should want to know of it. Though she may have been undertaking your business, I am passing what I saw to you. All Best etc. Clementina*

She seals the paper and picks up the bottle, fumbling off the cap and taking another sniff. The scent is unusual and quite the treasure, she thinks, and as she has just performed a service for Belle, the girl surely will not deny her. She has been wondering what to send to Constance von Streitz. Johann's grandmother was ever a woman who appreciated the unique, and the scent is certainly that. From her box, she pulls out a letter she has already written. She and Constance were known as the Beauteous Virtues in Leipzig because of their names, though Constance was called, her father once confided, after the lake near her mother's hometown, known in German as the Bodensee. 'In English it is Constance,' he said with a laugh, his accent making his daughter's name sound fricative. 'Not a virtue at all.'

Clementina adds a final line to her letter, which is full of reminiscences:

I hope this perfume diverts you. I have a young friend who manu-factures her own scents. I am not sure what it reminds me of – perhaps being young and in love.

The old woman signs the paper and seals in the small bottle. Then she scribbles a note to Johann, asking him to forward the packet in the diplomatic bag.

When the maid comes with the tea tray Clementina gives her the correspondence. 'Send it to town with Calum when he next goes,' she says. These days she prefers the young lad to Duncan, who appears to be carrying a heavy burden on his shoulders and will still not engage with her in the matter of his father.

When Elizabeth returns the old woman has poured tea and is humming Burns's 'Auld Lang Syne' to herself. 'The boy is in the music room,' she says. 'He is drawing water plants.'

Chapter Twenty-Nine

Before dinner Elizabeth makes her way to the Garden. She has no reason to do so other than the fact that she has an hour to spare and happens to feel like walking. The sky is blue and as she squeezes through the holly hedge and takes in the vista of the Garden below, it feels like a pastoral, though given what has happened she has to remind herself it is very far from that. There are, she thinks, so many flowers blooming just now. In winter, no doubt, this landscape will be a spectrum of green, studded only with berries, but today there is as much colour as a carnival. Still, not quite enough yellow now the aloe's golden blooms are gone.

Elizabeth has not allowed herself to miss Belle. She has kept extremely busy since that day on George Street. But now walking down the hill the smell of chamomile assails her, and she realizes that she has lost something she valued, even if she was wrong to do so. Not knowing what to do with this thought, Elizabeth dismisses it and strides past the glasshouses. She does not pass anybody. The gardeners work late but in the evenings they cool clay flacons of small beer in the pond and do not stray far from its bank. Mr McNab never joins them, for it would not be appropriate. He keeps to the north of the Garden, the direction in which Elizabeth now turns. As she emerges from the arboretum, however, she catches sight of him by the gate engaged in an intense conversation with, she squints with a leap of her stomach, Mrs Dickson. 'You cannot come here,' McNab hisses angrily at the old woman. 'I will meet you but not when the Garden is open.'

Elizabeth's cheeks burn and she makes to turn back but Mrs Dickson raises a finger and points straight at her. Damn the woman. She is like some kind of rogue element in a chemistry experiment, causing agitation wherever she goes. McNab barrels round. He looks sheepish.

'I have your catalogue ready to send, Mrs Rocheid,' Mrs Dickson calls. Elizabeth walks forward and thanks her coolly.

'I will return when it is more convenient,' the old woman says to McNab and turns on her heel. Out in the street they hear her geeing up her horse as she pulls away in the old cart.

'Mrs Rocheid,' McNab starts, stilted. 'I hope that . . .'

'That woman,' Elizabeth bristles. It is, she knows, unfair of her to blame Mrs Dickson for Belle's wickedness, but now the old seeds-woman appears to have discomfited Mr McNab as well.

'You saw me with her before,' Mr McNab admits. 'The first week you were at Inverleith House.'

Elizabeth does not want to pursue this. She does not want to lose Mr McNab's friendship as well as everything else and she has an instinct that is what will happen.

'We will say no more about it,' she says. 'The old woman had nothing to do with the theft of the aloe, did she?' she adds, suddenly nervous.

McNab gives a hint of a smile. 'Far from it,' he says, and his blue eyes light up. 'There would be no value to her in that.' He holds out his hand. 'Thank you. You have been a friend to me and my son and the Garden.'

He seems suddenly earnest. Elizabeth shakes the gardener's hand. She is not entirely sure why it has been offered.

'Was there something you wanted?' McNab asks.

'I am only out for a walk,' she admits. 'Though,' she adds, 'I wondered what to do with the aloe's flower. The one you cut for me to draw. Shall I press it?'

McNab considers. 'That is an excellent idea,' he says.

As she disappears back up the hill, McNab stares in the direction of the road. He has held off Mrs Dickson for the time being, explaining to her he cannot return her money. She retorted that she wants the value of it and a premium for the inconvenience. But what that means he does not know and before Mrs Rocheid appeared at the head of the path the old woman burst out that cuttings were not enough and went on to say something about 'closer ties'. He worries about what she has in mind.

Come dinnertime, Clementina's letter awaits Belle's return from Fountain Bridge on a silver-plated salver in the boudoir. As Miss Brodie settles, Nellie hurries to fetch a decanter of hock and a plate of sliced ham with mustard. The mistress clicks open the seal and reads. By the time Nellie returns, Belle is waiting for her. She hands over a note she has just written to Robert Graham.

'Send that, would you? Have Jamie take it.'

'I could go, miss,' Nellie offers, rather too eagerly, reading the address.

This, of itself, is not damning for Nellie often willingly proposes herself for tasks. Belle takes a sip of the hock.

'Let Jamie do it,' she says. 'Mr Graham, sadly, has the pox. Dr Morton has informed me.'

Nellie's eyes suddenly look empty. It is then that Belle knows. 'Come back once it is sent. I want to reorder the dressing room.'

Nellie takes her time while Belle nibbles her dinner and sips the wine. When the girl returns it is clear that she has been crying.

'I have deceived you,' Belle admits, 'but you have lied to me, have you not?'

Nellie pauses. 'Do you mean . . . he is well?'

'Mr Graham's health is, as far as I am aware, intact. You know I must sack you for this, don't you, Nellie? Really! I cannot have you dallying with gentlemen who come to call.'

'But Mr Graham is not one of your gentlemen,' Nellie objects. Her jaw is hard. 'Besides, I don't need this job. He wants to set me up.'

Belle laughs. 'Set you up?'

'He loves me,' Nellie vows stolidly.

Belle raises an eyebrow. 'If he wanted to set you up, you silly girl, up you would be set. And yet here you are fetching my dinner, sending my letters and sneaking off for grubby assignations in Mr Graham's coach. And you believe he loves you? Nellie, you must never fall in love, not in this business. You know that, don't you?'

Nellie's eyes fill with tears.

'Well, we shall see,' Belle says.

'What do you mean?'

'I have asked him to call at his earliest convenience.'

Nellie puts a hand to her hair as if to tidy it and Belle loses patience. 'There's little point in that. In all your time in this house I thought you might have picked up something!'

'I learned to steep pennyroyal,' Nellie returns cattily. 'And that you must give gentlemen what they want if you wish to profit.'

'Well, what Mr Graham wants of you has certainly been adequately demonstrated. You think you can be me, do you? You are soft as butter, Nellie. And he will eat you.' Belle cannot quite believe she is having this conversation with Nellie, who was so grateful for her place when she first came to Warriston Crescent that for a fortnight she prefixed every utterance with 'yes, miss, thank you, miss.' Changed days.

'He wants me,' Nellie insists stubbornly. 'And I am not so demanding as you. I do not want a house like this with all its finery. I am easier.'

Belle leans forward. This interests her. 'What is it you want, Nellie?'

Nellie's eyes fill with tears once more. 'I want to attend recitals at the Assembly Rooms. I want to join the church choir.'

'You think the church will welcome you if you make an arrangement with a married man?'

'Nobody need know. Mr Graham will take a room for me on Young's Street and my time will be my own.' The girl starts to cry in earnest.

'You fool! Everybody on the stair will know. On the street, too. You think they will not see the comings and goings of such a gentleman? Young's Street is close to Charlotte Square – right in town. You think it is by chance that I choose to live here, beyond the city limits?'

Nellie shrugs like a recalcitrant child. 'We will work it,' she says, but her voice has lost its confidence.

'And you like the work?' Belle asks, genuinely curious. 'Let me guess. He likes you to curtsy? He likes you to call him sir?'

Nellie's eyes harden. This arrow has hit home. 'I'm sure you wouldn't understand, but I am happy,' she declares. 'I can look after myself.'

'Nellie, listen to me. You will always be a maid to him.' Belle lays down her glass. If there is one thing Nellie has demonstrated it is that she cannot look after herself at all. 'What has he offered you?'

The maid does not reply.

'You have not made a deal? Oh Nellie,' Belle admonishes her. She is about to add that this is a man who cannot even pay a gardener properly. They are interrupted, however, by the sound of the front door below. Nellie looks nervously in the direction of the hallway. When Robert Graham enters, it is Belle who greets him.

'It seems you owe me a maid, Mr Graham,' she says drily.

Robert takes off his hat. Nellie drops a curtsy and puts out her hand to take it.

'Oh dear,' he says, like a child caught with his hand in the shortbread barrel.

'Oh dear indeed. I suppose the least I can do is oversee Nellie's covenant. She tells me you plan to set her up in Young's Street.'

'Well,' Mr Graham hesitates. 'Well. Yes. That is what I said.'

'In, I hope, adequate apartments.'

'I have heard there are rooms available. They will not be lavish, I'm sure, but Nellie will not want.'

'Not if you settle one hundred pounds a year on her.'

Robert Graham quails. The figure, as Belle calculates it, is not too ambitious but will see Nellie in food, clothes and other necessaries as well as a few luxuries. Or perhaps the girl will be sensible and save the excess. The arrangement is unlikely to last, but it might as well start right. Belle continues, negotiating smoothly.

'I understand the girl is keen to become part of the city's musical community. She will require tuition and an instrument. Is there an instrument you wish to play, Nellie?'

Nellie, wide-eyed, pale but in the full understanding that Belle is now doing her a favour, chimes in, 'I would like to learn the pianoforte, miss.'

'An excellent choice,' Belle says. 'I understand that Sir Walter Scott has upon occasion provided a pianoforte for a lady in need. I recall he sent an instrument last winter to a schoolteacher in Shetland. That being for the benefit of the community.'

Nellie looks hopeful. Despite her long sojourn at Warriston Crescent, she had no idea such things were possible. Miss Brodie's life always seems to her like a fairy tale but Miss Brodie was born a lady, not a maid. Now it is her turn to be the principal character. With a hundred pounds a year she can have a woman clean her rooms and wash her linens. She sighs. 'Oh sir,' she says, the moniker falling from her lips as if it were a name and said with awe, not as a lady might pronounce it.

Belle notices that fleetingly Graham gazes at the girl in the most ribald fashion. Perhaps Nellie has the right of it. Perhaps he is sufficiently infatuated to make the affair last. One way or another, the girl has certainly aroused him. 'Very well,' he snaps at Belle.

'And do you have any terms, Mr Graham?' Belle lays the floor open.

Robert shuffles. 'I do not want my wife to know.'

Belle's eyes dance. 'Of course.'

'My wife attends Saint Giles. I'd prefer it if Nellie frequented a different church.'

Belle notes that he is speaking about Nellie in the third person, though she is standing right next to him. 'Nellie?' she gestures.

'I will attend Saint George's,' Nellie says. 'For the acoustics.'

'Now that's settled you should pack your things,' Belle says. Nellie disappears through the doorway and Belle offers Mr Graham a glass of hock while he is waiting. He is quite the most ridiculous man, she thinks. He shakes his head and only reluctantly takes a seat when she invites him.

'Is there any progress on the missing flowers?' Belle asks.

Robert Graham stares at her resentfully. 'I thought at first that you might be involved,' he says.

'Me?'

'You liked the smell. At least it seemed you did. And you had asked me if you might pick the blooms. But I checked with Nellie and she confirmed you had no part of it.'

Belle feels her whole body tighten. How dare he? 'That's quite the thing to admit, Mr Graham. Given I am now the keeper of your greatest secret,' she says crisply.

Graham hangs his head. 'I did not think you would take Nellie's place from her,' he says.

Belle regards him slowly. 'Because I am a kept woman? A kept woman requires absolute loyalty. And it is clear Nellie cannot offer me that.'

'And to whom is your loyalty due, Miss Brodie?'

'To myself first,' says Belle. 'And then my gentlemen.'

'So I am holding your secret too, am I not?' Robert Graham eyes narrow. He dislikes the fact that Belle holds such power over him.

'Perhaps,' Belle says smoothly, 'we will hold each other's.'

He is a terrible cull. He is the sort of man who might change his mind in an instant. Would he have realized his desire for Nellie if he had not discovered that Ruari Innes had a mistress? And he clearly does not want to pay for her. In choosing a consort each man names his disgrace, she thinks, for he makes an admission. For someone of Graham's standing, to find his desires sated by a drab little maid is practically perverse.

Nellie appears in the doorway with her trunk – a small wooden box that fits under her arm. She owns little more than her Sunday best, a bible, a thin, silver neck-chain and a few ribbons.

'I can recommend Mr MacPherson on George Street for the making of financial arrangements,' Belle says.

'Arrangements?' Nellie repeats.

The girl does not have a clue, she thinks impatiently. 'He will be a go-between,' Belle explains. 'Make sure that Mr Graham takes you to formalize the arrangement he has agreed. You must go to Mr MacPherson's offices directly. Now. Do you understand?'

Nellie nods. 'Goodbye, miss,' she says.

'Goodbye.'

Belle considers giving the girl a gift. A bottle of oil, perhaps, but then Nellie never was interested in such matters and Belle has nothing musical to pass along. The girl has had the pick of Belle's small library but has never opened a single book. 'Perhaps I shall see you at a recital,' Belle says, without feeling, for she does not generally attend musical events.

She watches from the window above as Nellie leaves by the front door and John hands her into the carriage. Mr Graham does not look up as he follows her. For a moment she worries for the girl but it is not her business. Had Nellie come to her first, she would have advised the girl to make him work harder to win her, so he might value what she has given. To see to the lawyer's arrangements before anything, as Belle did herself all those years ago. Nellie has made a whore of herself rather than a prize. But, Belle thinks, she owes the girl nothing – Nellie told Graham what she thought she knew about Belle and the flowers, and that feels like a betrayal, albeit a lucky one. Belle blesses the instinct that prevented her from including Nellie in what she was up to. She flops down on the sopha and regards her empty hock glass. She has done her best.

She leaves it ten minutes and then rings the bell. She expects Mrs Grant to arrive to make an arrangement for a new maid. Perhaps they will promote Claire and find a new kitchen skivvy for the time being. That will be easier. So she is surprised when the door opens and it is Mhairi MacDonald who is standing, somewhat out of breath, on the threshold.

'Miss?' pants Mhairi. 'Oh, miss, I went to Tanfield and the boy is not there, and the shed is in disarray.'

Belle sits up. She feels as if she is living under a strange astrological combination. One primed for chaos.

'It is gone. Or at least, I cannot find it. The bottle of oil,' Mhairi continues. 'It seems to have disappeared.'

Belle lays her hand on the bell again. Whatever next? she thinks. She will send Jamie to find out what on earth has been going on.

Chapter Thirty

The morning the king's visit is confirmed, Johann von Streitz does not stand on ceremony but bursts from his carriage, waltzing up the steps at North Castle Street and through the front door. Sir Walter and Lady Charlotte rise from their breakfast as he comes into the room. 'We have nine days,' Johann announces, pulling the king's missive from his tailcoat. Scott laughs. He flings his arms around the German and kisses his cheek before dancing a jig with Lady Charlotte, right there at the breakfast table. The plates abandoned, he rushes out, his greatcoat put on by unseen hands. Johann follows. All their tentative arrangements must be immediately firmed. There is, as Sir Walter keeps saying delightedly, much to do. Still he cannot resist telling people he passes in the street, ordering the carriage to go slow and leaning out to spread the news as he spots friends on the pavement. Pedestrians on George Street, Frederick Street and Princes Street clasp their hands and change their plans in order to chase their tailor or have their coaches decked with Union flags. After all this time it seems so soon, so sudden.

The news spreads across the city more quickly than the day that Robert Burns's bastard was unmasked. Within an hour or two, pamphlets declare it, hot off the presses at Cowan's Printworks. In public houses spontaneous bursts of 'God Save the King' break out and reels are danced down the darkest closes. Sir Walter's full programme of royal events is made public at last and is talked of everywhere from New Town nurseries to Old Town garrets. The news is at last abroad that the Honours – the country's crown jewels, which were thought lost – have been tracked down by Sir Walter at George's command. The ruby sceptre, ceremonial sword and gem-studded crown were hidden from Oliver Cromwell's marauding troops more than a century before, walled deep in the bowels of Edinburgh Castle. This subterfuge was so effective that the exact location of the treasures had been forgotten. Now the Honours will be paraded around the city before being presented to the king. George is looking forward to it. He has scribbled, *I think I shall look rather grand wearing the crown of Scotland,* and von Streitz has allowed Sir Walter to read this part of the king's letter.

Left behind with the kidneys and eggs in the warming tray as the city explodes into activity, Lady Charlotte summons her maids into the morning room at North Castle Street and calmly enjoins them in the matter of her wardrobe. Material has been sewed into an array of new gowns and jackets, but these require final fitting. Her diamonds must be cleaned and all shoes and boots polished. The Scotts will stay at Dalkeith Palace for part of His Majesty's visit and the luggage must be readied.

'We have only a shade more than a week,' Lady Charlotte says. 'Everyone must work on Sunday.'

The maids grumble though they are more excited than most – the Scotts' personal servants stand a good chance of catching a glimpse of the royal party and, for that matter, meeting the royal servants. Still, it is not much notice and there will be little sleep now with everything there is to do. The Scotts' plump, Irish cook, Mrs Kelly, refills her pipe as she surveys the stores. 'The master will be known for his part in this,' she says thoughtfully, 'and we will not let him down.'

The news, however, does not reach Elizabeth and Clementina. At Inverleith House, tidings generally arrive because a member of staff brings them and nobody is out today beyond the bounds of the estate. Clementina does not take the *Scotsman* or the *Edinburgh Review*, sending for a publication only if there is something specific that she wishes to know. The guidance issued by Highland chieftains in the matter of wearing tartan – their ceremonial dress – has passed her by, but Clementina does not pay much mind to such things.

The sun is high by the middle of the morning and Clementina has arranged for Duncan to accompany her to the southern fringe of the estate, where the Water of Leith flows along the boundary. She has a plan to divert the water and create a fishpond on Rocheid land. Such an endeavour, if large enough, might be stocked with eels, and Lady Clementina has a fancy for elvers sautéed in butter more regularly than is currently managed.

'Mrs Rocheid tells me you have a sweetheart,' she says jovially as they walk across the lawn and down the slope towards the water. The coachman nods.

Clementina grins. 'You are your father's son,' she says wistfully. 'Have you ever considered penning verse?'

'No, ma'am,' Duncan says stoutly. 'Never.'

'Perhaps you might try. Think of the Allan Ramsays, father and son. These things run in the blood,' the old lady says.

Down by the rushing water, Clementina directs him to a patch of low-lying ground where a channel might be dug. 'We will need to move the lavender,' she says, indicating the site of Duncan's first meeting with Mhairi. 'But that will grow anywhere, and besides, it may be more useful to set it near the wash-house where the girls have most cause to use it. I shall instruct the gardener.'

Staring at the lavender bushes, Duncan does not, at first, see the old lady fall into the swell. The bank is muddy, and with a splash, she disappears down it almost like a magic trick. It is cold, Clementina thinks in some confusion as the water soaks her frock. She opens her mouth but discovers she can make no sound. Her voice will simply not obey her, and her body is quivering uncontrollably. One of her shoes comes off and is washed downstream. As she watches it, she wonders if she is suffering an apoplexy but cannot quite think her way to the end of that idea.

Duncan turns.

'Lady Clementina?' he says and hesitates for a moment, standing over her on the riverbank. She sees his face transmute into that of his father as if Rabbie Burns were before her, large as life. She hears a voice greeting the dead poet. It is her voice – not as it is now, in age, but as it was decades ago. 'Why, Mr Burns, you have every woman in the city a-quiver, I'm sure.' Did she ever say such a thing? Behind the figure of Mr Burns she sees David Hume, as she last remembers him, wearing a salmon-pink turban, bustling up the High Street, forever late for an engagement. Has he not been dead these last forty years? she thinks as he disappears down a vennel opposite the Royal Exchange. Her mouth fills with water. Her hair falls soaking around her shoulders. She cannot feel the cold anymore.

It crosses Duncan's mind that with nobody around he could have his revenge now, for his sweetheart is none of Lady Clementina's business and the old lady has done nothing the past weeks but torment him about his father. But his anger cannot induce him to leave an icy sheet unrolling over such an old woman for more than a second or two. That, he knows, would be murder. She puts up her hand to grasp a coarse wisp of long grass that trails in the water from the bank, but she is too frail to lay hold of it and Duncan wades in and hauls her to safety.

She feels the grass against her back where he lays her down, but she does not register when he slaps her lightly on one cheek and then the other. She wants to tell him that he is no longer in her service for she knows that he hesitated, only a moment, but still. She cannot form the words. 'Lady Clementina!' he says but though her eyes are open she does not respond. He hoists her over his shoulder as if she were a hock of ham and makes for the house, where he marches into the kitchen and lays the old woman on the table. The kitchen maid shrieks, and Cook chastises her. 'Fetch Mrs Rocheid,' she directs one of the upstairs girls, and then snaps at Duncan, 'Quick! Fetch the doctor!' He feels glad he can do something to make up for his hesitation.

As Duncan heads back out of the door, the staff rally, moving Lady Clementina upstairs into her bedroom, peeling off her clothes, drying her, and warming her nightgown by the fire before dressing her in it. Inside her mind, Clementina is dancing in and out of the rooms at Inverleith House as if there were a ball tonight and the musicians had arrived early. Only intermittently does she see Elizabeth's face, the tears in her cousin's eyes. And then Dr Fraser and James Rocheid, smoking in her chamber, such a cheek! She wants to tell her nephew that Mr Burns was rude. That he did not rush to help her when she fell. That he should take over her project for the fishpond for it will be to the benefit of the estate. But she can get out none of it, not even when James Rocheid calls for Duncan and rewards him with a half-crown for saving her from the swell. Rewards him indeed!

Dr Fraser bleeds her, but it is no use. She could have told him that, if only she could speak. She watches impassively as the pottery bowl fills with her blood and the doctor bandages her arm. She finds suddenly that she has much to say. To dear Elizabeth especially for she wants to counsel her. To the farmhands regarding the summer's crop of berries. To Duncan to berate him for treating her ill. To her nanny, who has been dead, now she thinks on it, these last sixty years. To Constance von Streitz in the matter of her grandson. To little Bobo, the terrier – her father's favourite hunting dog, skewered by a redcoat the year after Culloden. She has never had so much to say her whole life, it seems, as now, when she can get none of it out. But she knows that Elizabeth is sitting next to her and that the sky has darkened.

Elizabeth mops Clementina's brow with a damp muslin cloth and wets the old woman's lips with a Greek sponge soaked in water and brandy until finally, exhausted, she falls asleep in the chair. But Clementina does not want to sleep. She is afraid that if she does so, she may never wake. She only wants to break through the glass that appears to have settled around her, preventing her from moving. She opens her mouth, or thinks she does, and closes it again, like a fish caught on dry land.

Later, when Elizabeth wakes in the night, and shifts uncomfortably in the chair, Clementina is lying absolutely still with her eyes open like a corpse. The house is quiet. Beyond the window, an owl hoots. Elizabeth stands over the prone body of her cousin in the long, dark silence. This is the woman she came to Edinburgh for, she thinks, and now Clementina is leaving. Dr Fraser said the apoplexy was violent. James Rocheid left as quickly as he could. Elizabeth's eyes fill with tears, for she does not wish to be here by herself in this huge, empty house. In the hallway she can just make out the slow tick of the grandfather clock. She shivers and fetches a cashmere stole from the chest and a rug to cover her knees. It is a matter of waiting. Edinburgh tonight seems very far away and no company at all. 'I am here,' she whispers sadly, unaware that Clementina can hear her. 'And, without you I am entirely without friends.'

Long past midnight, Duncan creeps away from Inverleith House. Confused by his hesitation to help the old woman, and mired in shame because of it, he seeks sanctuary and for him that can mean only one thing – Mhairi. The couple take a moonlit stroll along the river, past the distillery. The darkness does not matter to Mhairi, but Duncan feels shielded by it, wearing the black sky like a velvet cloak. His soul feels heavy and his stomach turns. He might have let the old woman die and all because she mentioned Robert Burns overmuch and took an interest in his love for Mhairi. He feels ashamed, but the events of the day have incited him to tell his sweetheart everything. Tonight there might be absolution, unless she tells him to go and never come back.

'Mhairi,' he says, his chest heavy, 'I have something to say.'

Mhairi motions towards the riverbank. 'Shall we sit here?' she asks. The weather has been dry, and the scent of the lavender rises towards them. 'We could wade over,' she suggests.

'No,' says Duncan. All he can see is the old woman's eyes, glassy with lack of recognition as she lies unresponsive near the spiked purple of the bushes. 'If we are to sit, let's go to the grass by the rushes.'

They walk further along and settle on the bank. Mhairi sings a song in Gaelic, syncopated to the water's flow. His heart feels as if it will burst with love. When she falls to silence, he blurts it out. 'My father was a farmer,' Duncan says steadily. 'But my mother had a dalliance with a poet. Robert Burns.'

Mhairi's face lights. 'What? "Auld Lang Syne"?' she says. '"To a Mouse?"'

'Aye,' Duncan confirms. 'They say I am his bastard.'

'Why do they think that?'

'My mother said so. On her deathbed. I look like him, they say.'

Mhairi reaches out and feels his face but she cannot tell if it is true, for she has never seen the likeness of Mr Burns Senior. 'Why did you no tell me?'

'It's just what everyone assumes.' Duncan's temper rises. 'It's shameful and I'm sick of it. Dirty gossips the lot of them. People treat me as if it's their secret or it's not a secret at all it's just a . . . joke.'

Mhairi lays her palm on Duncan's chest. She feels his heart pounding through the linen. 'Wheesht,' she says. 'Who cares what people say? My parents never married. They made an irregular marriage, mind. But I like the kirk. The smell of wood and wax. Though my father would never step inside. I don't care who your father is or isn't, Duncan. Some would consider me a bastard too, you know.'

Duncan looks as if he might cry.

'You should hae told me,' Mhairi adds. 'If we are to marry.'

He chokes. For this is what he has wanted but has not been able to voice.

'Marry?' he repeats.

'You're not out with me past midnight for any other reason, I hope.'

He kisses her for the first time, full on the lips. She tastes of milk fresh from the cow, warm and comforting. Of hot bread and butter. Of goodness. She touches his face before pulling back.

'I want to,' she says frankly, 'but we maun be married first.'

Mhairi, it turns out, is more respectable than her parents.

Duncan takes her hand. He stares at the moon, waxing tonight though still thin. He wishes she could see the sky with its magnificent sprawl of stars. 'I'll have the banns read,' he says. 'I can do it tomorrow.'

'And then what?'

'We will be married.' His stomach jumps. He can scarcely believe it.

'Where shall we live?' she asks.

Duncan has not dared to plan any further than this moment. The thought of bringing Mhairi to live on the Rocheid estate, he realizes, is not appealing. He curses himself for not wading into the water sooner. The old woman is not dead, but she is haunting him.

'Where would you like to live?' he asks.

Mhairi considers. 'I'd like my own place,' she says. 'I am tired of working for Mr Stein and for Miss Brodie. Always being at the whim of others.'

'I have savings,' Duncan says. 'I could get us a place.'

'I have savings too,' Mhairi echoes. 'But what about your work?'

'I almost let Lady Clementina drown today,' he admits. 'I did not rescue her as quickly as I should have. I have had enough of working for the Rocheids.'

Mhairi lies back on the grass, listening to the soothing sound of the river. 'I would prefer my husband was not tried for murder,' she says smoothly. 'It seems that neither of us is suited to service much longer.'

'You have the right of it,' Duncan confirms.

'You'd have let her drown, you say?'

Duncan dissembles. 'I couldnae,' he admits. 'But I thought of it.'

'Och,' says Mhairi, 'we all do that! I have a mind to set up on our own. Not a distillery for that would be beyond our means. But should we start a wee brewery, Duncan? I shall make the beer and you shall barrel and drey it?'

'Here?'

'I have heard,' Mhairi says slowly, 'that there is land to be had near Holyrood, below Cowan's Printworks, and that it is not expensive.'

Duncan tries to recall where the printworks is located. It is run, he seems to remember, by a widow and has doubled in size since the death of her husband.

Mhairi continues. 'We could take rooms there too. I have heard there is fancy accommodation nearby at a cut price, now the gentry have moved to this side of the old loch.'

Duncan leans heavily on his elbow and searches her face. He kisses her neck and she bats him off. 'After,' she says, laying her hand seductively in his lap and giving his leg a squeeze. 'I have near forty pounds English,' she says. 'And more to come if only I can get Miss Brodie's perfume finished.'

Duncan watches the river flowing, the small white crests glowing in the darkness where the current breaks. 'A brewery,' he says. 'Aye. I don't have near the savings you do. Nine pounds, twelve shillings. But I could maybe get more. I saw Miss Brodie when the flowers were taken. And the magistrate's men have been asking about it. She's a fine lady and might pay for my silence for I am sure she should not have been abroad and was up to mischief.'

Mhairi hoists herself onto her elbows. 'Are you daft?' she says. 'I have another twelve guineas coming from Miss Brodie. You cannae turn her over. There's no elegance in that. I can see it will be me who will manage our business. Mind,' she adds, 'you might leave me to mention the matter and see if the lady would make my bonus fifteen guineas. For then it would not be a matter of blackmail.'

'You should push her to twenty,' says Duncan. 'I'm sure your perfume will be braw.'

The ton frustrates his understanding. If Duncan had money to burn, he would not be spending it on a bottle of scent, that is for sure. Mhairi reaches into her bodice and withdraws a tiny vial. She dabs a smear of oil just below her ear and it opens on the air, the smell of strawberry and cinnamon and gorse flowers. Duncan reaches over and strokes her neck, then he leans in and kisses it again. Mhairi sighs seductively.

'It's no right, though,' she says.

'I would never . . .' he pulls back.

She laughs. 'I meant the perfume. The kiss was grand. The scent is still coming.'

She gets to her feet and smooths her skirts. 'You best chum me home,' she says. 'I am tired and tomorrow we are malting barley.'

Duncan takes her arm and they walk back to the house where Mhairi lodges, each aware of the movement of the other's body. The landlady is dozing by the kitchen fire as they come in. The embers glow. The kitchen smells of carbolic soap and straw and the baking that has been done earlier in the day.

'Duncan's Daddy was Robert Burns. The poet,' Mhairi tells her when she wakes.

'I heard that,' the woman yawns. 'I didnae like to say though I can see it around the eyes. Very handsome.' She gets up from her chair and pulls a thick book off the shelf. *Collected Works of Robert Burns.* 'Would you sign it?'

Duncan finds that he does not tense at the mention of Rabbie Burns. He does not care. The old poet may be his father, or he may not. The only thing that matters now is that he is affianced to Mhairi MacDonald. He laughs. 'Sign it? All right.'

The woman fetches a pot of ink and a tatty quill and Duncan signs his name with a flourish.

'They say that Mr Burns had more than one bastard and where the mothers couldnae manage them, his wife took them to raise with her own bairns. But you were not raised in Ayrshire.'

'No,' Duncan confirms. 'My Ma looked after me, and her husband, my father, took me as his own.'

'She must have loved you.'

Duncan glows. She did. And his father did too.

'Mr Stein has asked me to keep him informed if Mhairi has gentlemen callers,' the woman admits.

Mhairi sits at the kitchen table. 'Oh, aye?' she says. Mr Stein sees her as an asset and a suitor might pose a threat to his interests. He considers Mhairi's talented tastebuds his property.

'Have you told him about Duncan?'

'No,' the woman admits. 'That doesnae seem right. A young couple like you. Now you're in, I'll to bed.'

They wait for the door to close and the sound of her footsteps on the stair.

'I'll post the banns tomorrow,' Duncan says. 'I'll find out about the land.' He lowers his head to her hand and kisses it.

'Our very own brewery. MacDonald and . . .' Mhairi hesitates. 'Duncan, what is your family name?'

'Tennent,' he says. 'That's my real father. Not Mr Burns.'

'MacDonald and Tennent,' she tries it out. 'Tennent and MacDonald.'

Duncan would like it to be Tennent's alone. It has a ring to it, but in Scotland a woman has the right to her own surname. He will not argue about that. He gets up.

'I'll leave you to sleep,' he says and kisses her cheek. 'Goodnight.'

He turns to go. The walk home this evening will feel like a dream. He will practically float his way back to the hayloft for Mhairi MacDonald will be his. She has offered him absolution and he has accepted it.

Chapter Thirty-One

Despite Belle's enquiries, the magistrate's men hold Edzel McBain in the Bridewell gaol for two days before admitting they have him. It is said that the cells at the Bridewell are cold as winter, no matter that it is summer now, and that the food is worse than at the old Tolbooth – porridge and sour milk twice a day and watery soup with stale bread. Yet, despite the two days of his incarceration feeling like the longest of his life, Edzel holds firm and refuses to answer their questions. After the first day they leave him alone save for a snide comment as the jailer passes. When Belle is finally allowed in with Jamie, Edzel stands so close to the icy iron bars that he almost gets frostbite. Belle looks quite the lady in the dim light with her leaf-green spencer and demure bonnet with wreaths of silk daisies. She looks like summer.

'Edzel,' she greets him gently and nods at Jamie, who hands Edzel some pies and a flacon of small beer wrapped in a linen through the bars.

Edzel breathes in. She is wearing the citrus blend. He has not smelled anything at all in the last day, which has been a relief, his nose becoming accustomed to the stink of unwashed bodies and the putrid latrine in the corner of the cell. Belle, on the other hand, smells as if she is made of nature, sweet and free. She smells of life.

'You remember my promise?' she asks.

He nods.

'You will be up before the magistrate tomorrow and I have engaged a man to speak on your behalf.'

'Tomorrow?' he repeats. He feels sick, a wave of dread flowing through him. His hand quivers.

'You should not have struck the officer, Edzel.'

'I know.' He panics that she will not be able to get him off. Is that what she means?

Belle leans closer and lowers her voice. 'Where is the oil? Do you know?' she whispers.

He nods. 'McNab has it,' he says. 'I asked him to keep it safe.'

Belle blanches. William McNab is the person outside her circle most likely to recognize the scent.

'I could not risk them finding it. It seemed the safest thing to do,' Edzel continues.

Belle accepts this. There is no measure in berating him now. She holds his gaze. 'All right,' she says.

She hopes at first the magistrate will be a friend of her brother's, but Joseph is a confirmed Whig and liberal magistrates in Scotland are rare. There is one fellow, she recalls, who she met whilst dining at Charlotte Square but he is out of town presently, visiting relations in Dorset for the summer, clearly disinterested in the melee that surrounds the king's visit. Nonetheless Belle instructs Mr MacPherson and confirms she will pay the boy's legal fees and any fine that Edzel's outburst attracts.

'He has a future,' she tells the solicitor.

MacPherson was recommended to Belle when she first arrived in Edinburgh as a man who not only could be trusted, but whom it was impossible to shock. He has handled Belle's business since her first transaction and has proved a tomb for his clients' secrets. She wants to ask him if Nellie has succeeded in her contract with Robert Graham, but she knows he will not answer such a question. As she tells him about Edzel, though, he raises an eyebrow. It is the first time she has ever seen him so animated.

'I have taken an interest in Edzel these last three or four years and have seen to his education,' Belle adds. 'I intend to fund him through a university degree in medicine, if he can pass the exam.'

MacPherson clears his throat and shifts behind his mahogany, leather-topped desk. The air in his office feels grey and powdery like an old solicitor's wig and he sits, pink and porky, contained within it.

'Why?' he asks. 'What is the boy to you?'

'He is useful running messages and he processes ingredients for the bathing oil I told you about. I like him. He has promise.'

MacPherson's eyebrow is exercised again. The bathing oil seems to him quite the unnecessary nonsense, even though the endeavour has of late enhanced Miss Brodie's already robust finances. It is, however, beyond the scope of his understanding. Most of his clients make their money from land or the sorry business of slaving in the colonies. Aristocrats every one of them. Belle is unusual. He took her on for the sake of her brother, though he has come to admire her enough to overlook what he views as her moral limitations.

'I will engage an advocate to speak for the lad,' he says. 'Although there is no question he is guilty. You know that?'

'He was provoked to attack the man. The officers were all round Canonmills asking questions for days. They baited him.'

'The boy had drink taken. I understand he bought a quantity of small beer from a hostelry nearby.'

'I will pay the fine,' Belle repeats. 'He's a good lad, Mr MacPherson. He does not deserve his life to be ruined over a single misdemeanour.'

MacPherson nods. 'We will try to avoid a custodial sentence.' He almost asks whether it is Belle's preference to allow the boy to be flogged, which will cost her nothing. But the scuttlebutt around the legal clubs is that the thief flogged on the High Street the other day will be the city's last. Flogging has too much of the theatre about it and is not considered in keeping with modern sensibilities. The criminal becomes a celebrity. The lad who stole his mother-in-law's candlesticks has not had to buy himself a drink since they released him off the scaffold. Belle draws the solicitor's attention back to the point.

'Think of the japes other young gentlemen get up to that are attributed to high spirits,' she says. 'This lad will learn his lesson, but we should not ruin his life just because his father is a porter rather than a lord. As I say, he has promise.'

Mr MacPherson takes a note. 'I will see to it that we procure a character reference from his tutor,' he says. 'I take it you will be willing to pay?'

'Yes. I shall give him a reference myself. He is a hard-worker and trustworthy. I have never had any trouble on his account before.'

Mr MacPherson pauses. He is unsure how to put it to Miss Brodie that a character reference from a courtesan is more like a character assassination when given in court.

'Perhaps we could arrange for your brother to speak for him?' he manages at length.

Belle understands immediately. 'I shall see to it,' she says. 'I shall go to Charlotte Square directly.'

It is to Belle's credit that she undertakes these arrangements for Edzel before making any attempt to retrieve her oil, but upon leaving her brother's house, having bent Joseph to her will, she instructs Jamie to make straight for the Garden. It is late in the afternoon and the men are eating bread and cheese near the hut as the carriage pulls up, its long shadow providing much sought-for shade.

'Miss Brodie,' McNab greets her.

Belle dismounts. 'I wonder, Mr McNab , if you would be kind enough to show me your poppy beds?' she says. The poppies are planted in the south-west corner of the site –far away from everything else. While all the plants in the Garden have medicinal purposes, these are the only ones that are regularly harvested and sold though the Garden grows the poppy in relatively small quantities.

'Of course,' McNab acquiesces.

Belle waits until they are out of the way. With the flowers in bloom everywhere the Garden looks magnificent. She feels someone ought to stage a concert here, among the colourful beds. As they round the corner, the poppies come into view – a flash of frail red petals like a burst of fireworks.

'I understand my boy left something in your care, Mr McNab?'

The gardener shakes his head. 'He left nothing with me.'

Belle bites her lip. She likes McNab, and if he wishes to play it this way it will be awkward.

'I am prepared to pay to retrieve the item,' she offers. 'It is only right.'

McNab assures her that he has no knowledge of the matter to which Belle is referring and therefore cannot claim payment. 'I understand your servant was taken. That there was an affray?' he asks, changing the subject.

'He had drunk too much and the magistrate's men taunted him. I have engaged a lawyer to speak on his behalf. It is most peculiar, for Edzel told me, Mr McNab, that he entrusted the item to you.'

McNab cannot respond to this. He stops, for they have reached the limit of the poppies, which are swaying in the breeze. 'They have no scent, you know,' he motions towards the flowers. 'Was there something you wanted to know about them?'

Belle hovers. 'I wanted to speak to you,' she admits frankly.

McNab looks uncomfortable. He likes Miss Brodie, but he is aware of her profession. 'Mr Graham, I'm sure, would want me back at my post,' he says.

Belle considers. 'Mr Graham owes you a pay rise as I understand it.'

McNab blushes.

'I did not mean to make you uncomfortable, Mr McNab. But Mr Graham is a gentleman who does not always recognize the true value of things.'

'What do you mean?'

Belle loiters. 'I have a piece of information that may help you secure what I know he has promised and not delivered. I do not endorse blackmail . . .'

'Blackmail?' McNab sounds alarmed.

'Mr Graham has engaged my maid,' Belle tells him. 'He is setting her up in rooms on Young's Street, or at least he said he would.'

'What kind of rooms?' McNab frowns.

'The kind that are furnished with a bed.' Belle's eyes are gleaming. 'The girl has taken my profession.'

McNab finds that he is angry. Nellie is not eight years older than his eldest daughter, Catherine, and has always seemed a fine, honest girl. 'You sold her off? Miss Brodie, that is unconscionable.'

'I did not. I would rather she had not left my service, but a love affair was started, and Nellie was complicit. The point is, Mr McNab, that Mr Graham is paying her an allowance. It is equal to the sum he promised you by way of salary.'

McNab clenches and unclenches his fist. That Robert Graham would spend such a sum on his floozy devalues all the years of his own hard work. The night before, late, to placate Mrs Dickson, McNab allowed the old woman free run to take cuttings, not only of the aloe but also of the rarer plants that have come to the Garden recently from America and India. However, she chose to avail herself of little and is clearly still not satisfied. This morning she sent a curt note demanding he meet her again. He does not want to, but meet her he must. It feels as if keeping his head above water is a constant struggle.

'And he has taken rooms for her?'

Belle nods. All McNab can think is that he has a wife to support and several children and that he is a good twenty pounds a year short on being able to feed, clothe and educate everybody. Belle's maid is a slip of a lass and alone.

'Thank you, Miss Brodie,' he says.

Belle bides her time. 'What Edzel left with you is important,' she adds, trying one final time.

McNab sighs. 'I do not have it. I have not so much as seen the lad for weeks and then only in the street, by Tanfield. I thank you for what you have told me, but we must go back.'

He leads her along the path that runs below the arboretum in the shade. The sun today feels as if it has burst its bounds and is bleeding heat across the sky. The men have returned to work and on the doorstep of the hut, James McNab is whittling a stick with a small, sharp knife. McNab thinks that he must approach Mr Graham with the information Belle has imparted to him, but he does not wish to make himself a blackmailer. Perhaps he can find a way to shame the keeper into doing what is decent, which is after all the very thing that Graham said he intended all along. Still, it will be difficult to bring him to the point in such a way as to allow him dignity. McNab will need to employ all his diplomacy.

'I'm sorry I couldn't help you, Miss Brodie,' he says.

Belle gets into the carriage, handed up by Jamie, who gees the horses to take her home. At Warriston Crescent he hands her down again, only to be accosted by little James McNab, who appears as if out nowhere.

'How did you get here?' she asks, looking back in the direction of the main road as if the boy has cast a spell to get here.

'I jumped on the back, miss,' James explains. 'Edzel said you would give me a coin if I hid the bottle. He said you would be pleased.'

Belle feels her heart leap. 'Yes!' she says pinching his cheek. 'I am pleased. I am. What kind of coin would interest you, James? How about a silver sixpence?'

James has not the wit to negotiate. When things are offered, he generally accepts them gratefully for he is his father's son. 'Sixpence,' he says with a grin. 'Very generous, miss.'

Belle holds out her hand. 'Give the bottle to me, then.'

'I do not have it. I took it to Inverleith House with a thought to hide it among Mrs Rocheid's painting things. The bottle is not dissimilar to some that she uses.'

Belle's stomach sinks.

James continues. 'When I got there Lady Clementina took it and said she would keep it safe.'

Belle is briefly buoyed by hope. Clementina would at least receive her were she to call. But then she recalls that the old woman has taken ill. Mrs Grant heard it from one of the maids at Inverleith House who she met at the blacksmith's when she took a copper pot for repair. 'The old woman cannot speak. They have tried everything, but she just lies there,' the housekeeper told her. 'She did not even hear the news – you know, about the king coming.' Belle hopes fervently that Clementina has made some kind of recovery.

Nevertheless, she pays James the sixpence and retreats into the house, calling for Claire as she enters. It has been quite the day, though she is closer to all the things she would like to happen. It is only a matter of pushing on.

Chapter Thirty-Two

Johann von Streitz ought to be busy with preparations but such is the industry of Sir Walter Scott and the comprehensive nature of the plans already agreed before His Majesty sent word of the royal arrival, that he finds that even though a date has been set, he still unexpectedly has time on his hands. The great and good of Edinburgh are in a state of frenzy and his correspondence pile has more than doubled. Anne Melville has taken to sending him dispatches that do not include invitations – merely updates upon the state of the family's readiness for His Majesty's visit and the excitement of her daughter, Jane, who will be coming out during the king's sojourn with the Buccleuchs. His Majesty, on the other hand, has become a less regular correspondent. Johann assumes that given that they will see each other in only a few days, there is little need for communication until then.

So when he hears from Dr Fraser, one of the palace's grace and favour tenants, what has happened to Clementina Rocheid, Johann immediately calls for a mount and makes for Inverleith House. Outside, he tarries, for he has not seen Elizabeth since she rejected him so roundly. Still, Clementina is a friend of his grandmother and he cannot countenance withholding service to a family friend in need. He sends word upstairs.

It takes a long time for Elizabeth to descend. James Rocheid, having rushed to the Inverleith estate when his aunt's health first failed, realized quickly he could do little other than pay Dr Fraser's bill, and returned quickly to his business in the New Town, which is to say, talking politics in the club room at the Royal Society and gambling after dinner. It did not cross his mind that he was leaving Elizabeth to nurse Clementina alone. She has seen nobody but the staff for the last two days. Clementina remains prone and silent. When his message reaches her, Elizabeth's cheeks colour that it is Johann von Streitz who should first consider her. She does not want to see him, but the message mentions the friendship between his grandmother and Clementina and that she cannot deny. She has not washed or changed her linens and she decides that she must present herself better than this to the immaculate Johann von Streitz. Currant Bun is sent to fetch a bowl of hot water.

Downstairs, waiting in the drawing room, Johann admires the sunny view over the city, the sky a milky blue. As time passes, there is movement at the door and he is disappointed to see the figure of Belle Brodie, loitering in a smart, pale spencer and dark hat.

'Herr von Streitz,' she says. 'You are calling on Mrs Rocheid today too?'

Johann bows. 'She has been a while,' he admits. 'I am not sure she wants to see me.'

Belle sighs. 'She definitely does not want to see me,' she says. 'It is awkward but Lady Clementina has something of mine. I hesitate to call for it but the matter is urgent.'

Johann wonders what can be urgent enough to disturb a woman recovering from an apoplexy. Belle looks around. She pauses at the door to the music room where she can see the table with Elizabeth's painting things, abandoned these last days. The small brown bottle is not upon it. Nor is it anywhere to be seen in the drawing room – on the mantle or any of the side tables. She can hardly rummage in the drawers and in a house of this size there is no telling where Clementina may have stowed the trinket.

'I wonder if I might leave you this,' Belle asks, proffering a note that she pulls from her reticule, 'to give to Mrs Rocheid when she comes down?' It is sealed with an embossed Brodie crest in green wax. 'Might you pursue the matter on my behalf? I do not wish to offend Mrs Rocheid by my presence . . .'

'Of course,' he says.

Belle looks relieved. She hands over the note. 'Well, it is best not to tarry,' she adds. 'It is nice to see you, Herr von Streitz. If Mrs Rocheid can bring herself to it, I should like the item returned to Warriston Crescent as soon as possible.'

Outside, Belle's carriage pulls away and Johann sits on the sopha with the note in his hand. Belle Brodie is bullish for having come on such a mission. Waiting here, he now feels a fool for having offered his service. He cannot understand why Elizabeth disdains him so. Nor why she fell out with Belle, with whom she had seemed such fast friends. The clock ticks and his attention turns to the note left by Belle. In all his time at the king's service, Johann has never read another person's sealed correspondence, but he is intrigued at what has passed between the women. He checks the hallway to be sure that nobody is about, then he opens it.

Dear Elizabeth [it says], *I am sorry to hear the news of Clementina's failing health. I know you will not wish to hear from me but an item of mine was entrusted to the dear lady by James McNab before illness overtook her. It is a small brown apothecary's bottle. I hope I might have it of you. Belle.*

Johann considers a moment and pockets the letter. It is not kind of Belle to pursue such a trivial matter at this time.

For all his doubt, when Elizabeth comes down he knows he has made the right decision, for it is apparent that she cannot tolerate further distress. She is thin and pale and looks tired, but his heart still leaps at the sight of her. He bows awkwardly.

'Herr von Streitz,' she says formally, her slim fingers fluttering as she readies herself to tell him that she is too occupied to receive callers. He does not let her continue.

'I came to help,' he says simply. 'That is all.'

'Help?' she repeats.

'You are alone, as I understand it. You should not be alone when your aunt is so ill.'

She steels herself to disagree and say something about the staff or that the doctor calls early each day and spends ten minutes inspecting Clementina, during the course of which Elizabeth discourages him from purging the old woman, who would never have welcomed such an intervention were she conscious. In any case, she finds she cannot get out the words and instead starts to cry and to her shame cannot stop. The nursing of the elderly is a lonely and trying business.

Johann gently takes her arm, but she pulls it back. 'I am not a whore,' she sputters. 'Please do not touch me.'

Johann blanches. Is that what she thought he was asking of her? He cannot quite believe it.

'You, Mrs Rocheid, are a lady. I hope there has not been a misunderstanding for you are the best lady I know,' he says soberly.

She continues to cry but lets him lead her to the seat beside the fireplace. He does not try to stop her weeping, merely kneels next to her as the tears stream down her cheeks and she gasps for breath. 'She's going to die,' Elizabeth says. 'I know she's old and it's part of God's plan, but I am fond of her. And I will be quite alone, you see.'

'If you felt I disrespected you, Mrs Rocheid, when I spoke the other day, that was my error.' He bows.

Elizabeth regards him, her face wet with tears. His words appear to have momentarily comforted her, until he adds, 'You must not forget to look after yourself,' and then she starts crying again. When she has control of her emotions at last, he suggests they ring for coffee.

Elizabeth sniffs. 'I fear Cook's coffee is not what you may be used to.'

He manages to stifle a smile. 'Ah yes,' he says, 'I recall the sandwiches.' The only meal he ever took at Inverleith House, a snack on the lawn a few weeks before – ham wrapped in a kind of vellum.

'Cook has improved,' Elizabeth cuts in. 'In her baking, at least.'

'You have instructed her?'

Exhausted and careworn, she merely nods. Johann thinks that she is the very model of accomplished womanhood. His mother could not have tutored the kitchen staff. They ring for tea, which arrives with syrup biscuits, a pleasant surprise.

'I see what you mean,' he says, biting into one and letting out an appreciative murmur as the sugar melts on his tongue.

'I do not know what to do,' Elizabeth admits. 'That's the worst of it. I simply sit there, next to her.'

'Perhaps you might allow me to read to Clementina?' Johann suggests. 'She likes poetry, does she not?'

'You could read to her in German. I'm sure it would remind her of her youth.'

'Gladly, if you have a book of German poetry.'

She gives a slim smile.

Although they cannot find any German books on the library shelves, Elizabeth admits him to Clementina's bedchamber and he recites some lines of von Goethe and Schiller that he remembers. Clementina lies impassive, pale upon the sheets, her breathing shallow. Elizabeth dallies in the bedside chair, listening to Johann's voice. 'What does it mean?' she asks, and he translates one of the Roman elegies.

Strength, generosity, courage become a man,
Ah, but deepest reticence becomes him more.

The time passes quickly and before he leaves, Johann asks if they might pray. It is the thing he most remembers from his grandfather's sick bed, his father leading the family in prayer as they kneeled around the frame. Elizabeth is moved. They pray, standing together, as if this is quite natural.

Then, taking his heart in his hands, he raises his eyes. 'I want you to say you forgive me,' he ventures. 'If I offended you it is my fault.'

Elizabeth hesitates.

'Please,' he insists.

'You must be busy,' she replies. 'I hear the king is coming.'

He will not be distracted. 'His Majesty is not here yet,' he says and promises he will call tomorrow and bring coffee beans so they might brew them together.

As he rises to leave, she touches his hand as he brushes past her. 'Perhaps it was I who misunderstood,' she says. Then she watches from Clementina's door as he sees himself down the stairs and when he's gone she sinks into the bedside chair and has to admit to her silent cousin that she feels braver.

Buoyed up by Elizabeth's forgiveness, Johann is nonetheless not one to let business slide. He makes a stop at Warriston Crescent to talk to Belle about the matter of her little bottle, but he is informed that Belle is not at home. Claire, the newly promoted maid, who, he notes, is not as pretty as Belle's last girl, declares that she cannot possibly say where the mistress has got to, nor when she might return. He decides not to wait but leaves his card, thinking he might catch sight of her carriage for the New Town is not very large and there are limited places a lady might go.

Belle, however, is not in the New Town this afternoon. An hour previously, she crossed the chasm of the old Nor Loch, which is slowly transforming from a mud pit into passable gardens in which the residents of Princes Street might promenade. The trees this year have grown beyond the spindly saplings that were first put in and provide at least some shade and interest. Lawns and herbaceous borders have been laid. On the mound, men on ladders are putting up bunting for the royal visit as Belle's carriage turns towards the magistrates' court where, this afternoon, Edzel's case will be heard. Jamie, who has delivered supplies to the boy daily, reports he is holding up and most grateful to Miss Brodie for keeping her word. Stout, she thinks, is the right word for Edzel. She is coming to admire the boy's fortitude.

Inside, the courtroom smells like an old church, of musty parchment and dusty robes. It is sunny outside which makes the interior feel shady. Mr MacPherson the solicitor is in place already sitting next to the advocate he has engaged on Belle's behalf, at a table in front of the bench. The magistrate's officers loiter in the doorway, ready to give evidence. As Belle slips in, past two or three casual observers, she realizes she is the only woman. She nods at Mr MacPherson, who looks like a pale pink ghost in the gloom, one comprised entirely of powder and black tailoring. The Reverend Mathieson enters and greets the lawyers, only nodding in Belle's direction. He is carrying a book, which he starts to read rather than talking to her. The reverend has always been torn, she thinks, accepting her money despite what he knows of her profession, which is precious little but enough for him to judge.

The magistrate enters and everybody rises. Gordon Strang Philips is sixty-two years of age and well-suited to his post. He is a man unencumbered by pity, who accepts no excuses for poor behaviour, not even his own. His whole life he has had an appetite for young men, but has never pursued it, marrying instead a dowdy woman, the daughter of a burgess, and siring three children by her, on three separate occasions. Of this matter, Mrs Strang Philips has made no complaint, being as much wed to her duty as to her husband and so devout that Sundays in the Philips house are rendered extraordinarily dull – 'the most boring place in Scotland' one of Philips's cousins called it when he had cause to stay.

Magistrate Philips pours himself a small glass of madeira and sips it joylessly before addressing the court. He peers at his notes. 'Bring in the prisoner,' he says. 'Edzel McBain. Charged with affray.' He sips again.

Edzel is pale in the dock. He has not washed since they took him and his jacket has become frayed. His skin is smeared in grime. He gives a nervous half-smile in Belle's direction and she curses that she did not think to bring him fresh clothes. She spent some time choosing her own outfit, a muslin dress with a plain, pale lemon spencer and a sober black hat – for she recognised it was important for her to look demure for this occasion. Edzel stands grubby but solid, turned towards the bench, his brown eyes steadily cast down. He sneezes and blows his nose on a rag.

The case proceeds at first as Belle expects. The officers give their evidence, buttering the pudding as if Edzel were a madman who had attacked them unprovoked. The magistrate questions them. 'What were you seeking when you interviewed Mr McBain?' he asks and they talk about their enquiries into the stolen flowers, a case which, they admit, has not yet been solved.

'So Mr McBain was under suspicion?' the magistrate asks.

The men shift. 'We interviewed several householders near the Garden,' the clean-shaven one says.

'But this boy was not under suspicion for the crime?'

The moustached officer seems suddenly much smaller. 'Mr McBain makes soap,' he says, 'and thus has an interest in flowers. His dwelling was on the likely path of the thieves back into the town.'

'Soap?' The magistrate caws as if he were a crow.

'Scented soap, sir.'

'The prisoner does not look as if he has been anywhere near soap. Not in some time.' Philips lets out a dry laugh that might be mistaken for a cough. 'And you were of the view that Mr McBain, having professional expertise in botanical matters and residing close by, may have been concealing something?'

The moustached officer nods. 'It was an instinct, sir.'

'Did you uncover any evidence?'

'No sir,' he admits. 'Mr McBain attacked us.'

'But you must have interrogated him after you had subdued his violence? Searched his . . .' Philips consults his notes, 'shed?'

The men remain silent.

'So we must assume that Mr McBain attacked you for some other reason than concealing a crime.'

'He had drink taken, sir.'

'I see.' Philips gulps down more port. It is going to be a long afternoon. 'Mr McBain?'

Edzel has been told not to speak. He looks up, however. The advocate jumps to his feet. 'Sir,' he says. 'As I understand it, Mr McBain had drink taken as the man says, and he admits that freely. But the officers baited him considerably and he lost his temper. This is uncharacteristic of the lad. Might I call his tutor, Reverend Mathieson, to attest to the boy's habitual sobriety?'

Philips looks Edzel over with a bemused expression, 'Tutor?' he says faintly.

'Yes, sir. Mr McBain is a promising student who hopes to pass the matriculation examination at the Medical Faculty in the coming year.'

Philips's gaze lingers on Edzel's frayed jacket. 'Indeed,' he says, dubiously. 'And how might he manage that? Does he have a benefactor?'

Magistrate Philips has always considered the practice of sponsorship of young fellows at the university suspect. He cannot see why a philanthropist might choose to pay fees for another man's son. Such arrangements have a whiff of intimacy that he finds quite terrifying. The advocate, however, is unaware of the magistrate's secret desires.

'Yes,' he confirms enthusiastically. 'He will be given an allowance by his current employer.'

'The . . .' Philips checks his notes again, 'soap manufacturer?'

Belle cannot stand the tension. When will they get to the point? She rises. 'I am his employer,' she says. 'I make the soap. And it is I who hope to see Edzel improve himself through hard work and education.'

Philips peers at her over the top of his notes. Mr MacPherson casts Belle an animated glance, and motions her discreetly to sit down. His sternness takes her aback.

'And your name, madam?' the magistrate asks.

'Isabel Brodie,' Belle trots out.

The advocate jumps up once more. 'Miss Brodie's brother has given a sworn affidavit as to the good character of the young man,' he says, with the paper in his hand. 'Might you like to see it?'

'Her brother?'

'A gentleman. Joseph Brodie of Charlotte Square,' Belle adds. 'The point is, sir, that Edzel McBain damaged neither property nor person. He was harassed by the officers and made an error of judgement. He should not have done so, but he has learned his lesson. I am sure of it. Have you not, Edzel?'

Edzel looks worried. He would never want to ignore Miss Brodie, but he has been told not to speak. Mr MacPherson impressed this upon him with great lucidity.

The magistrate takes Joseph's affidavit from the advocate. He surveys Miss Brodie. 'Why is your brother giving testament to the boy's character if you are his employer?' he asks. It is a fair question. Women, after all, in this Enlightenment city have legal currency and the right to speak up. The advocate coughs. The courtroom stops while he heaves and splutters. Mr MacPherson pours him a glass of burgundy and he downs it. 'Are you quite all right?' the magistrate asks.

'Yes, sir,' he says, but he sounds panicked and it is left up to Mr MacPherson to slowly rise and say something, anything, to move the issue on.

'What is it?' the magistrate is losing patience.

MacPherson looks apologetic. He glances at Belle. 'Miss Brodie sought Mr Brodie's help in this matter because of his standing,' he says. 'Mr Brodie is one of three investors in the New Town Building Company and heir to his father's concerns on the Leven Estate in Jamaica. Miss Brodie is his . . .' MacPherson coughs, 'well, she is Mr Brodie's half-sister.'

Philips takes a moment to absorb this information. The penny drops, albeit in slow motion. He looks at Belle with fresh eyes, surprised he was not able to ascertain from the moment of her entry into his domain that she was born on the wrong side of the bedsheet. Belle feels the discomfort like a weight on her chest.

'You may sit down, Miss Brodie,' the magistrate says coldly.

The officers stir, as if they want to add something but MacPherson anticipates them. If the magistrate finds out Belle's profession it will go badly for Edzel and, once spoken in court, will tarnish his own reputation as her solicitor. 'I would ask that we spare the lady's blushes and add no more to the matter of her involvement as it is not relevant. None of us, I'm sure, would seek to waste the court's time. But sir, what I would say, if my colleague would allow . . .'

The advocate motions for MacPherson to continue. He might as well now he has taken the floor.

'Miss Brodie has been a client of mine for some years. She is a lady who has broken the bounds of the circumstances of her birth. And she wishes to help this young man break his. This is Mr McBain's first offence. Not many boys from his background might say that. He is in steady employment at the soap manufactory and shows promise in his studies. He has genuine prospects and is not usually prone to high spirits. He has also admitted his guilt in the matter and has repented.'

The magistrate's eyes flick towards Edzel, who does indeed appear sorrowful.

'Very well,' he says. 'I cannot have boys attacking my men, however. He shall serve another week in the Bridewell and pay a fine of six shillings, which, as I understand it, his employer has agreed to cover on his behalf.'

The moustached officer lets out a yelp. 'But sir,' he says. 'That woman is . . .'

'Silence!' Philips booms. He will not have insubordination in his courtroom. 'And get the boy out of here.'

Outside, Belle waits for MacPherson and offers him a lift in her carriage back to his office.

'I have business to finish here, Miss Brodie,' the old solicitor says coldly. 'You have made matters most difficult. I asked you not to speak. You came close to losing us the case. You must try to contain yourself.'

'He is the one who almost lost it,' Belle snaps, pointing at the advocate. 'He did not make Edzel's case. Not one bit.'

'Please!' MacPherson proclaims, his cheeks more pink than usual. Belle thinks, annoyed, that he looks like a sausage in a wig. 'I shall arrange for the fine to be paid forthwith,' MacPherson continues. 'You will have your boy back in a week. That is an end to it.'

Belle turns tail and mounts her carriage, fuming at being treated like an incalcitrant child. It takes her until she crosses the highway at Queen Street Gardens to recall that both she and Edzel are in fact guilty of the greater offence of theft. And they have got away with it. Edzel need only last another few days in jail and Jamie can be sent to ease that with food, a book to read and a thick woollen blanket. Then he will have his freedom and Belle will add a small sum to the boy's allowance for his loyalty. This success, however, is muted for there remains work to do. They may have stolen the flowers and extracted their scent but she still does not have the oil.

As she closes the door behind her at Warriston Crescent, Belle feels a wave of weariness overtake her. She is sick of having to hide what she does. People are such snobs. It is ironic when she knows what most of them get up to. At least, she tells herself, she is honest, or honest enough. Her heart feels heavy and even the familiar scent of cinnamon and the burning of beeswax candles cannot soothe her. She climbs the stairs and hands her spencer to Claire, managing a smile, but she wants to crawl into bed and pull the Irish linen sheets over her head though it be only five of the clock.

'Bring my tisane,' she says.

'Miss . . .' Claire starts, but does not finish her sentence before Belle walks into the sitting room, where Mhairi MacDonald waits on the sopha.

'Mhairi,' she says. 'What are you doing here?'

Mhairi jumps to her feet, her hand on her stick. She has been waiting for over an hour and has had time to consider exactly how to phrase what she wants to say, though it be difficult. 'Miss Brodie. I am concerned about our scent. I have made twenty wee pools of it, but it is not . . .' Here she pauses, searching for the word.

'Real,' Belle comes to her aid. 'It does not feel real, does it? What we are making must have substance.'

'Exactly that,' Mhairi continues. 'It is as if there is no heart to it. It is a strange business this receipt. Perhaps I ought to start again with mint and cumin.'

Belle shakes her head. 'That will not work,' she sighs, falling onto the more comfortable chair. Mint affects women more than men and cumin does very little other than settle the stomach, and then only if it is swallowed. 'It must be strawberry, cinnamon and the pink peppercorn. It must be effective.'

'To be warm, you mean?'

'To invoke love. The smell of it. As we discussed.'

Claire comes into the room with tisane on a tray.

'Might I have the girl fetch you something?' Belle offers.

Mhairi shakes her head. 'What is that smell?'

'Pennyroyal. I drink it daily,' Belle replies but does not explain why.

Mhairi pauses.

'Was there something else?' Belle asks. 'I have located the oil but am yet to retrieve it. Tomorrow I will set myself to the task in earnest.' She can bear no more today.

'Well,' Mhairi starts, waiting for Claire to leave and close the door. 'I also came to assure you of my loyalty.'

'Indeed?'

'I am promised to a coachman. We are to be married,' Mhairi continues.

'Congratulations,' Belle replies drily, unsure where this is going.

'He was on his way home from calling upon me on the night of the robbery at the Garden. He has confided, miss, that he saw you and Edzel McBain at three of the clock or thereabouts, walking along Warriston Crescent from the highway.'

Belle's jaw hardens. 'Did he now?'

Mhairi's voice is like honey. 'I have assured him that a lady such as yourself would never be involved in anything underhand . . . and that you are a good employer. A generous employer. I admonished him not to cause any trouble. I hope I have done the right thing.'

Belle has had enough of today. It feels as if everyone wants money. Money, she knows, is the least interesting thing, and quite undervalues her true talents. 'I will not be blackmailed,' she spits.

Mhairi flusters. 'There is no question of blackmail. It is loyalty that had me silence him, miss. It is loyalty that brings me here. I have not asked for money. Save my agreed bonus, that is.' She waits a moment. 'Twenty guineas, was it?'

Belle sighs. 'The job must be completed before that will be paid, Miss MacDonald,' she points out. 'And as you say, we are a way off yet.'

'But I have remembered the sum correctly?' Mhairi presses.

Belle demurs. 'You can go now,' she adds coldly. 'I will send a message when I have the oil.'

For almost an hour Belle sips her tisane in silence. It is the closest she might come to prayer. Her books lie unopened. The periodicals on the side table remain unread. She does not think of bottles or paintings or instructions for the seamstress. She does not think of schemes to arouse Ruari or if she will seek a new second gentleman. The royal visit is irrelevant to her. She simply sits and sips.

When later she flops onto her bed without removing her dress, she hopes tomorrow will be a better day. She is about to pull up the quilt when Claire comes in.

'This just arrived, miss.'

Belle lets her pumps slip from her feet. They land on the carpet with a dull thud. She turns and takes the sealed note as Claire bustles off to put the shoes away. The letter is sealed with Ruari Innes's stamp. Belle clicks it open, hoping that he does not intend to call tonight. Now that she thinks on it, it has been more than a week since she saw him. And then he was not as enthusiastic as usual.

Inside the folded paper there is no note, only a banker's draft for a hundred guineas. She reads the draft slowly twice and turns it over, checking again inside the packet. No, he has included no explanation, not even a signature. Ruari, it seems is a coward. And one who has, she assumes, returned to his wife.

She remembers the night Elizabeth came to call, when she described Ruari's clumsiness with the ratafia. He caught himself out, she thinks, and lays the bank draft on the side table to deal with in the morning. A carefully worded letter from her should elicit a proper settlement, to which, in truth, she has no objection. She has been tired of the situation for longer than she realized. But now she must sleep. She lays the pillow under her head with a growl of frustration and focuses on the fact that Edzel will be free in a short while and that Elizabeth will hopefully send the small brown bottle upon which so much now depends. As languor grips her, she summons the vision of Mr Lunardi's balloon and climbs slowly aboard.

Chapter Thirty-Three

At night, with Clementina still prone on her mattress, the old lady becomes Elizabeth's confessor. The staff are abed, the household unsettled by her illness, for a dying woman is considered unlucky by some. Johann visits daily and Elizabeth is grateful for his company. Together they brew their own coffee and eat the biscuits she bakes in secret. In the dark Elizabeth has the curtains in Clementina's bedroom left open and the moon casts both light and shadow over the thick carpet in strange, sharp-edged patches. In this cold half-light, Elizabeth finds that she can talk frankly about her life with William, how he slapped her when she asked him where he'd been, how he assaulted her. 'I know he was your favourite,' she tells the old woman as she straightens the cover, 'but William did not like me, Clementina. Nor I him. Though I am glad my marriage brought me here. To this house and to you.' She squeezes the old woman's fingers as she talks about the little house in Richmond and counting pennies, hoping they would be enough, and baking her own bread. She sounds, she realizes, almost wistful. Then she runs over what happened on George Street with Belle. 'For money,' she laments. But, she confesses, 'for shame,' and despite Belle's profession, she finds she can say in the darkness that she misses the intimacy of their conversation. When she talks about Johann, she becomes coyer. 'He does not appear grand for all he lives in a palace,' she says. 'I wish you could tell me more about his grandmother and your youth. I wonder about Leipzig . . .' At last, all talked out to the cushion of silence, she falls asleep in the chair beside the bed.

The next morning the sky is blue as a field of forget-me-nots and Johann arrives at Inverleith House earlier than usual. Elizabeth is still at her breakfast – a tray of tiny pastries studded with plump raisins and a pot of coffee made at the table. He joins her. 'These are excellent,' he says, savouring his final bite. 'You have quite reformed the place.'

'In good ways and bad,' she admits, stirring a lump of sugar in her cup. 'I recall when I arrived the house was far tidier.' She stops. 'The first day I came, Clementina had run away from the maids. She was barefoot on the lawn.'

Johann smiles at the thought. 'How is your cousin today?'

Elizabeth looks less careworn than when he first called, but a shadow now crosses her face. 'The same,' she says. 'We cannot get any food into her. Dr Fraser says not to worry about it.'

Johann does not want to say this is a sign the old woman is quitting the world. 'Margaret managed to spoon in a little beef broth,' Elizabeth continues. 'It would not keep a cat alive.'

'Let's go and see her,' Johann says.

Upstairs the window is open in Clementina's room and Margaret sits by the bed, darning. She curtsies and excuses herself. There are two chairs at the bedside – the one to the left has become Johann's, while Elizabeth sits closer to the old woman, where she can stroke her hand. The breeze from the window is warm and smells of violets.

Johann is more sombre today. 'When the king arrives, I will have duties,' he says. It has been on his mind.

'You have been so kind,' Elizabeth replies.

He wants to tell her that it isn't only kindness. But he is afraid to startle her as he did before. Besides, a deathbed proclamation is hardly romantic. She has enough on her mind.

'How many days will His Majesty spend in Edinburgh?' Elizabeth asks.

The king's progress has been published in the newspapers and little else is spoken of abroad. It is touching, Johann thinks, that Elizabeth does not know.

'Ten days or so. Maybe twelve. His Majesty is his own man. I expect you will not wish to come to the ball now? Poor Clementina, she was looking forward to it.'

Elizabeth nods. 'You can tell me about it afterwards,' she says. 'I should like that.'

Johann pauses. 'When the king leaves, I will go with him,' he admits. 'I am at His Majesty's convenience.'

'To London?'

'He normally spends September in London but . . .'

'He is his own man,' Elizabeth finishes the sentence with a smile.

'He likes the pavilion at Brighton and sometimes a week at Windsor,' Johann says. He does not tell Elizabeth, but in Brighton the refurbishment of the Royal Pavilion has taken decades, and has as good as bankrupted the nation. Louisa Adams, wife of the Secretary of State of the United States of America, declared the building more erotic than a Turkish seraglio, a remark that greatly pleased His Majesty. 'You lived in London, did you not,' he asks, 'when you were married?'

'Richmond,' Elizabeth blushes. 'It was hardly London and more modest than this house. My husband left me in meagre circumstances. The Rocheids took me in.'

She looks forlorn as she admits this.

'I do not like to think of you that way, Elizabeth,' he says.

'What way?'

'In need.'

Elizabeth gets up. She opens the window a crack further. Two laundry girls are making their way to the banks of lavender at the Water of Leith to air linens in the sun. 'You will have the honour of accompanying the royal party, will you not?' she says.

'Indeed,' he confirms. 'The king will reside at Dalkeith Palace. I have seen the rooms and they are magnificent. The Buccleuchs have a dining chamber on the first floor. I know His Majesty will like that. He is fond of palaces and always looking for new ideas for his own.'

'Do you like palaces?' she asks simply.

It occurs to Johann that he has never considered the matter before. For the most part, he realizes, he does not. 'I was brought up in a palace,' he admits. 'A schloss, in fact, but to be frank I think I prefer something smaller.' He decides to risk saying it. 'Like here. There are adequate rooms, a good stable and a deal of privacy.'

She is about to say something about her own preferences but is halted as Clementina stirs in the bed. It is the first time she has moved since she was tucked in. Slowly, the old woman lifts one hand, opens her eyes and squints at her fingers.

'Clementina!' Elizabeth proclaims joyfully and rushes back to the bedside. 'You are awake.'

Clementina stares at Elizabeth, then past her towards Johann, but her gaze is vague.

'Let me help you,' Elizabeth insists. 'If you sit up perhaps you might take something to drink?'

Clementina grips Elizabeth's arm tightly and pulls her urgently down. 'You have been with me. I have known that you were here,' she says hoarsely.

'You heard us then? When we were reading to you?'

'All of it,' Clementina says with finality and Elizabeth feels a flush of shame and terror that Clementina will tell Johann what she said in the night. She thinks she might die if the old lady does.

'First,' croaks Clementina, 'James should not have given the half-crown. Let me be clear about that. I will leave you to see to it.'

Elizabeth's forehead wrinkles. She has no idea what Clementina is talking about.

'Second,' the old woman presses on breathlessly, 'I bequeath you my jewels. There is no written will. The Rocheid amethysts, my garnets and the pearls. They are in my jewellery case. The girl will show you. You are the last Rocheid lady, Elizabeth, and I will not have James selling our family legacy or giving my things to some lassie he will never marry. It is my property and I leave it to you with no entail upon it. You must witness this,' she says to Johann. 'And my capital besides. It is not much but you shall have it. *Verstehst du mich?*'

Elizabeth turns to Johann.

'I understand,' he says solemnly. 'I shall stand witness.'

'Now you must go,' Clementina dismisses him, her breathing becoming increasingly laboured. 'I want to speak to my cousin.'

Johann bows formally and quits the room. Seeing him leave, Elizabeth feels suddenly bereft. Clementina is not normally so directive. There is something stark about it. It scares her.

'We should send for Dr Fraser,' Elizabeth says.

'That sawbones!' Clementina gasps with some effort and gives a rattle that passes for a laugh. 'I hope you do not expect me to call for a minister.' Her breathing is becoming more shallow. 'I have failed you,' she says.

'Failed me? Clementina, you saved me. If I had not come here . . .'

'Bread and water,' the old lady cuts in. 'A bed. That's all we offered you. What you needed was goodness. I see that now. Nobody ever believed in you, my dear, and that is what a woman needs more than anything.'

Elizabeth finds she is crying as Clementina continues.

'I lost a friend once because my father did not approve. She was Hanoverian, which did not play well with him. And she was a bawd, or so he judged her. A kept woman. I regret cutting her now though she is long dead. Time is so short, you see.'

'But . . .' Elizabeth starts to protest, but the old lady tightens her grip.

'The people who matter are the people who notice. Who listen. The gowns do not matter. The titles neither. The opinion of society. It is nothing. Nothing at all.'

'We must try to get something into you,' Elizabeth says desperately, for Clementina is pale. She turns to the side table where the decanter of brandy has sat unopened these last days. Her hands shake as she pours a glass. Clementina's breathing sounds like some-body climbing a set of rickety stairs. Elizabeth holds the glass to her lips and Clementina sips.

'Poor, dear Mr Hume,' the old lady smiles weakly. 'He so enjoyed brandy.'

'Let me call for a bowl of broth.'

Clementina shakes her head. 'Tell Herr von Streitz to pass an account of my death to his grandmother. She will want to know. Tell him I remember her. I have wasted these last years. I should have been in company . . .'

'In company?'

'Say I hope she enjoys the scent. Say it reminded me of talking with her by the fireside.' The old woman coughs. 'That is why I had him dispatch it to her.'

Elizabeth reaches for the bell but has no sooner rung it than the old woman suddenly stills. Her breath is her only animation as it slips low and thin over her lips. Elizabeth grasps her hand but there is no strength in it. 'Please . . .' she implores.

The door opens on a maid who loiters in the frame. 'Ma'am?' the girl says.

Tears are coursing down Elizabeth's cheeks. There is nobody she can send for, she realizes. Nobody who can help. She is the one who will be here for this. 'Send for Mr Rocheid,' she says. 'And the doctor.' She knows it is too late. Even riding like the wind Duncan will not fetch them in time.

The girl disappears. Johann, who has been waiting in the corridor, steps back into the room.

'May I?' he asks.

She nods. She's never been so glad to see anybody. Johann puts his arm around her shoulder. 'She's gone,' he says. 'I am so sorry.'

Elizabeth heaves a sob and in despair wraps her arms around his neck. He holds her as she cries.

'She never said where she wanted to be buried,' she whispers.

'Mr Rocheid will know. Don't worry about that,' he soothes her.

'I don't care about the necklace,' Elizabeth continues.

'I will tell James. Please do not worry. I will see to it all.'

Silently he curses that the king is coming. Time is too short. He wants to stay and help but he will be called away soon.

Later, Elizabeth cannot be induced to eat but she sips some tea once James Rocheid has departed. The maids have laid out Clementina's body and messages have been sent to arrange her burial at St Cuthbert's, where all the Rocheids lie. 'I don't know what to do with the old place now,' James says, motioning around the drawing room before he leaves. 'Do you want to stay?' he asks Elizabeth carelessly.

Elizabeth nods. 'For a while,' she says. 'If it will not inconvenience you.'

'Are you coming back to town, old man?' James asks Johann.

'I will sit with Mrs Rocheid a little longer,' he says. Once James has gone, he stays by Elizabeth's side.

'I hope you will not mind being alone here tonight,' he says.

Elizabeth looks up. There is little alternative. 'Thank you for everything you have done. I will be fine.' She thinks she will ask Currant Bun to bring a mattress into her mistress's chamber and sleep on the floor.

William McNab judges there is a storm coming. Betty was up last night with the feel of the air. The woman is a veritable barometer. It often goes this way in summer – settled for days, weeks even, and then a sudden storm. If cloud masks the sun it can feel like winter this far north even at this time of year. He is sure that in two days there will be wind and rain and plenty of it. The water at least will be good for the planting. The news of Clementina Rocheid's death was delivered to the Garden by the Rocheids' undergardener, Calum, when he was sent with a notice for the minister at St Cuthbert's. The Rocheids' servants do not gossip as a rule, but the boy knows that Clementina was fond of the Garden and that Mr McNab is acquainted with the mistress.

'I'm sorry to hear it,' McNab says. He wonders if he should send condolences to Mrs Rocheid, alone now in that big house. He will keep James away a few days, he decides, but to pass his condolences might seem presumptuous however much he liked the eccentric old woman and her obsession with fruit trees and root crops. McNab is acutely aware that he hovers in the strange space occupied by educated people in service, the governesses and estate managers who do not belong fully to one class or the other.

As the sun sets like a pool of melted toffee, the gardeners leave one by one and McNab loiters in the shed, considering the measures he must take for the coming of the storm. The trees in barrels must be tied down. He has told the watchman to come late tonight but perhaps the old man can lay out the ropes. All the while he listens for Mrs Dickson until he hears her horse stamp as she pulls up her cart in the darkness, not on the road, but in the yard.

'McNab!' she calls, and he opens the shed door, casting a slice of candlelight onto the mud.

She is enjoying this, he thinks, cursing her.

'I have it,' she says as she approaches, 'I know what I want. And you will hear me out.'

He hopes that she does not expect to take cuttings of the Highland flowers. Mr Graham will notice if she does.

'I know what will be most useful,' the old woman prattles. 'The boy!' she exclaims delightedly. 'Of course, you ought to pay me to place him, but I have seen his talent and the catalogue will benefit from line drawings in black and white. He has some skill, I admit it, and I will educate him in the seeds. He already has some learning . . . not in practical matters, but still . . .'

McNab suddenly notices the smell of pine needles on the air and the sound of Mrs Dickson's horse snorting, which startles the sleeping pigeons and sends a rustling through the trees. Then silence.

'James,' he says incredulously.

'The new catalogue will go to press at the end of the summer. It is not as far as it feels. And your debt will be cleared,' replies Mrs Dickson.

McNab's cheeks burn. James will not be a seedsman. He is the son of the head gardener at the Royal Botanic Garden and as such will be qualified to take part in botanical expeditions and someday manage a garden of his own. A garden of some significance, too.

'You cannot have him,' he says.

Mrs Dickson chortles. 'Why not? Are you going to pay back my money?'

McNab wants to hit her but he will not strike a woman. 'I can pay you by turns,' he says. 'In time.'

Mrs Dickson's gaze is both frank and cold. 'You cannae afford it. That's why you came to me in the first place, McNab. I will keep him a year or two is all and he will learn a good deal at my hand. He can sleep with the other apprentice and I'll let him home on Sundays. I'll start him tomorrow. I will fetch him myself.' Her composure is regal as she dispenses her orders. 'The monkey puzzle cuttings are taking well,' she adds, as if the matter is concluded. 'Can I give you a lift home?'

McNab shakes his head. He watches as she climbs back into the driving seat and turns the cart, lifting her hand to say goodbye. The sound of the horse's hooves and the creaking wheels takes a minute to recede.

Once all is silent again, McNab lifts a lantern, locks the gate behind him and starts along the dark highway with some determination. He does not leave instructions for the watchman, Richard Eyre. At the bridge he passes the turn for the toll road south to Leith Walk, instead following the path into town. The lamp becomes less necessary as he climbs the hill, the lights from the long windows up Pitt Street casting crisp squares onto the paving stones. Once he passes Queen Street Gardens, he blows out the candle. It is a warm evening and many windows here are open, the sound of two violins being played snaking onto the street punctuated by staccato laughter. He turns down Thistle Street, where a group of men are drinking beer on the pavement, quite the hubbub. When he crosses to Young's Street it is quieter for the terrace is comprised of houses, not flats. He enquires of a maidservant, loitering at the corner of the lane, if a lady has moved here of late.

'Mrs Lindsay has a new tenant. Number four,' the girl says helpfully. 'They had a pianoforte delivered yesterday and had to hoist it through the window for it would not fit up the stairs.'

McNab thanks her. He crosses the road and examines Number 4, a flat-fronted stone house, three stories high. There is no service basement. On the second floor the squares of the window are yellow as butter pats and he can see from the shadows that there is movement inside. He settles to wait. It is past eleven of the clock when Robert Graham emerges, banging the front door behind him. He has no horse tethered nor John in the carriage waiting. In the winter he has decided he will carry his own hanway and walk between his home and his mistress's lodgings, to avoid being noticed as far as it is possible.

McNab follows the Regius Keeper to the corner and pulls alongside. 'Mr Graham,' he says, rather too loudly.

Graham jumps. 'McNab,' he almost squeaks. 'What are you doing here?'

'I came to talk to you about money.'

Robert Graham bristles. 'At this time of night? For heaven's sake, man. I will petition for you. Only be patient.'

'Matters have become urgent, sir.'

'You must not press me,' Graham complains and makes to head down the hill.

McNab realizes that he has in fact never pressed sufficiently. Not his whole life. Until now.

'I disagree,' he replies ominously, his face set with a new determination. 'You will help me. You will do so this minute. I have waited long enough.'

Not an hour later, Mrs Dickson is roused by a banging on the door of her house on London Road. McNab has relit his lamp and when she opens up wearing her nightgown, he is standing there, large as life in a dim puddle of light.

'You have roused me,' she snaps, her capless hair a white bird's nest. 'What is it?'

McNab lifts a leather pouch. It clinks as he holds it in the light. 'Your twenty-five pounds,' he growls. 'I do not see that we will be doing business again.'

Mrs Dickson is no fool. She knows the tone of a man's voice when he is decided. Besides, she has an array of new cuttings to keep as her interest on what she will come to think of as a loan she once made. She takes the money.

'You'll leave my son alone,' McNab warns. He does not wait for a reply as he steps away, striding past the building site at Hillside and down Leith Walk, homewards.

Elizabeth relishes the darkness tonight. It does not scare her that Clementina's body is lying upstairs in the bed where she died. At first Elizabeth thinks she ought to be tired and that she should retire early for a long, deep sleep, but after sitting in the drawing room alone following Johann's departure she realizes she is not sleepy at all. Looking out across the lawn, she decides to take the advice of the dead.

She smooths the crumpled sketches she made of Belle into a leather portfolio and the pressed aloe flower. Then she calls for Duncan to ready the coach.

'Where will you go, ma'am?'

'Warriston Crescent, please,' Elizabeth says pulling her cloak around her. 'To Miss Brodie's.'

The staff, she knows, are unsure of what will happen. The death of the mistress of the house calls their service into question. James has not said anything to reassure them of their places. It is like him, she realizes, only to consider himself. She is surprised that he asked her if she intended to stay and wonders how quickly he will change his mind about allowing her to be there, if he is offered good coin for the house and land. She is in no doubt that he would sell off the whole Inverleith estate if it made him enough gold. This prospect does not scare her though, for now, for the first time in her life, she has her own funds. Clementina might have felt her portion was not generous, but it is more than enough to live on, with a maid and a cook besides. Ten times what she has from William's pension and enough to run a small house, perhaps on Northumberland Street or one of the new terraces due to be built nearby.

The night air is fresh though there is still a little heat in it. Claire opens Belle's door and admits her. Upstairs Belle is supping late, on a fine Derby achette of blue cheese, Muscat grapes and soft, white bread. 'Elizabeth?' she says, surprised.

'Belle.' Elizabeth takes a breath. It takes courage to say what she intends to. 'I am here because I wronged you,' she gets it out. 'I judged you and I had no right.'

Belle smiles. 'You need judge me no more. My state is changed. I have not a single gentleman to my name.' She motions around the room. 'I'm glad to see you. Will you sup with me?'

Elizabeth shakes her head. She cannot imagine eating. Tasting and chewing and swallowing is quite beyond her. 'Clementina died this morning.'

Belle puts down the scrap of bread in her hand. 'I'm sorry,' she says gravely. 'That is a loss for you. For us all.'

Elizabeth sits. 'What happened to your . . . gentlemen?'

'They settled with me.'

This is true. Ruari Innes sent a revised notice today which was half a dozen times more generous than his original gift. Gentlemen, Belle knows, always pay for discretion and she is happy to offer them that, both in the bedchamber and afterwards. She considered briefly allowing him the right to one more night at a time of his choosing – any night in the coming year. Such a clause, she knows, would torment him for Ruari loves to anticipate pleasure. But she decided against it, for it would only be a form of cruelty, and in the end she gave him what he wanted – a clean break.

'What will you do?' Elizabeth asks.

Belle shrugs. 'I had thought to travel,' she says vaguely. 'What about you?' She has calculated that given the money her gentlemen have paid, the ladies' bathing oil will provide enough income – for the time being. She will come to some kind of settlement with the apothecary for a lump sum in due course. 'I'm not entirely sure where I will go. If you had the whole world, Elizabeth, where would you set sail for?'

It has not occurred to Elizabeth till now that she need not settle at all and might go wherever she wishes. 'I can see you would enjoy travelling,' she says. 'Mr Rocheid has said I can stay at Inverleith House for a while.'

'And will you stay? It is not a bad position.'

Elizabeth sits back on Belle's comfortable cushions. 'That depends,' she says. It is a pleasure, she realizes, just as Clementina said it was, to have a friend who listens.

Belle pops a spherical, honey-green grape into her mouth. 'I thought you might have come to return my perfume.'

'Perfume?'

'Clementina was taking care of it. James McNab entrusted it to her. I expect it must be among her things. As I wrote to you.'

Elizabeth frowns. 'I did not receive a letter. I do not think she had such a thing. I have not seen it.'

James Rocheid insisted on surveying Clementina's possessions that afternoon – the jewellery and the dressing table and the wardrobes. 'None of this will be any use to you, my dear,' he said, 'the dresses are so out of date.' Still, she thought, she might remake some of them. There was no perfume. Not an ounce. Then she realizes.

'My God,' she says, 'I think Clementina may have given it away.'

Belle stops eating. 'To whom?'

'Johann von Streitz's grandmother.'

Belle cocks her head. Her sigh, when it comes, is long. All her trouble, it seems, has been for nothing. Mhairi has tried the scent a hundred other ways. None of them is right.

'Perhaps Johann can have it from her?' Elizabeth suggests.

'Johann? That is exceeding familiar,' Belle smirks.

Elizabeth blushes. 'He has been very kind.'

'He had an eye for you from the start,' Belle declares. 'I saw the way he looked at you.'

Elizabeth brushes this off. Johann is younger. And handsome. And well-connected. 'I do not enjoy such intimacies,' she says.

'That is not true,' Belle replies. 'You did not enjoy them with your husband. That does not mean to say you would not enjoy them with someone . . . better.'

She pours a glass of port and offers the decanter. Elizabeth nods slowly and accepts a measure. 'We should toast Clementina,' she says, and the women clink glasses before they take a draught. 'Here,' Elizabeth adds, handing over the portfolio. 'I have brought you the drawings I made of you. I crumpled them up after our falling out. And that aloe flower – the one McNab cut for me. It is drying between two papers. I thought you might like it.'

'Thank you,' says Belle and admits she is considering replicating Elizabeth's design of her, but in oils. 'What do you think?'

'It will be grand!' Elizabeth says and realizes she would never think to have a portrait of herself painted and then wonders why.

The women sit in Belle's sitting room beyond midnight and Elizabeth swears she will help Belle find the perfume she has lost, and Belle promises her friendship.

'I have met the minister at St Cuthbert's,' Belle admits. 'He is a dry old stick, but Clementina will be with her people there.' The women toast to that, among many other things, until the bottle of port is done.

Chapter Thirty-Four

Now the king has embarked on his journey north, Holyrood Palace is in considerably more disarray than when the work started on the new throne room some weeks ago. The hammering, already distracting, has become quite frantic as tradesmen work through the night, the lamps still burning as dawn breaks over the park, grey this morning and damp. One or two of the more radical debtors have made complaints to the prison authorities about the noise, or at least did so once the rumour was scotched that the king intended to forgive all debts to celebrate his visit. George IV is better at seeing to it that his own debts are forgiven – the price of a thousand items of gilded furniture and a hundred lavish feasts. The grace and favour occupants of the palace grumble among themselves about the inconvenience but it is George who grants them the right to live there on little or no rent so they will voice no real objections to his coming.

The town is practically awash in bunting now – festooned all up the mound and across the palace gates. This morning, it is dripping with dew. Some of the grander houses on Princes Street are set to fly the Union Jack and the Lion Rampant on parallel flagpoles erected from the drawing room windows. Scotland is almost ready to go to the party. The visit is becoming known as the Daft Days.

The women arrive early in Elizabeth's carriage, which pulls up on the palace's forecourt as the last of the throne room's new carpet is delivered on a dray. They peer out of the open door, held by Duncan. They might reasonably have expected a footman or even a door boy at a royal residence but there are only several rough-looking porters shouting at each other as they manhandle a roll of red carpet, the last left in the city.

Inside, they come across an elderly cleric making his way, out of the palace, into the world.

'Excuse me,' Belle accosts him, 'we are looking for Johann von Streitz?'

'Who?' the old man thunders. 'Never heard of her.'

Belle takes Elizabeth's arm and the women stifle their giggles. At length they spot a footman struggling to place a large vase in an indent. He directs them up a flight of stairs to the correct door, which Johann answers.

'Ladies!' he says, with obvious pleasure at their visit. 'Please, come in!'

Inside, his suite is unassuming. Sir Walter sits at the table and rises to greet them, tendering his condolences to Elizabeth on her cousin's death. He looks tired.

'It is not long now, until the royal visit, Sir Walter,' Elizabeth remarks.

'A matter of hours,' the writer replies sagely and checks his gold pocket watch. 'Twenty-six hours, perhaps.'

'I'm afraid we have come with a request at this busy time,' Elizabeth says. 'Before Clementina sickened it seems she wrote to your grandmother, Johann.'

If Sir Walter is shocked by Elizabeth's familiarity with the king's man, he does not show it.

'She sent a small bottle of perfumed oil with the letter. The oil belonged to Belle. We wondered if we might have it back?'

'I have brought a bottle of perfume for your grandmother – something more suitable with lilac and violet,' Belle cuts in, removing a cut crystal vial from her reticule. 'I am sure she will like it.'

Johann catches Sir Walter's eye. 'I recall the missive. I dispatched it yesterday to Leith in the diplomatic bag.' The papers had piled up and he wanted to clear them. When he got back from Inverleith House, it gave him something to do.

Both Elizabeth and Belle's faces drop. 'Oh no,' says Belle weakly.

'How is the diplomatic bag dispatched?' Sir Walter enquires, for he does not like ladies to be disappointed.

Johann pauses before answering but he can see no harm in telling them. 'The Dutch Consul at Leith sends it on a packet. From Holland it travels overland into the German states. We have an arrangement.'

'Dutch indeed?' Sir Walter sounds surprised though of all the foreign ships at Leith the Dutch are the most reliable, being a great nation of seafarers whose achievements, Johann has noticed, the English often choose to ignore.

'You believe it will have embarked?' Belle sounds downhearted.

Sir Walter's eyes light up. 'Well, von Streitz, I don't see how you can be sure the ship has sailed. You must help the lady to retrieve her property if you can.' He pulls the pocket watch from his waistcoat once more. 'The next tide will be in an hour, if I judge it correctly.'

Sir Walter is probably Scotland's greatest expert at the moment on the tides at Leith. The time of His Majesty's arrival is uncertain, but it must chime with the sea and Sir Walter has educated himself in detail about the Forth's tidal flow.

'Do you have a carriage at your disposal, ladies?'

'Yes!' Belle squeals.

'I shall stay here and oversee the carpet,' Scott adds. 'Off you go.'

The three of them clatter down the stairs in an unbecoming fashion and Johann climbs up on the box next to Duncan as the women pile inside.

'To the port!' he says, and Duncan gees the horses as the mulberry carriage speeds through the gates, past the track that leads to the cemetery and up the hill towards the two-mile highway to the water. Beyond the fields, Leith is busy, the Kirkgate thronging with deliveries. The owners of buildings along the king's route into the city have procured hard coin for reservations to gawp at the king's carriage. All possible places are reserved and rumours circulate that some wealthy fool has paid a hundred guineas for a prime vantage point from which his party can witness the king step onto the dockside, which will be strewn with flowers for the royal welcome to Scottish soil. Chairs and tables for the lords and ladies and cases of brandy and fortified wines block the doorways as they are delivered.

'Where at the port, sir?' Duncan asks, peering at the confusion.

'The Dutch Consulate.'

'Where's that?'

Johann freezes. He disembarked at Leith only a few short months ago, but does not know the town's geography. Of course, it makes sense that Duncan does not know its location either. The Rocheids have no business here and Belle always sends Edzel McBain. Johann stands on the box and calls down to a man in the street for directions. He is pointed towards The Shore. Progress is slow. Belle puts her head out of the window and calls up to Duncan, 'There will be a coin in it for you if we get there in time!'

Three doxies on the street take an interest in the carriage. 'You're too early for Georgie boy!' one shouts, 'he isnae here yet!'

The carriage grinds to a halt, unable to move for a rubbish cart and a dray delivering a large, mahogany dresser held down by ropes. There is no way around.

Belle loses all patience. She opens the door and jumps onto the street, which, she notes, is quite filthy and has not yet been cleared for the king's arrival.

'Where is the Dutch Consulate?' she snaps at one of the doxies.

'You offered him coin,' the woman nods towards Duncan.

Belle fishes a shilling from her reticule. The woman eyes it dubiously. Johann appears at Belle's side and Belle adds another shilling to her offering.

'Come on!' she says.

As the woman issues directions, Johann turns to close the door of the carriage. 'Follow us with Duncan,' he says to Elizabeth, but she protests, and steps onto the street, which, strewn with rubbish, marks her hems badly.

The doxy takes Belle's coins and the three of them cut down a laneway following her instructions, Johann keeping his hand to the knife in his belt that he has not had to use during his stay in the New Town.

It has started to drizzle, and the air is chill. The smell coming from the waterside is most unpleasant. This port feels a million miles from Edinburgh with its castle and wide, clean streets, and more like the Old Town but on the sea. The passageways lead to The Shore where ships are bobbing on grey water and porters scurry along the setts.

'What does it look like?' Belle snaps for she can see no sign of the Dutch anywhere.

'Look for a red, white and blue flag – the Dutch Navy's jack,' Johann replies.

But there are red, white and blue flags aplenty, hoisted for the arrival of the king. A veritable sea of them along the dock, ornamenting almost every building.

It is Elizabeth who spots it – not the consulate but a tidy packet flying the right colours.

'There!' she shouts and they clatter along the dockside. Two sailors are just casting off and Johann shouts at them to stop, but they ignore him.

'I must come aboard,' he yells. 'I am the envoy of His Majesty George IV. Stop what you are doing! I must speak to your captain at once.'

The men pause at this. A gangplank is lowered, and Johann disappears up it. There is the sound of raised voices on deck – a language that sounds like German only with the edges smoothed. Then someone snarling in English, 'We must get away, sir, there is a storm coming on the next tide. We must leave on this one to get ahead of the weather.'

Belle passes a hand over her face which is wet with smirr. She looks at Elizabeth and the two women start to laugh. Their dresses are streaked in the drizzle, the hems filthy and their shoes smeared in mud. Elizabeth spots the mulberry carriage at the other end of the dock. She waves to catch Duncan's attention, which only makes Belle giggle more for there must be a hundred people between the ship and the carriage, and all of them moving. But Elizabeth will not be put off. She gets onto the gangplank so the driver will spot her though one of the sailors berates her for it.

'My carriage is coming,' she says breathlessly, waving the man off.

Then she thinks of what Clementina would say about them dashing to the docks and ruining their stockings. All for a bottle of God knows what.

At length Duncan pulls up next to the ship, jumps down and opens the door, handing the women up. Inside, the carriage smells musty. Belle pulls down the window, keeping her eye on the deck until Johann comes into sight. He strides down the gangplank and pauses, his hand outstretched.

'The replacement?' he asks.

'You have found it?'

He smiles as she hands him the crystal vial through the window.

'The captain says that the king will not be able to disembark. There is quite the storm coming. We must inform Sir Walter,' he adds before disappearing again.

'I hope this smells good,' Elizabeth whispers to Belle.

Belle's eyes glint. 'It smells of true love,' she says. 'Why else do you think I am so keen for it?'

Elizabeth's expression tells her that she does not believe her, and Belle does not push the point. She does not want Elizabeth asking where she got the oil, or indeed, wanting to smell it. In any case, she needn't fear much, for Elizabeth's eyes are fixed on the gangplank, where von Streitz will re-emerge any minute.

'It is so many weeks since I arrived. I feel quite a different kind of lady,' she says dreamily.

'When you sailed north from the Thames was there a storm?'

Elizabeth shakes her head. 'It was good enough weather, though I felt ill for the first day. I'm sure His Majesty has excellent sea legs,' she adds diplomatically.

Belle thinks of the cartoons she has seen of George in periodicals – a fat sixty-year-old with thighs like ham hocks. She does not say this, however. Elizabeth, it seems, is fast becoming a royalist.

Johann is breathless when he comes back, the gangplank removed immediately he steps off it and the casting off of the ship resumes. He gets into the carriage and sits opposite the women, banging on the box for Duncan to get going.

'Warriston Crescent?' he checks.

Belle does not care where the carriage is headed. 'Did you get it?' she asks, like a child desperate for a treat.

He pulls the small brown bottle from the pocket of his tailcoat and hands it to her. 'Oh, thank you. Thank you,' she says, hugging Elizabeth and grasping Johann's hand. Everyone is laughing. 'If there is ever anything that I can do for you. Anything at all, Herr von Streitz . . .' she says and notices that Elizabeth is looking at the German as if he were a god.

Duncan takes the new route along Constitution Street, which has been laid expressly for the king because there is no cleaning the Kirkgate, and back in town they drop Belle at her door. She has a job to do. She sends a note to Mhairi to summon her to Tanfield and changes into workaday clothes to meet her. The sky is as dark as an evil fairy's portent and as she unlocks the shed with the large, iron key, it seems strangely deserted without Edzel, who still has two days of his sentence to run. He is missing the payoff, she thinks, but perhaps that is for the best. Inside, she lights the lamps and puts on her linen wrap, setting out the mixing things on the bench and lining up the bottles – cinnamon, strawberry, gorse, pink peppercorn, star anise and the final elixir, *Agave americana*. They do not look like a set, more a rag-taggle collection of brown bottles and green ones of different shapes and sizes. Edzel did not know they were meant to go together any more than she did.

It is tempting to start, but instead she loiters impatiently at the door, waiting for Mhairi who hurries along the path as the wind stirs the long branches of the chestnut trees on the opposite bank. The girl dips her hands into the cold, flowing riverwater and dries her fingers carefully on her skirts. 'I got mash on them,' she explains. 'It smells gey sour.'

The shed creaks in the wind as the women stand at the bench. Mhairi's hands are steady though her fingers are pink with the cold. Belle can tell she is nervous. She has mixed this scent before, or almost, but tonight the last ingredient is irreplaceable. She has to get it right. The cinnamon smells sweet, but it isn't really. It's the strawberry and the gorse that bring that intrigue, the cinnamon only amplifies it. Once this base is in place, she drips the peppercorn carefully and adds the star anise. The girl's concentration reminds Belle of Elizabeth when she is drawing – an art and a science at once. Belle holds her breath as the aloe goes in, first one drop, then two, then a spoonful. They open the door without a word and stand outside in the start of the rainstorm till their noses are clear. Then they go back in and Belle places a tiny drop of the mixture on her forearm. They both lean in to smell it.

'Ah!' says Mhairi delightedly. 'That's it! Much better. It has the . . .' she struggles to find a word to describe the scent, but Belle is more worldly.

'Sex,' she says. 'It smells deflowered.'

Mhairi leans against the bench. Her brow furrows. She grasps Belle's arm, bringing it once more to her nose. Then she makes for the shelf. 'Aye,' she says, 'the heat of it. The need. But there is something more.'

The glass almost full of liquid glows like honey in the lamplight as Mhairi sniffs her way through the bottles.

'It is enough,' Belle says, judging by eye that she will be able to fill all four of her red, glass vials.

But Mhairi will not be put off. 'You were right,' she insists, lifting the bottle of pine oil.

'You'll spoil it,' Belle panics but Mhairi does not waver. To near a half pint of perfume she adds a mere three drops of pine and then mixes.

Belle opens the door once more. She repeats the ritual, clearing her palate, then smearing a drop, this time on her other arm. It is as if the scent has been lifted by magic into another realm. A better one. 'Three drops of pine oil,' she says in wonder. 'Alchemy.'

Mhairi's smile widens into a grin. 'It is worth my twenty guineas,' she says, satisfied, for she is a woman who expects to earn her money.

'Yes, yes, twenty guineas. You must come to the house for I have no coin upon me.'

Belle does not take off her linen wrap. She carefully stoppers the mixture and the women leave the door unlocked behind them as they walk into the dreich evening, Belle insisting on carrying it herself. The rain has started in earnest and puddles are forming on the bridge. Inside, at her desk, Belle hands over the money. 'You will see to your coachman, then? He will keep the confidence?'

Mhairi acquiesces. 'Soon he will be my husband,' she adds and allows herself to be dismissed.

There must be, Belle thinks, something in the air. This reminds her that she has a friend to consider. Before she fills her red bottles she chooses a tiny, crystal flacon from her dressing table, cleans it with alcohol and drips in no more than a dozen drops of the precious potion.

'Take this to Mrs Rocheid,' she tells Jamie. 'Find out where she is. If she is not at Inverleith House, you must seek her out with Herr von Streitz and Sir Walter Scott.'

Jamie looks through the window at the Water of Leith swelling in the rain. It is a miserable night, but he does not complain and goes to fetch his oilskin and saddle the horse.

When he leaves, Belle calls for hot cider to ward off the chill. To be ordering that from the kitchen in August seems strange, but the sky is getting darker by the hour and the temperature is dropping. His Majesty, she thinks, must be at the Tyne Estuary by now, hoping to harbour at Leith late tonight. Belle picks up the portfolio case Elizabeth brought and peruses her friend's sketches. She will surely have a painting done in oils for now she can afford whatever she wants. She decides to have the artist add a pine tree to the vista through the window – there is no reason, she thinks, not to include all the ingredients. But she has work to do for she, like Mhairi, must earn her money.

With a sneaky smile she opens her writing box. She takes a piece of paper and considers before she inscribes it. She has never met the Melvilles, but they are the richest family in Scotland, and they have a daughter about to come out. It is said a pamphlet that drew the girl as a plain Jane was recalled by her father, which is to say, the family bought every pressing of the image and paid the printer to make no more. The timing, she thinks, could not be better.

> *Dear Mrs Melville* [she starts], *I have a treasure that I hope might interest you, for as I understand it, you are seeking a match for your girl among the gentlemen arriving tomorrow to accompany the king . . .*

In North Castle Street, Sir Walter, Lady Charlotte, Johann von Streitz and Elizabeth are gathered in the drawing room, a fire crackling in the grate for the first time since May. Every weather sage in the city swears the storm will last a day and Scott has spent the latter part of his afternoon working out how to retain as many events as he can, with one day less to carry them out, for until the storm abates there will be no way to get the king safely ashore.

'I think it is romantic,' Lady Charlotte enthuses. 'Nature is a force that sweeps man along. Like an elopement.'

'What do you think, von Streitz?' Sir Walter sighs.

'I think His Majesty will be frustrated.' This is diplomatic to say the least. The king being prevented from doing whatever he desires has in the past prompted temper tantrums that would put an infant with a fever to shame.

'Perhaps,' Sir Walter says, drawing on his vast imagination, 'we could make a picnic of it somehow.'

'A picnic?'

'We cannot risk the life of the sovereign in the storm, but we can send entertainment. Make the royal yacht a . . . location. We can go ourselves.'

Lady Scott looks alarmed. 'Walter,' she says gently, as if waking her husband from a fretful nightmare. They have recently decided it is too stormy a night to allow Mrs Rocheid to venture home in her carriage, and that involves no larger body of water than the Water of Leith, over which there is a sturdy stone bridge, albeit one that sometimes floods.

When Jamie arrives sodden with Belle's packet, they wait impatiently for the maid to show him up.

'Quite some night to be out,' Elizabeth says.

Lady Scott cuts in. 'The kitchen will give you a toddy,' she instructs him.

'Ma'am,' Jamie bows and makes the delivery. Elizabeth opens the folded paper and then the tiny crystal vial. Belle's hastily penned note says *Wish me luck, for if this works as I hope it will, I shall be on my travels . . .*

She sniffs and slicks some of the oil at the pulse of her wrist and the base of her neck.

'Is that the oil your friend wished to rescue?' Johann asks.

'I think so,' she says.

As the scent opens in the air, his gaze is drawn towards her. His eyes light up and he feels suddenly inspired.

'We must make best use of the time,' Sir Walter continues, unaware of what has just happened. Lady Scott, however, is on this occasion more perceptive.

'Come, Walter,' she says. 'We should go into my day room. From there we will be able, perhaps, to see the sea, the site of His Majesty's arrival.' She grasps her husband's arm firmly and removes him.

Elizabeth finds her eyes drawn to the fire. Then the chandelier. She wonders if she should offer to play a piece on the piano but before she can do so, Johann sits next to her. 'Mrs Rocheid. Elizabeth,' he says. 'I upset you once by declaring myself, but I did so clumsily on that occasion . . .'

Elizabeth catches her breath. The memory of that day, what happened with Belle, now seems a kind of fable.

'I misunderstood you,' she admits, shame creeping into her voice. 'I know you would never . . .'

'Never,' Johann echoes. 'But I will return to London in less than a fortnight and I do not like to think of doing so, although I am committed to the service of the king. Dear Mrs Rocheid, I wonder if you might, entertain my feelings . . . if you might honour me . . .' His hand is shaking and he puts it behind his back.

Elizabeth purses her lips. 'I do not understand,' she says. 'Speak plainly.'

Having spoken so carefully, the words suddenly rush out. 'I should like you to be my wife,' he says.

'What?' Elizabeth asks in shock. She feels woozy.

'Will you marry me?' he asks solemnly.

The impossibility of his request makes Elizabeth's thoughts swim. 'But I am older than you are. I am widowed. I am not at all grand . . .' her voice trails.

Johann bows formally. 'Madam, there is nobody with whom I would rather spend my days. Eating little cakes,' he declares. 'If we marry, Elizabeth, you will have a place. You can resume your illustrations at Kew Garden if you wish. You would be an addition to His Majesty's court. Though I hope we will make our own home together in time. Here. Or in Saxony. Together as we have been the last several days.'

Elizabeth feels her cheeks glow as if she is sitting too close to the fire. She smiles. She cannot say that the last days have been pleasant, for her cousin passed, but what would it have been like without him? Suddenly she knows exactly what she wants.

'You are the kindest person I know,' she says simply.

'Yes? Is it yes?' He can't hide his hope.

Elizabeth nods. He kisses her and it is, she thinks, like the chiming of a bell, as if they are not here in the Scotts' drawing room on North Castle Street, but have passed into another realm. They are both surprised by the sensation, and only shaken back to the drawing room by the gasp of a maid who has come to stoke the fire.

'Oh, ma'am,' she says, mortified at catching them out. 'Sir! I'm sorry.'

Johann laughs. 'Would you please ask Sir Walter and Lady Charlotte to join us?'

The girl bobs a curtsy. 'Aye, sir.'

'Saxony is very fine in the springtime. I'm sure we could take a few weeks there next year. I would like you to meet my family,' he says when he turns back. He feels full of energy, as if he could take on the world.

'We shall see,' Elizabeth replies. 'But we are putting the cart before the horse, I think. We are not yet married!'

An elegant grin spreads across Lady Scott's face as she rejoins the party. 'Well?' she says.

Elizabeth is pale as a white rose and yet the picture of happiness. 'Johann and I will be married,' she confirms.

Lady Scott claps her hands, her long, kid leather gloves amplifying the sound. She notices it smells lovely in this room – not the geranium scent that came from the Grahams' but something more appealing. 'You will live in a royal palace, my dear.'

'Oh, I shall not mind that,' Elizabeth replies, and Johann's eyes settle on her happily. She is quite the most perfect woman.

Chapter Thirty-Five

Unlike the king, currently closeted in his yacht, and the Scotts and their guests, drinking champagne now by the fireside, Belle is about her business this stormy evening. A note received from Anne Rennie Melville, several hours after Belle's was dispatched, has cast her out in her carriage to brave the storm. Mrs Melville, the niece-in-law of the late Henry Dundas, erstwhile known as the King of Scotland and the woman whose invitations Johann von Streitz has so studiously avoided over the last few weeks, has summoned Belle to the family's grand house on St Andrew Square. The monument to Henry Dundas, raised the year before and paid for by seamen of the Royal Navy, towers over Edinburgh's city centre, imposing itself on the length of George Street. While Anne cannot admit she finds it overbearing, she has been known to remark that it is a perfectly fitting monument to Henry, without adding that is because he was the most overbearing man she ever met. Still, Robert Dundas, the new Viscount Melville, Henry's son, has been kind to her daughter and has settled on the plain and ungainly girl a fortune of 20,000 guineas.

Belle has never before visited the Viscount's home, and, though not easily overawed, she halts in the marble hallway with her mouth open as she takes in the sheer scale of the place. The high ceiling is so airy that it smells, she notes, of nothing. She pulls herself together and hands her fur-edged cloak to the footman. Many visitors, she tells herself, must have the same reaction she has had, for the hallway is grander than any cathedral and it is difficult to feign indifference towards such a showy display of sheer wealth. The footman turns and leads her up the wide staircase to Anne's private day room where a lively fire is set in the grate and Mrs Melville has hurried her toilette before dinner in order to meet Belle Brodie, whose brother she knows by reputation.

Belle curtsies very low as Mrs Melville regards her carefully from her gilded mahogany chair. Beside her a Black boy of no more than nine years of age is dressed in purple silk pantaloons and a matching turban, holding a plate of sweetmeats. Anne waves the child away. Tradespeople are always trying to sell the Melvilles their wares, but Belle's note has intrigued her. Jane, Anne's daughter, is fifteen. While the family intended to take the girl to London to parade her in search of a suitable husband, the king's visit has allowed what her father jokingly refers to as a 'preview, as in the theatre, my dear'. Jane is wilful, and loves to dance, though shows little grace, has a fascination with fine tailoring that does not suit her and is devoted to a small cat she rescued from being drowned by a farmer on the Melville estate to the south of the city at Lasswade. Sadly, she is an ordinary-looking girl at best and though her mother has ordered her a coming out trousseau of gargantuan proportions and quality, she knows that the settlement of 20,000 guineas notwithstanding, her daughter will need all the help she can get if she is to snare a man in possession not only of a fortune but also a high-ranking title.

Miss Brodie, Anne notes as she peruses Belle, is not exactly a tradesperson. She has never entertained a courtesan before, but looking at Belle, it feels more like a social call than she expected. She motions her to take a seat. 'Your missive fascinated me, Miss Brodie,' she starts. 'I had my husband's secretary look into your background. I myself am the great-granddaughter of the Duke of Rutland.'

Belle smiles.

'However, I am not a harlot,' Anne finishes crisply.

'Being a courtesan, my lady, brings with it a certain set of skills,' Belle replies smoothly and without shame.

'So Lady Liston writes to me . . .' Belle thanks Henrietta silently. 'Which, frankly, is the reason I have admitted you, for had that lady not praised you in the most glowing of terms I would not have entertained this . . . notion of yours. A love potion, is it?'

'I should be clear,' Belle says, 'that my perfume will not make an unwilling gentleman fall in love with a lady if he is set against it, but it is, shall we say, a strong encouragement if he is anyway inclined.'

'You have used it?'

'I use many perfumes in the course of my work.' Belle smiles in what she hopes is a mysterious fashion. 'Our senses read many signals. It stands to reason that those senses might be encouraged. A gentleman will be attracted to certain physical attributes – a lady's good looks or the sound of her voice. Why not her smell?'

'Or her dowry,' Anne adds.

'Indeed,' Belle agrees. 'I'm sure that will be a great inducement.'

'What does this perfume of yours contain?'

Belle will not say, though she makes mention of the fact that there are several exotic ingredients. 'A man might have died in the getting of them,' she adds mysteriously.

Anne sighs. 'May I smell it?'

Belle reaches into her reticule and pulls out a small walnut box. She unlocks it to reveal the midnight blue interior. Drawing the ruby glass stopper from its place she passes the bottle to Anne, who sniffs. 'It is not what I expected,' she says.

'Most perfumes are only flowers, which are most efficacious for covering less pleasant odours. But this scent has a purpose,' Belle says confidently. 'It will induce love, which is to say devotion, if the fellow is willing. It is a potion, not a perfume.'

Anne hands back the stopper between thumb and forefinger. 'How much do you want?'

Belle pauses. This is the nub. 'Three thousand guineas,' she says.

Anne laughs. She throws her hands in the air. 'For three thousand guineas, I would expect the heir to the throne delivered to me on a platter,' she says airily.

Belle shrugs. The heir to the throne is the present king's younger brother who is a good deal older than a fifteen-year-old girl might hope for her husband and is already married to a German noblewoman. 'That is the price,' she says. 'His Majesty will disembark tomorrow, and this will give your daughter an edge that no other girl out this season will have in Edinburgh or anywhere else.'

Anne motions the Black serving boy forward. She chooses a sweetmeat. 'I think not,' she says. 'There is no proof of the thing.'

She is right. But Belle is not yet willing to admit defeat. 'I have been making love potions for more than ten years. This is my finest,' she lies. 'And there will be only one bottle. The ingredient that is key is not generally available. The cost, madam, reflects that. It is unique.'

Anne pops the sweetmeat into her mouth while she considers. It is a lot of money even for someone as wealthy as she, but her daughter's future is in her hands. She considers this. 'No,' she says at length. 'I say no.'

Belle stands. 'I will not trouble you any longer then. I have other prospective clients.'

Anne laughs. 'Not many at that price, my girl.'

Belle does not appreciate being laughed at. 'I only require one mother happy to make the investment in her daughter's future,' she replies with hauteur and curtsies before quitting the room. She descends the stairs quite slowly, but Mrs Melville does not call her back. At the bottom, the footman folds her fur-edged cape around her shoulders and opens the door. Jamie is waiting sodden on the box. She gets into the carriage without the slightest sign of interest from the house. She sighs and knocks for him to gee up the horses.

It is only as she is about to pull off through the gates and into the muddy street that the front door opens and a girl in a strangely adorned peach dress and white dancing pumps runs into the dark. Jamie pulls up the reins and Belle lowers the window. Raindrops drench the girl's hair, so it is the colour of dirty straw. Her frock is girded by ribbons and fringing in the most extraordinary amounts. It puts Belle in mind of a curtain. She is a strange-looking creature. Behind her, a liveried coachman dashes outside with a hanway, which he holds, somewhat hopelessly, over the young lady's head.

'I am Jane Melville,' the girl curtsies.

'Miss Melville.' So this is the girl.

Jane looks over her shoulder. 'I am going to be late to supper,' she says. 'I wonder might I . . .?'

Belle opens the door of the carriage. The footman casts her a dirty look as if she might be kidnapping Miss Melville.

'Don't fuss, Lachlan,' the girl chides without looking round and climbs eagerly inside. She laughs at the state of herself. 'I can never stay tidy,' she admits. 'I know my mother rejected your offer,' she says, 'but I wonder if I might . . .?'

Belle brings the small box out from under her cape and opens it showily with its key, lifting the ruby bottle so that it glints in the light of the solitary candle that burns in the interior of the coach.

'It is very small,' the girl says.

'But a mighty weapon,' Belle counters, with a glint in her eye.

'I should like to smell it.'

Belle repeats the ritual, removing the stopper and handing it to Jane, who sniffs. The rain beats a tattoo on the roof as the smell fills the carriage. Jane searches for the words. 'I am green in the ways of the world, Miss Brodie, and I find myself awkward in the company of men. A lady such as yourself has experience beyond my understanding.'

'Are you seeking advice?'

Jane's eyes are wide if not entirely symmetrical. 'If there was anything you could tell me, I would value it.'

Belle pauses. This girl, it strikes her, is not ordinary. She feels suddenly maternal for she senses that the poor thing is frustrating to her elegant mother in much the same way, albeit for different reasons, than as Belle herself, a decade before, frustrated the women who were supposed to look after her. Jane smiles nervously, revealing oddly spaced teeth. She has the air of a puppy that has been washed and groomed and yet its ears point in different directions. Belle sighs. She's always had a soft spot for a stray dog.

'I should certainly comment that what you are wearing . . .' she starts.

Jane looks aghast.

'It needs less fringing,' Belle says. 'Come here,' she beckons Jane Melville across the coach and removes half the ornaments from her hair.

'There,' she says. 'Your gown is fine, but it makes you . . . unapproachable. You should allow a space here and there.' She tips the hair ornaments into the girl's hand.

'Is there anything else I may do to aid a gentleman's interest?' Jane says, her brow furrowed with concentration as if Belle is delivering a lesson in the schoolroom.

'I can send you a little oil. It is not the love potion but a drop or two when you bathe, and men will think kindly of you in general.'

Jane considers this a moment. 'Thank you,' she says. She sniffs the bottle and turns it over on her wrist, so the oil smears her skin. Though the oil is precious, Belle allows this. 'And it will make a man fall in love with me?' she asks.

'Not exactly. A love potion can only encourage a man already that way inclined,' Belle says. 'You need say little when you put it on, for it will talk for you.' She moves to close the deal for she has an instinct for such things. 'Have you come to buy it?'

Jane nods. 'This marriage is a terrible business. I have read all Miss Austen's novels. They terrified me.'

'The stuff of nightmares,' Belle agrees sympathetically.

'I know I am not Aphrodite,' Jane continues sadly. 'I need all the help I can muster, and the king is coming. I have a great chance, Miss Brodie. Most girls who look as I do could not hope for my advantages. I intend to make the most of them. My parents plan to donate a sizeable sum to build the Parthenon on Calton Hill, but another stuffy monument will not help my cause. They are calling the city the Athens of the North.'

'I have heard that.' She is a bright girl, Belle thinks.

Jane pushes down the window. Outside, the footman is still waiting. He has not sheltered under the hanway, but holds it to the side, in case Miss Melville might require it. 'Lachlan,' Jane says. 'Go inside and bring it.'

The footman turns back into the house and returns holding a strongbox.

Belle smiles. 'Miss Melville, did you steal this money? Is it intended to fund the monument?'

Jane does not answer this question. 'It is not three thousand guineas,' she admits. 'Only two but I assume you will happily make that bargain.' She holds out her hand. 'If I marry well, I shall remember your kind advice.'

Belle smiles. 'For you,' she says, 'yes I will sell it for that. I wish you married and married well within the year.'

'Within the sixmonth, surely, for I cannot stand the tension,' Jane concurs with a lopsided smile that renders her face if not pretty, at least slightly more attractive. Lachlan slides the strongbox into the carriage at Belle's feet. Belle hands the girl the perfume.

'Never forget that you are choosing your husband quite as much as he is choosing you,' she recommends. 'Observe every young gentleman's true appetites as if he were a dog. If he bites once, give him no second chance. You must be a goddess, not a redeemer, Miss Melville. I wish you luck.'

Lachlan helps the girl down. The hanway is quite useless in the westerly wind. The rain curls around it.

'Goodbye,' the heiress says and splashes back indoors.

As Jamie turns the carriage along George Street and down the hill Belle relaxes. The inside of the carriage feels damp, the light is low, but she might as well be Cinderella in her glass coach. She has done it!

Something about the storm lends urgency to everything. The city is alight with it, tipping over the threshold as it is into royal mania.

This evening heralds a two-week party that the capital has been thirsting for this August. Lady Charlotte, having spent so many weeks patiently supporting her husband's dedication to the king's visit suddenly feels she wants to celebrate. She orders a supper of fried goujons of sole followed by rhubarb posset and slices of creamy goat's cheese. 'Family style,' she says, acknowledging the intricacy of the last meal this company enjoyed together, Robert Graham's over-wrought menu served the night he sought an invitation to the king's ball.

'I think your engagement is romantic,' she declares dreamily over the port. 'Don't you, Walter?'

Scott casts his wife a glance that betrays his preoccupation with His Majesty not being able to get off his yacht in this storm.

'Walter,' she berates him, 'is it so long since we were first in love? Can you not recall how it felt?'

'I write about it all the time,' he blusters. 'But the king is almost arrived . . .'

Lady Charlotte holds herself in check, but her expression clearly betrays that, after weeks of listening to her husband drone on about the royal arrangements, she has had enough. However, that would be treason and Walter might never forgive her. She smiles lightly, hauling her temper back into place and taking a stand for romance. 'But dear,' she says, 'do you not think an elopement such as this is exactly like one of your novels? While His Majesty is stranded at sea, don't you see – this young couple, so in love, so beautiful. They are betrothed and must be wed.'

'But the banns must be published,' Sir Walter objects.

'In one of your stories would the characters wait for such a thing? Pah! If anything is to get His Majesty through what will surely be a tedious delay, it will be a story. It seems to me we must find a priest who believes, above all else, in love – to make that story great – to divert His Majesty, do you see?'

Elizabeth blushes but she cannot help smiling.

'See,' says Charlotte, suddenly impassioned. 'It is Mrs Rocheid's wish too. You will become Frau von Streitz,' she adds. 'Have you thought of that? Do you speak German?'

'No,' Elizabeth admits.

'Does Sir Walter speak French?' Johann asks.

'Little and badly,' Lady Charlotte confirms with amusement.

'But . . .' Johann halts the conversation, 'I must elicit His Majesty's permission. I am an officer of the royal household.'

Sir Walter considers the glass he is holding. It is crystal in the shape of a thistle. 'That is not entirely true. You have no official title.'

Johann does not mention that he is Keeper of the Royal Bastards.

'Technically, I mean,' Sir Walter continues. 'The post you occupy is not officially appointed. As I understand it?'

Johann smiles. 'That is correct. I am a German and the King of England cannot have foreigners among his personal staff.'

'His Majesty is King of Great Britain and Ireland,' Scott corrects him.

Johann bows to Sir Walter's point – today of all days. 'What do you say, Mrs Rocheid? Would it be fitting? Is it too soon?'

Elizabeth finds she cannot speak. Johann reaches across the snowy linen tablecloth and clasps her fingers. 'Yes,' she manages at last, finding she is more romantic than she might have imagined.

Sir Walter raises his glass. 'All right,' he says. 'We shall call on James Rocheid, shall we? It is only fitting you should have at least one of your relations present. And we will need to find a minister in this storm. Somebody who believes in love over custom for there is no time for the banns.'

'I don't want to rush you, Elizabeth. Your cousin after all has only lately passed,' Johann says carefully. 'Are you truly willing?'

She recalls the last conversation she had with Clementina about the seizing of life. 'I am,' she gushes. 'I do.'

'Well, in that case,' von Streitz replies, 'I might know the very fellow.'

It is dark and wet, but they call about the town collecting Elizabeth's people – James Rocheid in the club room at the Royal

Society on George Street and Belle counting her money on the sopha at Warriston Crescent. They make an odd party – the famous writer and his French wife, the man about town and the lately retired courtesan, and last of all Reverend Brunton, upon whom Johann calls in his rooms at the university, and willingly presses into the service of love. The carriages form a convoy that makes its way smartly down the Royal Mile and through the gates of Holyrood Palace, where, wrapped in oilskins and capes, they bustle inside and order the French chapel opened, much to Lady Charlotte's delight. The staff fetch candlesticks and incense and Reverend Brunton officiates by candlelight which emanates a truly golden glow, for the chapel's small altar is gilded and casts its warmth onto the red walls, reflecting the flames as if they are the summer sunlight on this dark evening.

James Rocheid gives Elizabeth away and Belle, fresh faced and delighted, is her bridesmaid. As she says 'I do,' Elizabeth can hardly contain her excitement. It was not this way before, she thinks, as she puts William Rocheid out of her mind for ever. Lady Scott weeps copiously as the reverend pronounces the couple man and wife and Johann pulls Elizabeth close and kisses her gently.

The party crowd the couple.

'I am so happy for you,' Lady Scott says, hugging Elizabeth as Belle jumps up and down like a schoolgirl.

'I'm proud of you, my boy,' Scott claps Johann on the back but it is Herr von Streitz who looks proud.

'Come,' Belle says. 'We must go up and open a bottle or two.'

Outside, the storm rages, but inside the wedding party sups burgundy in Johann's suite and as the news spreads the grace and favour residents come to offer good wishes.

'There is no cake,' Sir Walter complains. 'We cannot have that.'

Elizabeth swears she will bake one, but not now. Tomorrow, perhaps. And Johann sees to it that candied fruit is pilfered from the copious stocks laid in for the king's drawing room event, to sate Sir Walter's sweet tooth. Belle Brodie, the life and soul of the party, wants to stay up till dawn to celebrate her last night in the capital as well as her friend's marriage. Tomorrow she will tarry only long enough to make sure Edzel McBain is released from the Bridewell so she can set him to her service, by which she means he must make as much Dr Brodie's Most Efficacious Ladies' Bathing Oil in her absence as he can manage. Then she will leave for London, for she has business to attend to. Meantime Lady Charlotte dances with an old fellow from the upper floor – a marquis by all accounts. She laughs in delight and Sir Walter is glad to see his wife so happy. It has been a trying time, he realizes. He may have to furnish her with some rubies, after the royal visit.

'What do you expect His Majesty will make of your wedding, Herr von Streitz? ' Reverend Brunton asks.

'Sir Walter and I will row out and inform him. Tomorrow.'

'We shall make it through the storm to breakfast on the royal yacht,' Sir Walter proclaims.

Johann grins. 'I am not known for the ladies. I expect the king will be surprised.'

'Delighted,' Sir Walter says, 'he will be delighted.' He is sure of it.

Once the guests have left, the newly wed von Streitzes loiter around the table. Johann reaches for his wife.

'I have never seen much of the world,' she says.

'You will see it now,' he says gently, 'and you will take it at your own pace, my love. I promise.' And with that, he takes her hand and leads her to his bed.

Chapter Thirty-Six

The wind is still howling as the sun rises weakly on the greyest of mornings and Sir Walter and Johann von Streitz decide on a carriage for the two-mile drive to the dock. Anchored in the Firth, the royal yacht has attracted a few hardy sightseers on the shore despite the storm, including two small boys of noble birth who stole their mother's carriage and drove it to a vantage point where they shared a spyglass to make out the three masts of the *Royal George* denuded of sails on account of the gale. With this order of high-spirited behaviour being generally frowned upon, such is the city's excitement at the pending arrival of His Majesty that when he finds out what his sons have done, the boys' father merely exclaims 'Capital!' and joins them to have a look for himself.

Scott has arranged for four stout sailors and a young naval ensign to wait at the dockside next to an upturned wooden rowing vessel. There is no question of using a sail on a day like today. Here, to the north of the city, the wind whips even stronger, almost barrelling von Streitz into the swell as he steps out of the carriage. Scott grasps his friend's arm.

'I don't want to lose you,' he says with a smile. 'Your wife would never forgive me.'

They stare at the turbulent grey Firth beneath its troubled sky. It is a scene, Scott thinks, that even Mr Turner would find difficult to enliven. The ensign salutes.

'Sir Walter,' he greets the writer, whose face he recognizes from the flyleaf of his books. He is clearly unsure who the other fellow might be.

'Are your men ready?' Sir Walter enquires.

'They are volunteers,' the ensign says. His captain pronounced Sir Walter's idea 'pure folly' when he received the request the evening before, but he and his men are enjoined to the king's service and must drown for him if required.

Von Streitz stares over the side of the dock as they lower the boat. It seems, he thinks, too small in the face of this gale. And yet they must go. The storm is set to rage the whole day and there will be no backing down. One of the sailors raises the jack.

The ensign takes a whistle from his pocket and pipes his men into place, motioning Sir Walter and Johann onto the bench at the rear of the vessel before climbing aboard, so far to the front that he might be a figurehead.

'God bless His Majesty,' he says bravely and two of the sailors use their oars to push the boat from its sheltered position into the swell. Johann thinks that Elizabeth shall not be required to forgive Sir Walter if they both drown together. What seemed the night before a challenging prospect is now, he realizes, more extreme – a watery version of an army cavalry charge. As they cast off, he gives up a silent prayer that brings Alexander Brunton to mind and, for that matter, Clementina Rocheid's recently dug grave at St Cuthbert's.

They are all sodden in a snap. Beyond the shelter of the dock the waves are merely choppy for the first hundred yards before rising in more open water. Johann turns to Sir Walter to say something, but his words are whipped away on the breeze no matter how loudly he shouts them. At least the ensign's whistle pierces the ferocity of the gale. The first wave to crash over the side drenches their coats and knocks Johann's hat into the sea. The second penetrates his britches and undershirt, taking his breath away with its icy shock. This water comes from the North Sea and beyond its eastern shore joins the Baltic. He wonders if today, in Christiansborg Palace, the Danish royal family are sheltering from the other side of this freezing self-same storm. It seems so vast.

Each stroke of the oars moves the boat mere inches against the wind, but the ensign and his men do not seem to tire. They are like clockwork figures holding Scott and von Streitz safe. Such is the ferocity of the weather that while the *Royal George* is just about visible from the shore, here on the water they can no longer see it. Scott, always bluff, adopts a facial expression that might best be described as taciturn though like Johann his teeth are chattering and his hands shaking. It is not that the writer does not trust the young ensign but merely that in such conditions mistakes are too easily made. Scott has made a study of these instances – British army officers taking a wrong turn in Africa and losing the lives of fifty soldiers, naval captains misreading the compass and missing a safe port before running out of fresh water. He keeps these accounts, clipping them from the broadsheets, to use in his stories. Now he fears that he may become a cautionary tale.

One of the sailors loses hold of his oar, which is hopelessly swept away. The ensign's eyes hollow of all expression. He puts the man to bailing out while his fellows continue. Another freezing wave crashes over the side and Johann clings to the edge of his seat so tightly it grazes the palm of his hand. Then they see it, like a looming grey shadow. Von Streitz cannot calculate whether they have been on the water for five minutes or fifty, but the yacht is ahead of them, moving up and down in the swell as if it is sitting on the belly of a snoring giant. Two sailors lean over the side small as toys, pointing as they follow the rowing boat's tortuous progress. More men arrive on deck to witness this madness. Ropes are thrown up, ladders thrown down and the boat is tethered. Johann feels his heart pounding with relief and the men climb aboard to be greeted by the captain of the ship, pulling a greatcoat over his jacket as he emerges from his cabin.

'Good Lord,' he says. 'Sir Walter Scott!'

Scott laughs, mostly with relief. Both he and Johann are dripping. 'We came to welcome His Majesty to Scotland,' he says.

Below deck in the royal cabin the king has hardly slept and spent most of the night drinking rum laced with laudanum, which his doctor serves to quell His Majesty's seasickness. Things were fine until just off the Tyne, with George proclaiming proudly that he should use his yacht more. Now the captain is nervous that the king might decommission the vessel.

'Sir Walter,' George growls in a discouraging tone. 'Von Streitz.'

The sodden travellers bow very low. George's state room smells of sleep, stale sweat and vomit though they are both grateful it is dry. Von Streitz had forgotten the size of His Majesty's frame, which seems even larger here, with the king curled up in his nightgown and paisley wrap, which he has not yet forgone.

'Edinburgh is ready and at your pleasure, Your Majesty,' he says. 'Your subjects cannot wait to greet the king.'

'How did you get here?' George enquires. 'Look at the state of you.'

'It is some tale,' Scott promises. 'And one that includes a story of true love,' he adds, with a twinkle in his eye.

The king shifts. The last day has been, above all, boring, which is not a word he ever associates with the company of Sir Walter Scott. He softens.

'Well, let's have it,' he says as the cabin boy brings hot rum for the king's guests.

'May I?' Scott theatrically asks Johann.

'Please,' Johann bows his head, 'go ahead.'

George looks quizzical.

'It is, you see, a story of true love in which Herr von Streitz plays a leading role.'

The king grins. 'Young Johann!' He lets out a bark of laughter. Johann is useful but has never displayed a glimmer of interest in women, despite the role the king has bestowed upon him.

'It is Scotland herself, Your Majesty, that inspired him. Let me explain . . .'

Within the hour dry clothes have been brought to the shifting cabin and the king's table set with figs, honey and more rum. A game of piquet is promised over which the men will continue what has become a most jovial and ribald conversation. So delighted is His Majesty with the tale of his man marrying a widow, and an older woman to boot, that the matter of royal assent to the union has not even come up.

'I shall have to give you something,' George says. 'Or to your wife at least.'

Johann pauses. This is when most men ask for a knighthood or the gift of grace and favour accommodation. 'Well,' he says, 'there is something close to her heart. She is interested in botanical illustration and assisted in that capacity at Kew Garden for a number of years. Now she is connected to the university's Botanic Garden in Edinburgh.' George looks bored already. 'I wonder might I write on Your Majesty's behalf to commend the work of the Garden, which is run by a most competent man, making interesting advances.'

George sighs. Johann's new wife sounds quite as boring as he is. He had hoped for a more merry widow. Still, a letter will cost him nothing. 'Very well, if that is what Mrs von Streitz desires,' he says. 'Now, tell me about the Melville girl who is coming out. I have heard she is anything but a tasty little piece.'

Johann, having avoided all contact with the Melvilles, cannot answer, but Sir Walter steps in. 'I visited the other afternoon. She is a most individual young lady,' he says. 'Fearless in fashion.'

This sounds much more fun.

'Gossip!' the king declares banging the table. 'I demand gossip. Henry's niece, isn't she?'

Scott grins. This is his forte. 'The young lady has a dowry of twenty thousand guineas, I hear,' he starts, 'though any husband who takes her will earn that money. She is strong-willed, they say, and used to getting her own way.'

George swills more rum. As far as he's concerned, Edinburgh's welcome can wait. He is perfectly satisfied, here, sitting out the storm.

Two trees in the Botanic Garden have been felled in the wind and one of the greenhouses smashed at the east end. The *Agave americana* has been covered in waxed cotton and tied down with rope, which is the best McNab can do to preserve the final flower and its precious seed. McNab sheltered in the shed all night with two garden boys who, between snatches of sleep, did their best to see the Garden's plants through the ravages of the storm. Still, puddles have turned into pools, the lake has burst its bank and flooded the low ground around the willow tree and the delicate summer petals of the legume beds are smashed to pieces.

The gardeners arrive at the usual time and McNab sends the night boys home. 'Get some sleep,' he says.

'What about you, sir?' asks Jack, the eager water boy.

'I am the head man,' McNab says simply and dismisses him.

He sends one of the fresh boys for bread and ham and milk to warm. They cannot tackle this without fuel. Then he pairs the men and allocates them a section each to review now it is light for they must know the damage. 'We meet here again in an hour,' he says, 'to make a plan.'

Outside, as the gardeners set off, he is about to make his way to the greenhouses, fearing the worst, when James appears through the gate. The boy is sodden.

'What are you doing here?' McNab asks.

'I came to help, Pa.'

McNab smiles. There is limited help James can give but he's glad to see him.

'Get yourself dry in the shed,' he says.

'Where are you going?'

'I must assess the damage.'

'I shall come with you,' the boy replies solemnly.

Down the path it is worse than he feared. The ground around the aloe is covered in shards of glass as if there has been some kind of explosion. The oilskin has been whipped away by the wind and the great aloe's stem felled. There will be no seeds – none at all. The *Agave americana* has come to nothing.

'What do we do?' James asks with consternation.

McNab puts his hand on his son's shoulder. 'This is the game upon which we are engaged,' he says stoutly. 'A battle with all the forces of the world. Come, I must write Mr Graham a report. We will seek more seeds from America, if we can get them. In thirty years, God willing, you might be here to try again. I hope you make a better job of it than I have.'

The McNabs turn back to the hut. Waiting at the door, the under-gardener from Inverleith House, Calum loiters in the doorway.

'Everything all right at the big house?' McNab asks.

Calum says there are trees down, but nobody hurt, thank God. 'I am sent by Mrs Rocheid to offer help – hands or equipment from the estate, the horses if you should need them, sir.'

Elizabeth is truly an extraordinary woman, McNab thinks admiringly. He notices that Calum's cheeks are rosy – he seems delighted about something. 'The mistress married, sir, last night,' he adds. 'We are to call her Mrs von Streitz, now. She arrived home at dawn and immediately thought of the Garden.'

McNab lets out a laugh. 'Good for her,' he says. 'Send my heartiest congratulations – from both me and her little pupil here. And my thanks. But we have men and we can manage. We will welcome her again, I hope. When the weather is mended.'

Calum doffs his cap.

'Go through the holly,' McNab directs him. 'It's a shorter route.' Then, with James beside him, he turns his attention to the work of the Garden.

Nine days later

Margaret has spent the past few days in seventh heaven, for the mistress has removed her from Inverleith House to Dalkeith Palace, where the von Streitzes are staying with (Margaret quivers at the thought) His Majesty the King. Between seeing to her lady's wardrobe and helping her dress, Margaret, bursting with pride, has befriended the Duke of Buccleuch's first footman with whom this week, once the household is abed, she has taken to dallying near the dairy and sharing a plate of whatever is left over from the royal table – exotic fruits, sweet French sauces and the dregs of the claret. Mrs von Streitz's maid thinks that life cannot possibly get any better as she brings up her lady's breakfast and opens the curtains. She hoped her lady would marry the German gentleman from the moment it became clear he cared for her.

Elizabeth sits up. Johann left just after daybreak to ride out with some of the king's fellows. Alone, she inspects the tray – tea, a breakfast wine, two boiled eggs and warm rolls with curls of butter and a craggy mound of marmalade. Propped against the milk jug there is a letter on thick, creamy paper. She picks up the missive and clicks the seal open with interest for she recognizes the writing.

Regent Street
20 August 1822
My dearest Elizabeth

I have taken the most wonderful rooms for it seems that the ton is away. What with the king's visit and the weather London is half-empty, but this has bequeathed me many possibilities and I have engaged a seamstress who in the normal run can hardly be got. She is sewing me gowns in the Italian style and also turbans. Which, when you get to court, you will discover, are all the rage. The smartest ladies wear them trimmed with ostrich feathers and pearls. You will love it here. It so much more amusing in town than when you sojourned at Richmond, I'll be bound. Ladies are permitted at the Royal Society, only for some lectures but quite fascinating, there is a public art gallery opened at Dulwich and riding in Hyde Park is an education. I have had more than one proposal, but I shall confide in you when you arrive. If this is the slim pickings, I cannot imagine how much fun we will have when the king returns.

You will be glad to hear that your sketches have proved invaluable and I have commissioned Mrs Christina Robertson, no less, to paint me as you designed the picture, but in oils. I have asked her to work into the fabric draped behind, the little yellow flower you dried from the aloe and star anise on the wallpaper. She exhibited last year at the Scottish Academy summer show and I judge her most talented. She also has a deal to say about Scotland's great male painters – Sir Walter will have a fit. The long and the short of it is I will be here for some months – so come soon! I miss you and look forward to hosting you in my rooms when you get to Buckingham House, which it is said Mr Nash has almost finished to His Majesty's specifications.

Your friend
Isabel Brodie

Elizabeth pours a cup of tea. Her return to London will be better for having a friend, she thinks, with a prick of excitement, and wonders if Mrs Robertson might also paint her. Now she is Frau von Streitz it seems fitting, though perhaps not to be surrounded by flowers, as Belle will be shown, but in her own studio, with paints and charcoal, for Johann has promised she will have a place of her own. She sips the tea and directs Margaret.

'I will wear the sprigged muslin with the tartan sash, please.'

Currant Bun bustles out of the room and Elizabeth smiles, for she has not yet told her maid where they are heading, and she knows the girl will be pleased. There is a tentative knock at the door and Lady Charlotte Scott puts round her head.

'Good morning,' she greets Elizabeth. 'You are late abed for a lady of the royal household. The ball was a great success.'

'It was,' Elizabeth smiles. She had not thought she would enjoy to dance so much and the jugglers caused quite the commotion. Her confidence is growing, she realizes, and it feels as if she will never be a wallflower again.

'Do you find yourself tired, Mrs von Streitz?'

Elizabeth smiles again, for she relishes no longer being Mrs Rocheid. 'Not at all,' she says. 'Quite the reverse.'

'They say tonight there will be fireworks,' Lady Charlotte continues. 'Tell me, how is married life?'

Elizabeth tries to look nonchalant – sophisticated, like this older, wiser woman. 'Fireworks,' she whispers. 'And not only in the sky.'

Charlotte gives a little Gallic shrug. 'How poetic,' she says. 'I thought you might like to walk with me in the garden. The Buccleuchs' man is happy to give us a tour of his rarer plants, but we must go now.'

'How charming,' Elizabeth replies, putting the tray to one side. 'I am most interested in botany. I shall be as quick as I can.'

Author's Historical Note:

Late in 2019 I met an editor in Contini's restaurant at 103 George Street in Edinburgh. It was a chance encounter – my agent texted me from a booth in the front of the dining room saying she was with an editor who she thought I ought to meet. I texted by return to say I was up at the back. The editor, Emma Herdman, was tremendously patient as I gabbled about women's history during the tail end of the Enlightenment in the city – about the female artists, scientists, salonnières, writers, philosophers and sex workers whose legacy has been consistently underplayed. I ranted about the injustice of the fact that outside the window behind our table there were only statues of men (many of whom had lesser legacies and made fewer positive contributions than some of the women I mentioned.) We also discussed the move of the Royal Botanic Garden Edinburgh from its site on Leith Walk to Inverleith (which took place between 1820 and 1823) and the visit of George IV to the city in August 1822. The Garden, which was founded in 1670 was about to celebrate its 350th anniversary. Then, reader, in an act of faith, Emma commissioned this story – literally on a couple of paragraphs that I had jotted down. It was to be light-hearted, she said, but catch the spirit of the city at this fascinating time in its history. I promised to do my best.

We met several times after that – in Edinburgh and in London – and talked over the phone as well as emailing back and forth. During the Covid-19 lockdown we FaceTimed like gossipy Enlightenment schoolgirls. Whatever the medium, our interactions often had the synchronicity of that first meeting – at one point (out of lockdown) when I was staying in my daughter's flat in Highgate it turned out Emma lived less than a mile away and we could hook up for meetings in a convenient coffee shop nearby. This felt very Enlightenment.

I had written both fiction and non-fiction books set in the period 1819–1845 but I had never set one in my hometown. I can honestly say that every day of writing this book was an absolute pleasure for lots of reasons, among them the fact that it turns out I was ready to channel my passion for the city where I live (and its history) into a novel.

For me an historical novel is a time machine that takes a reader back to where they come from. It casts light on the modern world. I slid the fiction of this story right up against the real history of the summer of 1822. Many characters in this book existed in real life and some of the fictional ones have real roots. I hope I have not horrified anybody by employing this technique which was the best way I could think of, of bringing to life the spirit of the New Town and Inverleith in the run up to George IV's visit and the many extraordinary residents of this extraordinary town at that time. The melding of fact and fiction, I hope, serves to engage the imagination.

For clarity, however: the Rocheid family did live in Inverleith House, and James was real – by all accounts a flamboyant gentleman about town. The new site of the Garden was purchased in 1820 from him and he continued to live in Inverleith House on what then became the western edge of the Garden. Today, Inverleith House is a treasured exhibition space with an artistic programme that amplifies the Garden's environmental work.

I concocted both Clementina and Elizabeth Rocheid for my own ends. I named Clementina after Clementina Sobieska, the love of James Francis Edward Stuart's life and a Jacobite heroine, for I fancied the Rocheids had been Jacobites in the century prior to this story, when Clementina would have been born.

Belle Brodie is also fictional though I concocted her from tantalising glimpses of sex workers in the city who appeared in court, and others who are immortalized in records in London and in passing in the poetry of the era . . .

Ah, poets. Or for the purposes of this book – The Poet. Robert Burns fathered several illegitimate children and to my mind, it is unlikely that we know about all of them, so Duncan Tennent was an easy fictional addition to the story, as was Mhairi MacDonald who I created in memory of the thousands – literally – of women who brewed and distilled in the era. I like that she is someone who prospers despite her disability and is a Gael making good, when, sadly, so many 18th and 19th century Highlanders were subject to the grim genocide that was the Highland Clearances. It is a bugbear of mine that in most historical fiction working-class people exist in the story only in relation to their employers – often painted in two dimensional terms (good if they don't betray their masters, bad if they do). I wanted to make sure that my working-class characters had lives of their own – secrets, dreams and beliefs. So, alongside Duncan and Mhairi, Nellie Patterson, Belle Brodie's not-so-faithful maid, is a girl who loves music and longs for more of it in her life. She creates her own moral universe, as all the best people do.

Real-life characters William McNab and Robert Graham are both well documented. In his time, Graham was considered an ingenious and successful horticultural transplanter, and as a medical doctor, he co-founded the Botanical Society of Edinburgh and went on to establish the Garden's tropical Palm House. Under his supervision, like in the story, McNab invented a transplanting machine and transported mature trees across the city with the help of 12 horses. McNab himself was, by all accounts, an inspiring gardener, talented plantsman and excellent teacher. There is also real correspondence which documents McNab's mission to elicit the promised pay rise for his work at the Garden. He was not alone in being chronically underpaid. Beside the long hours committed to working in the Garden, several of the gardeners had side-jobs, including ones as far from the botanical world as Customs Officers. I always wonder (though there is nothing specific that leads me to this – only a novelist's spider sense) if Graham was really on McNab's side. Records show that in real life, McNab and Graham worked well together, and given all this, it seems to me Graham, who earned a thousand pounds a year in the Keeper's post could have pushed harder earlier on to support McNab's work. McNab certainly wasn't asking for anything unwarranted and in the book, I give him the helping hand of some fictional scandalous information to forward his case.

In the Royal Botanic Garden archive, I found letters where McNab was swapping seeds and botanical samples and specimens in return for food for his family. I also noted an instance of candles bought for the new Garden being put through on expenses that I suspect were ordered to augment the stingy 'candle and hearth' allowance given to McNab to run his home – the Botanic Cottage which has now been re-sited at Inverleith and is open to the public. This gave rise to the fictional sale of the seeds to Mrs Dickson (also real), a step further into the illicit than I found in real life. But it is no fiction that life for the McNab family (which consisted of McNab, his wife, Elizabeth Whiteman, and their nine children – five sons and four daughters) was financially challenging. Catherine McNab – only just into double digits when we meet her in the story – would later go on to write a book about the Botany of the Bible, having been bequeathed, alongside her sisters, all her father's inheritance because, as he put it in his will, in life he had dedicated the entirety of his financial resources to educating his sons. Catherine's brother, James, whose childhood botanical drawings are today held in the archive at the Royal Botanic Garden Edinburgh, would go on to scheme his way into the Head Gardener's post at the second big garden to be established at Inverleith (by the Royal Caledonian Horticultural Society – a plan alluded to by Belle in this story). As an adult, James McNab also undertook botanical expeditions abroad, contributed botanical artwork which engravers and lithographers used to produce botanical plates in journals, and contributed to several horticultural magazines and the general Edinburgh press as well as Scottish botanical and general science journals. I found myself immensely fond of the McNabs as I read the material relating to their real lives – I hope that comes across in the story.

There is also evidence which suggests that the real-life Robert Graham was quite the host. In 1826 when the naturalist and painter John James Audubon visited Edinburgh, he dined with the Grahams at 62 Great King Street and commented in a letter to a friend that the evening was 'embarrassing' by which he likely meant, 'extraordinarily lavish'. It is this letter that led me to cast the Grahams as hosts with an eye to social advancement and also had me writing into the emotional gap of insecurity that might have existed for Graham. It's this opening which, in the book, Belle Brodie takes advantage of, and the vanity of which leads him into his affair with Nellie. That being said, I have likely painted Graham as worse than he really was, for there is nothing to suggest that he was actually unfaithful, and he is fondly remembered in the Garden's archive as a well-loved Regius Keeper, who held the position between 1820-1845, when he died relatively young from a tumour.

One of my earlier novels, *The Secret Mandarin*, follows the 1840s career of Berwickshire gardener and botanist, Robert Fortune (one of the most stone-cold ambitious people I've ever found in the archive), who apprenticed at the Royal Botanic Garden Edinburgh in the 1830s. When I started writing this book it was in part knowing Fortune's story that meant this was a familiar world to me. I also discovered an intriguing and delightful connection when I was halfway through writing *The Fair Botanists*. I had already written another historical novel about Maria Graham, who travelled extensively in South America during the 1820s. Maria's first husband was Robert Graham's distant cousin. My novel, *On Starlit Seas*, features other female members of the Dundas/Graham clan (who were by all accounts quite snobbish, to be frank.) Maria remains one of my favourite historical characters of the period but, as she bears no other connection to Edinburgh apart from this one, I was unable to get her into this story except when Robert compares himself to 'his cousin' Thomas who is 'the adventuring sort'. Sadly, Thomas has already died by this time in Valparaiso, Chile, though the news has not yet made it home. All of these links demonstrate the wonderfully rich texture of late Georgian and early Victorian life and the interconnectedness of that world.

The competition with Kew Garden suggested in the book has its genesis in an article I found in a botanical journal of the 1830s which talked about how much better things were between Kew and its many sister institutions, since the changes made in the running of the institution focused more on the good of science and the country than that of private individuals. I suspect Sir Joseph Banks, while extraordinary, was not a generous man – certainly not to people who he may have considered merely of functional interest (gardeners and plant hunters alike).

Johann von Streitz is entirely fictional and came to me one afternoon in January 2020 while I was travelling by train to Glasgow. He is a concrete product of the Rocheid family's genuine historical connection to Germany and that of the Hanoverian elite. The character I came up with looks like an historical version of the well-dressed young man who was sitting opposite me on the journey. He reminded me of a modern-day Beau Brummell in understated and immaculate Doc Martens and a Norwegian jacket. I hope I didn't stare too much – I had to take it all in when I could. He was tremendously handsome.

Likewise, many ideas for storylines and backdrops emanated from real-life, though I have adapted them. McNab did move trees (the highest one a forty-three-foot alder) through the streets of Edinburgh. He would later write extensively about this extraordinary process. The last public flogging in the city did take place in the summer of 1822. There was a huge distillery just over the city boundary at the Water of Leith and there was a riot there in the late 1700s when the contingent delivering grain to the distillery was attacked by a working-class mob who were starving due to localised famine. The floor of a house on Picardy Place did fall in but not until two years later. 'Love potions' were a genuine focus of interest. Two Edinburgh shop boys were found guilty of trying to create one with which they literally poisoned a young woman – the key ingredient was 'Spanish fly' – in 1824. The father of the girl was a courier who lived on Thistle Street (like Edzel McBain's fictional and more drunken dad). While what the lads were attempting sounds more like a 'rhohypnol' incident than an actual attempt to make somebody fall in love, this in part, inspired Belle's idea to make her magical perfume. In other inspiration, strawberries (or as we know them, fragaria x ananassa) were a relatively new product of modern gardening in the early 1820s, though they did not engender the heady excitement of pineapple cultivation (most likely because anyone rich or poor could grow them whereas pineapples required heated greenhouses – a luxury beyond the reach of most). The smell of strawberries is sometimes pumped at a low level into gymnasiums as it enhances the physical performance of men (as Belle discovers). Of the other scents that Belle uses to manipulate those around her, many are used by retail outlets and in the hospitality industry today to encourage certain behaviours. The encouraging of behaviour by smell is a dark art. That's all I'm going to say about that.

The glorious Lady Liston was a real-life character too, one of Scotland's many botanical women, some of whose books I tip in the text. I took a liberty with her – she was born in Antigua and in real life never visited Bermuda. I wrote a short story about Lady Liston's return from Constantinople and her first encounter with Belle Brodie for the National Library of Scotland (where her papers are held). It is available online on the library's site, should a reader wish to hear more about her. She was extraordinary. In fact many such women whose legacies I greatly admire appear only as asides in the book. Clementina's 'poor, dear Mrs Brunton', whose novels I would contend are as good if not better than Jane Austen's (try them) and her husband Alexander, who never fully gets over his bereavement (though he tries to in fiction by engaging Belle). As in the story,

Alexander did become Moderator of the Church of Scotland in 1823. Also, the allusion by Clementina to Burns' poem to the 'Ferrier lasses', the eldest of whom, Jane, went on to make a valuable historical record of Stirling Castle that is treasured today and the youngest, Susan, who wrote novels that Sir Walter Scott claimed were better than his own. There is a strong case to be made that Sir Walter was right.

Sir Walter Scott is real, of course. He sat on the committee that was appointed to organize the king's jaunt to Scotland and quickly took over the organization of events with his extraordinary vision and indeed, sense of propaganda and contributed to the Victorian romanticization of Scottish history that so frustrates Scottish historians today. I like a lot about Sir Walter – he supported many women writers and good causes (including helping to found the Edinburgh Academy, just as it says in the text) although he made some dreadful misjudgements, among them not fully supporting the abolition of the slave trade. The idea that crosses his mind in Chapter Twelve is the building of the Radical Road around Arthur's Seat, a plan to keep dangerous radicals in employment that he put into action in real life after the king's visit.

In passing in the book we also catch glimpses of other real-life male Enlightenment figures Adam Smith and David Hume through the agency of Clementina's memory. It is a sadness to me that I have not managed to include Sir John Sinclair (of the Royal Caledonian Horticultural Society) who looks furious at his Highland garb in the contemporary portrait of him painted to celebrate the king's visit. There simply was no way to shoehorn him in, but it is a brilliant portrait in which he clearly wishes he was not wearing tartan (and a huge sporran). It's worth searching out.

This brings me to the greatest liberty I have taken with the actual history, which is the timeframe of the royal visit. Poor Sir Walter and the rest of the committee were literally given only three weeks to make the arrangements. George IV (as he appears in the book and in life) was mercurial and expected his court to jump at every whim.

Here I have given Sir Walter (and Scotland) an inkling that the king might be on his way, earlier than anyone would have had one, and certainly earlier than Scott could have made concrete plans. But for the purposes of the story (and the creation of Johann von Streitz) I went with that. The king was always going to leave London during August to go somewhere (he visited Dublin in 1821) so it's not unreasonable to think some of his close courtiers might have suspected he would be on the move northwards. Conversely, I denied Sir Walter his full three weeks' notice and allowed him only ten days or so to firm up the royal arrangements.

It should also be noted that the *Agave americana* is not these days considered an aloe at all, though it was referred to in the period as the Great Aloe. If you are a botanist I hope this doesn't drive you too crazy while reading, but I have stayed consistent with the terms used in the 1820s. Likewise, the word 'hothouse' isn't used any longer at the Botanic Garden where there are now 'glasshouses', though in the 1820s both terms were used, as in the text.

I would also like to add a short note about use of Scots. I have used quite a few Scots words during the course of the book, especially where working-class people are speaking. Clementina inserts Scots into her (largely English) patter as a matter of course. In her generation it was the lingua franca of all Scotland, though English was beginning to dominate by the time we get to 1822 at the end of her life. I have been asked in the past to remove Scots from manuscripts but in this case, the editors were understanding and appreciated that it provides a real flavour of speech at this time. I was glad to be able to do that though in real life, please note, there would have been more of it!

Lastly, I want to say for clarity that the Edinburgh I have written about in this book (the New Town of the city, that is) was built on the back of the Atlantic Slave Trade with all its horrors. This is a part of our history that Scotland is only just coming to terms with (not only in our capital city but across the country). This story is set in 1822 and though slave trading was abolished in the British Empire in 1807, slavery in British Colonies was not abolished until 1833. Legal cases in England and Scotland established that a slave could not be held in either country (except of course for the enslaved native salters who were not freed until the end of the century). Thus, the trade was still underway internationally and it was backed by many wealthy Scots whose families benefitted financially from the enslavement of others. Though this is not the main content of this book (if any publisher would like to commission a novel where this is the main storyline, please get in touch) I could not ignore it. So, I have mentioned that Belle's father owns a plantation and has 'taken advantage' of one of his female Black slaves (a move that Belle sees through). While the Black community living in Scotland was small in this era I wanted to represent their hidden history as much as I could so I also gave Belle a Black neighbour (who was born in Scotland for we tend to forget that there was a Black community here over many centuries, albeit a small one). The fictional characters of Jane and Anne Melville, the purchasers of Belle's perfume are relatives of the notorious Henry Dundas, Viscount Melville, an MP known contemptuously as the King of Scotland, whose work in the House of Commons delayed the abolition of slavery by over a decade. One historical argument makes the case that this was the best way to get the act through parliament but there is another view that Dundas did so in bad faith, allowing slave owners to continue to import African slaves and instigate breeding programmes on their plantations, thus circumnavigating the need for the transatlantic slave trade. Certainly, Dundas's ally William Pitt commented that the delay was the worst of all possible routes to abolition. Whatever Dundas's reasons, his actions at Westminster resulted in hundreds of thousands more Black people entering into chattel slavery than had slavery been made illegal more quickly. It is a shocking and horrible part of our history and my own view is that we need to own it properly. I hope we can find the courage to do so. While a plaque explaining Henry Dundas's involvement in the slave trade adorns his monument on St Andrew Square today it is my own view that the plaque should remain, but the monument be removed. Henry is Edinburgh's true Disgrace, rather than the monument on Calton Hill and we have, after all, very many extraordinary women who could be honoured in that prominent public space. I feel my fictional character Anne Melville would agree (though for entirely different reasons).

It was a pleasure and an honour to be commissioned to write this book. I have been visiting the Garden since I was a child and have fond memories of feeding the squirrels there with my younger brothers. The Royal Botanic Garden is such a resource for the people of Edinburgh. However, although I was aware of some of the Garden's history, I was delighted when diving into the archive to find such a rich and evocative part of our city's story of which I was unaware. It felt as if I was putting together a jigsaw puzzle that precursed my own memories – a link back to the previous residents of the city.

Thank you for reading and I hope, enjoying my foray into the daft days of the summer of 1822. Please forgive any lapses and mistakes I have made in writing about this rambunctious and exciting period. I hope Elizabeth and Belle and their adventures stay with you, an echo of our foremothers and the lives they might have lived, for history is endlessly complicated and full of secrets, and in my view is as much herstory as his one.

Acknowledgements

The kindness of all at RBGE but especially Paula Bushell, Leonie Paterson, Graham Hardy, Fiona Inches, Emma Nicolson, David Affleck, David Rae, Amy Porteous at Inverleith House, Laura Gallagher and Henry Noltie.

At the National Galleries of Scotland, Grainne Rice and Imogen Gibbon helped with tips for female artists and also tried valiantly to find a pictorial representation of the trees moving through the streets of Edinburgh. Ladies, we have to hope some brave soul makes a movie for history this time has let us down.

Jane Anderson, a fellow historical writer who told me the story of Christina Robertson, a Scottish painter who became famous in St Petersburg in the era. I mention her only in passing but Jane is currently engaged in writing a novel based on her story. One for my To Be Read pile.

Sutherland Forsyth who at the time I spoke to him worked at Holyrood Palace. Sutherland was fun, patient and helpful – thank you for all your help. Deborah Clarke also from the palace, who generously gave me hints and tips about George's visit and the geography and uses of buildings in the King's Park of 1822.

Ashley and Eilidh Douglas kindly helped me with my Scots – all errors are mine, of course, but Ashley and Eilidh are always generous in their support and always interesting in what they have to say! In real life, as well as in the text, they have helped up my Scots game and I so appreciate their input and sunny personalities.

Also Rachel McCormack, whose periodic historical food and wine tips always make my ears prick up; Val McDermid (ever the inspiration); Jenny Brown (a great agent and a great friend); Deborah Anne Reid, whose PhD thesis is full of amazing female gardeners of the period (and beyond). I bumped into Deborah quite by chance at an advance screening of Sue Kemp's excellent feminist documentary about the Edinburgh Seven and she generously chatted to me for ages as I fangirled her doctorate. Thanks are also due to Leslie Hills (always) who read an early draft of the book and gave brilliant historical feedback. Also thanks to the many who encouraged me on twitter – a quick shoutout in particular to Andrew Morton and Andy Arthur, who both sent maps I hadn't seen before when I needed them. You stars.

To Emma Herdman who commissioned the book and Kate Howard and Lily Cooper at Hodder who brought it to publication, thank you for championing this project over the difficulties of the Covid-19 crisis and the changeover of editorial oversight that occurred when Emma got her dream job and Kate went on maternity leave. Lily burned the midnight oil working through the edits and the final draft of the book is better for it. I didn't get to meet the other editors who tirelessly corrected my need to spell realise with an s and not capitalize His Majesty (cos I'm a republican) – thank you for ironing out my cracks!

Lastly to my family. This book was mostly written during the Coronavirus lockdown, when I foraged through the real history of Edinburgh's streets outside of the archive – in my imagination and on deserted afternoon walks – latterly, with Dotty the miniature wire-haired dachsund, a lockdown addition to our household. In that, this book was a saving grace – I loved flinging myself into it. I needed to. But it also made me difficult to be around at a time that was fraught with other difficulties for writing historical novels is an immersive venture. Thanks for supporting me always – Alan, Molly and Jon – the best non-conformist, creative posse a locked-in writer ever had. Persevere *et esse felix*. You lot are the only reasons I do anything at all.

The Interview

Edinburgh, December 1818.

It is just past dusk at four of the clock, and Mhairi is heading in the direction of the Cowgate, past the drinking clubs and whorehouses of the Old Town. It does not matter a jot that it is dark, for she navigates by means of smell and sound and the tap-tap of her stick on the setts. The stick has two purposes, for Mhairi is a pretty girl and from time to time people do not realise that she is not as vulnerable as they hope.

Now she pulls her thick, lambswool scarf over her coat; the dog days of summer so far gone that they seem a kind of myth. She hurries past the Royal Exchange where a carthorse tethered to an iron ring whinnies. Mhairi wonders, not for the first time, if it is true that thirty years ago, a person would not have been able to walk a clear block here without hailing a fellow resident and engaging in an interesting conversation. She came to Edinburgh six months ago and likes it well enough in service at a lodging house, but she is well aware that though this part of town houses the court and the college, it is not what it once was.

She swiftly bypasses the freezing straggle of beggars loitering behind St Giles and turns down a muddy close that smells like a sewer. The ground is even enough on the High Street but the hilly closes running off it are irregular. The place seems almost deserted this evening. She has no more formed this thought than a raucous babble of students bursts out of a doorway onto the blackened wynd. Mhairi skilfully dodges out of sight and waits for the gentlemen to pass. She is close here to the medical school's lecture rooms and the city morgue with its murky but necessary trade in illicit corpses. This time of year the place does not smell as bad. As the drunk voices recede, Mhairi pulls in again to let an old-fashioned sedan chair pass, lit by mounted candle lamps in the gloom.

The sedan stops. Then a man's voice. 'Mhairi MacDonald is that you?'

Mhairi can smell cheap spirits and fresh sweat but she does not recognise the man until he speaks again, this time in Gaelic, dripping with the familiar vowels of the croft where she was born, like the sharp tang of a seaweed shore. 'Nach eil thu eòlach orm?' *Don't you know me?*

'Seamus?'

A laugh like a creaking cart on a country track. 'Aye, lass.' He takes a breath, about to say that she looks well, perhaps, for folk say that to Mhairi often, with her glass green eyes and peachy skin even now, over the worst of the winter. Seamus, however, doesn't get the words out and instead a woman's voice slices through the icy darkness as the sedan chair's occupant pulls back the velvet curtain and leans out of the window. An old woman, Mhairi thinks, sensing the steely tang of freckled, elderly skin, musty lace cuffs and a rich, fur collar.

'James, why have we stopped?'

'Sorry ma'am,' Seamus says. Mhairi hears him howking the sedan chair higher.

'Who are you?' the female voice asks.

The girl curtseys and says her name.

The old lady pauses, trying to ascertain Mhairi's relation to the sedan-chair bearer, who is at least two decades older. The girl does not look like a huur. 'I'm Lady Miller of Howe,' the woman announces. 'You're a Highlander, are you?'

'I am, madam.'

Lady Miller inspects the girl in the flickering candlelight. The old quine has a nose for who is who and does not go solely by appearances. She has remained living here on what is now the wrong side of town, refusing to relocate to the double-fronted townhouse her family has secured at the fashionable end of George Street. For thirty years she has maintained that the New Town of Edinburgh will never catch on. 'It's too far from the palace,' she says when her son begs her to move into the suite he's had prepared on the second floor, overlooking St Andrews Kirk.

'Holyrood is a wreck, mother,' he bats back but Lady Miller of Howe will have none of his New Town nonsense. A mere twenty years ago refugees from the French court resided in the palace. 'Flibbertygibbet,' she dismisses him.

Now she inspects this young woman. 'Turn around,' she says, taking in Mhairi's tidy figure and her snub nose, pink with cold. 'Remove your scarf,' she adds, peering at a golden lock of hair that has escaped and deciding she wishes to see more of it. The girl is extraordinarily attractive, a trait which Lady Miller of Howe considers most inconvenient in a servant.

'Where are you working?'

Mhairi gives her address.

'Do you like it?'

'Well enough, madam.'

'What do you do?'

'I make soap,' Mhairi says. 'Lavender and goat milk with sea salt . I run messages and brew small beer for the gentlemen's breakfast.' It is not all she does, but these are the duties Mhairi enjoys.

Lady Miller of Howe raises a scant eyebrow. 'But you're sightless.'

'Yes, madam.'

'So how do you . . . ?'

'By the smell,' Mhairi says. 'And the feel on my fingers. Mistress Anderson says that she's never had soap as fine nor beer as gusty. I can tell how fresh things are from a sniff, you see.'

A snort of laughter from the carriage. 'How do you know James?'

Seamus cuts in. 'Mhairi's father and I belong to the same place.'

The lady's lips tighten. Highlanders are too dramatic. Belong to the same place, indeed. 'Well, you belong here now, James.'

'Aye, ma'am.'

'Because most people hire their sedan bearers whereas I employ mine,' the old lady emphasises.

'I'm grateful, ma'am,' Seamus assures her.

Neither of them adds that the arrangement suits Lady Miller as much as it does Seamus. Street-hired sedans are filthy and the bearers erratic. She must have her own chair, for horse drawn conveyances are useless in the Old Town's slim vennels and only a sedan can deposit you inside your house so that you need not step in the muck. This is another quibble she has with her son, who now has not one carriage but two of the damn things.

'I should like to try your soap, Miss MacDonald,' Lady Miller announces. 'Lavender, salt and goat milk . . . most intriguing.'

Mhairi pauses before taking her chance. 'I can bring some, ma'am, but barley and rose would be better for your skin. The gentlemen at the lodging house are students.' She does not say they are younger but that is what she means.

'Barley and rose? Extraordinary,' Lady Miller of Howe declares but the girl has caught her attention. The lady's mother had a rose garden of great blousy flowers that suddenly blows into the old woman's mind; a soft breeze she has not felt in years. There were barley fields too at Lasswade where she was brought up. 'You may bring some,' she pronounces. 'I'll not pay more than the apothecary's soap, mind.' She taps the side of the sedan chair. As Seamus moves off he winks, though Mhairi cannot see.

*

The following afternoon, Mhairi finds Lady Miller of Howe's residence, on the Canongate near Whitefoord House. The sky is spitting rain half-heartedly as she turns off the road. Lady Millar has the first and second floors down the vennel. Her neighbours used to be titled folk, but these days the close houses a blacksmith and a cabinetmaker. Mhairi finds Seamus whitewashing the stair. 'It's sixpence ha'penny an ounce for soap,' he says, climbing down the steps backwards. 'I checked what the apothecary charges.'

'Thank you,' Mhairi replies and does not add that she checked too. 'Shall I leave it in the kitchen?'

'Aye. The mistress is with Mrs Stein. Of the whisky,' he says, touching Mhairi's arm to lead her in the right direction 'Do you hear from home?'

The girl nods. 'My mother writes. I ask the gentlemen to read her letters. My mistress cannot nor the other maid nor Cook.'

'I'll do it,' Seamus offers. 'I'd like to hear about the old place.'

Inside, the warm air is scented with cock-a-leekie, yeasty bread and the smell of a plump woman with wafts of flour up her meaty arms. Seamus takes the parcel. 'Is this the blind girl?' Cook asks, as if Mhairi is deaf, not sightless. Mhairi curtseys and Cook stifles a chortle. 'Jemmy can take it in,' she says and there is a snap and rustle as a footman, Mhairi supposes, is dispatched. 'Would you like a cup of milk?'

'Yes please.' It is put into Mhairi's hand with an oat biscuit that smells of butter.

'Sit down,' Seamus says and she lowers herself onto a wooden seat as the first bite melts on her tongue.

'Deònach.'

'None of that nonsense,' Cook snaps. 'We'll have proper English here.'

'Delicious,' Mhairi corrects herself. 'Tasty,' as if she is reading the definition from a dictionary. She sips the milk. It is whole, not watered, but it is a day old, by her reckoning.

The footman returns. 'The ladies wish to see her,' he announces. Again, as if Mhairi is not there.

'I'll show Miss MacDonald in,' Seamus says. He doesn't like the footman, Mhairi thinks, and gets to her feet.

The room they go to smells of woodsmoke from the fire, which is crackling in the grate. There is tea on the side too, but the women are not drinking it.

'Miss MacDonald,' Lady Miller of Howe greets her. 'This soap smells like a summer garden, though it's on the soft side.'

'I use more fat than some.' Mhairi feels she must defend her process. 'It has to be soft,' she adds. 'For the Edinburgh water.'

The lady shifts. 'The water?'

'At home I used to make it harder,' Mhairi explains. 'Our burn has a peatiness, but here in town, the water comes from the reservoir and has risen through whinstone. A fattier mixture melts better into it. You'll feel the difference on your skin when you put the soap to use, ma'am.'

A silence which Mhairi cannot interpret falls on the room like snow. She wonders if she has said too much. The sighted do not notice such details. Then a different woman speaks. She leans towards the girl as if sniffing her out.

'Miss MacDonald, do you drink whisky?'

Mhairi stiffens. 'Sometimes,' she says carefully. The still her mother owned was illicit. The whisky one that is, not the one she made lavender oil in. The excise men believed both to be for flowers and declared Mhairi's mother as good as a witch. Not that they burn you for that any more, Mrs MacDonald said afterwards, making light.

'This is Mrs Stein,' Lady Miller introduces her friend. She does not add that Mrs Stein's husband, John, is Scotland's most famous distiller. The Stein brothers between them produce more than ten thousand pints of whisky a day and sell their wares as far afield as London. Mr Stein bailed out Mr Haig when he went bankrupt, not that the Haigs would admit it. In any case, they are known to be canny, though Lady Miller is well aware that Mrs Stein herself is the source of many of the family's famous innovations. The lady's father gave lectures in physics and her mother was cousin to Isabella Lovi, who developed a pioneering method of measuring liquid in the dairy that saw her feted in Edinburgh's most prestigious salons in the old days, before, the old lady sniffs, the fools moved the capital over the old Nor Loch.

'Do you mind me quizzing the girl?' Mrs Stein asks.

'Not at all,' Lady Miller replies.

'We shall play a little game then.'

The sound of the stopper on a crystal decanter. The sound of a splash into a glass. The ghost of it on the air as it gets closer. Mrs Stein says, 'Try this.'

Mhairi smells first. Always. It is from an old cask, something American. Bourbon, she thinks. She takes a sip. 'It needs water,' she says.

'Do you like it?'

'Aye. The barley is malted but not smoked. For preference I like it fired a little.' Her heart is pounding at being so frank, but Mrs Stein asked.

There is a short pause. Another decanter, or perhaps a bottle this time. Another glass and the whisky in it is toasted. 'This is from closer to home,' she allows herself a smile. 'The Black Isle I'd say.'

'And how would you know that?'

'The earth,' Mhairi says. 'The sand in it.'

'I don't see how . . .' Lady Miller of Howe starts but Mrs Stein stops her friend: The edges of this woman are more defined than anyone Mhairi has ever met. She pulls people into her orbit and commands the room like a conductor in charge of a symphony.

'What do they pay you where you work at present?' Mrs Stein enquires.

Mhairi stands up a little. 'Eight pounds a year,' she lies. 'And my board. I've one halfday a fortnight.' This is a lie too.

She can feel Mrs Stein smile as if a log has been put on the fire. 'I wager the gentlemen students are tiresome,' she says.

Mhairi gives a little shrug. 'They're only boys.'

'And if you were to work for me?'

'Making soap?' Mhairi enquires drily.

Mrs Stein gives a little sigh. 'Making whisky, girl,' she replies, 'A job you may find you were born to.'

'There's money in it, is there?'

'Ten pounds a year for you, Miss MacDonald. And I'll house you.'

Mhairi considers. 'Twelve guineas would be better,' she says. 'And a halfday each Saturday.'

Lady Miller of Howe lets out a snort as if this is outrageous. It is double what she pays her lady's maid.

'Where would I live?' Mhairi continues, smooth as a well-aged dram.

'Stockbridge,' Mrs Stein replies. 'Much more pleasant than living in town. My husband has a distillery there to the north of the city. Twelve guineas, Miss MacDonald, and you'd better prove worth it. I'll send a carriage for you the morrow.'

Mhairi curtseys. 'Thank you, ma'am.'

Lady Miller of Howe turns to her friend as if the girl is already out the door. 'But what of my soap?' the old lady objects.

Mrs Stein lets out a laugh that seems too carefree for the feel of her. 'Och, I'll get you soap, Margaret,' she says. 'Consider it commission.'

Mhairi makes her way back onto the Canongate. 'I'll bring my next letter, shall I?' she bids Seamus farewell, her breath frosting the air now she's outside again in the cold. As she turns west up the hill it starts to snow. The flakes melt on her cheeks and she thinks that the magic of the Old Town is just as it always was, if only you give it a chance. And bit by bit, she is sure, she'll make her fortune here. She'll have Seamus write the news and send it home the very next chance she has.

If you'd like another peek into the backstory of The Fair Botanists, the National Library of Scotland commissioned another story which shows the first meeting between Belle Brodie and real-life Georgian botanist, Lady Henrietta Liston, in the winter of 1821. Walk this way: https://digital.nls.uk/travels-of-henrietta-liston/long-reads/sheridan.html